Saba Kapur

AMBERJACK
PUBLISHING

Idaho

Amberjack Publishing
1472 E. Iron Eagle Dr.
Eagle, ID 83616
http://amberjackpublishing.com

Cataloguing-in-publication data available upon request.

Paperback ISBN: 978-1-944995-93-5
eBook ISBN: 978-1-944995-94-2

Cover Design: Stephenу Miller

For my mother, who said:
"You better dedicate this one to just me, I don't want to be grouped in with the rest of the family."

One

Renowned philosopher and poet Jay-Z once stated that he had ninety-nine problems, which, to anyone else, would seem like a hefty amount. But if you ask me, he's got it pretty good. He's married to Beyoncé, which basically means he's won at life, and he's rich enough to buy a pet dragon if he wanted to. I'm not talking about those tiny lizards, either. I mean the huge *Harry Potter and the Goblet of Fire* kind. So, forgive me, but I don't really see how his problems could add up to a number so high. Jay-Z has clearly never had to deal with the stress of being the teenage daughter of a Hollywood movie star.

My name is Gia Winters, and trust me, my life isn't as great as it seems in the fashion magazines. In April of this year, things got a little sucky. My dad's ex–best friend decided it would be fun to stalk me for months and then kidnap me at the Golden Globe awards. Everyone needs a hobby, and apparently his was being a full-time lunatic. As it turns out, his revenge plan was sort of idiotic because he was really the one to blame for his own failures in life. You don't sleep with your agent's wife and then expect to become the next Brad Pitt. For those of you who are rolling your eyes right now, believe me, I can't make this stuff up. I still have the emotional and faded physical scars to prove it.

Five months later, it's safe to say nothing is as it used to be. I made the choice to leave sunny Los Angeles for the full college experience in New York, which allows me the pleasure of being trampled by eight million people on dirty streets with skyscrapers. No palm trees. No tanned guys on skateboards. It's all briefcases, trench coats, and cheap hot dogs here. Leaving California wasn't just hard because I was saying goodbye to my dad, my brother, and all my friends. In fact, leaving my sixteen-year-old brother Mike was actually not an emotional experience *at all* because he's a huge pain in the ass. He only cared about my spike in fame when he realized I could potentially set him up with Cindy Crawford's daughter. Yeah, like that was ever going to happen. But finishing something means starting something new, only I wasn't convinced I was equipped for all the new things being hurled in my direction.

My therapist, Dr. Adele Norton, was one of these new additions. She was pretty, but in a plain-Jane sort of way. She wore a lot of beige, and she had a painting of a bouquet of flowers hanging in her office that made me feel uncomfortable. Sessions with her were like discussing your intimate secrets with a stranger while you're waiting to see the dentist.

"Gia," she said, taking a seat on the wine-colored armchair opposite mine. "I'm so glad you've decided to come back for more sessions this week. I wasn't sure I'd see you after our last conversation."

"You mean when I told you that therapy was a waste of time, and if I had any life problems I'd email Oprah?"

She gave me a small smile, the kind you give a small child attempting to discuss politics with you. "Yes, that one."

I shrugged. "Thought I may as well give it another try. Dad paid you for the whole month."

"Well, whatever the reason, I think you made the right choice."

I stared at her blankly. She was clearly thinking hard about something as she watched me in concentration. Maybe she was thinking that the money wasn't worth dealing with my sour attitude. Maybe she was wondering if her hair was wrapped too tightly in that bun on her head. Probably a bit of both, actually.

"So . . . are we going to discuss my parents' divorce or something now?" I asked, fiddling with the ends of my long, brown hair.

"Actually, I think we'll just talk for a bit." Dr. Norton placed her notebook down on the table that stood between us. She folded her hands in her lap and gave me another gentle smile. "Are you excited about starting classes this week?"

"Sure. Should be fun."

It was not going to be fun. It's not like I'd been chilling at home watching sitcoms all day since the little kidnapping incident. I mean, yeah, okay, I had been doing a bit of that, but I'd also been crazy busy with all my life changes. The idea of class and homework being crammed into my schedule seemed almost impossible to manage. I was going to have to compromise a bit.

"I know a few people who went to NYU," Dr. Norton said earnestly. "It's a great school. I'm sure you'll love it."

"Cool."

With any luck, she'd keep talking like that until the session ended and save me the trouble of actually participating.

"Are you nervous?"

"No."

Uh, yes. What kind of a stupid question was that? I dug my nails into my palms so that she couldn't see I had been biting them all morning. There goes that two-hour manicure I sat through just last weekend.

"College is very different than high school," Dr. Norton went on. "And you've only been in New York for a month. It's perfectly normal to be overwhelmed."

"Yeah, well," I began with a forced smile, "there's nothing really normal about me, now is there?"

Dr. Norton was silent for a few long moments, clearly thinking about her bun again. Probably. "Well," she finally said. "Not every college freshman has the same responsibilities as you do."

It was clear Dr. Norton was struggling to find a polite way to say "Not all eighteen-year-olds miss the first week of college because they were attending the most exclusive New York Fashion Week events." But, sure. Let's go with "responsibilities."

"Those are the perks of being Harry Winters's daughter," I told her.

Dr. Norton leaned over and picked up the notebook. Playtime was over. Time for business. She uncapped her pen, and I felt the dread build up inside me.

"How have you been sleeping lately, Gia? Have these past few days been any better?"

"Yeah," I lied. "A little, I guess."

"Still having nightmares? You mentioned you had quite a few last week."

And that was the last time I was ever going to tell her about them. I think one session was plenty for her reminders about "dealing with unresolved fear and trauma."

"I wouldn't call them *nightmares*," I mumbled. "I mean, yesterday I dreamt that I got married to Zac Efron, so that's good, right?"

Dr. Norton gave a quiet laugh. "Yes, I would say that's a good dream."

I conveniently left out the part where Zac Efron morphed into a faceless figure who shot me, and I got blood all over my Vera Wang wedding dress just before I said my vows. We never even got to the wedding cake or the moment where he serenades me with songs from *High School Musical*. But there was no need to make a big deal out of the little things.

"It's okay if you're still having trouble," she said. "This isn't always a quick process. Sometimes it takes time."

"It's been five months! I think my brain has had enough time to move on."

"Honestly," Dr. Norton said. "I don't think you've given it a proper chance to. You've certainly kept yourself busy enough that you don't really have time to cope with what happened to you. Do you think that's fair to say?"

I don't know, lady, I came to you for the answers. I shifted uncomfortably on the plush armchair. It's not like I hadn't thought about that. I mean, I didn't have full-on PTSD, but something was definitely off. It didn't help that the past few months had been devoted to publicity events and cramming my entire wardrobe into boxes. All the chaos and changes had uprooted whatever emotional stability I had left after the incident. I figured that pretending the problem didn't exist could potentially make it disappear.

I sighed. "Maybe. I guess. You're the expert; you tell me."

"It's important that you recognize where the problem is, so you can take steps to resolve it. I can tell you what you want to hear, but that won't solve anything. Ultimately, only *you* can overcome the anxiety you're feeling. Only then will the nightmares start to go away."

Other famous people had to deal with actual problems, like grand-scale custody battles or intense therapy after smashing their guitars on stage or something. And then there was me, considering sleeping with a night-light like I was a toddler.

"Gia," Dr. Norton continued softly. "I know it can be hard to open up to someone you hardly know. But this is a safe space; there's no judgment. I'm only here to help. But I can't do that if you don't have any faith in me. I'm asking you to trust me. Can you do that?"

I couldn't even meet her eyes. Her voice wasn't soothing or calming, it was patronizing. She said she wasn't going to judge me, but how could she not? Celebrities practically exist for the entertainment and judgment of others. Why should I be any different? I picked up my Roberto Cavalli bag, hiked it onto my shoulder, and rose from my armchair.

"I'll keep that in mind," I told her. "Thanks, Doc."

She looked down at her watch. "Our sessions are half an hour. You've still got half your time left!"

"You're still getting the full fee from Dad, right?"

Dr. Norton blinked at me. "That's not really the point."

"So that's a yes," I said, heading for the door. "Great. Everybody wins! See you Thursday."

"Actually . . ." Dr. Norton stood up, smoothing out the creases in her black pants. "I think we need more than one session a week to address your issues effectively. I'd like to schedule our next session for Wednesday, if that works for you."

I turned the door handle and pushed it open. "Sorry," I said.

"Busy that day."

"Gi—"

"Well, have a great day! Enjoy!"

I practically bolted down the hallway and past the receptionist as if I were being chased by a pack of rabid dogs. Therapy was a joke. I didn't need some middle-aged stranger in an armchair telling me I needed to solve my life issues. You want a problem to solve? Repaint your damn office. Taupe is never the answer.

I rode the elevator impatiently, hastily texting my driver, George, to bring the car around as soon as possible. I doubted Dr. Norton would follow me downstairs and drag me back to her office, but I was taking no chances. Luckily, George was already waiting for me when I stepped outside, opening the car door.

"Drive," I told him as I slid into the black town car. "And hurry."

In hindsight, that was a pretty unreasonable request for George, who had one too many wrinkles to hurry. It wasn't until he pulled away from the curb and into the traffic that I started breathing again. Goodbye Dr. Norton, and goodbye stupid beige blouse.

"The session finish early today, Miss Winters?" George called out from the front seat.

"Something like that."

The message-bank on my phone showed one new voice mail. I put the phone to my ear. "*Hi!*" came the voice through the receiver. "*Okay, so don't hate me. But I have to cancel for tonight. I know I've been doing this a lot lately, but one of the guys misplaced some of the paperwork, and the captain's really cracking down on us today. I'm so sorry, I'll make it up to you, I swear. Anyway, good luck for your first day of classes! Don't be nervous, you got this. I'll call you when I can.*"

The line went dead, and I dropped the phone back into my lap in disappointment. That was the only downside to having a boyfriend who was a police officer. You could never have long, romantic phone conversations, and he was *always* filling out paperwork. On the plus side, he looked super sexy in his NYPD uniform, and it was good to know that he had the ability to arrest people if they annoyed me. Even though he kept reminding me that I couldn't just have annoying people arrested, and apparently "that's not how the legal system works." But whatever. If it came down to it, he could probably fake a crime scene, and that was a useful skill to have.

Milo Fells was still a cadet when I met him, assisting on my stalking case back in April. Our first encounter had involved me gaping at his tousled brown hair and dimples while trying to control the urge to pass out. The next few interactions were about the same. Him smiling and being adorable. Me almost hyperventilating and mentally naming our future children. By some miracle of God, Milo decided my puns were hilarious enough that he wanted to actually be my boyfriend, which was great decision-making on his part. My puns really are hilarious.

Before Milo moved to join the NYPD, we were hanging in limbo. It was hard starting off something with so much distance in between, and a few frozen yogurts dates and stolen kisses barely counted as a relationship. But we finally decided that if we were going to do this, we were going to do this right. At first, I was a little scared that he'd run into Olivia Palermo while I was back in LA and decide I wasn't worth the effort. But my best friends, Aria and Veronica, were kind enough to remind me that Olivia Palermo's husband is a superbabe, so she was probably not going to be leaving him anytime soon. Still, a girl can never be too sure.

I stared out the tinted window impatiently. LA traffic had been bad, but this was unbearable. We were practically stationary.

"How far away are we?" I asked George.

"Hard to say, Miss," he replied. "NYU is only a ten-minute drive, but I'd say double that time with this traffic."

I checked the time. 11:26 a.m. Class was at noon, but this had been the only available time slot for therapy that day. As Dad liked to constantly remind me, Dr. Norton was very high in demand and was basically the "Justin Bieber of therapy." Honestly, I think he was just trying to form an argument in what he assumes is the language of the youth, because he actually said the word "yo" a couple of times during that discussion. That man was hopeless. Either way, he deemed Dr. Norton worthy enough of showing up late to school for, which is a huge deal if you know anything about my father. I would have happily avoided class altogether if I had a better alternative. But right now, even class seemed more appealing than suffocating in her office.

George blared the car horn at a pedestrian darting across the road, slamming his foot on the brake and stopping the car with a jolt. I was thrust forward in my seat. I put a hand over my heart, which was drilling into my rib cage from the adrenaline of almost flattening a man with our tires.

George turned to check on me with a small smile. He shook his head and gave a friendly laugh. "Welcome to New York, Miss Winters."

Two

Right away, it was abundantly clear how out of place I was going to feel at New York University.

Dr. Norton had mentioned that college was nothing like high school, and that adjusting was a challenge for lots of people, not just me. I tried to keep those reassuring words in mind as I scanned my surroundings. There were people scattered on the sidewalks as far as the eye could see. Everyone else had already settled into their schedules the week before, but you could still feel nervous excitement in the air. It wasn't hard to tell by the lost looks on many faces that I was definitely not the only person overwhelmed. I was, however, the only person wearing studded Valentino stilettos with my ripped skinny jeans.

Well, Gia, no time like the present. I took a deep breath, pulled up the campus map on my phone and began walking. Why in the heck was Washington Square Park located right next to the college? Nobody just builds a college around a park in LA. I was already having a hard enough time dealing with the street numbers and names. I didn't need extra greenery to confuse me.

"Hi," I said, stopping a girl passing me.

She pulled out her headphones with annoyance. "Yeah?"

"Yes, hi. Sorry. I was just looking for the fountain? I'm supposed to meet someone there."

The girl looked me up and down. "Are you a student at NYU?"

I looked almost apologetic. "Um, yeah."

She raised an eyebrow, a little piercing rising with it. "Keep walking left, you'll see it in about a minute."

"Oh, great. Thanks!"

She didn't return my cheeriness. Instead she gave me another once-over, pushed her earphones back into her ears, and walked away. Well, alrighty then. Fall in New York was a little chilly, but it was nothing compared to the icy attitudes of the locals.

I did as she said and continued toward the fountain, trying not to look as completely helpless as I felt. Luckily she was right. After only a minute or so, the huge fountain came into view with people chatting all around it. Great. This was a fantastic place to meet someone I had never laid eyes on before. There were only about fifty people here. Should be no problem. I blew out a sigh, scanning my surroundings. It was two minutes to noon. I was going to be late for sure.

"Gia?" A pretty blonde girl appeared in front of me with a perky smile.

"Yeah?"

"I'm Zoe! Hi! I'll be helping you out today!"

Just by looking at her, you could tell Zoe was a hugger. I, unfortunately, was not. Instead I offered her a formal handshake and a forced smile.

"It's nice to meet you," I told her.

"Likewise!" She looked down at the clipboard in her hand. A little purple and gold icon sat on the top left corner of the page, showing the NYU logo. "You're in building sixty-eight. That's right around the corner."

"I'm really late to class, aren't I?" I asked.

"Oh, don't worry about it." She waved her hand dismissively. "I had Professor Michaels last year, and he was always late. I think you'll be fine."

I hoped she was right, because there was no way I was sneaking in late to my first ever college class without drawing some attention to myself. Yet another unconsidered flaw when we had scheduled today's therapy session.

"Thanks again for helping me out," I said to Zoe as we walked.

"That's no problem," she replied pleasantly. "Everyone needs a hand sometimes."

"Does everyone get their own personal helper?"

Zoe flashed me an awkward smile. "Um, no. I mean, we have orientation. But I guess they wanted you to have VIP treatment."

Right. Of course. For a second there I had forgotten I wasn't some ordinary freshman trying to navigate their way to class. I was literally the exact same thing but with a more expensive handbag.

"Great," I said. "Cool. Fab."

"I hope you don't mind me bringing this up," she began cautiously. I immediately knew what was coming next. "But that . . . thing that happened to you? It really sucked."

Well that was the understatement of the century. Two minutes into a conversation and it had already been brought up. That may be a new record.

"Yeah," I mumbled, desperately hoping the ground would swallow me whole. "It did."

"I mean, when I first saw something about it on Facebook, I was like, there is *no way* that is happening. But then when I read about everything in the news the day after the Golden Globes, I totally freaked."

Yes, Zoe. I, too, freaked. In fact, I hadn't *stopped* being freaked by it yet. I decided to ignore her comment and instead motioned toward the wide, brick building ahead. Two purple flags hung from each corner, a flamed torch printed on each one.

"So . . . is that it?" I asked, stopping in front of a wide staircase.

"That's the one," she said with a nod. "I know NYU can be confusing because everything's spread out, but you'll get the hang of it eventually. You just have to go up the stairs. Your class is in the third room on the right."

I looked down at my watch with a grimace. The needle moved to 12:07. "Got it," I said. "Thanks again, Zoe."

"If you need any other help, here's my number." She unclipped a small piece of paper from her clipboard, a number neatly written on it. "VIP treatment, remember?"

I slipped the paper into my jeans pocket. "Right. How could I forget?"

"Okay then," Zoe said. She smiled at me silently, clearly working out a dilemma in her head. She finally took a step toward me and pulled me into a hug. "It's going to be okay! You'll have a great time!"

I just *knew* she was a hugger. I patted her back awkwardly. She was crushing my neck a little, but it didn't feel right to push her off.

"Um, thank you."

Zoe pulled away, nodding as if she were reconfirming she had done the right thing. I did some more polite thanking and watched her walk away, butterflies floating around my stomach. Okay, so it was just college. This wasn't rocket science. Unless of course you were studying rocket science, which I'm not even sure is an actual degree. It's not like I had been home schooled my whole life and now my parents had thrown me into a pool of perky blonde sharks. I could do this!

"You are Gia Winters!" I whispered to myself as I fiercely climbed the stairs. "You're a baller!"

Truthfully, I don't even know what I was hoping to achieve by repeating this to myself a million times as I walked into the building. But whatever it was, it seemed to be working, because by the time I reached the lecture hall door, I was actually eager to open it.

"You are Gia freakin' Winters," I told myself again, pushing the door open. "You got this, Babygirl!"

Apparently my warrior ferocity went a little overboard because the door opened with such intensity that it slammed against the wall inside, causing everyone to look up at me as I walked inside the room. I well and truly did not have this,

Babygirl.

The quiet chatter ceased as everyone's eyes fixated on me. There were easily two hundred people in the room, and I was sure some of them were already trying to figure out why I looked familiar. The door swung closed behind me with a loud thud, causing me to wince. On the plus side, Zoe was right. Professor Michaels clearly shared my lack of punctuality.

I headed for the staircase closest to me, keeping my gaze low. It looked as though every seat in the room had already been filled, but I was bound to find one near the back. The only problem was, everyone's eyes were following me as I walked up the stairs, and it was proving impossible to avoid their stares. There was no way in hell I was even considering the seats in the middle aisles; tripping over people's bags and giving them awkward apologies was not my idea of a good time. The clicking of my heels was echoing so loudly off the walls that I was considering just pulling them off and walking the rest of the way barefoot. This was not exactly how I wanted to start off my first class.

After what seemed like three years of painful searching, I managed to find a seat in the third to last row in the room. The row was almost completely filled, except for two seats at the end. Perfect. It was close to an exit. If all else failed I could fake a terminal illness and run out. I took a seat, and the chair let out a comically loud squeak as I sat down. There was one free seat next to me, right on the aisle, but I had left it empty just in case some other poor sucker walked in late and was as desperate as I was.

Hushed whispers broke out amongst the crowd, and I could see people stealing glances at me. Okay then. Clearly subtlety wasn't a valued trait here at NYU. The girl sitting next to me pulled out her phone and was Googling my name. I really should have saved her the trouble and just confirmed it myself, but that would have involved me actually talking. I was contemplating yelling out, "LOOK! IT'S BRADLEY COOPER," just to divert some of the attention away from me. But luckily, the lecture hall door swung open and a man ran inside, looking almost frantic.

"Sorry, folks!" he exclaimed, placing a small briefcase down on the table at the front of the room. "Got a little caught up. Are we all ready to start?"

Professor Michaels was probably in his mid-fifties, but his energetic demeanor gave off a much younger vibe. He was dressed in a casual brown suit and was rifling through his papers while muttering to himself. He was exactly what I imagined a college professor to look like. I hoped he was nice. After a few minutes, he put them down on the table and scanned the room with a smile.

"Gia Winters?" he said, and my heart stopped beating for a second. "Gia? Are you in here, Gia?"

Oh. Sweet. Jesus. This was actually a nightmare. Any minute now I was going to look down and shriek at my naked body before realizing it was all just a horrible dream, and then Dr. Norton would force me to talk about it next session. Unfortunately, the hundreds of people sitting before me were very real.

"No Gia? Ah! There you are!" Professor Michaels followed the trail of gazes and finally found me. I sunk lower into my seat. "I was told we would have our very own celebrity!"

I tried not to groan out loud, but I think it happened anyway. There was no way a discreet exit was possible *now.* If he was going to ask me to stand and bow for everyone, I was going to sue him for emotional trauma.

"Hi," I said quietly, offering everyone a meek wave.

"It is such a pleasure to have you with us, Miss Winters!" Professor Michaels exclaimed. He was practically bouncing on his heels. "I'm a huge fan of your father's work."

"Thanks," I said. "I'll let him know."

I would not let him know. He wouldn't care.

Professor Michaels stood with both hands and stuck out his chest as if he were Superman. "Sorry, Captain," he said in a low, intense voice. "The skies wait for no one!!"

The whole room was silent. A few people were exchanging questioning looks while others were trying to hide their laughter. I may have actually whimpered. He was quoting one of Dad's movies, *Skies Above.* Dad had played a brave, young pilot forced to save a plane when Russian spies took over. The movie, despite having a pretty poorly executed plot, was a huge success and ignited a lot of pilot fantasies within women around the world. I know because I had helped Mom throw away a ton of extremely scarring fan letters.

I forced a smile, although I'm sure it looked more like a grimace. "That's . . . great. You nailed it!"

Professor Michaels beamed with pride and said, "I've had years of practice for that one!"

I heard a guy a few seats away cough awkwardly, clearly trying to control his laughter. I could see him digging his chin into his gray hoodie, his hand covering his mouth in amusement. Nice to know one of us was having a good time.

"Well anyway, I think it's time we started on our class today! Welcome to week two!" Professor Michaels exclaimed, and I exhaled. Everyone was turning their attention back to him and away from me. "Quick reminder that this is Introduction to Psychology. If any of you believe you're in the wrong class, you can take this as an opportunity to leave now. A few years ago, I had a young man realize his mistake three weeks before the end of the semester. Needless to say, he did not excel in this unit."

A ripple of laughter went through the crowd. I even caught myself joining a little. "As I mentioned last week," Professor Michaels continued, "your major assignment for this subject is a group task. Each group is to choose one psychologist and construct a portfolio of their work. Be warned that this is not a simple copy-and-paste from Wikipedia job. Your portfolios will be judged not just on your understandings of theory, but also on how well you can *apply* these theories to modern psychological and social concepts."

Professor Michaels continued to explain the assessment as he set up his PowerPoint slides. A white slide popped up on the projector that read, "Week 2: Foundations of Psychology." I leaned down and pulled a notebook out from my tote. The gray hoodie guy sitting two seats away caught my eye, gave me an unimpressed look, and then turned his attention back to the front. Well, gee. Did I insult this guy's whole ancestral line by pulling out pen and paper? Like, at least get to know me before you start the judgy stares.

Professor Michaels was on a roll, flipping through the slides with the same gusto you would expect from a nightclub DJ. I wrote down whatever was on the screen hurriedly, trying to keep up with him as he practically bounced around the room. But my mind wasn't paying any attention. None of the words were really sinking in, and I kept checking the time, desperately hoping the minutes would tick by faster than usual. They didn't.

I examined the audience sitting in front of me. Most of the students were busy typing notes on their laptops or furiously scribbling in their notebooks. Others were discreetly texting their friends or scrolling through Facebook. Four rows down there was a guy who was clearly asleep. Everybody else was sneaking glances at me, whispering to their friends with excitement. If every class was going to be this painful every day, I was dropping out. I didn't even *need* a degree. What was the point of having rich parents if I still had to do homework? That is some next-level injustice.

After what seemed like twenty years of slow torture, the PowerPoint slides finally disappeared off the projector.

"Before we all rush off today," Professor Michaels said, "I'd like everyone to find four people sitting next to them. Left or right, it doesn't matter. We just need a total of five."

There was nobody in the aisle seat, so I looked to my left. The blonde girl sitting next to me whispered something to her friend, and they giggled. Then there was Gray Hoodie Guy, who was talking to someone on his left.

"Congratulations." Professor Michaels smiled. "You've just met your partners for your group assignment. I strongly recommend getting to know each other a little better. You'll be working closely together for the rest of this semester."

Professor Michaels snapped his briefcase shut, signifying that class had officially ended. Some people had already begun speaking to their group members, but mine didn't seem interested at all. Fine by me. I was considering never even coming back. I gathered my things, roughly shoved them into my bag, and headed for the back door.

"Hey!" I heard a girl call from behind me. "Um, Gia?"

I stopped, four stairs up. Apparently this clean break wasn't going to be so clean after all. I wheeled around, allowing people to push past me on the stairs.

"Yeah?" I said.

The blonde girl, her friend, Gray Hoodie Guy, and another guy wearing glasses were all staring at me expectantly.

"Um," the guy with glasses said. "I just thought we could introduce ourselves." The two girls nodded. Gray Hoodie Guy seemed even more unimpressed now.

"Right!" I said. "For sure. Introductions." I walked down toward my new group members, who were now exchanging weary glances. We were just about the only people left in the lecture room now, except for a few others at the front of the room, probably doing their own introductions. We stood in an awkward circle, silently waiting for another person to start. It sure as hell wasn't going to be me.

"So, I guess I'll go first then," the guy with the glasses said cheerfully. "I'm Kyle!"

I was half-expecting everyone to reply with a unified "Hello Kyle," as if we were sitting at an Alcoholics Anonymous meeting. Instead, the blonde girl spoke.

"I'm Hannah," she said simply, pushing her shoulder-length hair out of her face.

"I'm Michelle," the girl next to her said, her jet-black hair pulled neatly into a braid.

"Jamie," Gray Hoodie Guy said simply. He pushed his sleeve up on his arm a little, and the edges of a tattoo peeked out from underneath.

"I'm G—"

"Gia Winters," Jamie said with a smirk. "Yeah, we know."

"I don't think you really need an introduction," Hannah added. "*Everyone* knows who you are." Kyle and Michelle laughed politely, but there was nothing really funny about the way she had said it.

"So," I said, ignoring the anxiety gnawing at my insides. "Do you guys all know each other?"

"Hannah and I went to high school together," Michelle said. "But I think everyone else is new."

"Coolio!" Oh my god. Did I just say *coolio*? When was someone going to put me out of my misery? I was never great at awkward social situations before this, but moving states had removed any little abilities I had possessed before. Next class, I'd just pretend I had lost my voice in a freak accident and it was never coming back.

"I *love* your shoes!" Michelle said. "They're amazing."

Shoes. Now *there* was something I could actually talk about normally. "Oh, thank you! Valentino gave them to me."

"You mean someone gave you a pair of heels from Valentino, right?" Hannah asked, although she already knew that wasn't what I meant.

"Um, no," I replied, suddenly embarrassed at how flippant I had been. "Valentino gifted them to me on my sixteenth birthday. He's sort of friends with my parents."

"Oh my gosh!" Michelle's eyes widened with awe. "You are *so* lucky! I would die if that ever happened to me."

I snuck a look at Hannah, who was eyeing my shoes with a look of disdain.

"So anyway," Kyle piped up, clearly sensing that the Valentino topic wasn't getting us anywhere. "I guess we have a couple more weeks before we need to worry about the assignment, but if anyone has any theories or psychologists they really want to focus on, feel free to suggest them. It doesn't hurt to get a head start."

"What about Freud?" Michelle said. "I know he's an obvious choice, but his theory will give us a lot to work with."

I nodded. I had a fear at the back of my mind that they would be throwing around names and I'd be standing there blankly. I had spent half of class discreetly googling psychologists every time Professor Michaels had mentioned them in class. What the hell did I know about psychology? That was the whole point of taking the introductory unit! Professor Michaels had said that we'd be studying the theories in detail over the coming weeks, but nobody seemed as lost as me. Freud, luckily, I knew about. Creepy things about loving your parents in a sexual way and something about an iceberg. Things were looking up already.

"I don't know," Kyle replied. "Lots of groups might choose him thinking that he's an easy option, and then we won't stand out."

"I agree." Jamie added. "Freud is too easy."

Hannah nodded enthusiastically in agreement. It didn't matter that her friend's suggestion had just been majorly shot down. It was practically written on her forehead that she was into Jamie. Unfortunately for me, that meant I had officially run out of psychological knowledge.

"Any other ideas?" Kyle asked.

"What about something a little different?" Hannah said. "Like, Slavoj Zizek?"

Um, who?! Surely this was just a joke and they were testing to see if I would pick up on it. I glanced around the group. Everyone else seemed to be evaluating her suggestion as if they knew who she was talking about. I nodded thoughtfully, hoping that the panic inside my chest wasn't showing on my face.

"Isn't he a philosopher?" Kyle finally said. "I don't know if he counts as a psychologist."

"Well, technically speaking, yeah, he's a philosopher." Hannah replied. "But he *did* contribute a lot to psychology. And plus, his work is really relevant to modern society. We'd have a lot of modern examples to apply to his theories."

Michelle said, "His work is pretty complex, but what if it doesn't fit the brief?"

"What do you think, Gia?" Kyle asked.

Everyone turned to look at me expectantly.

I narrowed my eyes as if deep in thought and said, "Hmmm. Yes. Well, I myself am a great fan of . . . uh . . . that philosopher. But I think his work might be *too* complex for this assignment. We don't want to overwhelm people with a really heavy theory on, um . . . life."

"Yeah, I agree." Kyle said, pushing his hair away from his glasses. "I don't think it's worth the risk."

"Same." Jamie said, and Michelle nodded.

Wow. Really? That actually worked? Hannah shrugged, but she was pouting a little.

"What about Carl Jung?" Kyle suggested.

Carl Jung. I remembered that name from the lecture slides, but I had zero idea what he was about. Plus, his last name had been spelt with a 'j' but Kyle had pronounced it as "young." Why couldn't psychologists just have normal names, like John Citizen?

"That could work," Michelle replied thoughtfully. "His theory is pretty easy to explain. Not too complex."

"But remember," Hannah said. "We have to keep it relevant to modern society. Do you think Jung's work is too old and outdated?"

"Well, I mean he's still *Jung* at heart," I said.

Once more, all eyes locked on me. I let out a small, nervous laugh. Sweet Jesus. Why couldn't I just shut up for one minute and not give everyone even more reason to dislike me? Michelle smiled a little, but I think her amusement was directed more at me than the joke. I glanced at Jamie, who had his eyebrows raised. This was getting more painful with every minute that passed.

"I think it's actually pronounced *yoong,*" Hannah told me.

"Anyway," Kyle said, stepping in once more to diffuse the situation. "I got to run to my next class, but let's give it some thought, and we can decide next week."

I gave a small sigh of relief. Judging by the way Hannah was looking at me, Kyle was going to have to play mediator a lot this semester. Everyone exchanged polite goodbyes and stiff handshakes, as if we had been thrust into a group speed-dating session that was coming to an unsuccessful end. Kyle had already run out of the hall, checking his watch frantically. Students from the next class were already piling through the front door to take their seats, filling the room with chatter. Michelle, and Hannah disappeared into the crowd on the stairs below.

Jamie looked at me, expressionless, for a few seconds before turning to leave. Just as he turned, a pen fell from the pocket of his brown sling bag.

"Hey!" I called out, and he turned to face me. I bent down to pick up the pen that lay a few steps ahead of me, but he had already grabbed it.

"Don't worry, I got it," he said, both of us still kneeling. "Wouldn't want you to break a nail, now would we?"

He rose and stuffed the pen back into the pocket of his bag. I gave him a stunned look. "Excuse me?"

The room was loud, but there was no way I had misheard him. But he didn't reply. Instead, Jamie gave me a two-fingered salute, continued climbing the stairs, and disappeared through the exit. Well, jeez. No need to be nice or anything. It's not like I'm a human being with feelings. I blew out a sigh, my heart still pounding from embarrassment and anger.

Day one of classes, and I had already made some enemies. Maybe college wasn't going to be *that* different from high school after all.

Three

I rode the private elevator up to my Fifth Avenue penthouse with zero patience. It was a twenty second journey, but it was twenty seconds too long that day. All I wanted to do was run through the doors, grab a slab of chocolate on the way to my room, crawl under the covers and never come out again. Agoraphobic people had the right idea about life. Daylight and socializing were *way* overrated.

The elevator let out a small ding as the doors opened. I stepped out and sped down the small corridor before pushing the doorbell with such intensity that I was scared I was going to break it. I tapped my foot impatiently, waiting for Val, my housekeeper, to answer. The door finally swung open, and I let out an impatient sigh.

"Finally!" I declared with relief, dropping my bag onto the nearest table.

"Is everything okay?" Val asked. She did a quick scan of the hallway before closing the door. The way I had hurried in, she had probably presumed someone had been chasing me.

"No," I said, flopping onto the sofa dramatically. "Everything sucks."

Val walked over to the sofa and looked down at me with her kind, brown eyes. "Bad first day?"

"*Bad* doesn't even begin to describe it."

She gave me a sympathetic look and said, "Sorry, G. There's always tomorrow."

I pressed a cushion to my face and tried not to scream. Tomorrow there would be another day of college, and yet another day where I'd want to disappear into a sinkhole. I could hear the gentle pattering on the floor as my Yorkshire terrier, Famous, trotted about the place.

"Chocolate," I whimpered, my voice muffled by the pillow. "Now."

I listened as Val's footsteps faded. Sometimes I wondered if she had a resignation letter ready to go whenever I got on her nerves too much. She was far too young to be babysitting me, and far too old to be dealing with my tantrums. I saw her as a big sister. She probably saw me as a pain in the ass. But, then again, she really worked for my mother and not me. If she hadn't quit after all the trauma Mom must put her through, she definitely wasn't going to desert me.

My ringtone blasted from inside my bag, and I removed the pillow from my face with a groan. I checked the caller ID.

"You're late," I said simply, placing the phone to my ear.

"I'm here now, aren't I?" came the reply.

"I even told the front desk to let you up without asking, and you're still late."

"You just got here yourself!"

"No, I didn't. I've been here for, like, an hour."

"Your doorman told me you just got here."

Goddamn it. I knew I couldn't trust Phil. "Just hurry!"

"Alright, alright! Stepping into the elevator now."

I hung up without a goodbye and peeled myself off the sofa with all the energy I had left. Finally, something to look forward to after this horrible day. Val emerged from the kitchen with a sealed box of Ferrero Rocher.

"I think this is all we have," she said, holding up the box to show me.

"It'll do," I replied, dropping it onto the sofa.

The doorbell chimed, and I rushed to the front door, tugging on the gold handle with excitement.

"I bring gifts from the land of Chinatown!"

Jack held up two big plastic bags, the delicious smell of noodles wafting through the penthouse. I moved aside to let him into the house, closing the door behind us.

"I thought we were supposed to go out?" I said.

"Yeah, well," Jack replied, placing the plastic bags on the dining table. "Change of plans."

Typical Jack Anderson: make a plan and then change it last minute without letting anyone else know. Sometimes I wondered why I even kept him around, but I knew the answer to that was simple. Jack had been my bodyguard when Frank was stalking me. We hadn't liked each other much when we first met; he thought I was a spoiled brat, and I thought he was an arrogant jerk. Neither of us were really wrong about the other, but we had found a way to work around it. He had jumped in front of a bullet for my father and had put up with a lot of my complaining over the months. So, sure. He could be extremely stubborn, and sometimes I caught myself staring at his perfect blond hair and bright blue eyes a little longer than I should. But he was one of my best friends now—really, the only one in New York. Except Zoe, of course, but I don't think one forced hug counts as friendship.

I walked over to the table with a pout, watching as Jack pulled out little white boxes from the bags. "We were supposed to do fancy Italian tonight."

"And now we're doing common Chinese takeout." He handed me a pair of packaged chopsticks. "Keep up."

"Oh, hey Jack!" Val said, walking out of the kitchen in her plain black dress and ballet flats. She had a small purse hanging on her shoulder. "I thought you guys were going out tonight."

"We *were*," I told her. "But then Mr. Change of Plans over here decided we were having Chinese takeout instead."

"You want some?" Jack asked Val, bending down to pet Famous.

"No thanks. It's a little early for dinner, isn't it?"

Jack cocked his head toward me with a smirk. "Tell that to

everyone in LA."

I gave him an offended look. "It's, like, seven o'clock! How is that early?"

"This is New York, Gia," Jack said, and Val let out a giggle.

I rolled my eyes. "Thanks for the reminder."

Val told me she fed Famous and said, like, four other things about cleaning the house that I didn't really care about, before letting me know she was heading home for the day.

"Enjoy your takeout," she said brightly.

Jack yelled out a goodbye just as the door clicked shut. He turned to me with a raised eyebrow. "You know I think she's really hot, right?"

"You know I think you're disgusting, right?"

"You may have mentioned that on occasion, yes."

Rice, noodles, veggies, chicken, and pork. I inspected the feast with a frown. "This better be the best Chinese takeout in the city," I told him.

"I've never tried it," Jack replied. "But my friend Scott said it was life-changing."

"He actually said 'life-changing'?"

"Actually, I think he described it as 'dangerously cheap but excellent quality.'"

"Anything that combines the words *dangerously* and *cheap* doesn't go near my mouth." I held up my finger just as Jack began to say something. "Don't!"

He clasped his lips shut, smiling at whatever dirty joke was still at the tip of his tongue. "I wasn't going to say anything."

"Good, don't."

Jack handed me a pair of wooden chopsticks. "Just eat it, Princess. Chances of food poisoning are, like, 20 percent. I'm kidding. Jeez! Just eat it."

I cautiously nibbled on some noodles as Jack watched with excited anticipation, as if he had made them himself.

"Well?"

"They're pretty good. But you and I haven't had the best luck with Chinese food in the past."

Jack laughed. "This isn't the Dumpling Hospital, don't worry."

Boy, that was a relief. After Frank Parker, or "Dr. D," as he called himself, was "robbed" of his one chance at making it big in Hollywood, he had traveled to the place everyone would least expect to find him: China. He spent most of his life there before returning to LA, taking over a rundown Chinese restaurant called The Dumpling Hospital and, of course, stalking me intensely for two months. Jack and I had paid the place a visit, hoping to find some answers. And answers we found, along with possible stomach infections.

As we later found out, while I was conveniently tied to a chair in the middle of a Universal Studios set, Dr. D had ruined his own chances of ever becoming a star when he had an affair with his agent's wife. Like I said before, I can't make this stuff up. Not only did Frank Parker have a poor business sense, he was also an absolute idiot. But it always made me smile a little thinking about how ridiculous his restaurant looked. It was the place Jack and I had begun our investigation and maybe even our friendship.

I picked up two white boxes and carried them to the sofa, which was so big that if I sat all the way back, I could stretch my legs out almost completely with only my feet dangling off.

"Are you sure you want to sit there?" Jack asked, balancing the rest of the takeout boxes in his hands. "If I accidently drop a noodle, I don't want your mom to kill me because I stained a pillow or something."

"Mom's not even here."

"Yeah, but mothers have a sixth sense about sofas being stained. Especially white ones."

"Don't worry, we have good cleaners."

Jack sat on the edge of the sofa, carefully placing the food in between us. "Why is everything in this damn place so white, anyway?"

He had a point. Mom's interior designer had gone a little nuts with the pearly white. The plush sofas were white, the walls were white, the stairs were white, and the doors were white. The rest of the penthouse consisted of fluffy gray rugs, gold-plated handles, marble sinks, and beige wardrobes. Lots of room for error. Lots of room for stains.

"Okay, I'll admit it," I said, reaching for a piece of broccoli. "This is delicious. Tell Scott he has my seal of approval."

"See! Doesn't this beat your fancy Italian food?"

"It really doesn't, but I can deal."

Jack kicked off his shoes and eased himself further up the sofa, crossing his legs as if he were sitting in a kindergarten classroom, waiting for story time.

"How was your first day of college?" he asked, stealing a few noodles from the box I was holding.

"Ugh."

"That sounds promising."

"It was *terrible.* I got lost a zillion times, and everyone kept staring at me like I had a unicorn horn attached to my forehead."

"People like unicorns."

"Yeah, well, apparently they don't like me."

"Oh, come on," Jack said. "You're famous! Who doesn't want to be friends with a famous person?"

"I can think of a few people."

"Hey, you can't win 'em all. Some people just suck."

Those were definitely words to live by. I gave Jack a quick rundown of my classes, describing my professors and how people kept trying to sneak a photo of me any chance they got. I told him about my group assignment in psychology, and Hannah's smug smile, and Jamie's little comment. Jack said he sounded like an ass, and I suggested the two of them would probably get along just fine then, and then he tried to throw a mushroom at me, but he was too scared it would fall on the sofa. If there was one silver lining, it was that my Foundations of Criminal Theories professor was a quiet woman who didn't really care that much about my celebrity status. She had enough sensitivity not to call me out and quote my father's movies to me in front of hundreds of students, all of whom were already ogling at me like I was a science experiment. She had simply come up to me after class, introduced herself as Professor Weber, and told me I should probably avoid joining a sorority during Rush Week.

"After all of that," I told Jack, "I had to go to Steph's office for a meeting."

Jack choked back a laugh, swallowing a mouthful of food. "Yikes."

"Yikes" was probably the most accurate way to sum up my publicist Stephanie. Before the kidnapping, Dad had a strict rule that Mike and I weren't allowed to interact with the media in any way. No magazine cover shoots, no TV interviews, no radio, nothing. It was a rule Mike and I were pretty comfortable obeying, but after the Golden Globe Awards, everything changed. People swarmed outside our LA mansion as if we were throwing hundred-dollar bills from the balcony, and I was hounded every time I stepped outside the house.

When it became apparent that the spotlight wasn't going away anytime soon, Dad decided to take charge of the situation. It wasn't a way to make extra money; it was just an opportunity to set the record straight about what had happened. Rumors had been flying in every direction, some worse than others, and I guess Dad got sick of hearing them all. A thirty-minute exclusive on *60 Minutes* was all it took to clear the air. Frank Parker was labeled a scorned lunatic; I was labeled as helpless and innocent, and that was all that needed to be said. Kind of. The interview offers continued to flood in, but we had said our piece. Suddenly all these magazines that I had read cover-to-cover my entire life were calling Dad's assistant nonstop. Apparently getting kidnapped is trendy, because everyone wanted me as their representative. The magazine cover shoots were approved after much persistence on my part. If everyone was going to talk about me, then I wanted it to be on my terms. I never answered any more questions about the incident, and they never outright asked. Instead I just posed happily and gave some generic spiel about overcoming difficulties and staying positive, like I was some kind of expert.

When I had made the decision to accept NYU's offer, I had been so excited. I was dying for some more freedom from Dad. But when that feeling wore off pretty quickly, I figured a few distractions might help. So after much convincing, Dad hired Steph, an overzealous thirty-something woman with way too much enthusiasm for her petite frame. As long as I wasn't selling stories about Frank to strangers or train surfing, I could do what I wanted. Just as long as Steph and my dad approved, of course.

"She wants me to do this volunteer project," I told Jack.

"That sounds nice."

"Yeah, except it's in Haiti."

"Like, *the* Haiti?"

"No, the other one."

"Tell me you said no."

"I didn't have to say no; Dad said no for me. She was just 'double-checking.'"

"That reminds me . . ." Jack put down his chopsticks. "Your dad called me."

I tried not to groan out loud. I had a feeling this was going to happen. "Really?" I mumbled, innocently shoveling more food into my mouth. Somewhere behind us, Famous was wrestling with his squeaky ball.

"He said he called you a few times, and you never picked up."

I took my time chewing before I swallowed. "I didn't get any missed calls."

Jack leaned across me to where my phone was and grabbed it before I could snatch it away. He pressed the home button, and the screen lit up. It showed five missed calls from Dad among a few text messages on a group chat that I hadn't even checked yet.

"My phone was in my pocket. New York is so loud; sometimes it's hard to even hear myself think."

Jack gave me a pointed look. "He told me you called Reggie and said you didn't need him today."

"I gave him the day off. He looked a little tired."

"I know Reggie, and Reggie doesn't tire easily."

It was not a pleasant thought that my father was venting to Jack about how disobedient I was. Next, they'd be starting their own book club and going golfing on the weekends together. My only solace was that because of this new movie keeping him busy, Dad didn't have the time to call and check up on me twenty-four-seven. Once they actually started filming, I'd be completely free.

"I don't even need a bodyguard!" I exclaimed. "It's a waste of everyone's time, especially poor Reggie's. I mean, I'm thinking about what's best for all of us."

Jack gave me a *you can't be serious* look and said, "I remember you saying you didn't need a bodyguard when you first met me, and look how that worked out."

"Okay, that was totally not the same thing," I argued. "I was being stalked. No one's stalking me now."

"Are you kidding? *Everyone* is stalking you now! You've been on the top-trending hashtags on Twitter for five months!"

"Reggie's scary," I pushed on. "He has, like, five hundred muscles, and he's weirdly tall."

"Reggie is a great guy," Jack said patiently. "I've worked with him plenty of times. He's a gentle giant."

"Well, if he's so gentle then why did we hire him as my bodyguard!"

"Because he has five hundred muscles, and he's weirdly tall!"

I gave an exasperated sigh. "Why can't *you* just be my bodyguard?"

Jack practically choked on the cashew nut he was eating. "Uh-uh. No way. Hard pass."

"Excuse me? What is *that* supposed to mean?"

"It means I was your bodyguard once, and it was terrible. We fought the entire time, your ex-boyfriend got poisoned by a dumpling, and I got shot in the arm. So thanks, but no thanks."

"Oh, come on! The bullet didn't hit any bone!"

"Either way, I think I'll sit this one out."

I hugged my knees to my chest in defeat. He was right. The whole experience had been a complete disaster. Just thinking about Jack lying unconscious with blood everywhere made me shudder. It was an image that had never fully left my mind.

"Fine," I said reluctantly. "I'll use Reggie. But only for the important stuff! I don't need any more attention on myself in class. So I guess you're off the hook this time."

Jack put a hand over his heart. "Thank god. For a minute there, I was scared my other arm was a goner."

"Besides, you're my only friend in the city, you better take care of more than just your arms."

He reached across the sofa and grabbed the box of chocolate. No point in delaying dessert. Here was a man who knew the proper way to live. "I know someone who'd be interested in being your friend," he said with a casual shrug.

"Jack," I said. "One interview with Anderson Cooper doesn't make us friends. Although, trust me, I'd be up for it. His hair is flawless."

Jack blinked at me, almost looking concerned. "That's not what I meant. And also, I don't think your therapy is working, because you still clearly have issues."

"Tell me about it."

"I meant Lucy."

Oh. Crap. This again. Apparently pretending that Jack's girlfriend didn't exist had achieved little success, because he kept bringing her up every chance he got. Can't a girl just eat some dangerously cheap noodles without being harassed into meeting her friend's girlfriend? What kind of world do we live in?

"Right," I said, hoping my tone wasn't giving my feelings away. "Lucy! Of course. How could I forget?" No, really. How could I *possibly* forget?

"You've been here a month and still haven't met her yet," Jack said, fiddling with the wrapper of his chocolate. "I know things have been kind of intense for you lately, and she's been really busy. The timing just never seems to match. But she's really excited to meet you!"

Um, why? No girl is ever *really* excited to meet her boyfriend's female friend, especially if her dad is a Hollywood movie star and her mother is an ex-Playboy Bunny. Hell, I hate me right now just thinking about it. Besides, I hadn't even known about her until Jack had moved back to New York. He hadn't mentioned her *once* while he was working for me in LA and then casually sprang it on me over the phone like it wasn't a big deal. Clearly he didn't care *that* much about us two being friends. But he was emotionally blackmailing me with his perfect blue eyes, looking all hopeful, and I could practically feel my barriers breaking down.

"I'm excited to meet her too," I told him unconvincingly.

"I guess we've just been unlucky with the timing." That, and I'd been avoiding this at every freaking turn.

"How about this Friday night?" Jack asked. "She's having a get-together at her place. Nothing fancy or anything, but it'll be fun."

"Do people still say 'get-together'?"

"You should come."

"Friday's no good," I lied. "I already have schoolwork to catch up on. And 2 Chainz is filming his new music video, so I should probably be there to support him. You know, as a fan and all." Lordy lord. I should have stuck with my fake life-threatening illness excuse. But I don't think the symptoms would be that aggressive in, like, four days. Plus, I'd have to Google diseases and cry a lot. Not really worth it. Jack was staring at me with puppy dog eyes that rivaled Famous's when he really wanted a treat. No one was immune to those eyes.

"Fine," I finally said, and he smiled. "I can do Friday."

"Great!" Jack said. "You can even bring Milo."

Thank god. At least someone would be there to save me from slipping into madness. I aimed the remote at the TV, eager to move on from the discussion.

"So anyway," I said. "Suggestions for movie night?" I always liked to ask, but we very rarely reached a consensus. It had been months, and he still refused to watch *Breakfast at Tiffany's*, no matter how many times I had tried to convince him. But I was still holding out hope that one day he'd just give in.

"You're just going to make me watch some boring movie from fifty years ago," Jack said, settling into the sofa cushions. "Why can't you just watch mindless Seth Rogen movies like a normal teenager?"

I gave him a look that almost resembled pity. "Oh, Jack. I too was once naïve and uneducated like you."

"Rude."

"These aren't movies, they're a cultural experience!"

"I'm pretty sure *Magic Mike XXL* isn't a cultural experience, but you still made me watch that."

"I disagree. Anything to do with Channing Tatum taking his clothes off is a work of art."

"Fine." Jack gave a sigh of defeat. "But if you put on anything remotely related to Nora Ephron, kissing in the rain, or slow dancing, I'm leaving."

If this man hadn't saved my father's life, I would have kicked him out ages ago.

Four

IT WAS TUESDAY MORNING, AND I WAS FEELING SURPRISingly chipper given the events of last night. Once again, I had been blessed with a nightmare that involved me being chased through an abandoned parking lot while some unidentified person tried to run me over. At some point after I had woken up sweating, I pretty much gave up on going back to sleep. But even with five hours of rest and dark circles under my eyes, I was feeling good. What doesn't kill you makes you stronger, your footsteps even lighter, your food taste even better. Or something like that. I'm a little murky on the song lyrics. So what if my first day had been a slight disaster? Tomorrow could always be better! The sun will come out tomorrow, bet your bottom dollar that tomorrow there'll be sun! I don't actually know what "bottom dollar" means. Is that when you lose a dime at the bottom of your jeans pocket? That Annie was a strange one.

I'm not entirely sure what brought on this newfound positivity, considering I hadn't seen my boyfriend in almost a week because he kept canceling our plans, my group members already hated me, I missed out on fancy pasta, *and* Dad hadn't budged on the whole bodyguard thing. Reggie would now be accompanying me to all my classes for the first two weeks *at least*. Emphasis on those last two words.

"It's just until people get used to you. Then we can dial it back," Dad had said on the phone last night, like I was some kind of plague being unleashed on the townspeople. But I was so optimistic about my day's events, I decided to take a bit of a walk in the morning before class. Fall was in full swing, and auburn leaves were beginning to appear on every tree. It wasn't quite home yet, but it was pretty all the same. Just looking at New York's beauty was already cheering me up. I had a feeling I was going to have a great day.

As usual, I was wrong. Reggie and I had been spotted by a small group of paparazzi on the way to getting coffee, and I spent four blocks trying to ignore their cameras being shoved roughly in my face and pointless questions being hurtled at me. Eventually Reggie had to step in and tell them to back off, and it almost worked for, like, thirty seconds. But then they just crossed the street and continued from afar, and by then a few more had joined in. It was such a relief when we finally ducked into Starbucks. At least I didn't have to listen to the sound of camera shutters buzzing around my ears any longer.

"Come on!" I groaned as I stepped inside, looking at the impossibly long line. "I'll be ninety-five by the time I get a muffin!"

Reggie did a quick scan of our outside surroundings, frowning at the photographers still a distance away. "It's nine-thirty on a Tuesday morning," he said in his deep voice. "Peak coffee time."

I swear, only bad things happen when you wake up before eleven. Lesson learned. The employees were clearly working as fast as they could, roughly scribbling names on paper cups and frantically passing them around to their coworkers. But the sheer volume of customers was proving to be a problem. There were people everywhere—collecting drinks, placing orders, men in suits typing furiously on their phones. It was chaos.

"This was a terrible idea. I don't know why I suggested we come here," I told Reggie.

"I recall you saying you wanted to 'drink the beverages of the common people.'"

"Honestly, their blueberry muffins aren't even *that* good."

Reggie raised an eyebrow. We both knew that was a lie. The blueberry muffins were amazing, and I wasn't fooling anyone with that line.

"Let me handle this," Reggie said. "I know a shortcut to the front."

"This doesn't involve stepping on people, does it?"

"Not physically."

There was a huge part of me that didn't feel great about Reggie plowing through a group of people just because I wanted a muffin and a hot chocolate and couldn't be bothered waiting. People like Jamie already thought I was the type of girl who would sidestep lines because I had money. Which is a complete lie. *I* wouldn't be sidestepping; it would technically be Reggie. I did some quick moral evaluating, told Reggie my order—the muffin included, of course—and handed him some money. I added a little extra so he could get something too. "Does this make me a bad person?"

"No. It just makes you rich."

That I could work with. I scanned the place for a free table while Reggie worked his magic. In the background I could hear him say, "Excuse me, super famous and important person coming through" while everyone else groaned. Great. People were really going to love me now. Although the place was packed, nobody had looked up and noticed me yet. Everyone was too busy making use of the Wi-Fi and enjoying the three pounds of whipped cream added to their drinks. Either I was giving myself far too much importance, or free internet just trumps the chance to meet a celebrity. I had finally spotted a tiny table near the back when I heard a familiar voice behind me.

"Excuse me, ma'am. I'm going to have to ask you to put your hands in the air."

I smiled and turned around. "Do I have to wave them around like I just don't care?"

Milo hooked an arm around my neck and pulled me against

him in a hug. "Smart-ass."

I reached up on my toes to kiss him. Even with three-inch heels, he was still too tall. "Loving the choice of outfit, Officer," I said, stepping back to appreciate his uniform in full.

He grinned. "Oh, this old thing? Threw it on last minute."

If I haven't already mentioned how sexy I find my police officer boyfriend, let me take a minute to say it again. My boyfriend is not only super hot, he's a super hot *cop*. You'd think after all this time I'd be used to it by now. But every time I see the slick NYPD printed in block letters, I get butterflies. Milo Fells commonly has that effect on people.

"Where's Reggie?" he asked.

I gestured toward the cash register and said, "Taking care of business."

"And working overtime?"

"Are we only going to speak in song lyrics and clichés now?"

"Apparently."

Milo sank into the armchair closest to the window. There were only two seats, and we were a bit cramped sitting so close to the wall, but it would have to do. Plus, it was the only spot that offered us a tiny bit of privacy. Reggie wouldn't be sitting. He'd be doing whatever he does, which usually involves strolling around the place and pretending he's having more fun than he really is.

Milo picked up a folded newspaper lying in the corner of the table. I couldn't quite make out which newspaper it was, but it had been folded onto an entertainment section. "Oh, great," Milo said in a flat voice.

He held the folded page up to show me. There was a small photo of Milo and I holding hands, smiling at each other as if sharing some inside joke. I couldn't remember what we were so pleased about, but it was clearly something special. Milo was in jeans, a gray sweatshirt, and a loose beanie. I was in a Stella McCartney jumpsuit and glossy pink Louboutin heels. We looked entirely mismatched yet completely happy. My eyes skimmed the small description underneath, which said something cheesy about how my boyfriend was keeping me warm as the seasons began to change.

"They're getting sneakier." Milo dropped the paper on the table with less care than I liked. "I didn't even notice this one."

"So annoying," I added with a nod.

After the Golden Globes incident, people suddenly wanted to know everything about me. Whether they liked me or not was irrelevant. My life didn't belong to myself anymore. I was public property, and as a result, so was Milo. Going to the movies and having ordinary dates didn't last long. Once the press caught a whiff that I was dating one of the police officers on my case, one that looked *that* good, it was like the world plunged into hysteria. We were all anyone was talking about. Our first proper date in the public eye had been right before Milo had left for New York. We had been hounded by so many paparazzi when leaving the restaurant, we had barely made it to our car in one piece. That was the day Milo decided he hated any attention from the outside world. It had been a pretty full-on moment, so I agreed. But I didn't really mind when random fourteen-year-old girls would tag me in their Instagram posts of us with their #couplegoals. It didn't even bother me when they made "he can arrest me any day" jokes in the comment sections of my selfies with him. I didn't love the extra pressure and prying eyes everywhere we went, but I was kind of used to it, watching my parents go through the same for years. For me, it was a minor inconvenience I had to deal with on a daily basis. For Milo, this was a life-changing adjustment.

He eyed me up and down with a smile. "You look great! Got a fancy photo shoot after this or something?"

"Nope," I replied with a shrug. "Just thought I'd put some extra eyeliner on today." That, and Tony, my hairstylist, did my hair in perfect Blake Lively beach-waves at seven in the morning while I lay half-asleep in my chair. But I didn't bother elaborating on the minor details; men will never understand how much effort actually goes into the effortless look. My second day of college *had* to be better than my first. And on the off chance it wasn't, then at least I could celebrate how hot I looked. People will always try to tell you confidence comes from within, and they're 100 percent right. But those people never had to look at the perfection that is my mother. My confidence comes with a little extra mascara.

"What time do you have to go back to work?" I asked.

"In about an hour, if we're lucky."

"If we're lucky."

Milo gave me an apologetic look. "I know, I know. Things have just been really crazy lately. We're just waiting for that stupid paperwork on the perp transfer. My partner and I were all ready to go, but apparently the cops at the other precinct weren't." He mumbled something in frustration while I nodded, pretending I understood what he was talking about. "Anyway," Milo continued, "catch me up! How was your first day?"

I grimaced. It's not like I wasn't expecting this question to keep popping up, I just didn't have the energy to keep reliving the horror. I told him the same story I told Jack. He listened intently before reassuring me that nobody really hated me, and I was just being paranoid. Easy for him to say, you'd have to be dead not to like Milo Fells. Thankfully, he seemed equally outraged at Jamie's smug little comment.

"I know you can't have him arrested, but can't you, like, send him a police warning or something?"

Milo stifled a laugh. "For what? Being a sarcastic tool? That's not a crime you know."

"It should be."

"If it were, I might have to give one or two of your friends a warning."

I gave him a pointed look, not buying into his innocent smile. We both knew exactly who he was referring to.

"Order up!" Reggie announced, placing two coffees down on the table carefully. "And your muffin, of course."

"Hey man," Milo said, shaking Reggie's hand.

"Lookin' good, Officer."

"Lookin' pretty slick yourself, as usual."

"Ah, you know." Reggie gave a humble shrug. "New pants."

Jeez, man. Get a room. As far as I could tell, he was wearing the exact same black pants and black t-shirt he had worn since the day I met him. Maybe he just bought them in bulk to avoid confusion.

"Thanks, Reg," I said, reaching for my hot chocolate. "I owe you."

"Maybe stop telling the agency you don't need me every second day," Reggie said. "That oughtta make us even."

Hilarious. Nice to know one of us thought this encroachment on my personal space was entertaining.

"I love that guy," Milo said, watching Reggie walk away with his own coffee in hand.

"He's great. I just don't need him to be great every minute of every day." Although, judging by my first day at college, he might end up being my only friend this semester. It was probably worth keeping him around a little more. I'm not sure how good his gossiping skills were or if he was interested in getting his nails done with me. But in case I ever decided to try my luck in an out-of-control bar fight, he'd really come in handy. In the meantime, I had devised a genius plan to solve my little group work dilemma. Magnolia Bakery. Hard to turn down friendship when it's coming in the form of a red velvet cupcake.

"By the way," I said, breaking off a chunk of the muffin. "You and I have plans this Friday and you can't bail, so don't even pull the whole 'my city needs me' excuse, Batman."

"What's this Friday night?"

"Jack's girlfriend is having a get-together and we've been invited."

"Are people still saying 'get-together'?"

"And before you ask if we can get out of it, I tried, and it didn't work."

Milo sighed and leaned back in his armchair. "Great. I was really looking forward to spending some more quality time with Jack."

"Why can't you two be civil?"

"I *am* civil! He's just a . . ." Milo trailed off. I could only imagine the infinite possible ways he could have ended that sentence.

Every time those two were in the same vicinity, my heart threatened to implode from anxiety. It wasn't exactly a surprise that Jack and Milo didn't get along. Back when Milo was working my stalking case, he had been stuck on the idea that Jack was in fact Dr. D, or at least a well-disguised accomplice.

Needless to say, that theory pretty much blew up in his face when it turned out to be completely inaccurate. Although to Milo's credit, Jack's behavior could potentially have been classified under the category of *serial sketchy dude.* That's an official police term, I'm pretty sure. He was always conveniently absent when the threatening phone calls were taking place, which, of course, turned out to just be a coincidence. And then there's the issue of his trust fund, which contains millions of dollars, still untouched. Jack has never really explained it, and I've never really asked. His business is his business, and I've got to respect that. Okay, I've totally looked it up online like a million times, but I couldn't find anything.

I'm pretty sure Milo knows more about Jack's life than I do. He's got an unfair advantage, what with all those fancy police resources. But we've never discussed it, and I don't intend to start that conversation anytime soon. At a bare minimum, they were polite around each other, exchanging formal hellos and how's it goings. But their conversations usually consisted of sarcastic comments and a lot of eye rolling, the latter mostly done by me.

"There's no guarantee I'm even free," he continued. "I've got Friday night off, but the way things are going at work, they could pull me in at any time."

"You practically live there!" I exclaimed. "How could they possibly pull you in any more?"

"Oh, they have ways. Trust me." Milo ran a hand through his dark brown hair, and I suddenly noticed how tired he looked. It wasn't just the normal sleep deprivation that goes with the profession. Something was bothering him.

"Is everything okay?" I asked. "You know. With work?"

"Yeah," Milo replied with zero conviction. "I guess so."

Oh, please. I was the queen of the *I guess so* reply. I placed my drink down on the table and put on my best impression of Dr. Norton's *I am a great therapist with a beige blouse and a tight bun* face.

"Alright, Officer, what seems to be the problem?" I said.

Milo's lips almost twitched into a smile but didn't quite reach the full way.

"I just feel like I'm going to be stuck at the bottom forever. I mean the cases I'm working are ridiculous! I'm not an idiot. I know I'm still pretty fresh out of the academy, and they're not going to assign a rookie the big stuff. But the cases I'm working right now are ridiculous! I can actually feel my IQ dropping."

"Like you said, it's only been a few months since you graduated. You just have to work your way up."

"I know," Milo let out a frustrated sigh. "But everyone's fighting for the good stuff, and I feel like I'm getting left behind. There's this guy, DeLuca, who graduated around the same time as me. Last week, he chased a guy for six blocks, threw him to the ground, cuffed him, and carried him to the nearest precinct with no backup. The guy was armed too. Apparently he caught him trying to rob an electronics store."

Sweet lord, that sounded amazing! Seriously, how did this guy not have his own TV show? I, of course, did not say this to Milo, who now looked twice as agitated just remembering the incident.

"Big deal," I told him with a shrug. "You could do that too! If you're looking for an armed thief, I just passed like forty-five on the way here. I could introduce you."

This time, Milo's dimples appeared. "Thanks for the offer, but I'll pass. You should have seen the way the boys treat DeLuca now. Some of the higher ups actually congratulated him! Which is a big deal, considering they try not to even talk to us unless they're dumping more paperwork on our desks. Want to know what I was doing last week while DeLuca was kicking ass? I was helping an old lady cross the street. I'm not even kidding. I was *actually* helping an old lady cross the street. And then she thought I was trying to mug her so she smacked me with her bag."

I took a big sip to hide the giggle that was threatening to escape between my lips. "But that's cute!" I exclaimed.

"I don't want to be cute, I want to be a good cop! I need to be taken seriously, or else the captain won't put me on the big case I want. And that's never going to happen if he keeps throwing freaking noise complaints at me!"

Milo placed his empty cup down and ate a bite of my

muffin. He so defeated, even after venting some of his stress, but I wasn't sure how to help. I could tell I had only heard a small percentage of it. I felt bad for him. I knew he wanted to be good at his job more than anything, and it sucked watching all his effort go to waste.

"Well, what's the case you want?" I asked, hoping to brighten his mood. Maybe if he talked about something that excited him, he'd cheer up.

"You know I can't tell you that. It's confidential."

"You tell me about cases all time!"

"Yeah, but only the little stuff! Just the petty crimes."

"Oh, come on! Who am I going to tell?"

"Uh, Jack? Aria. Veronica. Reggie. The guy working at the counter. Jack."

"You said Jack twice."

"I meant Jack twice."

"I won't tell him, I swear!"

I was definitely telling Jack. He should just be glad I didn't have him on loudspeaker already.

"Please!" I begged him, dragging out the word childishly. "Just tell me the little stuff! I don't need to know it all."

Milo was silent for a few seconds as he deliberated. Not that there was much of a point—we both knew where this was headed, and it wasn't in his direction.

"Okay, fine!" he said. "But only the little things, and you have to keep it on the down low."

"Got it."

"You really are *great* at getting your way."

"It's probably my only talent."

"Okay," Milo said in a hushed voice, and I scooted closer to hear him better. "The department's getting a lot of pressure from the colleges to crack down on the drug problem. It's not the basic stuff anymore, like ecstasy and weed. People ave started mixing things on their own and selling them to fraternities. The NYPD have set up a task force to deal with the issue."

"That's it?" I said, slightly disappointed.

"What do you mean?"

"No offense, but it's kind of an open secret that frat boys

like their party drugs."

"True," Milo said patiently. "But it's harder to manage if we don't know who's making the new drugs, and it's still unclear what's actually in them. Campus police are getting fed up, and they're saying the problem is getting out of hand. In February, a student almost died from one of these new pills, and since then, two more have been hospitalized. Nothing fatal, but we're not sure how lucky the next person will be."

"Okay, wow," I said, and Milo nodded grimly. "So which college is it?"

Milo paused. "I don't know."

"Oh, come on."

"No, seriously!" he said. "I really don't. We have a list of potential schools, but we're still working on it. The hospitalized students were from different colleges in New York, and the drug is showing up at different parties. We don't even know if it's just one college responsible."

"Just tell me this," I said. "Is NYU on the list?"

Milo bit his bottom lip. I already knew the answer, but I just wanted confirmation. There was no chance in hell that NYU *wasn't* on that list. It was one of the top schools in not only the country, but around the world. There was no way a growing drug trade was going to ignore a market like that.

"Maybe."

Maybe was an absolute yes. I had a sudden vision of Milo kicking down doors like in the movies, pulling out some full martial arts moves on the unsuspecting drug dealers. Of course, I'm not even sure he knows martial arts. But that's irrelevant.

"This is so exciting!" I exclaimed. "I mean, not for the people in the hospital obviously. Like, that sucks big time. But everything else sounds *so* cool."

"Now you see why I want in on the task force so bad? This could be an amazing opportunity for me!" Milo's phone buzzed, and he pulled it out, reading a text. "Damn it," he mumbled.

"Let me guess. You have to go?"

"Yep."

I looked at the time. It had only been a half hour.

"I guess they finished their paperwork early," Milo told me.

"We have to go pick the perp up. My partner will be here any second."

My shoulders dropped in disappointment, but Milo already looked guilty enough.

"It's okay," I said, offering him a half-hearted smile.

"I promise I'll make it up to you. I know I've said that a lot lately, but I really do mean it."

"Sure."

"Aidyn's here," Milo said, rising to his feet as he turned to face the entrance.

Milo had mentioned his partner Aidyn a few times in passing, and based on the stories, it was obvious they got along well. I had only met a few of Milo's buddies from the precinct, but I had never met Aidyn, despite them often working closely together. So if you, like me, were expecting Aidyn to be a young, stocky guy in a police uniform with decent hair and too much confidence, then you, like me, would be completely wrong. As it turns out, Aidyn was very much not a stocky guy. Instead, a slender girl who looked just a few years older than me walked through the door toward us. Her tanned skin was flawless, and although her dark hair was pulled back into a tight ponytail, you could still make out a reddish tinge streaked through the ends. She was dressed exactly like Milo, in the slick, black NYPD uniform. Except of course, she had breasts. That was a kicker of a difference.

"Gia Winters," she said, beaming at me with a grin that reminded me a little of the Cheshire Cat.

I rose to my feet reluctantly. "That's what they call me."

"I'm so glad I finally get to meet you! We've heard so much about you back at the precinct."

"All good, I hope."

"Oh, of course!" Aidyn turned to Milo with approval. Even with little makeup, her eyelashes almost touched her eyebrows. "She's even prettier than the pictures."

Milo gave an embarrassed smile, as if he was introducing his girlfriend to his grandmother.

"I have to be honest," I told her. "I wasn't expecting an Aidyn that looked like . . . you."

Aidyn gave me an understanding smile, as if this wasn't the first time someone had brought this up. "I get that a lot," she said. "It's Aidyn with a 'y' instead of an 'e.' Dad's from India and Mom's from Cali. I guess they couldn't compromise so they just went for a name that was out of the box."

"You're from California?" I asked with surprise. "Did you graduate with Milo?"

Aidyn shook her head, her ponytail swinging to and fro. "Mom grew up there, but I did a bit of moving when I was younger. I only did one year of the academy in LA and finished the rest in New York. Guess I've got a little more experience with the tough streets than Fells over here."

"Hey!" Milo replied. He was feigning an offended look, but his laughter was giving it away. "I do okay on the streets."

"Yeah, I'm sure the elderly population of Manhattan are forever grateful for your services," she said teasingly, and Milo's grin widened.

Cool. No problemo. Pretty sure my boyfriend was flirting with his hot female partner right in front of me, but that's fine. No biggie. Did I mention that she was hot? I'll mention it again. I mean, it's almost impossible to look attractive in those hideous, bulky black shoes. *This* was who Milo was spending twenty-four-seven with every day? I had known her two seconds and I was already at risk of falling in love with her. What hope did the male population have?

"So anyway," I said. "Didn't you say you guys had work to do?"

Aidyn nodded with a sigh. "I was hoping for a little extra down time."

Milo shook his head with frustration. "I don't know what they were doing down there."

"We both know what Miller was doing," Aidyn replied, and Milo gave a short laugh.

Alrighty then. So they had inside jokes. Whatever. People have inside jokes all the time. In fact, it was a good sign. She clearly had a sense of humor, which is always good. This positivity approach was working out great!

Milo glanced at his watch and said, "We'd better go. We've

got a billion more boring tasks waiting for us at work."

"The perks of being a civil servant," Aidyn added with sarcasm. "It was so great to meet you, Gia! We have to do this again when we have more time."

"Absolutely!" I replied, giving her a warm smile.

We would not be doing this again. Ever. Although given my current situation, I'd die alone at this rate. Maybe trying to be friendly wasn't such a bad idea. Besides, if she just happened to take the spot Jack was trying to force Lucy into, then it was a win-win. Aidyn looked like a nice enough person. As long as Milo didn't fall in love with her, she was cool.

Milo leaned across the table and gave me a quick kiss on the forehead. "Gotta run," he said as Aidyn reached the entrance. "I'll message you later, okay?"

"Okay."

Milo left, passing a group of new customers as he walked through the door, and disappeared into the traffic of pedestrians, Aidyn by his side. I picked up the newspaper and eyed the photo of Milo and me. It *was* a cute photo. I may be lacking in the perky ponytail department, but Milo and I were solid.

"Who was the girl with Milo?" Reggie asked, appearing at my side. He must have seen Milo leave.

I dropped the newspaper back on the table. "Aidyn. She's his partner."

"Damn," Reggie said, nodding thoughtfully. "She's cute. I mean, you don't see a cop like *that* every day."

This positivity thing was turning out to be a real bitch.

Five

By the end of the week, not even the Annie soundtrack could save me from the impending doom of meeting Lucy. I had successfully survived my first week of classes, even though the loud whispers and stares followed me everywhere I went. Reggie didn't help much on that front. It's kind of hard to blend in when you've got a six-foot-four tower of muscle trailing you.

Either way, there was no getting around this "get-together." I would have to befriend Jack's girlfriend and spend the rest of my life making friendship bracelets and going on brunch dates. Well, maybe not the rest of my life. Even though Jack had claimed he had a girlfriend "since always," he never really went into the specifics of that. Truthfully, using the word "girlfriend" and Jack in the same sentence still felt a little foreign to me. He was a serial flirter who had the ability to charm an unplugged lamp into life.

Come Friday night, Milo and I stood outside Lucy's front door, hand in hand and dread evident on both our faces. Jack's invitation had casually failed to mention that Lucy lived on West 42nd Street, home to some of Manhattan's most expensive apartments. The golden doorbell was so fancy I almost didn't even want to push it, out of fear that I might leave a fingerprint on its slick finish. So we could safely assume Jack's girlfriend was rich. This wasn't a complete surprise, given his mystery trust fund. Birds of a feather and all that. If Lucy was as rich as her doorbell was shiny, I could totally handle her. I know rich people. Rich people are my niche. Hell, I'm a rich person. But the equal anticipation and reluctance of finally meeting her was still gnawing away at my insides. What if she was mean? What if she hated me? What if she was super nice? I couldn't tell which was a worse outcome.

"This isn't going to be one of those nights where everyone brags about how many diamonds they have and then sacrifices a servant or something, right?" Milo asked, eyeing the brass door handles with uncertainty.

"What? Of course not! What do you think rich people do all day?"

"Brag about diamonds and sacrifice the poor?"

"In 1840 maybe! Now it mostly consists of pretending our shoes are comfy when they're not."

"Fair enough."

"Well, no time like the present."

"If she's anything like Jack, this should be a *great* night."

Milo reached over and pushed the doorbell. I winced as it bounced back into position. No fingerprints.

"It'll be fine," I said, talking more to myself than him. "Jack said it was just a casual hang."

Milo opened his mouth to reply but was cut off by the door swinging open. A fairly short middle-aged woman in a little white dress smiled at us.

"Here for party?" she asked. I couldn't quite make out her accent, but it sounded Scandinavian.

Milo and I looked at each other, as if confirming our answer. "Yeah," we said in unison.

The woman stood aside and pulled the door open a little wider. I gave her a nervous smile and walked through, never letting go of Milo's hand. The woman in the white dress closed the door behind us.

"Through here," she said. "Follow, please."

The front of the apartment didn't give away too much of its décor. There was a small table with a vase full of lilies and a coat closet to the right. Straight ahead, I could only see the edges of furniture, as well as a small section of what seemed to be a much larger window. But turning the corner was a whole different story. Lucy's apartment was *beautiful.* It was modern and chic, but not cold and impersonal. The window almost took up her whole apartment, giving a panoramic view of the skyscrapers outside, all lit up as if it were Christmas. The living room, connected to the roomy kitchen, was full of velvet sofas and shiny silver lamps, with photos hanging on every wall that wasn't taken up by the window. There was a small bar set up in the back with colorful bulbs hanging from the corner of the room. It looked almost childish in comparison to the rest of the slick décor, but it seemed to fit perfectly all the same.

I only had a few seconds to take in the surroundings before my eyes landed on the group of people scattered around the place. All conversation ceased as their eyes fixated on Milo and me. Even the waiters held their trays in silence. This was a serious case of déjà vu. Milo and I stopped in front of our audience, glancing at each other apprehensively.

"Hi!" I squeaked to no one in particular.

The room remained silent for a few long seconds before an excited voice emerged from my right.

"Oh my gosh, Gia!"

So *this* was the Lucy Fields I had heard so very little about. Even without a formal introduction I could tell without a doubt it was her. She walked toward us in a pretty burgundy dress, bandaged around her painfully perfect figure. For a second, I was sure she was walking in slow motion with a wind machine somewhere in the distance. Her black Louboutins were the only sound echoing off the walls. Her hair was a slightly darker shade of brown than mine and sat in loose curls halfway down her chest. She held a champagne flute in one hand with a huge smile plastered on her face.

"I'm so excited you're here!" she said, pulling me into a one-armed embrace. "This catch-up was *so* overdue!"

I'm not sure you can even call it a catch-up if you have literally nothing to catch up on. But I hugged her back stiffly, fully aware that everyone in the room was still watching. Lucy smelled like she had bathed in daisies that morning.

"It's so great to meet you," I told her when she finally pulled away.

"And you must be Milo!" Lucy exclaimed with equal excitement, reaching over to hug him.

Apparently she wasn't into handshakes. I thought New Yorkers were known for being unfriendly. Why was everyone suddenly a hugger? Milo and Lucy broke apart from their hug, and Milo held up the large bouquet of pink roses.

"These are for you," he told her, eyeing her champagne glass. "But it looks like you've got your hands full . . ."

"Oh, how sweet!" Lucy replied, placing a perfectly manicured hand to her chest. "Thank you so much! You can just hand that to Helga."

As if on cue, the housekeeper who had opened the door emerged from behind Milo and took the flowers from him with a meek smile, disappearing once more past the kitchen and down the hallway ahead. Lucy beamed at me, clutching onto one of my hands. It was as if we were best friends, reuniting at the airport after a year apart.

"Everyone," Lucy announced to the room. "This is Gia and Milo!"

The guests blinked at us silently. A few of them gave us polite smiles, but the rest eyed us up and down as they sipped their drinks. Quiet whispers broke out across the room, and suddenly everyone seemed to resume their conversations, stealing quick glances at Milo and me.

"Come meet everyone!" Lucy exclaimed, practically bouncing on her five-inch stems.

"I'm so glad you made me wear this blazer," Milo whispered as we stepped amongst the small crowd of party guests. "This is some other kind of fancy."

He was right. I was lucky I had a tendency to overdress for every occasion, or else we would have had a real problem. Rich people in LA were all about the plastic surgery and stilettos, but these people were a different ball game. Everyone looked to be in their early twenties, but dressed far beyond their age. The girls were in expensive tight dresses and the boys in well-fitted suits. One girl who walked past was actually wearing a strand of pearls. This was going to take some getting used to. I couldn't even imagine what was going through Milo's head right now.

Lucy led us to a small group of girls standing near the kitchen island. They grinned at us as we approached, sipping their drinks classily.

"Gia Winters!" one of the girls said. "In the flesh! I'm Nicole."

Lucy placed her champagne glass on the kitchen island and motioned toward the other two girls. "And this is Sophie and Madeleine. These are my girlfriends!"

Both girls greeted me with similar air kisses, taking in Milo under their heavily made-up eyes. Based on the way Lucy had hooked her arm through Nicole's bent elbow, it was clear that these two were best friends. That meant Nicole was one to watch for. The only thing more daunting than meeting your friend's girlfriend is meeting *her* bestie. There was no doubt I had come up in their martini sessions over the past few months. Girls. We're all one and the same when it comes to these things.

Milo greeted Lucy's girlfriends with a formal handshake, steering clear of the air kisses which, I'm sure, disappointed one or two of them. Lucy pulled two champagne flutes off a tray held by a passing waiter and handed one to Milo and one to me.

"I can't believe you're actually here," Nicole said. "When Lucy told us you were coming, we didn't believe her at first."

"Well, here I am."

"And we're so glad!" Lucy said. "Jack talks about you all the time!"

"Really?"

I'm sure Jack would have mentioned me occasionally, but *all the time* seemed a bit out of character.

"Oh yeah!" she replied. "He was so excited for you two to come tonight."

The last time I had seen Jack so excited, he claimed to have found his favourite hot dog vendor who had disappeared for a few months. Jack was never going to be excited about a party like this, especially when Milo was going to be present.

"Where is he, anyway?" I asked, scanning the room. "I don't see him."

"He just went to the bedroom to get something. He should be out any second."

The bedroom. Not *my* bedroom. I was overthinking things, obviously. But the image of Lucy and Jack sitting in bed at night like an old married couple was an unsettling one.

"Oh, there's a cake," Milo said awkwardly, eyeing the beautifully decorated purple cake in the corner of the kitchen. "What are we celebrating?"

"My birthday!" Lucy replied cheerfully. "Well, technically it was last week, but whatever. Same thing."

Milo and I exchanged looks. I was going to *kill* Jack.

"I'm so sorry," Milo said. "Jack never mentioned it was your birthday! We would have done a lot better than the roses."

"Don't be silly," Lucy replied, waving a hand dismissively. "I told him not to say anything. I wanted tonight's focus to be on meeting you!"

"Wow," I said. "That's . . . wow."

Wow was about the only word to describe the situation. Lucy was so blasé about her birthday; she was the complete opposite to me. My birthdays were always a grand affair. Balloons, confetti, presents, the works. I wanted it all. Mine was still months away, and I had already begun planning. I especially wouldn't put those plans aside for someone else, unless Chris Pine wanted to grab some fro-yo the very same night or something. Jack's birthday had been two months ago, and I missed it. I had felt terrible and had his birthday Rolex delivered to his door with a ton of balloons. But he assured me he barely even celebrated it. Some ambassador's son from the Middle East was on holiday, and Jack couldn't get out of work. I didn't know if that was a lie or not, but it made me feel better.

"Gia!" Jack said, suddenly emerging from the growing crowd of guests. "I didn't know you guys were here!"

Jack leaned over and gave me a hug. We were close, but we didn't hug often. Ever, really. It felt animated and unnatural, as if both of us were conscious of every movement we were making. I pulled away with a forced smile.

"Milo," Jack said, shaking his hand. "Glad you could make it."

"Thanks for the invite."

I shifted from one foot to another in discomfort. There was no way Jack hadn't complained about Milo to Lucy. He was always complaining about him to *me*. Both men's hands fell to their sides in silence, looking to me in hopes I would carry the conversation. I just stared back at them tensely. Jack looked so freaking good, I could barely look him in the eye. He was dressed in black pants and a crisp white shirt. In typical Jack fashion, he had the sleeves rolled up to just below his elbows, adding a casual touch to his look. His hair was perfect, as usual. But even though he was dressed nicely, he still seemed out of place at the party. Maybe I didn't know everything about Jack, but I knew this wasn't his scene.

"We were just talking about Lucy's birthday," I told Jack. "The one you failed to mention."

"Yeah," he replied sheepishly. "Sorry. I was sworn to secrecy."

"Oh!" Lucy said, looking over my head toward the entrance. "Izzy's here. Hold on a sec, I'll be right back."

She gave me another smile and planted a quick kiss on Jack's cheek before walking away. Jack refused to meet my eye. Why was this so weird? It was like we had this huge secret hanging above us, only we weren't in on it ourselves.

"I think I need another drink," Sophie said, holding up her empty glass.

"Same," one of the other girls agreed.

"Care to join us, Milo?"

Milo looked at me cautiously, as if asking for my approval. I raised my eyebrows, suppressing a laugh at his expression.

"Uh, sure," he said, glancing at his barely touched champagne. "Why not?"

Milo gave me another long look before walking off, Madeline and Sophie looking extremely pleased on either side.

"So . . . 'small get-together,' huh?"

"I would have gone with the fancy party theme, but I didn't

want you to show up in a ball gown."

I gave his shoulder a playful shove. It was so bizarre. The moment people disappeared he was the normal Jack again. Why were we so automated and self-conscious around Lucy and her friends? Jack pulled the champagne flute out of my hand and took a sip without even thinking twice.

"How much did you pay Milo to show up tonight?" he asked.

"Nothing much. Forty grand."

"That's it?" Jack exclaimed, feigning an outraged look. "Wow, you're cheap."

"Gotta save something for shopping, you know."

Jack laughed and looked around the room, seemingly unimpressed. "You must feel right at home. These are your people."

I swallowed a slightly larger sip of champagne than first intended and felt it go down my throat at a painfully slow rate.

"Right," I practically choked. "Home sweet home."

Two hours into the party, it was crystal clear that these were anything *but* my people. Was it just me, or was everyone in New York crazy smart? Where were all the drunken pool parties, Pitbull songs, fake tans, and thousand-dollar bikinis? Trust fund or no trust fund, this definitely wasn't Jack's preferred crowd. It just didn't seem to fit his personality at all. At least if Aria and Veronica were here, we could have made fun of all the pretentious people who only wanted to talk about things like museums and art. Does it look like I know anything about Van Gogh? No wonder the dude cut off his own ear; he was so tired of hearing people discuss "the bold definition of his brushstrokes."

Don't even get me started on the political debates across the room. Apparently yelling out "Team Obama" wasn't considered an actual contribution to the discussions, based on the looks of disdain I received. Needless to say, I was not upholding the good name of LA's upper class.

"So what's your opinion on the European Migrant Crisis?" A girl in a pale pink poodle skirt asked me. "I'd love to hear what you think."

"Sure," I replied, nodding vigorously. "That is a tough one."

"I'm a bit on the fence about it," her friend said, sipping a cocktail.

"Same." The two girls blinked at me, encouraging me to continue. "Um . . . you know on one hand, they really should improve the quality of medication. But on the other hand, it could promote addictions to prescription pills."

The girl in the poodle skirt looked confused. "I'm sorry, I don't quite understand."

Yeah, you and me both, sister. "I mean," I continued, "we all know how *that* ends. Anna Nicole Smith. Heath Ledger. Even Elvis! It gets the best of us, you know? Such a tragedy."

They did not know. Both girls stared at me blankly, struggling to come up with a response.

"Are we talking about the same Migrant Crisis?" Green Dress finally said.

Oh. My. God. If there was ever a moment where aliens wanted to abduct me, please let it be now.

"Oh," I replied, the color rising in my cheeks. "I thought you said *migraine* crisis."

"No." Poodle Skirt took a long sip of her drink to hide her judgment.

Well, jeez. It was a perfectly valid mix-up. I just figured that a bunch of French people had had too much wine and had given themselves perpetual headaches. If it really had been about migraines, then I totally made some valid points. Plus, if she had wanted my opinion on the skirt she was wearing then I would have had *plenty* to say. This wasn't the fifties, and pale pink for an evening party? Yikes.

"If you'll excuse me," I said haughtily, sticking up my nose. "I think my boyfriend is looking for me."

I stalked off toward Milo before they could ask me about the Arab Spring. I found him standing alone at the bar, watching the now packed apartment with evident boredom.

"There you are!" Milo exclaimed. He looked around hastily and lowered his voice. "No offense or anything, but this party kind of sucks."

"I feel so dumb here! I never thought I'd say this, but I actually miss the wild parties in LA."

"If I had known they were only going to serve cocktail shrimp and cheese cubes tonight, I would have grabbed a slice of pizza on the way over."

"They're hor d'oeuvres! What, were you expecting a buffet?"

"I was expecting not to starve to death!"

"We can leave after they cut the cake," I assured him. "I'm not leaving without cake."

I took a big sip of Milo's drink. It was some kind of whiskey, and it made my insides feel like they were on fire, but I took another gulp anyway. Lord knows I needed a little extra energy to get through the night.

"Do I have to have the underage drinking talk with you tonight?" Milo asked, prying the glass away from me with a smile.

"I think we both deserve a free pass for tonight," I said. "I'm dying out there with Lucy's friends."

"Honestly, some of Jack's friends aren't unbearable. Will is actually really funny. I'm surprised. I didn't think I was going to get along with any of Jack's crowd."

"You and Jack don't even have a proper reason to dislike each other anymore! All you do is make snide comments and argue over stupid things."

"I just can't have a conversation with him! I feel like he just disagrees with everything I say."

"You know he only does that to piss you off. He just wants to get you riled up."

"Well, it's working."

"Officer Fells!"

Two guys wearing black suits strolled over to us, cocky smiles on their faces.

"Tim," the first guy said, extending his hand so Milo could shake it. "This is Logan."

Milo did the whole manly handshake thing and offered them a drink from the bar, as if it were his own party and he was picking up the tab. Both men helped themselves generously.

"So, we hear you're a cop," Logan said. "That's cool, man."

"My brother had a run-in with the NYPD once," Tom said, running a hand across his slicked-back hair. "DUI. It's a good thing my dad knows a senator, right?"

Both guys laughed as I concentrated hard on not throwing a drink in their faces. Milo was keeping his cool, smiling politely and staying quiet.

"I wanted to be a cop once," Logan went on. "But then I decided it would never work. I don't think I could live off eating donuts all day."

Logan gave a small shudder as Tim snickered. Okay, hold up. It's one thing to pretend the police don't matter because daddy knows a senator, and it's another thing to besmirch the good name of donuts. What the hell had donuts ever done to him? Milo opened his mouth to respond, but I jumped in before he got the chance.

"I, for one, could never be a cop," I told them. "It's *so* dangerous. All the guns and crime lords! I would crumble."

Tim raised his eyebrows, looking amused. "Really?"

"Oh yeah!" I continued with a nod. "Especially this case Milo's working on now. I mean, I can't say much because it involves the Mafia. But I don't know how he does it! He's sort of an expert in this field."

Tim and Logan looked extremely sceptical about Milo's Mafia expertise, given his young age. But I could see they were curious. Milo looked at me like I was crazy. I gave his arm a gentle nudge with my elbow.

"Right," he said finally. "Yeah. The Mafia."

"So are they really as screwed up as the movies?" Tim asked.

"More!" I replied quickly. "You should hear some of the stories Milo's brought home from work. If they're not too confidential, of course."

Both men looked at Milo expectantly. They were officially hooked.

"Uh, yeah," Milo said, looking to me for support. "Sure."

"Gia!" Lucy exclaimed, appearing at my side. "There you are! Can I steal you for a moment?"

I would much rather have stayed and bullshitted some more, but I knew that wasn't an option.

"I'll be back," I told the boys, reluctantly leaving Milo to do the rest.

Lucy linked her arm through mine and said, "We haven't had a proper chance to talk yet!"

Yeah that was kind of the plan, bud. I let Lucy drag me over to a group of girls in the corner of the apartment chatting by the large window. I recognized Sophie and Nicole from before, but I hadn't spoken to the others yet.

"Oh my gosh!" a girl with curly brown hair said, eyeing my feet as I approached. "I love your shoes! Are those the new Ralph and Russo heels?"

I looked down at my royal blue stilettos with a pleased look. I just knew they'd be a great accompaniment to my lacy black Christian Dior dress.

"Yeah."

"Lucky! I'm still on the waiting list, but I'm trying to pull some strings. They look incredible!"

"So is it true that you're going to be the new face of Marc Jacobs?" Sophie asked.

"Well if it is, then it's news to me."

"I have to say, Gia," Nicole said somberly, "I so wish all the terrible things that happened at the Golden Globes weren't true. I can't believe how brave you were."

I made a sound a bit like a whimper, but it was quiet enough that no one noticed. Truthfully, I don't know why I thought I could make it through the night without Dr. D popping up in conversation.

"It was nothing really," I said. "Jack and Milo did all the work."

Actually, it would have been pretty awesome if Jack or Milo could have stepped in right then. But apparently they were too busy impressing assholes with fake cop stories and discussing the work of Beethoven, or whatever Jack was doing.

"You're just being modest," Lucy said. "Jack said you handled it really well."

"He did?" I asked with surprise.

"Of course."

Wow. Jack was just full of surprises tonight.

The girl with curly hair said, "You were so brave! I would have been scared out of my mind!"

I wasn't sure what the girls had read or heard about the event, because I *was* terrified out of my mind. I hadn't stopped being terrified since. There really hadn't been much chance to display bravery through all the panic and fear.

"Lucy here is a bit of a badass herself," Nicole said, and the other girls exchanged smiles.

"Stop!" Lucy said with an embarrassed laugh, but her friends were clearly urging her to continue. "It's really nothing. This guy tried to mug me last Christmas, but I stopped him."

I'm not saying it was a brag, but it was totally a brag.

"I was coming out of this event in SoHo," Lucy explained, watching my eyes widen with disbelief.

"She's an event planner!" Curly Hair explained quickly.

Great. Maybe she could plan my great escape from this party.

"I was just finishing up my internship, so I was super excited about this huge launch party I helped plan," Lucy continued. "Anyway, so I walked outside and was waiting for the car to pull up when this guy pulls out a knife, presses it against my throat and tells me to hand over my handbag."

"No!"

"Yeah! Wild, right?"

"I mean, obviously I freaked!" She continued. "It was really late at night and there weren't many people in the area, so I did what he said. The moment he touched the bag, he took the knife off my throat. But I still had a hand on the bag too, so I yanked it back toward me, kneed him in the groin then basically just kept whacking him with my bag until he let go and ran away."

"That'll teach him to touch a Birkin," Jet-black Hair smirked.

Lucy shrugged, as if her story was a daily occurrence. "Guess I'm a New Yorker through and through."

"That's incredible," I managed to squeak.

Okay, so she hadn't been drugged and tied to a chair like I had. But I had to give her points where it was due. If someone came at me with a knife, I'd sign over the deed to the house, my brother included. I wouldn't even think about saving my handbag. But Lucy was not only super hot and smart, she was apparently also a badass. What had I done in my time of crisis? Sat and cried until Jack and Milo came to rescue me. I mean, sure, I had backed a chair into Frank's little henchman. But Dad was the one who broke his nose. I don't think I could take credit for those injuries.

"At least your creep's in prison now," Curly Hair said, turning the conversation back to me. "He can rot in there forever."

I nodded timidly.

Don't get me wrong, twenty-five to life in prison was definitely a welcomed decision. His accomplice had gotten half that and cried when the sentence was handed down. I had been to both hearings, forcing myself not to break down every time I entered the courtroom. The media had been ruthless; I had never seen so many cameras aimed at me in my entire life. Frank gave a half-hearted apology. I didn't accept it. A tiny part of me almost felt bad as he was marched out in handcuffs. But that part of me was so insignificant, I never thought about it again.

"I can't get over how beautiful your apartment is!" I told Lucy, deciding that an abrupt change in conversation was necessary.

"Thank you!" she replied. "Hopefully the next one will be as great. Finding good real estate in central Manhattan takes a miracle."

"Oh, you're moving out?"

"Maybe. Jack and I were thinking about getting a place together, but we haven't decided anything yet," she explained. "You know, somewhere that's *ours* and not just mine or his."

"Wow," I struggled to form a sentence. "That's a big step."

"Not for these two," Sophie laughed. "Lucy and Jack have known each other since they were, like, thirteen."

"Yeah, we all thought they'd be married with kids by now," Nicole added, and Lucy gave her a playful slap on the arm.

It felt like someone had suddenly sucked all the air out of the room, and I found myself wishing I had some more champagne in my hand. Lucy and Jack had been holding hands and frolicking while I was still learning long division. I was half expecting one of the girls to tell me Nicholas Sparks was basing his next novel off their love story.

"That's amazing," I managed to say in a strained voice. "So great. So, *so* great."

I swiped a glass of Moscato from a passing waiter and downed half of it before he could even walk away. Jack and Lucy had a fairy-tale romance, and I had to practically book an appointment to get coffee with my boyfriend. Who, let's not forget, was partners with the most adorable officer I had ever seen.

"It must be so comforting having Milo around," Lucy said. "You know, leaving your life in LA and moving here."

It might have been a side effect of the drinks, but suddenly everything Lucy was saying made me want to roll my eyes. She was so condescending. She kept looking at me with wide-eyed encouragement as if I were learning how to sing the alphabet.

"He's been really great," I told her. "Jack's been a huge support too."

"I'm so glad!" Lucy said, and I tried not to scoff. "He really wants to make sure you're comfortable. I know how close you two have gotten."

"Yeah," I said, almost as a challenge. "We've definitely become close."

"Well, after everything you've been through together," Lucy continued, "how can you not be? You're practically family now. Like his little sister!"

If someone had swung from the chandelier and punched me square in the face, it probably would have stung a lot less than the word *sister*. Okay, fine. I had liked Jack back in the day when he was around me twenty-four-seven. But it was a vulnerable time, when I couldn't even look directly at his hair in the sunlight. And then Milo came along, and it was obvious Jack wasn't interested. Clearly because of Lucy, which I had only found out later, of course. But that was okay. I didn't like him anymore. There was just residual jealousy and the occasional moment of weakness when he was wearing that black t-shirt he looked so hot in. But that was harmless. I mean we were friends, but I still had ovaries.

"Gia!" I heard Jack's voice from behind me.

He emerged from the small crowd with his arm around another guy, smiling at me excitedly like a proud parent. The two boys squeezed into our little circle, and I recognized his friend as the guy Milo had been laughing with before. I had no clue where Milo was now, but I hoped he was still crushing Tom and Logan's souls with some badass Mafia stories—even if they were fake.

"Jack!" I exclaimed with so much enthusiasm that the remainder of my wine almost went flying all over Jack's friend.

Yeah, okay. I was a tad tipsy. But I needed a savior in that moment, and Jack's timing had been impeccable. That get-to-know-Lucy session had left me feeling spiritually broken, and I was about ready to smash through the giant window and perform a Spiderman-style descend into the streets.

"This is my best friend Scott! The one I've told you about."

"The dangerously cheap Chinese food Scott?"

The guy next to Jack laughed. "That's me. Sorry I'm late, Luce."

"This is why I told you not to bother with law school," Jack said teasingly.

"Us common people gotta work hard for that scholarship, man."

Scott was cute, but not eye-catching like Jack or Milo. His light brown hair was cut short, and his smile was immature but pleasant. He just looked genuine and friendly, and I immediately liked him. Most of all, it was kind of a new experience to watch Jack so comfortable around someone else. He and Scott seemed less like friends and more like brothers.

"These two have been best friends for, like, seven years," Lucy said.

Please show me on this map where I asked for your input, Lucy.

"That's one year in dog years," I said for no reason whatsoever.

Scott gave Jack an affectionate pat on the back. "This dog's been trailing me for a long time now."

I couldn't believe that Jack had a best friend, and that I was actually meeting him. I just had this image of Jack living alone forever, yelling at little kids who passed him, and flirting with any woman who looked his way.

"So how do you guys know each other?" I asked.

"High school," Jack replied. "Tenth grade, was it?"

"Ninth, I think."

"Oh, so you all went to school together?" I said, motioning toward Lucy and her friends.

"Nah," Scott replied with a grin. "I'm not one of those snotty rich kids."

Jack slung his arm around Scott's shoulder and said, "Scott and I met at my second high school. The school for the common and ordinary."

Both guys laughed, as if sharing an inside joke. Lucy's friends didn't look half as amused, but they seemed used to it. In fact, the girl with black hair had somehow managed to light her cigarette during the conversation, and was blowing little rings of smoke into the air.

"So, Gia," Scott said. "Is this party any match for the ones in LA?"

"Sure, this is crack-a-lackin."

The only thing that was "lackin" was my sobriety at this point.

I must not have delivered my line with enough conviction, because Sophie gave me an understanding look and said, "This isn't really the best example to go off. You're in the Empire State! We *invented* parties."

"Don't bother," Jack said dismissively. "Gia's still on team LA."

"That's not true! New York is great!"

It wasn't a *complete* lie. I mean, I would never get used to the sound of car horns blaring no matter where you went. But New York was beautiful. And only three homeless people had called out to me inappropriately so far, which actually seemed like an achievement considering it had been over a month since moving. Sure, the people could be a little hostile and impatient, but you were always a corner away from meeting an interesting character. Just last week a lady dressed in a full psychic uniform, minus the crystal ball, told me to "get my life right" as I crossed her on the street. I was trying, random psychic lady. I was trying.

"I have a great idea!" Lucy exclaimed. "Why don't we have a proper night out? Just us girls! We can show you what the city's party scene is really like!"

The other girls murmured their agreements.

"Fine," Jack said. "Scott and I will have our *own* girl's night. You'll all be sorry then."

"I'd like to see you try," Lucy replied with a smile, reaching across the circle and pulling Jack toward her.

I watched them play fight for a few seconds before turning my focus back on the drink in my hand, which was now almost empty. Lucy and her makeshift group of Spice Girls were making me want to throw up, but my footwear was far too expensive to risk it. I zoned out of the conversations around me, trying to ignore the way Lucy had her arms wrapped around Jack lovingly.

My gaze trailed off to the little table behind them and landed on the framed photograph that sat next to a Jimmy Choo clutch and an empty martini glass. Jack and Lucy were kissing in the photo, pressed against each other with their lips were locked. They were standing under a large banner that read: Happy New Year! Lucy was trying to stop a party hat from sliding off her head, and Jack was holding a small balloon in his free hand. The photo looked to be a couple of years old, but Jack and Lucy looked as perfect together as they did now, standing in front of me.

"Well, I think it's time for some toasts!" Nicole said, breaking into my thoughts.

Lucy had somehow gotten a hold of another champagne flute, as did Jack, who was now smiling at me. I looked away. Who knew where that much champagne was coming from. I alone had gotten through enough for a small city.

"To new friends!" Nicole continued. "May they be just as precious as our old ones."

"We're so glad you're here, Gia," Sophie said, raising her glass. "You're going to fall in love with New York, I just know it."

"To falling in love!" Scott piped up, exaggerating the romance in his voice.

"To getting into trouble," Jet-black Hair added. Her glass joined the others in the center of the circle.

"I like that," Lucy said with a tinkling laugh. She lifted her champagne flute so that it was directly in front of me. "To new friends and new loves. And, of course, to trouble."

Jack was my friend, but he didn't belong to me. I had no right to be so overprotective. And if he liked her, then surely she couldn't be all that bad.

I raised my glass with a smile I hoped looked genuine.

"To trouble," I said.

Six

Dr. Norton was scribbling aggressively on her notebook as I tapped my foot impatiently on the carpet. My head felt like it was ready to split into two. I had definitely hit the champagne a little hard last night. In fact, I was quite impressed with myself for even rolling out of bed and throwing on clothes just so I could sit and talk about my feelings to a complete stranger. Maybe this new city, new Gia thing was working after all.

"Sorry," Dr. Norton finally said, turning to a blank page on her notebook. "My last client had a *lot* going on."

"No problemo."

Great. At least someone else was more screwed up than I was.

"So," Dr. Norton said with a gentle smile. "I'm glad to see you're feeling better today. It was such a shame you couldn't make our session on Thursday."

"Yeah, sorry. That sore throat came out of nowhere."

I coughed twice, hoping to add some credibility to the lie. Dr. Norton didn't look the least bit convinced, but she didn't push it. At least the dark circles under my eyes added to my sick person look. I knew those had to come in handy one day.

"So, you've survived your first week of classes," Dr. Norton said. "How was it?"

Oh, great. Here came the coffee-shop small talk approach. Why couldn't she just get to the point and start examining my subconscious while I lay on a couch and told her I had dreams of my teeth falling out?

"Good," I told her. "My teachers are nice."

"That's great!" Dr. Norton said. "And what about your classmates? Have you made any friends?"

I felt like I was talking to my mother after my first day of school. Only if this were actually Mom, who was still frolicking in Greece somewhere, she would have asked if any of the guys were cute and whether or not I could set her up with a hot professor.

"Gee, I don't know. In between the hushed whispers and not-so-subtle photos in class, I don't think anyone's really had the time to come and actually talk to me like a human being yet."

"It's only been a week. I guarantee there are lots of other people still navigating their way around college like you are. Once they get used to you, the excitement will die down."

Alternatively, I could use the Jack Anderson approach and force my girlfriend onto people without giving them a choice. I slumped lower into my chair, fully aware Dr. Norton was waiting for some continuation.

"So . . . I met Jack's girlfriend last night," I finally said, fiddling with the charms on my Tiffany & Co. bracelet. "You know, my friend Jack? He used to be my bodyguard."

"Yes, I remember. And how was it?"

"What?"

"Meeting Jack's girlfriend."

Gee, funny you should ask that question. I only wanted to kill myself twice throughout the night, so that was an achievement. I had gotten super drunk, completely failed at intellectual discussions and stuck my head out the window on the way back home like a puppy, attempting to rap a Nicki Minaj song I clearly didn't know the lyrics to.

"It was great!" I told her. "She's great. So great."

"That's wonderful." Dr. Norton looked a little sceptical. "I guess you've made a friend after all."

"Oh yeah. We're *best* friends now. I'm probably going to be maid of honor at the wedding."

"They're engaged?"

"Well, not yet," I explained. "But it's inevitable, right? I mean, they've known each other since they were thirteen. They're planning on moving in together."

"You must be happy for them then," Dr. Norton said. "It sounds like things are going well."

"I'm *so* happy for them!" I exclaimed, with almost maniacal enthusiasm. "She's perfect. They're perfect."

We watched each other in silence for a few seconds, allowing me to stew in my thoughts. There. Now she had plenty to write about in that notebook. Happy patient, happy therapist.

"I mean, sure," I continued, as if my brain had lost control of my mouth. "Do I think they're a little mismatched? Yeah."

"Why do you say that?"

"I don't know. They're just so different! They've known each other forever, but she's so . . . and he's just . . . I mean I *know* Jack and . . . well, I guess she knows him better, but . . ."

I trailed off as a scary thought popped into my head. Was I so unsettled because Lucy reminded me of myself? Was this just some weird snapshot into what Jack and I would be like if we . . . nope. Nope times a million. Better not go down that road at all. Time to put a big cross through that thought and banish it forever.

Dr. Norton blinked at me for a few seconds without giving away a hint of emotion. When she realized my thoughts were not going to unscramble anytime soon, she continued. "People often underestimate the power of familiarity. You might be right in assuming their personalities aren't very well matched. But they've grown up together. I suppose they've evolved side by side. It can be hard to break a bond like that."

See, this is why I don't open up to Dr. Norton. She starts making sense and then I feel like crap.

"But familiarity doesn't always mean compatibility, right?"

"No, but I suppose it can help." Dr. Norton paused. "You don't think she's good for him?"

"Of course I do!" I said quickly, hoping she couldn't see right through me. "She's pretty and smart. She's brave too! This guy tried to mug her once and she totally fought him off until he ran away! It was like an episode of *Buffy* or something."

Actually, she had sort of just whacked him and yelled until he got spooked enough to give up. I'm pretty sure Buffy never slayed any vampires with that method. Dr. Norton made a sound that was a little like a laugh, but I wasn't sure therapists were actually allowed to laugh, so maybe she was just suppressing a sneeze or something.

"Wow," she said. "I hope she wasn't hurt."

"She wasn't," I assured her. "And she was by herself too. She didn't need any rescuing or anything."

"But you do."

It took me a minute to overcome my surprise. "Is that a question or a statement?"

Dr. Norton leaned forward in her chair a little. We were clearly getting into the deep therapy mode now.

"Lucy didn't need anyone to save her, even when she was in a position of danger. But when you were in great danger, you had a lot of help."

Go ahead. Kick a girl while she's down, why don't you?

"Where are we going with this?" I asked, starting to feel a little flustered.

Dr. Norton paused, no doubt for dramatic effect. "Your situations were very different, so it's unfair to compare them. But you feel ashamed that you had to have others rescue you, when Lucy was by herself and managed to not only escape danger, but also remove the threat. That makes you feel inferior."

Oh my gosh, maybe Dr. Norton was secretly the psychic I had passed on the street. I hadn't even thought about why I was so unnerved until she said it. But for some reason, it just made me even more defensive. Dr. Norton didn't know me. She couldn't act like she had me all figured out from a few sessions.

"That's ridiculous. I don't feel inferior to Lucy just because she stopped a guy from stealing her Birkin! She just got lucky."

"Perhaps."

"What are you trying to say? That if I was smarter, then I could have prevented what happened to me?"

"Not at all." Dr. Norton shook her head. "I think that's how *you* feel. But what happened to you was very different. So really, there's no reason to engage in a competition."

"I'm not in any competition with Lucy!" I exclaimed, my cheeks brightening. "I didn't even bring up the comparison. You did!"

"You endured an extremely traumatic experience. It's okay to accept your vulnerability. It's perfectly justified."

I rolled my eyes with a frustrated sigh. "I am not weak!"

"I'm not saying you're weak," Dr. Norton replied patiently. "Being vulnerable doesn't make you weak. It makes you human."

Okay, now she was just quoting *The Hunger Games*, I was sure of it. What did Dr. Norton know about how I was feeling? If she was such an expert then I'm sure she could tell my brain was practically disintegrating as we spoke and that I desperately wanted to run out the door.

"So what?" I said hotly. "You want me to just accept the damsel in distress role? You want me to just sit there and wait to be rescued?"

"Gia," Dr. Norton pushed on. "What happened to Lucy was scary, yes. But it was extremely different from your ordeal. You endured two months of torment, only to be kidnapped on one of the most important days of your life. It's okay for you to still be scared, or even angry. But you can't direct those feelings toward yourself. You're letting it take a toll on your self-worth and confidence. *You* are not to blame for what happened, and there was nothing you could have done to stop it. There's no shame in asking for help. But don't ignore what you're feeling, or you'll never have any closure."

Ah, closure. The magic word we had all been waiting to hear. Next she was going to give me a pamphlet to some ashram in India so I could find my inner peace and recommend a great store for flowy pants. I gave up. There was no point arguing or I'd be a senior citizen by the time she let me leave. I looked down at my wrists. The scars were so faint, you'd never even notice them at first glance. But if you looked close enough, you could see the marks where the rope had dug deep into my skin, leaving it bleeding and raw the night of the incident.

"Do you see Frank Parker in your nightmares?" Dr. Norton asked softly, and I looked up at her with a sigh.

"I don't see anyone in my nightmares because they don't exist, okay? Can we drop it, please?"

Dr. Norton sat back in her chair. She didn't seem convinced with the discussion, but thankfully she seemed to have given up ,for this session at least.

"Remember, Gia," she said. "A person's strength isn't always measured by their physical capabilities. Even Buffy had her off days."

I slammed the front door, throwing the keys on the little table beside me. They landed on the small stack of *Seventeen* magazines that had been delivered the day before with my smiling face practically glowing on the cover. It looked nothing like the half-asleep, yawning version of me who promptly showed up for their shoot at the 7:00 a.m. call time.

"Val!" I yelled out. "I need Advil! Like, *now*."

There was silence for a few seconds before I heard footsteps coming from the kitchen. I was expecting to find Val, but instead Jack padded out, holding two plates of food in his hands.

"Oh good," he said casually. "You're home. Perfect timing."

I blinked at him. Was I still drunk?

"You're not Val."

"And you're not Megan Fox. I wonder who's more disappointed here."

"Hilarious."

"Val's upstairs dusting the windowsills or watering the plants, or whatever housekeepers do."

"What are you doing here?" I asked, watching him place two hearty sandwiches on the dining table. "How'd you even get past the front desk?"

"Saving you from your hangover," he replied. "And don't ask.

I have my ways."

I didn't doubt it.

"What makes you think I'm hungover?"

"You're wearing your shades inside, your heels are under three inches, and you just called out for Advil."

I pulled my sunglasses off and dropped them onto the dining table. Apparently Jack was learning a thing or two about detective work from Milo.

"I'm not hungover," I huffed. "I just have a slight headache. I was up early this morning reading up on European politics."

Jack took a seat, pulling a plate toward him. "And why were you doing that?"

"It's important to expand your knowledge on international affairs, okay?" I snapped, dropping into the chair opposite him. "Can't a girl read up on European foreign policy on a Saturday morning!"

Jack raised his eyebrows and said, "Alright, cranky pants! It was just a question."

I hung my head in my hands and let out a groan. My whole body felt like it was running in slow motion. Was I dying? Oh great. I'd be the only celebrity in history to have died as a result of too much dessert wine and champagne. That would do wonders for my rock-star image. If anyone even considered me a rock-star to begin with. Some random guy trying to sell me tickets to the Empire State Building two weeks ago had asked if I was dating "one of them kids from One Direction." I had politely said no, but I was secretly thrilled he thought I was worthy of Harry Styles's romantic attention. That's got to count for something, right?

"You look like crap," Jack said, chewing noisily on his sandwich.

Actually, I looked like a corpse, and I could feel my pulse beating behind my eyeballs. But close enough.

"Remind me again why you're here?"

Jack pushed the other sandwich toward me. "Have some. My Uncle Tom says a BLT can fix any problem in the world."

I lifted my head up and inspected the plate uncertainly. Bacon was falling all over the place, and there was a pile of french fries mounted beside the sandwich. It looked like heaven.

"I can't eat that," I told him. "I'm on a diet."

"Since when?"

Um, since your girlfriend is a sex goddess and her stomach is as flat as a pancake.

"Since today."

"Is this related to European politics by any chance?"

"Not directly."

Jack shrugged and took another bite of his sandwich. "Your loss."

I eyed the sandwich through parted fingers. Did I want bacon, or did I want the body of a slender swan? Rhetorical question. I wanted the bacon.

"Okay, fine! Give me the damn sandwich."

I made a mental note to start the diet tomorrow. Maybe I'd even go for a run. Steph had more than once strongly suggested I take up a gym membership to maintain my figure. She even landed Khloe Kardashian's personal trainer to do the job. I lasted a month and a half before almost dying on top of the elliptical. What the hell was Photoshop for if I actually needed to work hard for my body? When I mentioned this to her, she replied with a cautious smile and said, "There's a fine line between Photoshop and straight-up CGI." I should have fired her right then.

"I take it you enjoyed yourself last night?" Jack asked me.

My liver felt like it was in a coma, but it wasn't a complete disaster, I suppose.

"Yeah, it was fun."

"Well, what do you think?" Jack said, watching me expectantly.

"I'm seriously considering marrying this sandwich."

"Not that! About Lucy!"

I momentarily forget to chew before swallowing, choking unattractively on the piece of bread lodged in my throat. Jack watched me with alarm, as I concentrated on not suffocating because of a freaking sandwich. I knew I should have stuck with my diet.

"Sorry," I spluttered, a hand to my chest.

"Are you okay?" Jack asked hesitantly.

"Yeah, I'm good," I replied, dropping the sandwich back onto the plate. Great. Now I had lost my appetite.

"So, Lucy . . ."

Well, jeez. A second ago my life was flashing between my eyes while a piece of bread was scraping against my esophagus. But by all means, let's focus on your love life instead.

"She's nice," I said vaguely. "I liked her dress."

"And?"

What did he want? A customer satisfaction survey?

"She's, um . . . pretty," I continued, avoiding his gaze. "And she smells nice. Her hair smells like coconut or something. Maybe it was her shampoo. Actually, could you ask her where she bought it? Because mine smells like raspberries, but I was thinking about mixing things up a bi—"

"Gia," Jack cut me off. "Do you happen to have anything else other than a detailed report of her shampoo?"

"I spoke to her for, like, ten minutes. I don't really know her well enough."

"And since when has that ever stopped you from forming an opinion?" I threw a french fry at Jack, who lifted the corners of his mouth in a small smile as it hit his plate. "But seriously. You liked her, right?"

I looked at Jack. He was practically sitting at the edge of his seat. It was clear he was looking for my seal of approval, but I couldn't decide if I was ready to give it yet.

"She's awesome," I assured him with an internal sigh. "You guys are great together."

Jack's smile widened into a grin. "Thanks. I'm glad you like her."

Yay for him. Meanwhile I was concentrating so hard on not throwing up, my eye was beginning to twitch.

"So you and Scott seem close," I said, attempting to change the topic.

"Yeah, he really liked you," Jack said. "He told me about your passionate interest in studying hieroglyphics."

I froze. If only the champagne had drowned out that tiny incident. It was near the end of the night, after a tall glass of some pink drink and about three slices of cake.

"I may have mentioned that I was interested in ancient history," I said.

Jack looked amused. "I believe your exact words were, 'I love those stick-figure thingos that the Egyptians drew on their walls like a million years ago.'"

Membership in the upper class was completely wasted on me. If only Dad had invested some of his millions in teaching me when to use the small fork at fancy dinner parties, or how to interpret art. As far as I could tell, the only difference between Monet and Manet was the letter after M.

"I didn't happen to share any other pearls of wisdom, did I?"

"I think at one point you described George Clooney as the 'savior we all need but don't deserve.'"

"Oh god."

"Sorry I missed the rest of that conversation. I could have saved you."

I narrowed my eyes at Jack and said, "Right, because you think I always need someone to rescue me?"

"No, I just meant—"

"Because apparently I can't even manage a conversation without someone *saving* me!"

Jack opened his mouth and then closed it again, probably out of fear that I'd try to use the club sandwich as a weapon. Truthfully, I didn't mean to go off at him like a rabid dog. But it had been a tough morning, my head was still throbbing, I was probably PMSing and those three bites of bacon I had gotten through had probably already clogged an artery or two. Unfortunately, Jack was collateral damage to a much larger war.

"So . . . how's therapy going?" he finally asked after a minute of listening to Val humming pleasantly from upstairs.

Gee, I wonder where his sudden interest in my mental state appeared from.

"I want to learn self-defense," I declared.

"What?"

"Self-defense. I want to learn it."

"No, I heard you. I just don't know why."

"Because," I said. "I think it's an important life skill. I mean,

I'm terrible at parallel parking, and I can't really swim—unless you count breaststroke, which isn't even swimming, if you ask me, because you're basically just kicking your legs around the place like a frog. I should know *some* basic life skills, don't you think?"

Jack stared at me in silence for a few seconds, trying to formulate a response. He finally settled on asking, "Is this about therapy?"

"No!" I replied haughtily. "It's about me being able to survive in the world! Do you know how dangerous New York is? Last year, there were almost seven hundred homicides in just Manhattan alone!"

"That seems *wildly* inaccurate," Jack said, looking doubtful.

"Okay, I may have just made that statistic up. But I bet I'm not far off the real one!"

"Gia, why do you need to learn self-defense?" Jack asked, looking more perplexed by the minute. "You have a bodyguard! That's what Reggie's for."

"So? There are billions of restaurants, but people still cook, right?"

"But you don't cook. You can barely open a packet of chips without help."

"It's a metaphor, Jack!"

"Okay . . ."

"It's especially important for us girls to know how to defend ourselves," I pushed on. "We're most at risk. And you know who's to blame for that?"

Jack looked a little scared, like he was expecting me to point a finger in his direction and yell out "YOU, JACK ANDERSON. YES. YOU."

"Who?" he asked cautiously.

"Patriarchy. And the government. And . . . consumerism."

"What?"

"You heard me!"

Honestly, I had no clue what I was even saying at this point. But it sounded smart, which was kind of new for me, so I rolled with it. I'm sure I was probably making some valid points. If I continued with enough confidence, then maybe I could really sell it.

"Alright, fine," Jack said, exasperated. "Great. Sign up for a class or something."

"Why would I sign up for a class when you can teach me?"

Jack's eyes widened with either fear or surprise. Maybe it was a bit of both.

"Me?" he said. "Why me?"

"Why not you?"

Jack blinked at me, clearly stumped. He thought about it for a few seconds, evaluating his next move.

"You haven't been watching *Straight Outta Compton* again, have you? You got insanely riled up last time, especially for someone dating a police officer."

"I like the lyrics, okay? Sue me!"

"You were ready to start throwing furniture at the wall."

"Are you going to teach me to fight or not?"

"Okay," he said, pushing away from the table and standing. "Let's do it."

"What, right now?" I asked.

"Why, do you have somewhere to be?"

Well, I had sort of been hoping to crawl under my blanket and live there for the next week. I had even rescheduled my meeting with Steph, who had spent a good half hour on the phone to convince me to do an ad for a Portuguese brand of orange juice. But I couldn't very well back out after my huge patriarchy speech. It would go against all of the principles that I just made up on the spot. I rose from my seat reluctantly.

"I don't think I'm really dressed for a fight lesson right now. Maybe this is a bad idea."

Jack considered my tight corset top, cardigan, and jeans. "That top is always a good idea, trust me."

Jeez Louise. You have to give a girl some warning before you launch a move like that.

Jack and I stood facing each other between the dining table and living room and far away from the sofas, lamps, and anything else we could do some physical damage to. There wasn't a lot of empty space, but it was good enough for an impromptu lesson in self-defense. I glanced up. Val was peering down from the stairs, trying to look busy, but clearly curious as to what was happening. When I wanted an Advil she was a ghost, but every other time she was front and center for the show.

"Okay," Jack said. "Put your wrists together like I'm about to handcuff you."

I raised my eyebrows. "You're teaching me self-defense, right?"

"Just put your hands up, wiseass."

I bent my arms up obediently, pressing my wrists together like he said.

"Good." Jack wrapped his hands around my wrists, and I felt a bolt of electricity shoot through my veins. He tightened his grip. "Okay, now twist your wrists so your palms are facing me."

I turned my wrists, at first struggling to move them under Jack's firm hold.

"Now press your palms against my chest."

I widened my eyes. Jack and I were standing so close together, you'd have thought we were learning how to do the waltz. He looked at me expectantly, and I hesitantly placed my hands on his chest. I was not nearly emotionally or physically equipped to be feeling his rock-solid body today.

"Um . . . now what?" I asked.

"Now push me backwards, and then immediately jerk your hands back toward you. Make sure you bend your elbows upwards, so your hands slide out of my grasp. Don't be afraid to use a little force."

I took a deep breath and looked at Jack, who was nodding at me with encouragement. I pressed my palms harder against his chest and gave him a shove, yanking my hands back toward me as he had instructed. My wrists barely managed to escape his clutch, as I took a step backwards.

"I did it!" I exclaimed proudly.

"Not bad, Princess," he replied, looking mildly impressed. "But that was an easy one."

He took a step toward me, as I shamelessly thought about how if my potential attacker looked anything like Jack, I'd probably be nervously asking him out for coffee rather than pushing him away from me with intricate palm actions.

"Okay," Jack said. "Now the pressure points."

He stepped forward and pushed some of my hair behind my shoulder. My entire body went stiff as he placed two fingers on my neck. They were cold, but that wasn't the reason for my jumpiness.

"This feels weird," I told him, suppressing a nervous laugh.

"Concentrate!" he replied. "I'm teaching you the pressure points."

I made a big show of moving my arm slowly toward his neck, giving him my best don't-mess-with-me look.

"What are you doing?" he asked.

"That's my don't-mess-with-me look."

"Yeah, we're going to need to work on that later."

Jack spent the next fifteen minutes showing me the pressure points, like the eyes and the nose, and explained how I could inflict the most damage. He showed me how to break someone's nose using the base of my palm, how to kick the side of an attacker's knee to push them off balance, and three other ways to get out of someone else's grasp. I reenacted everything he showed me like an obedient puppy learning tricks, and I was actually beginning to enjoy myself. Kicking ass wasn't nearly as hard as I thought. I pictured myself in a grunge denim jacket, parading down the streets fearlessly with a bounce in my step. I'm not sure why my imagination had conjured up a cross between *The Outsiders* and *Westside Story*, but it seemed to be a happy medium.

"This is your reminder to stay on my good side," I said, practicing another kick.

Jack gave me a half-smile and said, "Calm down, Jackie Chan. You've still got a lot to learn. Now turn around."

Jack placed his hands on my shoulders and wheeled me around so that my back was to him. A second later he had an arm wrapped around my waist. I immediately jumped away from him, as if someone had tried to dunk me in a bathtub filled with scalding water.

"What are you doing?" I asked, my voice becoming shrill.

"What are *you* doing?" he replied impatiently. "Turn around! I'm teaching you how to defend yourself if someone attacks you from behind."

I chewed on the inside of my lips nervously. I whirled around slowly, wincing as Jack placed his arm around my waist once more.

"Alright." His voice tickled my ear. "If someone grabs you from behind, then it's obviously harder to get out of their grasp because you can't see them. So, your main focus is to get them off you."

Actually, my main focus was making sure I didn't rupture a lung with all my heavy breathing. But I nodded silently and let Jack feel me up in the name of self-defense. I was sort of hoping he would let go so I could run into the bathroom and fan myself for the next three hours until my heart rate dropped to a normal level. But Jack had a different plan, because instead of releasing me, he placed his other arm across my chest and over my arms, pressing himself completely against my back. By this stage, I had just given up on breathing completely. There was no point. I was probably going to die from my hormones running into overdrive, and I couldn't even complain that it was a bad way to go. I could no longer see Val by the stairs, but I hoped she wasn't secretly live streaming this footage on YouTube.

"Is this the tree-climber approach?" I said, feebly attempting a joke.

"Close enough," Jack replied. "A good trick is to jerk your head backwards and into the attacker's nose. It's basically a reverse head-butt."

"This is ridiculous. You're basically just sniffing my hair."

"Yeah, it smells like raspberries. Now tilt your head back!"

I did some eye rolling and tilted my head back until I could feel Jack's face basically buried into my hair.

"There. Happy?" I was so glad Jack couldn't see how red my cheeks were.

"Good," he said, but he didn't let go of me. "Okay, last tip for today's lesson."

Jack moved his arm up from across my chest and rested it a little higher, just under my collarbones. Every muscle in my body contracted.

"Is this really necessary?" I asked.

I was practically going into cardiac arrest.

Jack ignored me and said, "This one's kind of a combination. It's sort of a three-step process."

If one of those processes involved Jack's hand sitting right above my boob, he was pretty much nailing that step.

"First," he continued, "press down on the attacker's foot *really* hard. Second step, dig your elbow backwards into the solar plexus."

"The what?"

"Just underneath the breasts, right in the center."

"What if my attacker doesn't have breasts?"

"You know what I mean."

I did as he said, folding my arm and gently digging my elbow into his torso. I was probably a little off the mark, but it was close enough.

"Okay, good," Jack said. "The final step is the head-butt I just showed you. It's actually pretty easy, if you think about it."

Uh, yeah. Only because Jack was playing the role of the world's most attractive and kindest attacker. I doubted I'd have this much guidance if the real scenario ever played out.

Jack slowly removed his right hand, but my skin still felt like it was burning. He moved forward so that he was next to me, and we looked at each other silently for a few seconds, tangled in our own thoughts. I could practically hear my heart pounding against my rib cage. What a cliché. I was half expecting Mills and Boons to call and thank us for inspiration. I looked at the floor, afraid that my nerves were written all over my face.

"Cool, cool, cool. That's um . . . thanks for the lesson."

"Yeah! No problem. You did great."

We locked eyes once more, unsure of what the next step was. Whatever we were doing, it was worth the rise in blood pressure. Jack opened his mouth to say something but never got the chance, because we were interrupted by the sound of the doorbell echoing off the walls. I hadn't been expecting to hear the noise out of the blue, and reflexively whipped my hand upwards as I jumped, accidently smacking Jack in the face.

"Ow!" he cried out, clutching his nose.

Not exactly how Mills and Boons would have wanted the moment to end.

"Oh my god. I'm so sorry!"

Jack clasped his eyes shut for a few seconds, and thankfully I couldn't see any blood through his parted fingers. I watched with growing guilt and he sat on the top of the sofa, hands rubbing the bridge of his nose. Val was on the top step, ready to answer the door. But I assured her that I was closer, calling out another apology to Jack as I hurried toward the door.

"Milo!" I exclaimed with surprise.

Of course it was Milo. He was the only person the front desk let up without even bothering to ask me first. Although based on Jack's surprise visit today, they were letting anyone parade up to the penthouse these days. Milo stood in front of me in his NYPD uniform, eyeing my flushed face and glancing at Jack, who was still groaning quietly in the background. He raised an eyebrow.

"Am I interrupting something?"

I gave a laugh that was almost maniacal and waved a hand dismissively.

"Of course not! We were just having some jolly good banter!"

Oh great. Just what the situation needed. My horrendous British accent that forcibly popped out whenever I was extremely nervous or flustered. I had managed to make it through Jack's hands all over my body without it making an appearance, only for it to announce itself proudly when my boyfriend arrived moments later. Like *that* wasn't sketchy at all. Milo stepped inside, looking over at Jack suspiciously as I swung the door closed behind us.

"So what brings you to Casa Winters?" I asked.

What the hell was I even saying? I could barely handle the situation in English!

"I needed to talk to you." Milo said, eyes still on Jack, who seemed to be slowly recovering. "What's going on here?"

"Charades," I replied quickly. "Jack guessed the wrong

movie, so I had to slap him."

Milo looked at me with alarm and said, "That's a little extreme, isn't it?"

"Go hard or go home, right?" Jack said, massaging the tip of his nose.

"Anyway," I said, my gaze dropping to the big, white envelope in his hand. "What did you need to talk to me about?"

"Right." Milo turned back to me distractedly. "I need your help."

"Great!" I replied with concerning happiness. "Fabuloso! What do you need?"

Milo looked like he was considering injecting me with horse tranquilizer but instead lowered his voice and said, "It's kind of private. It's about that case I was telling you about."

"Wait, you got the case?" I asked, and a look of mild excitement appeared on Milo's face. I flung my arms around his neck. "That's so great!"

"Don't congratulate me just yet," Milo said with a little laugh. "Technically I'm sharing the case with De Luca, McCall, and Aidyn." Milo walked over to the dining table, briefly bending down to give Famous a cuddle. He pulled out the contents from the envelope in his hand and dropped them onto the table.

"What's all this?" I asked, as he rifled through the pages.

"This," he replied, "is what I need your help with." Milo looked over my head at Jack, who was still resting against the top of the sofa, watching us curiously. "This is sort of confidential, man. No offense or anything."

Jack gave him an innocent smile and said, "Don't mind me. I'll just be here watching the Disney Channel."

Jack reached for the remote, but didn't turn the TV on. Instead, he went back to watching us carefully. Milo rolled his eyes.

"Does he have to be here for this?" Milo whispered to me.

I turned to Jack with a *help a sista out* look, and he put his hands up in defeat.

"Alright, fine. Nickelodeon it is."

Milo didn't say anything until Jack had turned the TV on,

disappeared behind the sofa, and put the volume high enough to drown out our conversation.

"You're probably just going to tell him everything I say anyway, right?" Milo asked, giving me a knowing look.

"No," I replied.

"Yes," Jack called from behind the couch, and Milo gave another eye roll.

I assured Milo that we were sworn to secrecy and even offered to make a blood pact just for extra measure. He declined and said that wouldn't be necessary and asked why I was so drawn to violence today. I told him I had cramps and he nodded, more than happy to stop asking any more questions.

"Here's the deal," Milo said, clasping his hands together like a teacher ready to begin a lesson. "Last night a student at a party in Baruch College was hospitalized. Aside from almost drinking herself into a coma, she also took one of these."

Milo held up a piece of paper with two large photos on it, placed side by side. The first was of a round, orange tablet, and the second showed a small, cellophane packet with the black silhouette of a bull printed on it. I took the paper from him and inspected the bull's horns.

"What's that?"

"They call it 'Stag.' It's that drug I told you about the other day; the one that's made up of pretty much everything imaginable. The guys at the lab are still looking into it."

"How'd you get this?"

"Lucky for that girl, she pretty much threw up most of her insides before the drug could do any serious damage." Milo pointed to the paper still in my hand. "And lucky for *us,* she still had this in her pocket. Said some guy she was flirting with gave her a little packet with two orange pills and bragged about how he had helped make it. I guess she only got through one pill before things went downhill."

"So who's the guy who gave it to her?" I asked.

"That's the thing," Milo replied grimly. "She can't remember. Or maybe she can, and she's just trying to cover for him. We're trying to track him down, but I seriously doubt we'll get anywhere. Her description of him was pretty vague. Tall, brown hair, medium build. It doesn't really help us narrow it down."

"That sucks," I told him, placing the photos down on the table. "What are you going to do now?"

"Actually, I'm here about what *you're* going to do. She clearly couldn't remember much," Milo said. "But she did remember the guy telling her he was a student at NYU."

Oh, great. Dad would be so pleased that I chose the college where an up-and-coming drug lord was carrying out his life ambitions. That wasn't going to come up at the dinner table at all.

"I hate to break it to you," I said. "But NYU is massive. You can't honestly expect to find this guy based on this much information, right?"

"Like I said before, our hopes aren't high. But it gives us a good place to start."

"Only if she was telling the truth," I reminded him. "And who's to say that guy really did help make the drug? Or that he even goes to NYU. He could have just been bullshitting."

"You're right. But it's the first good lead we've had in months, so it's worth looking into."

I didn't want to burst his bubble, but it didn't really seem like much to go on. I hadn't had much experience with the manufacturers of shady drugs, but this guy was clearly an idiot if he was bragging about his contribution to the trade.

"What do you need me to do?" I asked, ignoring the sound of Jack flipping through channels in the background.

"We managed to get a few statements from some people at the party," Milo said. "No one else is admitting to taking the drug, but a few saw the packets going around. A few others said they saw the picture of a bull printed on a button pinned to some people's shirts. They couldn't say for sure who the buttons belonged to, but they definitely recognized the symbol going around."

"So you want me to find out about the button?"

"I want you to keep an eye out for it. There's no guarantee you'll even see it. Like you said, NYU is massive. But if there's any chance you do see it, I need you to let me know."

One self-defense class and the universe was already giving me a career as a badass! Maybe I'd get an honorary badge if I helped solve the case. Milo and I could be the power couple I always dreamed about.

"Sorry to interrupt," Jack said, his head popping up from the sofa. "But I'm just having a hard time believing that your Captain thinks this is a good idea."

"There's no way I'd ask Gia to do something if she was going to be in any danger," Milo replied roughly. "I wouldn't even be involving her if she didn't go to NYU."

"Exactly!" I said. "I just need to look out for the bull symbol."

"Right."

"And if necessary, take the drug dealers down."

"No!" Milo corrected me quickly. "That's not what I said. You just *look* for the button and that's it. You won't be taking anyone down."

"This sounds like a bad idea," Jack said in a singsong voice.

"And why's that?" Milo asked irritably.

"Don't you remember what happened last time Gia got excited about investigating? And now you're voluntarily bringing her in on a case. That's a recipe for disaster."

"Hey! My investigations were great, okay?"

"There's not going to be any investigating!" Milo said loudly, as if he were delivering an announcement to a crowd. "Gia, all you have to do is keep a lookout for the bull symbol, and if you see the button on anyone, let me know."

"Got it. And take them down if necessary."

"No! There will be no taking down involved! Do you hear me?"

I smiled in reply. Finally. An actual reason to show up to class every day.

Seven

The next week went by with little excitement. No Lucy, no bull symbols, and no escape from my therapy sessions. According to Dr. Norton, my "increasingly closed-off nature" was going to "deeply affect" my healing process if I didn't open my mind up to our sessions. As if the risks of me being messed up were only becoming apparent *now.* My mother spent a large portion of her career wearing nothing but bunny ears and G-strings, and my dad's ex-best friend tried to kill me on a movie set. The screwed-up ship sailed ages ago.

What I really wanted was some company. Val was cool, but she was hardly a roommate. The only thing Steph wanted to talk to me about was PR opportunities, and Mom was God-knows-where in the world, considering she called about once a week for thirty seconds. At least Dad picked up the phone when I called, but with the movie in pre-production stages, he was busier than ever. Milo was great, but now more than ever, he was consumed with work. The Stag investigation wasn't moving forward at all, so he was basically working double-time to try and outshine the other junior officers working the case.

There was always Jack, of course, but even he was busy with work. On top of that, I had been trying to avoid him as much as I could out of fear that he'd spring another surprise meeting on me and introduce me to his accountant or gardener. I was going to have to accept that the only friends I had were the ones I could reach through three-way calls. It wasn't completely satisfying, but I was in no position to be picky.

"They're going to hate me!" I groaned into the phone, trying not to topple the cardboard tray of coffees in my hand as I hurried down the street.

"They're not going to hate you." Veronica's voice came through the receiver.

"Yeah!" Aria said. "You're only a little late."

"Try forty minutes late!"

"It was a business meeting. They can't get mad at you for that. It's your career!"

"Veronica, I hardly think my overnight spike in media attention counts as a career."

"It's close enough," Aria said. "I don't see any of them getting interview requests from Jimmy Kimmel."

"I am officially lost!" I declared, glaring at the street signs with frustration. "Why is New York so confusing? It's been weeks, and I still have no clue where anything is."

"The grid system is so stupid. Like, why can't they just put all your buildings into one campus, like a normal college?"

"They're going to hate me," I repeated, cradling my phone between my ear and shoulder as I adjusted the coffees. "They didn't want me to come to this study session in the first place. I had to practically force them to invite me, and now I'm forty-one minutes late!"

"Well then what are you worried about?" Aria said. "They didn't even want you to come, so they won't miss you."

"Maybe I should pretend I saved a puppy's life or something. They can't be mad that I'm late if it involves puppies."

I took a sudden left and almost knocked over a group of people passing. God, I really hated the city right now.

"I think you're overthinking this," Veronica told me. "Just be yourself! You don't have to try so hard to befriend them. If they don't like you for yourself, then it's their loss, not yours!"

"Besides, you don't even know that they don't like you," Aria added. "You're just being paranoid."

"Oh, I'm not paranoid, trust me. Some of them aren't so bad. But Jamie and Hannah are the worst! They always look so smug. I feel like they have this private joke, and instead of laughing with them, *I'm* the punch line!"

"Gia, don't worry!" Veronica said, but I could definitely detect pity in her voice. "Making friends takes time. It's only been a few weeks. They're still getting to know you."

Easy for her to say. Her and Aria had made their own new friends already and uploading cute pictures with them at beach parties. It was only a matter of time until they replaced me for good.

"I don't get it," I lamented, slightly out of breath from all the rushing. "I thought everyone wanted to be friends with celebrities! Selena Gomez's birthday party was great! Everyone was so nice to me."

"That's because everyone there was already famous," Aria reminded me. "They've had much more practice with expensive vodka and air-kisses. You can't expect the same from a bunch of normal college kids. It's just two different worlds."

"You're a great person!" Veronica was saying when I finally found the street I was looking for. "You are adorable, and you have great hair!"

"Oh no," I said, anxiety filling my entire body. "I'm here, guys."

I looked a few yards ahead, where Jamie, Kyle, Michelle and Hannah were sitting at a wooden table, aggressively typing away on their Macbooks and occasionally looking up to speak. I doubted they even noticed my absence.

I told the girls I loved them, exchanged a quick goodbye, and hung up. This was ridiculous. Why was I so nervous just to talk to a bunch of my classmates?

"Gia!" Michelle said with surprise as I hurried toward the table.

"Hey!" Kyle added, looking equally taken aback. "You're here. We missed you at our study session last week."

"Yeah," I said. "I was um . . . sick."

Liar. I wasn't sick. I was in SoHo, working on a beauty piece for Refinery29.

"Anyway, I'm *so* sorry I'm late," I continued. "I got caught in traffic. Those taxis are a real pain, am I right? And then this tiny puppy just wandered onto the road . . ."

I trailed off, watching my group members blink back at me expressionless. Veronica's words rung in my ears. I just had to be myself, and if that wasn't enough, then it was their loss and not mine.

"Actually," I said, "my meeting with CoverGirl went a little overtime. I'm really sorry I'm late. But I brought you guys coffee to make up for it!"

I placed the cardboard tray down on the bench with a hopeful smile. Everyone looked at it blankly and then back up at me.

"Thanks, Gia! That's really nice of you," Kyle finally said.

He reached for a coffee and took a quick sip of it before placing it next to him. Michelle also pulled a cup from the tray and gave me a grateful, albeit slightly hesitant, smile. Jamie and Hannah inspected the coffees suspiciously. You'd have thought I'd placed a platter of poisonous apples in front of them.

I looked down at the table awkwardly. Kyle and Hannah were sitting across from each other, with Jamie and Michelle beside them respectively. There didn't seem to be too much room left on the table with all the laptops and notebooks sprawled everywhere. I eyed Hannah's handbag that was sitting beside her on the edge of the table. If she removed it and scooted over, there would definitely be a place for me. But she didn't remove it. Instead she looked up at me sweetly.

"No Reggie today?" she asked.

"Nope, just me. Decided to go solo."

Actually, Reggie had come to the meeting, but I had sent him home immediately after. Dad's two-week deadline was up, and no one even seemed remotely interested in approaching me, let alone harming me in any way.

"That's a shame," Jamie said. "I was starting to like him."

Really? He was *already* warming up to a guy he had met

once who was made up of 90 percent muscle? And here I was buying cupcakes and coffee for everyone like an idiot. Had I known that's all it took, I would have hit the gym once or twice.

"So are you going to be a CoverGirl?" Michelle asked excitedly, and for a fleeting second it actually felt like she liked me.

"I don't know yet! We're still negotiating a contract. Here, you guys can have these!"

I pulled out a handful of mascara wands and small eyeshadow palettes from my Burberry purse, dropping them onto the table next to the coffee. Looking at them together, I felt a little stupid. It was like I was a pushy sales rep, throwing products into the air and hoping someone would buy something.

"Thanks, but I've already got that mascara," Jamie said, deadpan, and everyone gave a little chuckle.

Hilarious. No, really.

"So what did I miss?" I pushed on, accepting that I would have to stand for the remainder of our study session.

"We've allocated different parts of the assignment to each group member. It just makes it easier to manage," Michelle said.

"Awesome! We've decided on Jung, right?"

I hesitated on the name. I didn't want Hannah going off on me again for improper pronunciation and burst a forehead vein or something. Kyle nodded and launched into his breakdown of our assignment roles. He explained how he and Michelle would be researching the key points, Jamie would be working on twenty-first century references, and Hannah would be focusing on pop culture in relation to his theory.

"We're actually pretty much done here," Kyle told me.

"Great! So, what's my role?"

Everyone exchanged quick glances, trying to avoid my gaze. It didn't take a genius to figure out that no one had even considered that I'd be contributing to the assignment.

"You can do background info!" Hannah piped up, looking pleased with herself.

"Yeah. Like, his childhood and stuff," Jamie said.

"But that'll take me like three seconds. I could literally just look that up right now."

"We just figured you'd be busy doing . . ." Michelle trailed off. "What you do."

I almost scoffed. "And what exactly do you think I do?"

"Let's face it. We both know we were doing you a favor," Hannah said, evidently dropping whatever charade the group had been playing. "You're Gia Winters! You don't have time to be researching some psychologist. You're too busy having dinner with Kendall Jenner and signing autographs outside Barney's."

Okay, she was wrong on so many levels, it was outrageous. Dinner with Kendall had been months ago, and it hadn't happened since. She was sweet, but we didn't know each other well enough to form a solid friendship just yet. Plus, she was far too attractive to be around for extended periods of time, and the selfie of us she had posted on Instagram made me look like her homely cousin who had never felt the touch of a man. And I had signed autographs *once* outside Barney's; it wasn't, like, a full-time gig. It just so happened that my every move was captured and plastered online, so it made it seem like I was having lunch dates with Marc Jacobs every day. In reality, I spent any time I had off eating junk food and watching reruns of *The O.C.*, hoping that Seth Cohen would come to life.

"Do you think I'm dumb?" I asked the group. "Do you think that just because I'm famous, I can only manage to read my credit card statement instead of a textbook?"

"Of course not," Kyle replied quickly.

He looked so apologetic that I actually felt a little bad for him. But I was too focused on not bursting into tears to care about how he was feeling. Michelle looked equally uncomfortable, but Hannah looked as smug as ever. I glanced at Jamie, who was staring at the table, avoiding all eye contact with me.

"I don't get it," I told them. "I just wanted you to treat me like a normal student. Is that so much to ask?"

"Oh, please!" Hannah scoffed, and I was a little shocked by her brashness. "You can save the poor little rich girl act. There are no cameras around. You aren't going to find a PR opportunity here."

Hannah's words hit me like a speeding truck. I could practically hear something inside my brain snap as my eyes narrowed with anger. She figured I was just a rich bitch, pretending to be wide-eyed and innocent, begging for all the attention she could get. But Hannah didn't know me. None of them did. They only knew what they read about, or what was said on TMZ. They thought they had me all figured out, and I was sick of it. I was sick of Hannah and Jamie and Dr. Norton, and even Kyle and Michelle, who at this stage looked about ready to die. So Hannah thought she knew me? Fine.

I picked up one of the remaining coffees from the tray, pulled the plastic lid off the top and calmly poured the contents of the cup onto Hannah's bag. She gasped, jumping up in her seat to avoid the coffee spilling on her. Kyle's jaw dropped, and I think I actually heard Michelle whimper. Jamie looked up at me in shock. I placed the empty cardboard cup back on the bench, amidst the spilled coffee, with a tight smile.

"What the hell do you think you're doing?"

"Now that I have everyone's attention," I said formally. "I'd like to say something."

"You're a lunatic!" Hannah cried with outrage.

"I have been nothing but nice to you guys ever since I met you. Yes, I am the daughter of Hollywood movie stars. Yes, I have Robert DeNiro's number saved as Uncle Bobby. And yes, this shirt-dress I'm wearing *is* Gucci. But that doesn't mean I don't deserve to have friends, which is all I really wanted! I just wanted you to be my friends. And if that seems like too tough a task, then the least you can do is show me the same amount of respect I've given to you!"

"You think *this* is a good way to make friends?" Hannah exclaimed.

"I think you made it pretty obvious that you were never going to give me a chance. I guess you just decided that it wasn't worth actually getting to know me before passing judgment." I leaned in a little closer with a steely glare. "Honey, I practically *invented* that game. You wouldn't last one second in my world."

I'm not going to lie, I felt pretty proud of myself in that moment. I had never called anyone "honey" in a patronizing way before, and I felt like a boss. But that moment didn't last long. My stomach was still in knots, and looking at four dumbstruck faces blinking back at you is actually quite nerve-racking. I forced a fierce look on my face and hiked my bag strap higher onto my shoulder haughtily.

"So, if we're all done here," I said steadily, "I guess I'd better get going."

"You just got here," Kyle practically whispered, looking slightly dazed.

"Oh you know, rich people things to do," I replied airily.

"You completely ruined my bag!" Hannah exclaimed angrily, gesturing toward the coffee dripping off the table.

I pulled out a twenty-dollar bill from my bag, trying to stop my fingers from shaking as I laid it onto the table. I didn't care that the corners were quickly drowned in the coffee.

"That ought to cover it, don't you think? Although, let's face it: we both know I was doing you a favor."

I looked down at the denim bag with an almost pitying look, making my distaste as evident as possible. Hannah gaped at me. She couldn't seem to come to terms with what had just happened, and I couldn't blame her. She was likely used to the pettiness of ordinary high schoolers. But I had special training—growing up amongst the youth of Hollywood. She never had to go up against people like Meghan Adams, my archnemesis for all of high school. Hannah had no idea what she was getting into before taking that leap of faith. I turned dramatically on my heel and stalked off, leaving my group members to clean up the aftermath of my meltdown.

I always knew they didn't like me, but I wasn't expecting *that*. Hannah's sneer kept popping into mind as I walked, making me angrier with every step. I couldn't believe how unfair it was. I had tried my best to be kind and show them I was friendly, and I had literally nothing but spilled coffee to show for it.

It's not like I was expecting the whole world to love me. Watching my parents both rise and fall had taught me not to be naïve. But still, I couldn't understand the hostility. It was one thing to sit behind a keyboard and say I looked like a "try-hard skank," like some awful people had mentioned in their online comments. It was a whole other thing to be a complete cow to my face. I was a nice person! Heaps of people thought so! People like **gary_rulez1992**, who had commented on a selfie of mine yesterday, claiming I was "da light" of his "lyf," and that he "lyked" my "bootay." If I was good enough for Gary, then why wasn't I good enough for my own classmates?

I was blinking back tears when I heard someone call out my name from behind. It was probably Kyle, trying to play the mediator again, but I marched on. The voice grew louder, as I heard footsteps pounding the pavement behind me.

"GIA!"

But when I finally spun around, I was surprised to see it wasn't Kyle. It was Jamie. I had figured he was already pinning a photo of my face to a dartboard, so he and Hannah could bond over their hatred for me on their first date.

"Wait up! The coffee's going to spill."

Jamie jogged toward me, holding one of the coffee cups in his hand.

"What?" I demanded angrily. "Are you here to humiliate me some more? Go ahead. Get it off your chest. I'm listening!"

Jamie took a few seconds to steady his breathing and said, "I'm not here to humiliate you, I swear."

"Then what do you want?"

Jamie held up the coffee cup and gave it a tiny shake. "I thought you could use this. Go on, take it. It's not laced with anything. I mean, you did buy it yourself."

I narrowed my eyes, pulling the cup away from his hands. "Why are you giving me this coffee?"

"I figured you were having a shitty morning and you could use some caffeine. Plus, I don't think Hannah's bag is thirsty anymore."

Jamie gave me a small smile, but that only made me wearier.

"That's awfully nice for someone who's spent the last few weeks giving me judging glares every time they see me. What is this, a peace offering?"

"Uh, no. I still don't like you. This is just so you don't snap and throw the coffee in *my* face next."

"Can I ask you a question?" I asked. "Why don't you like me? Because I can't seem to figure out what I've done wrong."

Jamie looked uncomfortable again, like he was mentally evaluating the consequences of answering my questions.

"Look, I'm sure you're a nice girl," he said carefully. "But I just think you're a little . . . fake? I just don't really believe you."

Fake? I dug my nails into the cardboard cup. If Jamie was going to say he thought the whole Frank Parker thing was a lie, then I really was going to throw the coffee in his face. Last week, I had overheard two guys discussing that very theory in so much detail, you'd have thought they were auditioning for *CSI.* It had taken Reggie all of his strength to stop me from walking over and smacking them with my Versace pumps. Evidently some people thought the Winters family had too much time on their hands and were looking for some extra media attention. Short of calling Dr. D up in his prison cell and getting him to corroborate the events of the stalking, I wasn't sure how I was going to convince everyone that it had really happened.

"Not that I have to explain this to you," I began heatedly. "But what happened to me *did* actually happen. So if you think I'm faking it, then that's really not my problem! It's yours!"

Jamie gave me a confused look and said, "What? No, not that! I just don't really buy this whole thing you've got going on."

"What *thing?*"

Jamie gestured toward the coffee in my hand. "This! Buying coffee and cupcakes every week. The whole sunshine gimmick. I don't really believe you're actually like that."

"Because I'm rich, I can't be nice? I thought you liked cupcakes! Everyone likes cupcakes! Excuse me for thinking you're a person who likes baked delights! I mean, I'm clearly a monster!"

Jamie rolled his eyes and said, "Cupcakes are great, but you can't *buy* friends with them. You can't make people like you like that."

Well, jeez. It's not like I had bought him a yacht or something. If someone had bought me a cupcake, then I'd have made a friend for life. In fact, most of my friendships had been built on the foundation of sweet treats. Maybe it was a New York thing. Maybe people didn't like you unless you were complaining and smoking cigarettes in a black beret.

"I was just trying to be nice."

"That's your problem! You're *trying* too hard. I just don't believe it."

I gave a frustrated sigh. "So I can't win either way! You don't want me to be mean, and you don't want me to be nice."

"I don't want you to be anything but yourself."

"You sound like my therapist."

"Yeah, how's that working out for you?"

"Great! Can't you tell?"

"Look," Jamie said reasonably. "One minute you claim you want to be a normal college kid, and the next you're talking about your designer footwear and dunking coffee in handbags like a maniac. You can't expect me to not be confused."

"Why can't I do both?" I replied. "I'm not going to apologize for having different emotions. And I'm definitely not going to apologize for my shoes. I can't help that I'm Harry Winters's daughter. I c—"

"That's what I mean! You still see yourself as just Harry Winters's daughter, but that's not true anymore. You see that guy over there?" Jamie pointed behind me, and I cast a look over my shoulder. "That guy's been aggressively taking photos of you on his phone for the past two minutes. He's probably texting his buddy right now about how you're standing two yards away."

I watched the guy he was referring to, who was trying desperately to be discreet in his photo taking. He quickly looked away when he saw our eyes on him, pointing his iPhone in a random direction.

"You're not just Harry Winters's daughter anymore, Gia," Jamie said, as I turned my attention back to him. "You have your own fame now."

"Okay, this is a little too *Chicken Soup for the Soul* for me," I told him. "So if you've got a point, I suggest making it now."

"The point is you're never going to be a normal college kid. You think it's okay to wear four-inch heels to class, you'll never have to line up for movie tickets or eat shitty plane food in coach. The sooner you stop trying to make yourself into someone you're never going to be, the happier you'll feel."

Jamie must work part time at some mental health hotline, because he was dropping life lessons on me like it was his day job.

"That's very insightful, but I still don't see how that's a reason to not like me."

Jamie adjusted the strap of his sling bag on his shoulder and gave a little sigh. He looked at me like he was trying to argue his case to a brick wall.

"You want my advice?" he asked.

"Not particularly, but go on."

"Choose one version of yourself you like best and stick to it, rather than morphing into what you think other people want. Not everyone is going to like you, and you're just going to have to accept that. You're a child of Hollywood, Gia. You of all people should know that you can't please everyone."

Jamie gave me a little shrug, as if to tell me he was done with his on-the-spot philosophy lesson, and turned to walk away. His words floated around in my head. On the one hand, he was right. I had always been a little insecure, but moving to New York had made me crave validation from everyone, which had been bothering me for a while. On the other hand, he had basically just reminded me that he still didn't want to be friends, and that I should just suck it up. Which, honestly, stung a little. I'll admit, I kind of wanted to win Jamie over. There was something about him that just drew me toward him. Aside from his whole brooding bad boy thing, something told me we could actually get along.

He had only been walking a few seconds before something on his black sling bag caught my eye. I squinted, hoping to get a better look in the sunlight.

"Hey!" I called out impulsively. "Nice button!"

Jamie stopped, turning to look at me. He inspected his t-shirt, as if I were talking about the buttons on his clothing.

"What?"

There was no denying it. The image of the bull was still fresh in my mind, and now it was staring back at me, attached to Jamie's bag. He glanced down at the button and then up at me, before turning his back to me once more and walking away without a word.

What were the odds? Surely this was a sign. Maybe the heavens above were trying to tell me that I didn't need to add Jamie into my small group of friends. I needed to add him to a police suspects list.

My phone began buzzing in my bag. I pulled it out and looked down at the caller ID excitedly. Milo really did have the best timing in the world.

"Milo," I said into the phone. "You'll never believe what I just saw!"

"Hey Gia! It's Aidyn."

"Oh! Sorry, Aidyn. I thought you were Milo."

I pulled the phone away from my ear to double-check it was in fact Milo's name that had popped up on the screen. It was.

"Yeah, I borrowed his phone to call you. I hope you don't mind," Aidyn replied, stress evident in her voice.

"Is everything okay? Where's Milo?"

There was a short pause on the other end, and I waited for her to reply expectantly. Why was Aidyn calling me from Milo's phone?

"I don't want you to panic," she said weakly, "but I'm calling from the hospital. There's been a little incident."

I clutched onto the coffee a little tighter.

"Incident?" I repeated. "What happened? Are you okay?"

"I'm fine! But . . ."

"But what, Aidyn?"

"It's Milo. You should probably come down here."

Eight

In Aidyn's defense, she didn't want to worry me on the phone so she tried to keep the details to a minimum. But that was also a terrible idea, because about a thousand gruesome and terrifying scenarios popped into my head after she gave me the hospital address and hung up the phone. Despite her assurance that Milo was in no life-threatening danger, I couldn't erase the images from my head.

My nerves were in overdrive as I rushed out of the hospital elevator and toward the reception desk, Reggie close behind. I had called him right after getting off the phone and asked for some backup. There was no doubt that someway, somehow, the paparazzi would have caught a whiff of Milo's injury and were impatiently awaiting my arrival. These things always tended to *mysteriously* leak out into the public sphere. Sure enough, there were a group of photographers camped outside the hospital, cameras ready the moment the soles of my heels hit the pavement. I trudged past them with my sunglasses on, trying to wipe all expression off my face as Reggie handled the crowd. Truthfully, I was about ready to cry. This had been a nightmarish day so far, and I didn't need anyone capturing it on camera.

I ran over toward the nurse standing behind the desk. The hospital was so loud. There were phones ringing in the distance and you could hear hurried footsteps hitting the polished floors. Everything was white and pale blue, and it made me feel sick just being there.

"Hi," I said breathlessly, practically crashing into the desk in my haste. "Milo Fells. I need to see him."

The young nurse had her mousey hair in a loose ponytail, and she was cradling a telephone between her shoulder and her ear. She looked up at me and gave me a small nod of acknowledgment and said "okay sure" a few times into the phone before placing it back on the receiver. I tapped my foot impatiently.

"I'm sorry, what was that?" she said, looking up at me.

"Officer Milo Fells. What room is he in?"

"Are you family?"

"I'm his girlfriend."

"I'm sorry, I'm not permitted to allow nonfamily visitors just yet."

"Is he in surgery or something?"

"No, no. It's not that serious. The doctor is with him now. You can see him soon."

"Look, I know you said no outside visitors yet," I said, "but I'm basically family. I'm pretty sure I'm listed as his emergency contact."

The nurse looked down at a clipboard on the desk, lifting up a few pages and scanning the documents.

"Actually," she said. "We just have the police precinct listed here."

"Is he okay?" Reggie asked.

"Oh, yes. The doctors are keeping him for the night, but there shouldn't be anything to worry about."

"Well if there's nothing to worry about, then why can't you let us see him?" Reggie said.

The nurse gave us an apologetic look. "I'm sorry. You'll have to wait for the moment. There's nothing I can do—it's just hospital policy. Family members only at this time."

"Do you happen to know who I am?"

I know, I know. But why even have the family name if I wasn't going to use it in emergencies? And this was definitely an emergency. We were standing in the ER! Can't get more of an emergency than that. The nurse looked at me uncomfortably.

"Er, yes," she said. "But unfortunately, there's still nothing I can do."

Reggie gave a little sigh as I folded my hands on the desk. "Tell me . . ." I peered at the name tag pinned to the nurse's scrubs. "Wendy. Do you like working here?"

Wendy glanced at Reggie, and then looked back at me uncertainly.

"Um, yes?"

"Yeah? The location is pretty good."

"I can walk to work."

"That's great!" I smiled at her sweetly and said, "Wendy, I would really *hate* for you to have to take the subway to work once you've been transferred."

Wendy looked at Reggie again, who gave her a sympathetic look, similar to mine. He was clearly catching on.

"I'm not sure I understand."

"I would suggest you let me see my boyfriend now. Unless, of course, you're open to being squished in a metal tube rushing through an underground tunnel every day. I heard those railings are a breeding ground for disease."

"I—"

"We both know I'm not bluffing, Wendy. Take my advice. Walk to work."

Wendy gave Reggie one last look, reassessed my confident smile, and pressed the clipboard against her chest.

"Follow me, please," she said.

"Nice," Reggie whispered as we trailed after Wendy down the corridor.

"It was a necessary evil."

Wendy finally stopped in front of a large brown door with a slim glass pane for a window.

"Members of the police force don't share rooms," she informed me, as if I were about to start yelling at her for poor accommodation.

"Thanks, Wendy. And sorry about going dragon lady on you before. It's been a tough day so far."

"It happens. We had a guy come in this morning who swallowed a plastic doll."

"I'm not sure I want to hear the rest of that story."

Wendy was still looking slightly apprehensive about my friendliness, but she finally walked away. For a minute, I felt guilty. Here I was complaining like a child that I wasn't making friends, when Wendy was dealing with people who were literally eating toys. God, I was a mess.

"I'll wait out here," Reggie said. "Maybe I can convince one of the nurses to give me a lollipop or something."

"Wendy seems like she'd be down for that."

"Only because you put the fear of God into her."

"Desperate times."

I left Reggie on his lollipop mission and pushed open the brown door. Milo was sitting on top of a thin bed. He still had his uniform on, but his shirt was unbuttoned. The bottom of it was ripped and had patches of blood on it. His bottom lip was slightly swollen, and I could tell it had been bleeding. His hair was disheveled, his cheek was scratched, and there was a large square bandage on his lower torso. He took one look at me and sighed.

"Gia, I'm fine!" he declared, before I could launch into my meltdown. "Seriously, Aidyn shouldn't have called you."

The door closed behind me with a soft thud as I walked toward the bed with an incredulous look on my face, taking in his battered appearance.

"Are you kidding? Of course she should have called me. Look at you!"

Milo winced in pain as he adjusted himself to a slightly higher sitting position. "It's not as bad as it looks, I promise."

"Good, because you look terrible! What happened to you?"

Milo let out another pained sigh, as if he knew the answer to that question was one I wasn't going to like.

"I just have a bruised rib and a little cut," he replied, buttoning up his shirt. "There was this call that came in from some neighbors who said they could hear strange noises from the apartment next door, so I went to check it out. It turns out the place was being robbed. The two guys got away."

"And they gave you a bruised rib as a parting gift."

I walked over to his side helplessly. I knew for a fact it *was* as bad as it looked, but Milo was trying to avoid a full-fledged panic session on my part. Milo was about to continue his reassurance when the door swung open and a friendly looking man in a lab coat walked in.

"Miss Winters!" he said pleasantly. "I was wondering when I'd have to lock out the paparazzi."

"Sorry about that," I replied, blushing in embarrassment.

"Not at all. It's always good to have some excitement."

I was about to point out that a man swallowing dolls was pretty exciting but decided the moment wasn't right. The man introduced himself as Dr. Paulson, and we exchanged polite handshakes.

"How deep was the cut?" I asked Dr. Paulson.

"Gia, honestly, it's not even a big deal," Milo said.

"It could have been much worse. But Officer Fells got lucky. His rib only just managed to keep away from a fracture, and the stab wound isn't very deep."

I blinked at him. It felt like my heart traveled to my throat.

"I'm sorry," I said weakly. "Stab wound?"

Dr. Paulson looked at Milo uncertainly and then back at me. "Uh, yes. It's not very deep."

"You were stabbed!" I repeated in a shrill voice, turning to Milo.

"Only a little!"

"What is that supposed to mean? How do you only get stabbed *a little?*"

"The knife didn't really . . ." he began. "It just sort of just slashed. Let's call it a slash wound."

"It's technically a small stab wound," Dr. Paulson said, and Milo gave him a look that hinted he was ready to strangle him. "But, uh, yes. Not very deep, as I said before."

"Milo, look at you! Do you have to do this for a living?"

"Well, I don't *just* do specifically this for a living, you know."

"You're already getting a black eye, your lip is twice its

normal size, you have an almost fractured rib, and you've been stabbed!"

"Only a little!"

I sank into the chair beside the bed, putting my head in my hands and shaking it.

"Really, Miss Winters, there's nothing to worry about," Dr. Paulson said. "We've already given Officer Fells his stitches and some strong medication for the pain. He'll need to take at least a week off work and get some rest for his rib, but he's going to be fine."

"See? I'll be fine!"

"We'd like to keep him overnight. I want to make sure the stab wound, uh . . ." Dr. Paulson glanced at Milo's hard expression. "It's really just a precaution."

"I really don't think that's necessary," Milo protested. "I'm honestly fine!"

"Why, do you have any experience with *slash* wounds?" I asked.

"Um, no."

"No. So you're staying overnight."

"Smart choice," Dr. Paulson added, watching Milo sink lower into the bed in defeat.

Dr. Paulson was smiling at me like Milo had somehow won the lottery by being stabbed by some degenerates trying to rob an apartment. I appreciated that he was trying not to worry me more than I already was, but he needed to tone down his happiness.

"I'll leave you to get some rest," Dr. Paulson said. "Please help yourself to some cafeteria Jell-O, Miss Winters. I can't guarantee its quality, but it does the job."

We thanked him and watched him leave silently, only speaking when the door had closed behind him.

"Were you just never going to tell me how bad it was?" I demanded. "A 'cut'? Milo, someone tried to plunge a knife into your body! That's hardly a cut."

"This is exactly why I didn't want to tell you! I knew you'd freak out."

"Of course I'd freak out! And didn't you have any backup?

What are police officers doing all day?"

"Fighting real crime!" Milo said. "Not taking calls from old ladies who hear things that go bump in the night."

"That 'bump' earned you an overnight visit to the hospital. This is what happens when you want to be John McWayne!"

"It's actually John *McClane*, but I appreciate you trying to drop in a *Die Hard* reference."

"So how did Aidyn find you then?" I asked him.

"I called her from the apartment," Milo explained. "Luckily she was close by, or else it could have been a lot worse."

I gave an involuntary shudder. Just thinking about how much worse it could have been made my insides feel like they were shriveling up.

"Is this about that story you told me the other day?" I asked him. "That guy who made that big arrest right out of the academy? Because you're just as good of a cop, Milo. You don't need to play the hero."

"I wasn't trying to play the hero!" he exclaimed. "It's not like I went looking for an armed robbery! I was just doing what I always do, dealing with noise complaints. I just so happened to get hurt in the process. It could have happened to anyone."

"Yeah, but I know you want to prove yourself right now with this task force. But I don't want you to take extra risks just to do it."

Milo's face softened. "Gia, I promise you I wasn't trying to be stupid. There are going to be times when I'm going to get hurt, okay? I'm a police officer. It comes with the job."

"Yeah, b—"

"Just listen. I'm not complaining about getting hurt because I know it's not always something you can avoid. And I may get frustrated about my stupid paperwork and complaints from old ladies, but I *know* I'm better than that. And like you said, one day I'll get to prove it. Everyone starts at the bottom, right? So if that means I have to take on a knife once or twice, then so be it. Today they got away. Tomorrow, they won't be as lucky. Or maybe I'll be smarter. Either way, I'm not taking any extra risks, okay? I'm just doing my job. So please don't worry about me."

It was a great speech, no doubt. And it did seem to appease

my panic a little. I admired him for knowing exactly what he wanted to do, even if it came with lots of paperwork and a few bumps and bruises. Milo would never have nightmares about marrying Josh Duhamel and then getting shot in a wedding dress. He was probably a badass even in dream form.

"Also, you didn't even bring me 'get well soon' flowers!" Milo said, feigning a hurt look. "How am I supposed to get well soon if I don't have encouragement flowers?"

"I was a little busy trying not to have heart failure! Flowers didn't really cross my mind. But can I interest you in some nasty cafeteria Jell-O?"

"The only kind I eat, to be honest."

"You're a real catch, you know that?"

"You haven't even seen me in the hospital gown yet."

I left Milo to groan in pain as loudly as he wanted, now that he could be alone in the room. Since venting to me in the coffee shop that day, he had clearly taken a new stoic approach to his career, which I respected. But the man deserved a minute or two by himself to secretly whine about being attacked with a knife. That was the least I could offer him.

"How is he?" Reggie asked, as the heavy door closed behind me.

"Stabbed, actually," I replied, and Reggie's eyebrows shot up. "Or slashed, or whatever. You can go in and see him if you want. I'm going to go get him some Jell-O."

"I'll come with you," he said. "Don't want the nurses to start asking for autographs on the way to the cafeteria."

My gaze fell on Aidyn, who was talking to another police officer. Her face lit up when she saw me, and she finished up her conversation quickly and walked over. I guess she had decided to make a wild decision with her hair, because instead of a high ponytail, it was a middle ponytail today.

"Gia! I'm so sorry about that phone call. I must have completely freaked you out, but Milo kept telling me not to tell you all the details on the phone."

"Thanks for calling me, Aidyn. I really appreciate you helping him out."

"Don't thank me! We always have each other's backs."

I decided I liked Aidyn much better than the few officers Milo had introduced me to since moving to New York. They were all so arrogant and sarcastic. Which, I know, is basically the title of my memoir. But she did seem genuine. Not at all like Lucy, who made me want to roll my eyes just thinking about her smile. Plus, Aidyn really did have Milo's back, and today was definite proof of that. I gave a quick introduction of Reggie, who said a quiet "How's it goin'?" and then went back to pretending he was part of the wall.

"The doctor said Milo will have to take some time off," I said, and she nodded.

"At least a week. But it's Milo we're talking about, so that's a little easier said than done."

We both gave each other pointed looks, as if we were the parents of a troubling child who was likely to throw another tantrum in the next five minutes.

"I'm planning on bribing him with Netflix and dessert," I said.

"Chocolate cheesecake, of course," Aidyn laughed. "I swear, it's an addiction."

Okie-smoky, then. They were police partners; of course she would know his favorite dessert. That must have been an icebreaker activity on their first day of the job. Practicing with their guns and learning each other's preferred chocolate treats. Perfectly standard.

"Right," I said, trying to push past the awkwardness. "Well, I'm going to the cafeteria. You want me to grab you something while I'm there?"

Wherever *there* was. It looked like the thick, brown doors traveled down the hallway for an eternity. It can't have been on this floor. There was nothing but gloominess and phones ringing here.

"I'm good, but thanks." Aidyn wrapped her hand lightly around my wrist. "And I just wanted to tell you that I think you're really sweet. I never believe any of the nonsense I read about."

I glanced at Reggie, as if he could help clarify what exactly she had heard. He gave me a tiny shrug.

"Nonsense?"

"Nothing particular," Aidyn assured me. "Just in general. The media can be such pigs. They just choose their next victim and then say whatever they want."

"If this is to do with that rumor about my mom potentially splitting up Michael Douglas's marriage, then I wouldn't believe what you read. I'm like 80 percent sure that's a lie."

Aidyn's eyes widened in surprise. "That's a terrible rumor! I would never believe your mom is a home-wrecker."

"Oh no, that part you can believe. But her type is much younger. It's unlikely that she would go through the trouble for a man twenty-seven years older than her."

Twenty-five if we're *really* honest. But I'm pretty sure Mom had the age on her passport officially amended to suit her denial. Aidyn briefly opened her mouth and then closed it again, unsure of how to respond. Her eyes flicked to Reggie, who just nodded.

"Well," Aidyn said. "I think you're awesome. You're being so cool about this whole thing. It's so great that you're not uncomfortable with Milo and I working so closely. I would totally get it if you were."

I looked at her, surprised. "Aidyn, that's sweet. But it's not like I'm going to stop my boyfriend from talking to other girls. Especially if he's your partner!"

Let's just ignore all the internal pettiness I was constantly harboring. We don't need to bring that up.

"I know," she went on. "I just think it's great how you don't mind your boyfriend working so closely with his ex."

For a few seconds I stood there gaping at her, not sure what to say. So Aidyn was Milo's ex-girlfriend. No problemo. None whatsoever. I could deal with that. It's not like I was ready to strangle someone with her perky-ass ponytail or anything. Reggie coughed awkwardly, taking a few steps backwards. He was obviously preparing for a nuclear explosion on my part.

"Ex?" I repeated.

"What, didn't Milo tell you?"

"Of course he told me!" I lied. "But he mentioned that it was a really long time ago. Ages, really. Practically centuries.

Historians have written about this kind of stuff."

"It wasn't *that* long ago," she replied lightly. "Like a year, maybe?"

No, really, Aidyn. Add more salt to the wound. I beg you.

"Well, here we are."

"Here we are."

We stood in silence for a few long minutes, staring at the ceiling and passing doctors. I was half hoping a truck really would come out of nowhere so we'd at least have something to talk about, other than the fact that my boyfriend was glued to his ex seventeen hours a day. Aidyn's phone started ringing in her hand.

"I'm so sorry," she said. "I have to take this. I'll catch up with you in a bit?"

"Go ahead! I have to go, um . . . food. Jell-O. It gets the job done."

As if things weren't bad enough, I was now losing my ability to form coherent sentences. Aidyn gave me a little wave and answered the phone, turning on her heel and walking away.

"Oh boy," Reggie said with a chuckle.

I pushed the brown door open again. I was feeling a little sick all over again, and it had nothing to do with the strong smell of sanitizer that hung in the air.

"No nasty Jell-O?" Milo asked, lifting his head up from the pillow.

He sounded slightly groggy. The medicine was doing its job.

"Sorry, they ran out of the bad stuff," I said with a forced smile. "Didn't think you'd be interested in the quality Jell-O."

"Hospitals suck."

Oh my god, should I bring it up? No. Yes. No! Yes? Milo laced his fingers through mine, his lips curving up into a half-smile.

"I'm glad you're here," he said.

Okay, *definitely* not bringing it up now. The man had just been stabbed! No, *slashed*. Whatever, he was definitely hurt. I didn't have the heart to ruin the moment.

"The good news is you get a little vacation," I told him.

"The bad news is I'm definitely out of the running for

solving this Stag investigation."

The Stag investigation! With everything that had happened today, I had completely forgotten to tell him about my findings!

"I have something to tell you!" I said.

"If you're breaking up with me, this really is the worst time you could have chosen."

I practically hopped off the bed with excitement. "No, shh! I have a lead for you. I found someone who has the Stag button."

Milo opened his mouth, and then closed it again. He shakily pushed himself up into a higher sitting position, looking confused.

"You what?"

"You know that guy I wanted you to arrest because he was being an asshole?"

"You're going to have to be more specific. You want me to arrest everyone."

"The one who was a jerk to me in my first Psych class! Remember?"

"Vaguely. What about him?"

"He has an orange badge pinned to his bag with a bull on it. I saw it today!"

"Okay . . ." Milo began slowly. "And you're positive that it was the same symbol I showed you?"

"I'm like 99 percent sure."

"But you're still 1 percent unsure."

"It's the same symbol. I recognized it straight away!"

You could practically see the cogs turning in Milo's mind as his dimples appeared. On the outside, he looked like he wanted to sleep, but I knew his brain was alert as ever.

"This is so great!" he exclaimed, and I felt a small surge of pride run through me. "Now we have a place to start! We can put him on the surveillance list."

"Why don't I just do the surveillance?" I asked with a shrug.

"Uh, because you're not an NYPD officer and this is a police investigation?"

"Yeah, but I'm something even better. I'm in his class *and* I have a group assignment with him. I see him all the time! You're not going to get better surveillance than that."

"Gia, that's not how this works," Milo said. "What if you say something to him accidentally? What if he suspects something? He knows you're dating a cop."

"Milo, this guy doesn't think I'm smart enough to sing the alphabet. He's never going to make the connection."

"Keeping an eye out for a symbol is very different from interrogating a suspect."

"I'm not going to *interrogate* him," I said impatiently. "I'll just wait and see if he does something suspicious. At most I'm just going to ask him where he got the button from. If he acts super shifty, then you'll know that he's hiding something."

"That's your grand plan? Just asking him?" he said, looking almost amused. "Then you'll *definitely* scare him off!"

"Oh, right. But getting formally questioned by the police won't?"

Milo looked like he kind of wanted to laugh in disbelief, but decided against it. "There's no guarantee that he'll act suspicious. Plus, he could always lie to you about where he got it from."

"Well, if he's going to lie to me then he's definitely going to lie to you guys! So what do you have to lose?"

"Look, I appreciate you trying to help," Milo said. "But I can't allow it. I'll give the lead to Aidyn. Don't worry, I can trust her not to steal my thunder on this case."

Yeah, but it wasn't his thunder I was worried about being stolen. I knew I was being childish, but it bothered me to know Aidyn would get another victory. She got to spend all day with him while I practically had to beg for a coffee date. It was immature thinking, but at least it would he helping Milo in some way.

"Just let me talk to Jamie," I reasoned. "You can have him under formal surveillance if you want, but don't just give away your lead to someone else. You wanted to prove yourself, right? Well prove yourself! Let me help you."

I didn't press the issue anymore. I didn't have to. I could tell by the way Milo was biting his bruised lip thoughtfully that he was already considering it. And if he was considering it, then I had already won. I waited silently as he deliberated.

"Fine," he finally said, exhaling deeply. "You can look out for anything suspicious, but I don't want you talking to him about the case at all! I'm serious. Leave the rest to us. That's the offer on the table. Take it or leave it."

"Alright, alright! Relax, Officer. I won't do anything crazy, I promise."

Milo leaned back, looking only slightly more relieved. I had no doubt in my mind that if he weren't in severe pain, he would never have agreed to me helping. That, or he *really* wanted to prove he was a great cop and didn't have the heart to give his only lead to someone else. I suspected it was a bit of both. Either way, I was going to get him the answers he needed.

The door swung open before Milo could change his mind, and for a moment I was scared Aidyn would walk in. The shrapnel from her little truth bomb was now lodged into my brain, and I wasn't quite ready for another conversation about how freaking great everything was. But it was just a nurse.

"Thought you might be more comfortable in this," she said, holding up a paper-like hospital gown.

Milo groaned and said, "Oh no. I was hoping it wouldn't come to this."

"Go put your dress on," I said. "Reggie and I will go get you some real food. No offense to the cafeteria, or anything."

The nurse shrugged understandingly. "None taken."

I gave Milo a quick kiss on the cheek that wasn't bruised and headed for the door. The sooner I could get away from the smell of gloom and detergent, the happier I'd be. I had gotten Milo a lead on his investigation! Me! I had actually done something right for once.

"Oh, and one more thing," I said, pausing in the doorway.

"Yeah?" Milo said, reaching for the hospital gown.

"Aidyn told me that she's your ex," I said, and the color from Milo's face vanished as he blinked at me. "Okay, be back soon! Byeeee!"

I practically skipped out of the room. There. It was out in the open now, so I wouldn't have to obsess over it on my own. This way I could obsess over it to Milo's face. Either way, I'd be stupid to think I wasn't going to obsess over it a little. That ponytail was going to haunt my dreams.

"I think I'm going to need some stronger pain meds," Milo said as the door swung shut.

Nine

I WAS DESPERATE TO GET A START ON THE STAG INVESTIGATION now that we had a proper lead, but things weren't going as quickly as I had hoped. I had spent the whole of class eyeing the back of Jamie's head from six rows back, watching every movement. I was kind of hoping to catch a glimpse of something sketchy, like doodling pictures of bulls in his margins or counting stacks of money on top of his little desk. But all he did was take notes and occasionally scroll through his Facebook feed. The moment class finished, he practically bolted out the door before I could even pack my things up. If that wasn't enough of a failure, my group hadn't organized another time to meet up and work on our project. Or maybe they had, but I hadn't gotten an invite due to my little coffee catastrophe. Whatever. Hannah had it coming. And a denim bag? 1996 called, it wants its fashion back.

Milo was now trying to enjoy his time off work, but he mostly spent all day calling me and complaining about how bored he was. Stabbed or not, a week's vacation is always a good thing. As expected, the topic of Aidyn had come up a few times. Milo had pulled the classic "I didn't say anything because I knew you'd freak out" excuse on me. Boy, that's original. But I had pleasantly surprised him by saying it was perfectly fine and that it didn't bother me at all.

It was *not* perfectly fine, and it damn right did bother me. I wanted to ask a million more questions, like why they broke up or whether she was a better kisser. But now that I had pulled the maturity card, there was no way I could ask those. Instead, I kept myself busy trying not to think about them running toward each other in slow motion in a daisy field.

In fact, I had finished my first college assignment and officially submitted it, which was both exciting and scary. Why the heck did we need to cite our sources? It pretty much goes without saying that I didn't invent the Panopticon. Seriously, there was no chance of me plagiarizing. I had only just learned how to spell "plagiarize"! Concentrating on school was actually a decent way to keep my mind occupied. Plus, schoolwork was a legit excuse to avoid Steph and her "new marketing strategy" meetings. Her latest obsession was a book proposal, which was only made worse by her eagerness to land a movie deal.

"I'm barely able to write my essays!" I had told her. "You want me to write a whole novel?"

"Ghostwriters, Gia!" she had replied simply. "You don't even have to lift a finger. But people want to know your story!"

Why in the world people wanted to know my story was beyond me. *I* didn't even know my story. Sure, the kidnapping stuff might take up a few chapters. Maybe even the nightmares that followed. But the rest of it would just be pages filled my arguments with Mike, and that one time Dad suggested we join a family Pilates class.

College and potential press opportunities were keeping me busy, but none of that helped with Milo's investigation. By the time he had reached his fifth day of forced vacation, his impatience with the lack of leads had doubled. The little surveillance the NYPD had managed in that short while had come up with nothing noteworthy, and it was frustrating him to no end. I had finally grown so annoyed that I took matters into my own hands. Sure, it was going to have to be a little less subtle than Milo and I had discussed, but, technically, I wasn't doing anything radical. One little conversation wasn't going to do any damage.

I shared lunch with Zoe after one of my classes, pretending to pay attention while she complained about how "boys these days only want girls that know how to twerk." I felt her pain, but I really wasn't there to offer advice, so Zoe's love life would have to wait. I had a bigger fish to fry, and his name was Jamie. Just as I had hoped, he was standing outside the building of his class, casually leaning against the wall, twirling a pen between his fingers and laughing at something the dark-haired guy in front of him was saying. Oh great. I hadn't even considered the possibility of extra company.

I determinedly made my way through the sea of students passing by, rushing to get to their classes. It was 2:50 p.m. I only had ten minutes to get what I needed.

"I need to talk to you," I announced loudly, coming up beside the two boys.

Jamie's pen froze in his hand as he looked at me with surprise. "Gia" was all he said.

"Oh my god," his friend whispered, eyeing me up and down.

"Yes, hello," I said to his friend. "Sorry to interrupt, but I need to borrow Jamie for a second."

"I have class," Jamie replied. "Can this wait?"

"Uh, no. It can't."

"Dude!" his friend said, as if urging him to obey me.

"I'm Gia, by the way," I added quickly.

"I know. I mean, I'm Tyler! Nice to meet you."

I turned back to Jamie. "I'll be quick."

Jamie looked at Tyler, and then back at me. "Fine," he finally said.

By the way he followed me, you'd have thought I was dragging him to the dentist. I stopped a few yards away from where a very stunned Tyler was standing, although I probably shouldn't have bothered. There was no doubt Jamie was going to repeat the entire conversation to his friend afterwards.

"Listen," he began, before I could say anything. "If you're looking for another pep talk, call up the women on *The View* or whatever. They're more qualified for this."

"I didn't come here for more life lessons."

"How did you even know where to find me?"

"I have your class schedule. Took a lucky guess that you'd be waiting outside."

Jamie's eyebrows shot up in alarm. "Why do you have my class schedule? Scratch that. *How* do you have my class schedule?"

I pulled out a small piece of paper from the front pocket of my Balmain military blazer and cleared my throat dramatically before I began reading. "Jamie Hart." I paused, smirking up at him. "Gee, that's ironic. Psychology major, sophomore year. Oh look, you failed a subject last year. You should really apply yourself more."

"I'm not exactly sure what's happening right now."

"It turns out that Heather from Student Admin is a huge fan of my dad's. She was practically willing to gift me your social security number once I offered her a personalized autograph and DVD box set."

Jamie looked like he was a little scared of me. "You really got your dad to send her an autograph just to get my schedule?"

"Oh, please," I rolled my eyes. "I memorized my dad's signature in fifth grade."

"Okay, I'm a little freaked out right now. So you want to tell me what this is about?"

I was suddenly nervous. So much was riding on this conversation, and I didn't want anything to go wrong. Milo had practically laughed at me when I suggested I simply ask where he got the button from. I'm pretty sure that meant he didn't approve of my plan.

"Um," I said, pointing to the tattoo peeking out from under his sleeve. It was busy, with lots of little drawings and a large rose in the middle, as if it were sprouting up from his wrist.

"Nice tattoo," I said. "It's cool."

Jamie looked down at his arms, which were tightly crossed against his chest. "Uh, thanks."

"Fan of the flower?"

"Of the name actually."

"I see." I nodded slowly. "Girlfriend?"

This was good. I was easing my way in! Sure, the conversation jump was a little abrupt, but he already thought I was nuts, so there was really no losing here.

"Not quite," he replied, growing more impatient by the second.

"Ex-lover then? Sister? Cat?"

"As much as I would love to go into the specific details with you," Jamie said, uncrossing his arms. "I'm pretty sure you didn't bribe Holly from Student Admin just to discuss my tattoo."

"It's Heather, actually."

"Gia," Jamie said. "What do you want?"

Okay. Now or never.

"I wanted to ask you about that." I gestured toward the black bag slung low on his shoulder.

Jamie's eyes traveled down the long strap before looking back at me in confusion. "The bag?"

"The button, actually," I replied. "The one with the bull on it."

"What about it?"

He didn't seem defensive, but he definitely seemed wary. It was like my hidden motive was hanging in the air above us, but both of us were waiting for the other person to acknowledge it first.

"I was wondering where you got it from."

Cool as a cucumber, Gia.

"Why do you want to know? Doesn't seem like your preferred kind of accessory."

"It's not for me! It's for . . . Vogue. I'm doing a guest article. It's a huge deal, I wouldn't expect you to understand."

"Oh, really?" Jamie asked, looking amused. "What's the article about? Buttons?"

"No. It's about, um, college fashion. And youth trends. And . . . lots of other stuff, okay? Life-changing stuff. I saw your button the other day and I thought it was cool. So if you want me to put it into the article then just tell me where you got it from. Jeez!"

Alright, not quite as cucumber-like as I would have hoped.

But he was really getting on my last nerve. People around us were slowly starting to make their way into the building, and I knew I only had a few more minutes, five at most. Maybe even less if anyone recognized who I was and decided they were brave enough to interrupt. But Jamie didn't seem too concerned by class anymore. Instead he looked like he was enjoying watching me squirm. It was an expression I was all too familiar with, considering it was usually plastered on Jack's face.

"I can see you finally figured out what version of yourself you like best," Jamie said, clearly enjoying himself. "I don't know how much help I'm going to be for your article. The button isn't even mine, it's my roommate's. I'm just borrowing his bag 'cause mine broke the other day."

Crapola. Jamie was my one lead, and I actually had access to him! Granted my access was sort of forced because he didn't like me much, and I definitely didn't like him either. Even though he *was* kind of hot in a bad-boy I'm-totally-what-your-mother-warns-you-about kind of way. Not my mother, of course, she'd be all up in that. But this mystery roommate had really thrown a wrench in the works.

"Is that it?" Jamie asked, breaking into my thoughts. "I've got class."

He turned to leave before I could even reply. Most people had dispersed, but his friend was still waiting for him, trying to act subtle as he excitedly glanced over at us. Okay, I had three options. One, do nothing and just let him walk over to Tyler and tell him how nuts I am. Two, stop him and tell him the truth about the Stag investigation, but potentially risk everything blowing up in my face if he really was secretly involved. Three, come up with a new lie that would involve meeting the roommate. My chances weren't looking good, but mama didn't raise no quitter.

"Is he hot?" I called out, and Jamie turned around to look at me. "Your roommate, I mean. Wanna set me up with him?"

Oh, dear God. Mama clearly didn't raise Einstein either. Jamie was looking at me like he was in actual physical pain hearing me speak.

"What?" he exclaimed. "What about your boyfriend? I can't

even go online without fourteen articles popping up about your lunch dates or trips to Saks."

That was *one* trip to Saks. Milo got super bored and vowed never to shop with me again.

"I was totally kidding. Ha. Ha. Ha. Just a joke. You know? Humor."

Jamie looked a little frightened, like I was going to start psychotically laughing and go skipping around the campus or something. I couldn't even blame him; I was such a train wreck.

"I'm going to class," Jamie finally said. "You might consider reaching out to Dr. Phil. If anyone can help you, he can."

"No, wait!" I cried out before he could walk away again. He gave an impatient sigh. "Sorry, ignore all of that stuff. The truth is I need you to ask your roommate where he got that button from."

"What is it with you and this button?" Jamie narrowed his eyes suspiciously. "It can't just be for some stupid article. I don't know you very well, but I know for sure that this is definitely not what you consider fashionable. Why are you so obsessed with this thing?"

Milo had practically drilled it into my brain that discretion was key, and here I was, about to openly ask a potential suspect about a crime that he may or may not be involved in. But all my alternatives had disappeared, and backing away would make me seem even crazier than I already looked. I was out of choices.

"Okay, what I'm about to say is going to sound nuts."

"Uh, yeah. I guessed that part already."

"Have you ever heard of a drug called Stag?"

Jamie didn't even flinch. No signs of defense or panic. In fact, he looked bored.

"No. Should I have?"

"It's sort of up-and-coming."

Jamie gave me a disappointed parent look and said, "Please don't tell me you rich Cali kids are into pushing drugs on the East Coast now."

"What? Are you crazy? It's not me who's the drug pusher, it's your roommate."

Jamie let out a short laugh and said, "Right. And *I'm* the

crazy one?"

"I'm serious."

"So am I."

"Listen," I said firmly. "This isn't a game. A lot of people are getting hurt by this drug, and there's a good chance it's being manufactured right here at NYU. That ugly bull symbol you're carrying around is basically the official mascot. These people are wearing it around like it's something to be proud of. So if that button belongs to your roommate, then it's possible he's involved."

Jamie looked at me with a grim expression. Apparently my tiny outburst had registered somewhere in his brain, because the levels of sass had definitely come down from his end. If he was secretly involved, then he was doing a great job of pretending he wasn't.

"Look, that sucks," he said. "But this is just a button. Have you ever considered it might be a coincidence?"

"It's not a coincidence, trust me."

"You're basically telling me my roommate might be selling or making drugs."

"Or both."

"I'm just having a hard time believing that."

"I don't know anything for sure, but that's where you come in."

"What exactly do you think I can do about this?" he asked me.

"I don't know," I admitted. "Maybe you can . . . you know. Spy on him for me."

Jamie's eyes widened in disbelief and he gave a half-laugh. "You're kidding, right? You've got to be kidding."

I stared at him stone-faced. "Does it look like I'm kidding?"

Jamie stopped laughing and said, "I'm not spying on my own roommate! I'm not clinically insane!"

"I'll pay you! Five hundred for any information you find that's suspicious."

At this stage, I was just grasping at straws and hoping he would be interested. He well and truly wasn't.

"Are you listening?" he exclaimed. "I'm not spying on my

roommate! Besides, why aren't the police handling this? If he really was suspected of being involved then I highly doubt they'd send you to do the investigating."

"I don't have time to explain everything," I huffed. "But I really don't see what the big deal is. You share a room with him! You won't even have to put in any effort, and you get to make money out of it! It's a win-win for everyone."

"This might be a new concept to you celebrities, but there's something called privacy. Look it up."

"If he's not involved then you've scored yourself five hundred bucks and the peace of mind in knowing your roommate's not a weirdo!" I reasoned. "And if he *is* involved then you're basically helping to fight crime. You can't lose!"

"Typical." He shook his head. "You rich kids think throwing money at the problem will just make it go away."

"Okay, firstly, you just referred to yourself as a problem, so sick burn, man. And secondly, I'm not *throwing* money. I'm politely offering."

"I'm sorry, Gia," Jamie said. "Count me out. This is all just a little too wild for me."

"Wai—"

"I've got to get to class. I'm already late."

I watched Jamie walk away, feeling completely defeated. My only lead now officially thought I was nuts and was probably going to text his roommate the moment I left to send him a warning. If that button really did mean something to his roommate, he'd have plenty of time to bury all the evidence once he knew I was poking around. Not only had I gained zero new information, I may have completely blown the investigation.

Apparently I was engaged in some serious battle against the city. And so far, the city was winning.

Ten

I COULD SEE MILO'S REFLECTION IN THE BATHROOM mirror. He was trying to concentrate on tending to his injuries, but I had been distracting him by constantly changing my mind about our pizza order. After an intense argument about whether pineapple belonged on pizza, we decided to keep it simple and stick to Margherita. Whoever decided warm fruit should be a topping should be imprisoned for at least a decade.

It had been a long day. Classes had droned on, and afterwards I had spent a half hour twiddling my thumbs in Dr. Norton's office. She was trying her hardest to be patient with me, but I could tell she was starting to grow frustrated. Apparently talking about how much I love Chrissy Teigen and John Legend's marriage doesn't count as "making progress."

I considered telling Milo the truth about my conversation with Jamie but ultimately thought against it. He had already mentioned that the brief police surveillance on Jamie had come up with nothing of note, and I knew he'd be mad that I pulled such a risky move by talking to him directly. But there was still a huge chance Jamie's roommate was involved, and I couldn't just let that slip. So I casually mentioned Jamie's bag was a loan from his roommate. Whatever Milo wanted to do with that information was up to him.

"Do we have to watch *Game of Thrones*?" I asked him, nestling my face into Milo's pillow lazily.

"Yes!" he said, the bathroom door wide open. "There's no getting out of it."

"But I've already seen the first season."

"YouTubing Khal Drogo because you think he's hot doesn't count."

Agree to disagree on that one.

"Alright," Milo said, emerging from the bathroom in a pair of sweatpants and a t-shirt in hand. "Move over. It's GoT time."

I peered at the large bandage on his lower abdomen, watching as he carefully dropped the t-shirt over his head with a wince. His bruised rib was still a deep purple, but the color had softened since the last time I had seen it. He sunk into the bed beside me, painfully adjusting himself into a comfortable position as I fluffed the pillows behind his head. Now only a hint of a black eye remained, and the cut on his lip had all but healed.

"What are you doing anyway?" Milo asked, gesturing to his laptop screen.

"Looking through your photos!" I replied. "You need to spruce this room up a little. It needs more soul.

It was a cute apartment, albeit kind of tiny. But Milo spent barely any time in actually making it look like anyone lived there. His bedroom walls were painted a shade of blue that I would have preferred to be darker, and everything else in his room consisted of unruly stacks of papers, gaming consoles, and fancy-looking Bluetooth speakers. Boys and their toys, I swear.

"I'm never even home!" Milo argued.

I waved a hand dismissively, pressed the arrow key on his laptop, and watched the photos fly past quickly in their slideshow. He had all kinds of memories on there. Eleventh birthday party, first school dance, the day he bought his German shepherd, Woody. He was heartbroken that he couldn't bring Woody to New York with him, but he always loved any interaction he got with the police canines.

"Hey, if you happen to see any photos from my ninth grade Eminem phase," Milo said, "just go ahead and delete them."

I paused. "Are there jean shorts involved? Do you still have them? Oh my gosh, can I see them?"

"Baggy jeans and silver chains actually. And *no,* you cannot see them."

"That means you still have them!"

Just the idea of seeing cool and collected Officer Fells in jeans three sizes too big was too much to handle. I continued through the slideshow with so much laughter, tears were actually welling up in my eyes. But my amusement only lasted a few more photos before it died out. A picture of Milo stared back at me, looking far more grown up and without a reindeer sweater in sight. He was in between laughter, flashing his dimples with his eyes crinkled. Beside him sat Aidyn, one arm looped through Milo's and the other on a half-empty wine glass. Her grin was so lively, it practically brightened the entire photo.

I felt Milo cough before hurriedly reaching over and slamming his laptop lid shut. I only blinked when it made a soft noise from the impact.

"Okay, memory lane is closed now," Milo said awkwardly.

We both sat in silence for a few seconds, staring at the blanket scrunched in between us.

"It's okay to have photos of you and your ex," I told him in a hollow voice. "I mean I'm not bothered by it."

"Uh, good."

"I'm a very unbothered person right now."

"I can see that."

I rotated my body so it was facing his. "Why did you and Aidyn break up?"

Milo exhaled deeply, looking very much like he wanted the mattress to swallow him whole.

"Aidyn's parents are always moving around, and she wanted to be closer to them," he explained. "She applied for a transfer and finished her training at the NYPD academy. It just didn't make sense to keep dating if we were on opposite ends of the country."

"The only reason you two broke up was because she

moved?" I asked.

"In the most simplistic sense, yeah. I guess so."

I sank back into the pillows, staring at his ceiling thoughtfully. So Milo and Aidyn hadn't thought it was worth it to keep dating once she moved, but he obviously thought I was worth it. I'll admit, that was pretty reassuring. I may not have eyes the size of chestnuts, but I was clearly doing something right. Even still, there was a tiny sense of doubt nagging at the back of my mind. There was a great possibility that if things had worked out a little differently, they would still be together.

Milo put his arm around my waist and pulled me against him. He smelled like soap and faintly like cinnamon.

"Don't think too much about this, okay? We're just friends now, that's all. It's been good to have somebody familiar in the city after leaving all my friends back home. But that's all we are."

Ugh, fine. I believed him, even though it still annoyed me. And she could clearly back him in a knife fight, which I absolutely couldn't. They were friends, and I needed to accept that. I scooted toward Milo and kissed him firmly. He inched closer, closing whatever tiny space remained between us. He angled his body so that he was practically lying half on top of me, with our legs tangled.

"What about your rib?" I asked quietly.

"Eh," he said dismissively. "I've got a whole cage full of 'em."

Milo's lips met mine again, but the reunion was short lived. The soft sound of keys rustling and a door closing in the distance pulled us away from each other. Milo was listening, alert and confused. He reminded me a little of Famous whenever he was certain he could hear a treat nearby.

I stifled a laugh, and Milo put a hand gently over my mouth, his dimples peeking through his cautious expression. I could practically feel his heart beating on my own chest.

"Stop laughing! I'm trying to listen."

"What is the thief going to steal? Your silver chains?"

"Milo!" I heard a deep voice call out. "You home?"

We both froze, locking wide eyes.

"Crap!" Milo said, rolling off me with a little too much

force for his injuries. "It's my dad."

I shot upright, all traces of hilarity from the situation gone. "Your *what?*"

"Coming!" he yelled to his dad, roughly adjusting his t-shirt. "Come on, Gia! I want you to meet my dad."

Surely he wasn't serious. I couldn't meet his father wearing tight-as-hell pants and a cropped sweater with my hair looking like . . . well, looking like I had just been aggressively making out with my boyfriend.

"Right now?" I asked him weakly.

"Maybe pull your top down first."

Milo gave me an endearingly excited look before walking out of the bedroom, leaving the door slightly ajar behind him. I didn't move for a few seconds, letting the wave of emotions settle in the pit of my stomach as I gave a breathless sigh. I was about to meet the most important man in my boyfriend's life, and I was *wildly* unprepared. What if we had nothing to talk about? What if didn't like me? Had I known this was going to happen, I might have done some background research or written down some conversation starters on cue cards or something. Now I was just walking in head first!

"Dad!" Milo's voice was slightly muffled through the walls. "I thought you were staying the night with your friend in Jersey."

"Change of plans."

I couldn't hear the rest of the explanation because I was too busy rolling myself out of an entangled web of blankets, trying not to pass out from anxiety. I ran my fingers through my hair in a weak attempt to make it look presentable and smoothed down my *I'm definitely only wearing this for my boyfriend* yoga pants. Maybe I could just hide in his room the whole night. He had access to Netflix in here, so I would be fine. I would just text Milo to slide a few slices of pizza under the door.

"Gia?" I heard him call out from behind the door.

Crap. There goes that plan. I did some quick heavy breathing and finally swung the door open. Milo's dad was standing in the kitchen, which was really just an extension of the small living room. He gave me a friendly smile when he saw me, but there were no dimples in sight. Milo's mother was probably to thank for that. Mr. Fells was as tall as his son, and he shared the same dark hair, only his didn't look quite as colored anymore. The resemblance between the two was striking at first glance, but upon closer inspection, you could see time and experience had aged him. He was standing beside a grocery bag, placed on the small kitchen island beside him.

"Mr. Fells," I practically choked out. "Nice to meet you."

"Gia!" he replied warmly. "Nice to finally meet you! I didn't know you were coming over for dinner. What have you two been up to tonight?"

Milo and I exchanged glances.

"Nothing special. We were watching a documentary," Milo said, giving me a wink.

"Yeah. A documentary on . . ." I eyed the tap on the sink, which Milo had been complaining about being semi-broken all week. "Plumbing."

Milo looked at the floor casually, but I could see he was just avoiding my gaze to stop from laughing out loud.

"Plumbing?" His father looked understandably dubious. "Wow. That sounds, um, interesting."

"Oh, it is!" I babbled. "It's er . . . Hungarian. But we have subtitles of course. Bloody good show, if you ask me! Jolly interesting watch."

Fan-freakin-tastic. I was destined to live my entire life with this abhorrent British monstrosity, bursting out in literally the worst possible moments. I sounded like a drunk Julie Andrews.

"Is that a hint of an accent I detect?" Mr. Fells peered at me curiously.

I looked at Milo, who was watching me with his arms crossed and a wide grin on his face. He gave me an innocent *well, go on* look, and I narrowed my eyes at him the slightest bit.

"I spent some of my childhood in London," I lied.

"Oh," Mr. Fells said thoughtfully. "I didn't know that."

Yeah, neither did I until this very second. Milo finally decided it was time to stop torturing me and stepped in, helping his dad unpack the contents of the paper bag. He laid out a packet of spaghetti, a bottle of pasta sauce, and a few assorted vegetables.

"We just ordered pizza," he told his dad.

"You can't eat that junk all the time!" Mr. Fells replied sternly. "Take out is *not* real food. I'm making some real dinner. Now go make yourself useful and give me a knife!"

Milo laughed in reply. "Alright, old man. Jeez."

Milo obediently handed his father a large knife and a worn-out looking chopping board.

"Do your parents cook, Gia?" Mr. Fells asked me, as I tapped my fingers nervously on the kitchen island.

"Not really. My dad likes to think he's a MasterChef, but he's almost killed us, like, twice."

Milo swung an arm around his dad's shoulders affectionately and said, "Dad makes the *best* spaghetti. Seriously, you're going to love it."

Mr. Fells waved a hand as if it were no big deal, but I could tell he was pleased. "I'm sure Gia's used to eating pasta much fancier than mine."

He placed a few mushrooms on the chopping board while Milo pulled out a rusty steel pot from a cupboard. He wrestled with the sink tap for a few seconds before water finally began shooting out of it and into the pot. How did he even have all this equipment? If someone asked me for a spoon in the penthouse, I'd need Val to find it for me.

"Gia," Mr. Fells said, pushing the mushrooms toward me. "Why don't you chop these while I get the pasta going?"

Milo turned the tap off abruptly and stared at me over his shoulder. He looked like his father had just handed me a loaded gun and asked me to fire off a few rounds into the floor. I looked at the mushrooms uncertainly.

"You want me to cut these?" I asked. "Like, with that huge knife?"

Seriously, it was the size of my entire face! People on the Titanic could have used it as a flotation device.

"Or you can just boil the water?" Milo suggested. "I'll chop."

I flicked my gaze to the stove. It was dark and scary, and it hadn't even been turned on yet.

"You know what, I'll chop!" I said. "Bring on the mushrooms."

Milo and his father moved around the kitchen with such purpose, they looked like experts in the field of quick pasta making. The pizza finally arrived, but Mr. Fells dropped it onto the kitchen island dismissively, mumbling something about how our generation wasn't going to survive in the real world if we relied on pizza to keep our food pyramid afloat. I respectfully disagreed, but I didn't voice my opinion. It took me ten whole minutes to carefully slice two mushrooms. I didn't attempt a third; I didn't want to tempt fate. When I found that I had managed not to slice my entire hand off in the process, I was finally brave enough to carry a conversation.

"So Mr. Fells," I said. "How long are you visiting for?"

"Just a few more days, a week at most. I came down the moment I heard the kid was in the hospital."

"You've already been here a few days?" I asked with surprise.

"Dad, the water's boiling," Milo said quickly, but he wasn't quite meeting my eye.

Interesting. Milo had been home almost a week now and he hadn't mentioned his dad's visit once. He sure had the time to complain about NBA scores and players that I seriously didn't care about. But no mention of his dad.

"I wish Chris was here too," Mr. Fells said. "Milo's brother can't wait to meet you, Gia."

"He's seen the *Wolf* movies like a billion times," Milo added with a shake of his head.

Ah yes. The *Wolf* franchise. Somewhere between *Mission Impossible* and the *Bourne* movies stood an old-school set of cheesy spy movies, starring the one and only Harry Winters as Atticus Wolf. Mike and I had been forced to watch them once we were deemed old enough to see people's heads being blown off in film. I had never been good around guns before, and watching a lunatic threaten to shoot your father in real life hasn't helped that much. I don't think I'll be revisiting those movies any time soon.

"You know, Gia," Mr. Fells said, looking suddenly serious, "I just wanted to tell you I think whatever happened to you and your family was . . . well . . . indescribable. I guess I never got the chance to say that before now. But Milo tells me you're doing really well with it all, and I'm real proud of you."

For a moment, I was stunned. The entire energy of the room seemed to shift. I wasn't sure what Milo had told his father, but it was far from the truth. If he was going to be proud of someone, it should be his son and not me. I hadn't strapped on a bulletproof vest and burst into a warehouse. I forced a wobbly smile on my face, digging my nails into my palms.

"Thank you. I appreciate that."

"Anyway." Mr. Fells cleared his throat, probably sensing that I was ready to jump out of the window. "Is it true your dad is friends with Denzel Washington?"

It took me a few seconds to steady my heart rate before I replied, "Yeah, they have dinner sometimes."

"Careful," Milo said. "My dad has a serious man crush."

"Excuse me!" Mr. Fells replied. "Have you seen the guy? He's amazing!"

"I'll see if I can get you an invite to their next dinner party."

"Don't joke about this kind of thing, Gia," Milo said, leaning on the kitchen island opposite me. "Denzel is a sacred figure in our household."

Just looking at the two of them now, I could imagine their life back in LA, arguing over how much sauce to put on the pasta and debating which Denzel movie was the greatest. When Milo and I were first getting to know each other properly, he had mentioned his mother wasn't in his life. They spoke once every few months for five forced minutes, and she was always traveling to some corner of the country. Milo described her as beautiful and gentle, but "just not cut out for a family." It never seemed to bother him though. He said his dad was all he ever needed. On some level, I related to him. I was fortunate enough to have a mother who didn't abandon me, but even when she was present, she wasn't really *there*. Sometimes it felt like Dad was the only parent I had.

"So I heard your mom is filming a movie in Greece right now?" Mr. Fells asked, as if he had just read my thoughts.

I nodded. "She's been gone for a while, but she's loving it."

At least that's what she told me in the high-angled videos

she sent me of herself pouting seductively in Santorini.

"Well," he said. "If you're ever missing a slice of family, you can always knock on the Fells' door. We can't guarantee gourmet, but we do a pretty decent Monopoly night."

"Yeah, except he always cheats," Milo added.

"I don't cheat! Chris cheats!"

"Do we need to revisit the Missing Hundred Dollar Bill Incident of 2014?"

I watched as Mr. Fells playfully threatened his son with a spatula, laughing at how ridiculous their conversation sounded. Milo jumped out of the way and armed himself with a zucchini as his shield. Maybe it didn't matter that this introduction had taken so long to occur. In a heartbeat, Mr. Fells already considered me family, and that's all I could have hoped for.

"This is pathetic!" Mr. Fells said pleasantly, pointing to my roughly sliced mushroom. "You're as bad as he is. The youth of today, I swear."

"Go easy on her!" Milo told his dad. "She's a rookie."

"Now I'm just glad I didn't get you to put the water to boil." Mr. Fells dropped the raw spaghetti into the pot with a shake of his head.

For the rest of the night, all I heard was continual laughter and affection. I dreaded going back to the penthouse and its pin-drop silence. Milo didn't need photos in his room to prove there was human life in his place. The apartment already had twice as much soul as Mom's place. For a minute, everything seemed peaceful. Like the only real problems in the world revolved around stolen Monopoly money and cutting mushrooms.

For the first time in a long time, it felt a little like I was at home.

Eleven

It was early afternoon, and the temperature wasn't quite as warm as I would have liked. I pulled the belt on my Burberry trench a little tighter, curled Famous's leash around my wrist, and listened to the wind rustling the tree leaves above me.

"This had better be good," I grumbled to Reggie.

"If it's not, I'd be happy to punch him for you."

"I feel like you should do that anyway."

Reggie and I were in Central Park, ready to meet with Jamie. Trust me, no one is more surprised than me. But Steph had called about fourteen times, saying there was some guy that kept harassing her assistant Tamara into getting a message to me. Turns out Jamie had some burning desire to get something off his chest, and according to him I would be very interested in hearing about it. Yeah, right. He had probably written a haiku about how much he hated me and wanted some feedback from his muse. I had given my group members Tamara's number a few weeks ago, thinking that it was the best way for them to get in contact about the assignment. They never called, not even to prank the office, and I ended up forgetting all about it. That is until Steph's voice was screeching in my ear about how I have to be "careful with who I let in my inner circle." As if I hadn't become far too pathetic to even have an inner circle. Unless you count Reggie, of course.

"What do you think he wants to tell you?" Reggie asked.

"I don't know," I replied, letting Famous tug me along excitedly.

Why I had even chosen to accept Jamie's invitation was a mystery to me. Maybe I was curious. Maybe I just liked haikus. Either way, there was no turning back now.

Reggie nodded thoughtfully as we reached Greywacke Arch where Jamie told Tamara he'd be waiting. But he wasn't there. Whatever sunlight that wasn't blocked by the trees hadn't quite penetrated the darkness under the arch. It was quiet all around, except for the occasional chirping of birds.

"Well," I said. "This looks promising."

From the other side of the arch, I could see a pair of worn out sneakers and ripped jeans heading toward me. As the person got closer, Jamie's face appeared. He had a black sweater on, a red and black flannel shirt wrapped around his waist, and a snapback resting on his head. He looked like something out of an American Apparel ad, which isn't something I'm necessarily complaining about. He calmly walked right into the middle of the arch, blinking at me.

"You came."

"Indeed, I did."

I led Famous under the arch, my eyes taking a few seconds to adjust to the shade. It was much cooler now that the sun was completely blocked, and I gave an involuntary shiver.

"Was it really necessary to bring your bodyguard?" Jamie asked, looking at Reggie with a raised eyebrow.

"He's here to keep me safe."

"Against who?"

"You. The joggers. The tourists. But mostly you."

"So why'd you bring the dog?"

"Because it's a free country. And he's cute."

"He looks like a hamster with a collar."

I sucked in some air. It had been thirty seconds and I

already wanted to hit him.

"As much as I admire the place you've chosen to murder me," I snapped, "I have things to do and people to avoid."

"Yeah, I'm sure I'll hear all about it on *Gia Watch*," he replied with an eye roll.

"What the hell is *Gia Watch*?"

"Google it." He lowered his voice, as if he were about to divulge a secret. "Anyway, that doesn't matter right now. Something really weird is happening."

"Uh, yeah," I replied, looking unimpressed. "You harassed my publicist into getting me to show up here, you called my dog a hamster, and we're standing in probably the sketchiest part of the park. I'd call that pretty weird."

"Not that!" Jamie pulled a small round object out of his jeans pocket and held it up to show me. It was the Stag button. "It's about this."

Now *this* I had not been expecting. Could it possibly be that my lead hadn't given up on me as quickly as I thought? I handed Famous's leash to Reggie, who looked pretty unhappy to be babysitting my puppy.

"Okay," I said. "Start talking."

"Yesterday I was walking out of the library at school when I heard these two random guys call out to me."

"You'd never seen them before?"

"I didn't think so at first. One was sort of tall and lanky with black hair. The other one was built like a jock. Lots of bicep, not a lot of brain. Anyway, they point at my bag—at the button specifically—and the jock says, 'Congrats on being chosen.'"

"Chosen?"

"Yeah."

"So what did you say?" I asked.

Jamie shrugged. "I just said 'Um, thanks.'"

"You didn't even ask what they meant?"

"Can I finish the story without you interrupting me every two seconds?"

Behind me I heard Reggie give a quiet snort of laughter.

"Alright, J.K. Rowling! Chill."

"So the other guy, the lanky one, goes, 'I guess we'll see you at Andrew's on Saturday?'"

"Andrew? Who's Andrew?"

"I don't know."

"You didn't ask who . . . sorry, continue."

"I was *about* to ask, but they had already started to walk away. They told me to bring the button to Andrew's. They said I'd need it."

I let that hang in the air for a few minutes, not saying anything. A man jogged right past us under the arch drenched in sweat trying to keep his earphones in place. In that moment I was grateful to be standing in the shadows, where people couldn't recognize me without getting right up in my face.

"So that's it?" I asked Jamie. "*That's* your amazing information that you were just desperate to tell me?"

"That's only half of it," Jamie replied mildly. "I kept thinking the second guy looked kind of familiar, but I couldn't really place it. And then it finally hit me. I'd seen him talking to Craig a few times."

I looked at him expectantly. "Like, Daniel Craig?"

"Of course not Daniel Craig! Why would I know Daniel Craig?"

"I don't know! I don't know any other Craigs!"

"You know Daniel Craig?"

"Well, my dad does."

"I meant my roommate Craig! Remember him?"

Oh! This *was* interesting.

"Well, well, well," I said with a smug smile. "You were ready to check me into a psych ward when I suggested that your roommate had something to do with this Stag stuff. And now here you are, begging me to come to Central Park because your old pal Craig isn't as innocent as he seems. That's kind of funny, isn't it, Reggie?"

"Hilarious," Reggie replied from behind me, sounding equally smug. "That's some Comedy Central shit."

"Are you done gloating yet?" Jamie asked.

"No, actually," I said. "I'm not. You laughed in my face! And you called me crazy. Multiple times."

"Oh, come on, I was just kidding around."

I cocked an eyebrow up. "Really?"

"Eh. The coffee incident wasn't one of your finer moments."

"So what exactly do you want me to do with this information?"

Jamie shrugged and said, "I don't know. What do *you* want to do?"

"I want more information."

"Well this is all I have, so tough luck. I wouldn't even be telling you any of this if you hadn't harassed me outside class the other day."

I narrowed my eyes at Jamie suspiciously. "Why are you so eager to sell out your roommate all of a sudden?"

"What?"

"You seemed pretty loyal the first time I brought him up, but now here we are days later, and you're more than willing to throw Craig under the bus."

"I'm not throwing him under the bus," Jamie retorted. "I still don't know for sure if he's involved with anything. But he definitely knows someone who is, so I thought he would be useful to you. You know, since you've clearly convinced yourself that you're Nancy Drew."

Clearly he hadn't seen Nancy Drew's choice in clothing, or else he would never have made that comparison.

"I don't buy it," I said. "Reggie, do you buy it?"

"Nope. I don't buy it," Reggie said, coming up next to me as Famous ran around his legs in circles.

Jamie gave Reggie a frustrated frown.

"So what?" I asked. "*Now* you're interested in taking me up on my offer?"

"No way," Jamie scoffed. "I want nothing to do with this. I'm not going to spy on him for you, but I can introduce you two. After that, I'm officially out, and you can leave me alone forever."

"You're kidding, right? What, you want me to just march up to him and ask if he sells and possibly makes illicit drugs?"

"I don't see why not. That was your plan with me."

Well, he got me there. That *had* been my plan with him, and despite the initial speed bumps, it was actually paying off. Craig definitely knew something, even if he wasn't involved. A conversation with him wouldn't hurt. That way I could point Milo in the right direction, and all the other cops would love him! Gia Winters saves the day.

"Do you want to meet him or not?" Jamie asked, glancing down at the phone in his hand.

"Yes," I said begrudgingly. "I want to meet him."

"Good. Because I invited him here and he just texted saying he's, like, ten seconds away."

The color drained from my face. "Exsqueeze me?"

But Jamie was already looking over my head, along the pathway I had just come from. There was a young guy walking toward us, eyeing us uncertainly. He raised his hand and gave a half-assed wave to Jamie, widening his eyes with disbelief when he saw me. I watched his floppy brown hair bounce against his forehead as he walked over to us.

"What if I had said no?" I hissed to Jamie, just as Craig was approaching.

Jamie smiled. "Lucky guess."

"Hey Jamie," Craig said, stepping into the shadows with us.

"Hey man, how's it going?"

I was expecting Jamie and Craig to do one of those *bros for life* intricate homie handshakes, but when they just stood there blinking at me, I figured they weren't that close.

"Hi," I said awkwardly. "I'm—"

"Gia Winters," Craig cut in with a nod. "I know who you are." He looked at Jamie, clearly trying to suppress his excitement. "When you said you knew Gia Winters, I thought you were bullshitting, man."

Jamie looked uninterested as he shrugged back.

"Ahem," I continued. "This is Reggie, and that's Famous."

Craig fiddled with the strings of his hoodie absentmindedly, looking almost nervous as he said a quiet hello to Reggie. Famous was too busy bouncing on a leaf to even look up.

"Thanks for coming on such short notice."

Real short notice for some of us.

"No problem," Craig replied. "Any reason why we're

standing under this arch?"

"I'm uh . . . sunburnt. *Real* bad," I said.

Craig peered at me sceptically, and I took a tiny step away from him. "You don't look sunburnt."

"Nope, I definitely am. Trust me on this."

I laughed shakily, and Jamie rolled his eyes. Craig looked confused, but he blew past it quickly.

"Jamie said you wanted to talk to me?" he asked.

No wonder he thought Jamie was full of shit. I'm surprised he had even shown up.

"Actually it's really not even a big deal," I told him. "I just wanted to know where you got this button from."

Craig looked down at his hoodie, confused. "There aren't any buttons on here."

Jamie held up the Stag button. "Not on your shirt. On the bag that you let me borrow."

"That button," I nodded. "I wanted to know where you got it from."

"Why?"

Jamie and I looked at each other. That was a tricky little question.

"Because . . ." I began uncertainly. "I think it's cool. Bulls are awesome. Yay bulls!"

Craig wasn't buying it. Jamie wasn't buying it. Reggie wasn't buying it. Famous sure as hell wasn't buying it.

"I got the button from rush week," he said. "I don't even remember who gave it me. They were sort of just passing them out, so I guess I just stuck one on the bag."

"Was it the PDA?" Jamie asked.

"Who?" I said.

"Psi Delta Alpha," Craig replied for him. "They're one of NYU's top fraternities. They call themselves the PDA. You know, like 'public display of affection.' I honestly can't remember if it was them or not. Why do you ask?"

Jamie gave a light shrug and said, "No reason."

But there was totally a reason. I could have used my lame Vogue magazine article excuse again, but it hadn't really worked on Jamie, and I doubted Craig would be any different. I was taking a huge risk, but it seemed worth it.

"Craig, I'm doing an assignment for *Criminal Theory Foundations* and this button could really come in handy," I explained, hoping my lie sounded convincing. "I don't know if you know this, but that symbol is sort of linked to this drug called Stag. They think college students might be distributing and making it."

"What?" Craig said incredulously. "Who's 'they'?"

"Just . . . you know. People."

"The other day these guys came up to me and asked me about the button," Jamie told him. "I think I saw the PDA symbol on their sweatshirts. Anyway, the point is I kind of recognized one of the guys. I've definitely seen you talking to him before. Tall, dark hair, kind of wiry? Is any of this sounding familiar?"

"If you can remember anything that would be totally great. For my assignment, of course!" I added with a friendly smile. I didn't want him to think we were hurtling accusations at him.

Craig let out a sharp sigh and said, "Okay, this got weird, like, real fast. First of all, I have no idea what 'Stag' is and I didn't even know that bull was a logo. As for the guy? That sounds like it was Julian. He was in my physics class last semester. You probably saw me talking to him a few times because he used to borrow my textbook a lot. I don't really know him on a personal level or if he's part of a frat. Sorry, but that's really all I've got."

Jamie and I exchanged looks. It would have been awesome if Craig had just casually explained he was indeed involved with Stag, so that all my life's problems would be solved. What he had given me instead wasn't quite as perfect as that, but it was a new lead. Julian.

"Thank you so much, Craig," I told him sincerely. "Honestly, this helps a lot."

"No problem," he said. "So, all of this is for an assignment?"

"Yep!" I replied quickly. "They're trying to get us to do more hands-on learning."

Craig might have bought it this time. To be honest, that was pretty quick thinking, and I was kind of proud. There were a few seconds of heavy silence before Craig finally pushed his hands into the large pocket of his hoodie with a shrug.

"So this was . . . fun. But I've got to finish an assignment."

"Right," Jamie said. "Thanks for coming down here, man."

"Sorry I wasn't much help." Craig shrugged. "If I can remember anything else then I'll let you know. But I think that's all I've got for now."

"Thanks again, Craig." I smiled at him, thought about shaking his hand and then decided it was too business-like.

"Nice to meet you, Gia," he replied. "I wish I had a pen, I totally would have asked for an autograph."

"Oh, what a shame!" I said cheerfully. "Okay, bye now!"

We all stood frozen to the spot, silently watching Craig disappear behind the tall trees in the park. It wasn't until then that I realized I had been holding my breath.

"Well, it seems that my work here is done," Jamie said, looking pleased. "So I'll take those five hundred dollars now."

"You're kidding, right?"

"Uh, no. You told me you'd pay me for any information I gave you. I gave you a whole *person*."

"You got me a name. Not even a last name. Just Julian."

"The deal was that I get you information, and you pay me."

"You can't extort me in the name of freelance spy work! I'm not paying you a *cent*."

Jamie broke out into a grin. It was the first time I had seen him genuinely enjoying himself when he wasn't being sarcastic.

"I'm totally kidding!" he told me. "I just wanted to see if you would actually do it."

I shook my head in a mixture of both disbelief and bemusement. "Seriously?"

"Oh, come on, it's not personal. It's just business," he laughed. "Why are you looking at me like that?"

"I'm just trying to figure out which Corleone brother you are," I said. "Sonny or Fredo?"

"Please," Jamie said confidently. "If anything, I'm Michael."

"I don't see it."

"Well what does that make *you* then?"

I smiled brightly, slipping my oversized shades over my eyes with an airy shrug.

"You can just call me the Godfather."

Twelve

I WOKE UP EARLY ON SATURDAY MORNING FEELING anxious and unsettled. The clock said it was just before eight, which was unheard of on a weekend. Apparently, I had taken a few nights of good sleep for granted because the nightmares were evidently back in full force. The latest addition to my sleep horrors involved me suffocating in what felt like a black box barely big enough for me to stand in. Above me I could see a floating yellow light with a slight reddish tinge. But every time I had tried to reach up and grab it, the light would float a little further up. Just when I thought I truly couldn't breathe anymore, I heard the familiar sound of a loud gunshot ringing in my ears.

I'm a little fuzzy on the transition details, but at some point I'm pretty sure Snoop Dogg made an appearance, wearing a sweatshirt with the Stag symbol on it. I guess it was a nightmare for both Snoop and I, because not only did I have to suffocate in a box, Snoop had to wear a bright orange sweatshirt. This is what happens when you listen to rap music as you brush your teeth before bed.

After thrashing around restlessly for a while, I gave up and dragged myself to the shower. It was a bright, albeit slightly chilly morning in New York, and for the first time I had absolutely zero plans for the day. Jack was probably busy, and even if he wasn't, I felt like I was always hounding him for attention. I had filled him in on my impromptu interrogation of Craig over text, but he had no help to offer on the Andrew front, and had eventually stopped replying. That's the downside to having all but one friend. When they're busy, you basically run out of motivation to live. I figured I'd be productive and try to get some schoolwork done, but that lasted barely a half hour before I gave up on my assigned readings.

When Valerie walked through the door at 10:30, she was clearly shocked to see me sitting there, doodling love hearts and stars on my psychology notebook, dressed up like I was ready for high tea at the Waldorf Astoria. I had almost started crying with relief when I saw her come in. Finally, someone to talk to! The schoolwork thing was clearly a bust, and Milo still hadn't called me back. Val only worked half days on Saturday, so she'd be gone by early afternoon. But at least for the time being I had some distraction from my soul-consuming loneliness. What I really should have been concentrating on was my stupid assignments. What I did instead was force Valerie to teach me how to make chocolate chip cookies. The culinary experience with Mr. Fells hadn't been as much of a disaster as I had expected. Mainly because I didn't actually do any of the cooking. But I cut two mushrooms! Maybe that was my gateway to an undiscovered talent.

Val had kindly pointed out that I was perhaps a little overdressed to be baking, and my heels might be a kitchen hazard. But I politely reminded her that Nigella Lawson didn't become a star wearing ballerina flats. It took an hour and a half to shove twelve cookies into the oven, even though Valerie said that the recipe was supposed to be "super quick and easy." Either I was just a completely hopeless cook, or her recipe was majorly flawed, because I guarantee you, the process was anything *but* quick and easy. The oven was so damn hot and apparently actual cookie dough is far more dangerous to eat than Ben & Jerry's would lead you to believe, because you can get salmonella or something. On the plus side, I had actually baked for the first time in my life! And I had not one stain on my immaculate outfit. Yes, I had some flour in my hair, but I'll still take that as a win.

Just as it was time to pull the cookies out of the oven, the phone started ringing.

"I'll get it," Val told me, handing me the oven mitts. "You pull the cookies out."

"I'll get it," I replied, backing out of the kitchen hurriedly. "I'm closer!"

That, and I was totally afraid of the oven. I ran to the phone and pulled it off the receiver, pressing it to my ear. Nobody ever called on that phone; it was really only used to communicate with the concierge.

"Hello?"

"Miss Winters," Nadia at the reception desk said. "Mr. Anderson is here to see you."

"Jack?"

"Yes. Should I send him up?"

Had I forgotten about some plans I had made with Jack? Not that I was aware of. Maybe the universe had seen me flailing about the kitchen and decided to put me out of my misery.

"Um, sure. Send him up."

Val was carefully placing cookies onto a cooling rack when I returned to the kitchen.

"They're done!" I exclaimed with excitement.

Val smiled down at our handiwork. "They look great!"

And they did. Kind of. I mean they weren't perfectly round. Some of them looked like the crater of the moon. I'm pretty sure a couple of them were hexagonal. But that's actually a very difficult shape to accomplish without some kind of cookie cutter, so maybe it meant that I was a natural. All in all, they looked pretty decent.

The doorbell rang and I ran to answer it, leaving her in the kitchen that I had somehow managed not to burn down. Jack was standing there in jeans and a black Nike sweatshirt. His hair was, as always, perfect. His smirk was, as always, flirty. He looked me up and down.

"Going somewhere?"

"No."

"Didn't think so."

I stepped aside to let him in, but he kept a hand on the doorknob without closing it behind him.

"What are you doing here?" I asked.

"I have a surprise for you," Jack told me. "Actually, two of them."

I eyed his hands. Empty. Jack took a step back toward the door, calling out behind him but still facing me.

"You can come in now!" he said loudly, looking excited.

"You didn't, like, kidnap the Hemsworth brothers, did you?"

"Oh, trust me, it's better than the Hemsworth brothers."

I was about to point out that there are very few things that could be better than the Hemsworth brothers walking through the penthouse doors, but I never got the chance. Because as it turns out, my two surprises *were* better than that. They were my two best friends.

"Oh. My. God."

Both Aria and Veronica launched themselves at me, enveloping me in a tight group hug, full of jumping up and down and shrill squeals of delight. I clutched onto them, breathing in the familiar scent of Veronica's sweet YSL perfume and Aria's body butter that smelled like vanilla bean. I had barely even noticed the bellboy carry up a trolley full of luggage and slip quietly out the door without his tip.

"Jesus, girls. I think I lost the hearing in one ear!" I heard Jack say.

"You're actually here!" I cried when we finally broke apart. "What are you guys doing in New York?"

"It was Jack's idea," Veronica explained. "He messaged us last week and said it would be great if we flew down to surprise you. So Aria and I worked some stuff out and we booked our tickets. And here we are!"

I looked at Jack, speechless for a few long seconds. "I can't believe you did that for me."

"Hey, it's not like I bought the tickets," he replied with a shrug. "I just knew you'd been feeling a little down lately. So I wanted to cheer you up."

I actually had to put a hand over my heart to stop it from ripping out of my chest with the speed it was going at. He actually listened to all my complaining. He actually wanted to make me happy. Not only was I lost for words, I was slightly breathless.

"You look *fab* by the way," Aria cut into my thoughts, eyeing my outfit approvingly. "I'm loving this Grace Kelly look on you. Very Upper East Side."

I did a little curtsy for her. "Why, thank you! And you two look exquisite as ever."

And they really did. Veronica was dressed in a baby-pink sweater and a matching skirt, with her fire-engine red hair in perfect waves. Aria's long, brown hair was dead straight, falling almost to her hips. Her heeled boots came halfway up her charcoal jeans, and her dark eyeshadow was worthy of a rock concert. Two majorly contrasting styles. That was exactly why I loved them.

"Gia, did you want to try one?" Val appeared from the kitchen with a plate of cookies in her hand. "Oh, I'm sorry to interrupt."

"Guys, this is Valerie," I said. "She's my housekeeper and general confidant when Jack's not around to annoy."

"Which, apparently, I am always available for," Jack added.

Val and the girls introduced themselves, doing all the appropriate finger waves and pleasantries.

"Would you like a cookie?" Val asked, holding the plate out in front of her. "Gia made them herself."

Everyone's hands froze midair, and they cut their eyes to me uncertainly.

"Go on, try one!" I said. "They're really good, I promise. I made them all by myself!" Nobody's hands moved. "And Val supervised the whole thing."

Jack, Aria and Veronica all reached for a cookie, each taking a small bite apprehensively.

"It tastes . . ." Veronica began. "Um . . ."

"*Um*?"

"What?"

"You said 'um.' What does *um* mean?"

"I think she means," Aria answered for her, "that it sort of tastes like . . ."

"Sand," Jack said musingly.

"That's it!" Veronica said. "That's what I was thinking too."

"Oh my gosh, it totally tastes like sand!" Aria nodded.

"What! It does not taste like sand. Give me one."

I took a big bite of the still warm cookie and aggressively chewed on it. What were they talking about? It was amazing! Okay, maybe not amazing. It sort of just dissolved. You could feel it crumble into tiny pieces that sort of tasted like, well, sand.

"Oh, great," I said with defeat, placing my half-eaten cookie back on the plate. "My first proper time cooking, and I basically made baked sand."

"Hey, they're not so bad!" Veronica told me. "Once you get past the first few bites you sort of get used to the graininess. And the chocolate chips are a nice little surprise."

"They're chocolate chip cookies, V. The chocolate chips weren't supposed to be a surprise."

"Were they supposed to look deformed?" Jack said, inspecting his closely. "Mine sort of looks like a piece of a beehive."

"Mine sort of looks like it has a face that's crying out for help," Aria added, holding hers up with amusement.

"Val, just throw them out," I sighed.

Val opened her mouth to no doubt offer some words of comfort, but then took another look at Aria's cry-for-help cookie and silently retreated back to the kitchen with a nod. My three friends, bless them, had the good sense not to place their cookies back on the plate and were now reluctantly nibbling at them.

"So how long are you guys here for?" I asked once we had all settled on the sofas.

"Just until Tuesday," Aria replied. "We would have loved to stay longer, but assignments are really starting to pile up. This college thing is so not worth the trouble. Like, why are we paying for something we hate?"

"Hey, if all else fails," Jack said, straddling the sofa arm beside me. "You can always make it in culinary school. I'm sure Gia will teach you how."

Veronica, who seemed to have just shoved the remainder of her cookie down her throat almost choked with laughter.

I picked up a cushion and slammed it into his torso as hard as I could. Considering his abs were perfectly toned, I doubt he even felt it.

"So, Jack," Veronica said. "Do we get to meet this girlfriend of yours on this trip?"

We exchanged a quick look. After the amount of complaining I had done, no wonder the girls were eager to make Lucy's acquaintance and see for themselves.

"Maybe," Jack told her. "She's been pretty busy with work lately. I feel like I barely get time to see her myself."

"Well it's a good thing you're moving in together then," I said, without thinking.

Damn it. Maybe I wasn't supposed to mention that. I guess it wasn't a secret, but we had never really discussed it before.

Jack looked surprised. "Who told you that?"

"Uh, Lucy . . . She mentioned it at her party."

"I mean . . . we talked about it," he said. "But I don't know. Nothing's set in stone."

Don't ask me why, but the way his jaw tightened when he said that made me very happy.

"So how's *your* boyfriend?" Aria asked, wiggling her eyebrows at me suggestively.

Great segue, Aria. Thanks for that. I filled them in on the basics, summing up everything from his hospital visit to the meeting with his dad. It felt awkward with Jack around, so I kept the gushing to a minimum.

"You cooked for him?" Jack gave an exaggerated bark of laughter. "Did they press charges for attempted murder?"

I narrowed my eyes. "Ha. Ha. Very funny. Besides, I didn't even do the cooking. I was just the helper."

"Yeah, yeah. Tell it to the judge."

"I'm so happy it's going so well, G," Veronica said.

Only she didn't look happy. At all. She had this wobbly

smile on her face like someone was holding a gun to her head and forcing her to pretend she was excited, and her eyes were sort of misty. I glanced at Aria, who gave me a look that said *don't worry about it.*

"Just think about how great your future looks," Jack continued. "You, him, and your two boring kids that always eat their vegetables and never jaywalk."

"I know three self-defense moves, okay? Don't make me use them on you."

"Relax, Betty Crocker. You still have flour in your hair."

Seriously? I was still dealing with the glitter from the photo shoot the other day that was trapped in my scalp. I swatted at the side of my hair with frustration, but the way Jack was laughing, it was clear I had missed it.

"Here." He leaned over and gently ran his fingers through a tendril of my hair.

I think this sort of goes without saying, but I was kind of dying. At this stage, being this close to Jack was becoming a health hazard. Our gaze held for lingering second. His eyes probably would have burned holes right through my skull if I hadn't abruptly jerked my head backwards.

"Uh, you know what?" Jack said, replacing his hand by his side as he climbed off the elevated sofa arm. "I'm going to go check if Val needs some help in the kitchen. I'll let you guys catch up."

"Great idea. So marvelous!" I said. "Cheerio!"

Please don't comment on my nervous British accent. *Please, please, please.* Jack gave his head a small shake of amusement and walked off. I didn't start breathing until he disappeared out of sight into the kitchen, which I knew he was more than happy to do so he could go hit on Val a bit. It was a second nature to him now. I turned back to my friends who were blinking at me, looking dumbstruck.

"What?" I asked them.

"I'm sorry. Are we not going to discuss what just happened right now?" Aria said.

"What do you mean?"

"Don't 'what do you mean' me! Don't think I didn't pick up

on that little British accent you slipped in there. Not to mention you and Jack were basically having eye-sex!"

"Shhh!" I hissed, shooting a quick look at the kitchen to check if he had overheard. "We weren't doing anything! We're just fr—"

"Friends?" Veronica finished for me. "Yeah, I don't think so."

"*We're* friends, Gia," Aria said. "And if you started gazing at me like that, then we'd have a slight problem."

I rolled my eyes, but they knew I was flustered. They could see right through me. I blame the cheerio comment. It was my undoing.

"We were literally *just* talking about Milo and his dad," I reminded them. "Besides, Jack has a girlfriend, remember? They've been together for a million years."

"So?" Aria shot back. "Time doesn't always define the depth of a relationship. You can be with someone for years and then bam! Someone else can come along and everything can change in the blink of an eye."

Two very strange things happened just as she said this. First, she was actually saying some pretty deep stuff about relationships, which was a pleasant surprise. Usually she just shrugs and then makes out with the next foreign exchange student she meets. Secondly, Veronica burst into tears. Big time.

"Oh, V!" Aria sighed deeply. "I didn't mean you!"

"Oh my gosh! Are you okay?" I jumped up and came beside her on the other sofa.

"Aaron . . . and . . . I . . . broke . . . up!" she told me in between sobs.

I looked at Aria, who was clutching onto one of Veronica's hands comfortingly. She gave me a slightly pained look, but I immediately knew she had seen this before.

"When did this happen?"

"Two weeks ago."

"Two weeks?" I repeated in a shrill voice. "And nobody bothered to tell me?"

That was a comment I directed at Aria.

"She told me not to say anything!" Aria explained. "She didn't want to bum you out. We knew you were already feeling kind of down lately."

"Veronica, that's crazy!" I said, pulling her into a tight hug. "I'm your best friend! If I'm not going to be bummed out for your break-ups, then who is?"

I was having a really hard time wrapping my mind around this breakup, and I wasn't even part of the relationship. But Aaron and Veronica were the it-couple. The dream team! I'd always presumed they would get married and she would wear the perfect dress and I'd cry while I gave my toast, and then they'd have lots of annoying kids that I'd be stuck babysitting. Apparently Veronica thought so too because she was basically blubbering all over my lavender dress.

"Okay, slow down. Start at the beginning."

Aria wiped the tears from Veronica's face as she tried to compose herself and begin her story. It was the age-old tale. Things just started to feel different. Text messages started to go ignored, missed calls were never answered. *No, nothing's wrong, I'm just tired.* And then finally, the truth. He thought he had feelings for someone else, and he wanted to pursue them. I watched Veronica cry, my heart sinking. The only thing worse than someone breaking your heart is someone breaking your best friend's heart.

"This is crazy," I said, still shaken by the news. "Aaron is obsessed with you."

"Not anymore. He says he has 'chemistry' with this other girl."

"I didn't even know he was taking chemistry this semester," Aria said.

Neither Veronica nor I bothered to correct her. Sometimes it was better to just let Aria go with her thought process.

"Maybe he just needs some time to get his shit together," she continued.

"Aria's right," I nodded. "This might be a good chance to figure out what you both want."

"Oh really?" Veronica replied, and even through her tears I could see how unconvinced was. "So if Milo told you he met someone else and wanted to take a break, you'd be totally fine with it?"

Yeah, right. If that happened, he was getting a lamp thrown at his face.

"V, you can't sit here crying about him either," Aria said helplessly. "You were totally the best thing that ever happened to him! This new chick is just a sidepiece. He'll realize that soon enough."

"Maybe," Veronica said softly. "Or maybe he's just found better. Maybe I'm just not good enough anymore."

She buried her head in Aria's shoulder, her tiny chest racked with heavy sobs. I didn't know what to say. On the one hand, Aria was right. There was no way Aaron was finding better than Veronica. This was clearly just an error in judgment, a minor distraction. They belonged together. But on the other hand, was Veronica just supposed to forgive him when he finally came to his senses?

"V, it's going to be okay," I attempted half-heartedly, giving her hand a quick squeeze. "I'll go get you some more tissues."

I rose from the sofa, giving Aria a *please handle it* look. She gave me a thumbs-up in reply. It was a little selfish, but I needed to leave the room. I felt guilty for going on about Milo and Jack when my best friend was so torn up inside. And the worst part was I had no clue how to make her feel better. How could I have missed such an important event in her life?

I marched into the kitchen, where Jack was seemingly telling Val some hilarious story as he helped her dry the baking equipment with a dishcloth.

"We need to get out of the house," I declared. "Like now."

"Why? What's wrong?"

"Aaron temporarily dumped Veronica, and now she's an emotional wreck."

Jack raised an eyebrow. "Temporarily dumped?"

I waved a hand dismissively. "He thinks he likes some other girl. It's a whole shebang."

Jack handed Val a sparkly clean plate. "Sounds complicated."

"It is. Which is why you and I need to keep V entertained today. If she's too busy enjoying the city, then she won't have enough time to cry about Aaron!"

"Okay," Jack shrugged. "I'm down. What's on the agenda?"

"I'm thinking we should do the whole New York tourist thing. The Empire State Building, The Rock, Times Square."

"Well, alright then," Jack said, casually tossing the dishcloth onto the counter beside him.

I was feeling better already. Veronica was going to be having fun in no time.

"Maybe we can go to Jean-Georges for dinner." My mind was racing with ideas. "Better yet, Masa! They can totally squeeze us in for a booking if I use Dad's name."

"I'm pretty sure Veronica can be cheered up in a place that doesn't make me broke," Jack said pointedly.

"I can pay. Unless of course that hurts your manhood."

"It takes a lot to bruise my manhood."

I didn't doubt it.

"We can work it out later," I told him. "Besides, it's not like we're going to Andrew's tonight. That was *clearly* a failure."

"Good choice," Val piped up. I had almost forgotten she was in the room. "I heard that place is full of annoying college kids. *So* not worth the trip."

Jack and I blinked at each other for a few seconds, before diverting our attention back to Val.

"What?"

"Oh, sorry," Val replied, looking embarrassed. "I didn't mean to intrude. I just heard that it's a total letdown. My cousin used to work a few bars down and he hated the crowd that kept seeping in from Andrew's. I just figured I would save you the trouble."

"Wait, back up," Jack said, looking confused. "You know Andrew?"

"I know Andrew's, the bar. It's on Bleeker. Isn't that what you guys are talking about?"

"Andrew's," I repeated incredulously. "Jack, it's not a person. It's a bar!"

"We don't know that for sure," he replied. "You're just basing this off a huge assumption."

"It's close to NYU and Val said lots of annoying college boys hang out there. You know who qualifies as annoying college boys? Frat brothers!"

"It's definitely a hot spot for frats." Val nodded.

"Okay then," Jack said simply. "Tell Milo. They can go check it out tonight."

"Milo's not back to work yet," I told him. "And you said it yourself that it's a huge assumption. No other cop is going to take me seriously. I can tell him, but there's no chance the NYPD is wasting resources on what *I* have to say."

Also, I knew Milo would totally be down to stake out the place. But that would mean his partner-in-crime Aidyn would be right by his side, and despite his reassurances of their friendship, I wasn't fully aboard that train yet. Was I being petty? Maybe. Did I care? No chance, buddy.

"New plan," I declared. "We stop by the bar really quick before dinner. If we don't see anything useful, we leave. No extra investigating, no nothing. I won't even talk to anyone, I swear."

"I may as well just say yes because I know that's what we're going to be doing tonight either way."

"Now was that so hard?" I asked sweetly, and Val giggled beside me. "But for now, we need to focus on getting Veronica off my sofa and away from her heartbreak."

I was halfway out the kitchen when I heard Jack call out behind me.

"And what happens if you *do* find something useful at this bar? You call Milo for backup, right?"

I stuck my head back into the kitchen, spinning on my heel.

"Exactly." I gave him a light shrug. "Although I'm happy to kick some frat boy ass if need be."

Jack leaned against the kitchen bench, trying to suppress a smile but clearly failing. He sighed.

"That's my girl," he said.

Thirteen

JACK INSISTED THAT WE TAKE A CAB TO THE BAR. I wanted a limo, but he said it would only draw more attention to ourselves when we showed up, so I agreed. After the shamelessly touristy day we had, visiting all the sights and taking all the expected corny photos, I was tired of being in the spotlight. The photos from the day had given the press enough material to last their readers a month. I had offered to wear a disguise to the bar, but Jack told me I needed to chill out and stop giving myself so much importance. I threw a spoon at him. Jack had even invited Scott to come along to the bar, which was a pleasant surprise. I felt oddly proud, like I had just unlocked a new level of our friendship. That, or he was hoping I'd launch into my alleged love for ancient history again and make a fool of myself.

Spending the entire day with Jack and my two best friends had been so fun, I almost felt guilty. It wasn't like Milo and I didn't have a good time when we were together, but we were just never together much anymore. These days, all I had to look forward to were his voicemails and the occasional *can't talk right now* text.

When the five of us walked into Andrew's bar, we were all tired but still buzzing off leftover adrenaline from the day. The bar was dimly lit, with candles on every tall, circular table that stood scattered around. Everything was dark brown, contrasting with the mason jars that were hung in every corner, filled with little fairy lights. It was like having a candlelight dinner with a whole bar. The place wasn't quite full, but it had pulled a decent crowd. Despite the scarcely few middle-aged drinkers, it was obvious that everyone else was a student. Next to the unlit fireplace at the back, there was a makeshift dance floor, where people were enjoying some old school R&B as a background score to their conversations. It was such a different vibe to the LA scene, and I was surprised that I immediately loved it. Aria found a table close to the wide front window, giving us a great view of all the passersby.

"Oh god," I groaned over the music. "People are *so* going to recognize me here. I totally should have worn a wig."

"Okay, firstly, should I be concerned that you have a lot of wigs?" Jack asked. "And secondly, who cares if they recognize you?"

"I care! I'm not in the mood to autograph people's greasy bar napkins."

"It's real dark in here anyway," Scott assured me. "No one's even looked in our direction yet."

"Time for drinks!" Aria announced happily, throwing her arm around Jack's shoulders. "Tonight is going to be so lit!"

"We're not here to party!" I told her. "This is just a quick pit stop."

"Yeah, a pit stop with drinks. Come on, I know Scott wants to party! He can keep me and Jack company at the bar."

Wow. Subtle. Aria was never off her game when a cute boy was around.

"You heard the woman." Jack clapped his friend on the back. "Drinks time!"

Veronica and I watched them walk away, shaking our heads like the parents of mischievous kids. But it didn't take long for me to notice that Veronica had slipped back into her moody, pensive mode. She had cheered up a lot throughout the day, but

I could tell it was still at the forefront of her mind.

"V," I said, watching her fiddle with the candle. "I know you're upset. But you can't be sad the whole night. We're supposed to be having fun!"

"Can I ask you a question?" she said. "Do you think it's possible to be in love with two people at once?"

"Veronica, Aaron is *not* in love with this other girl. He's known her for, like, five minutes. He's just being an idiot."

"What if he's not?" she replied. "I mean, he clearly feels strongly enough about her to ruin our relationship. That's got to mean something, right?"

"No, it doesn't," I told her firmly. "He's just caught up in this whole college thing. He as no idea what a huge mistake he's made. He's not worth fighting for."

"Is Jack?"

I looked at her, surprised. "You mean Milo, right?"

She placed a hand over mine gently. "You and Milo are great together. But you can't keep pretending that you don't have chemistry with Jack."

"What are you trying to say?"

"I can hate Aaron now, but maybe it's better this way. If he has feelings for someone else, I'd rather he not lie to himself or sneak around behind my back."

"Jack and I aren't sneaking around!" I replied sharply, my cheeks rising in color.

"I'm not saying you are! But if there's any chance that you and Jack might be more than friends, then I don't know . . ." Veronica sighed. "Forget it, I don't know what I'm talking about it. I'm sorry, G. I'm just in a weird mood today. Just ignore me."

But I couldn't. Her words fell to the pit of my stomach, like someone had just made me swallow a bag of stones.

"Alright ladies! Round one!" Scott announced, emerging with two colorful shots. Jack and Aria rejoined the table and the five of us gently touched our tiny glasses together and downed the contents in one swoop motion.

"Okay, time for business," Aria declared, putting her empty glass down. "Keep your eyes peeled."

"What are we looking for?" Scott asked.

"Frat boys doing things they shouldn't be."

"Gee, that narrows it down."

"So you don't know what this Julian guy looks like?" Veronica asked me.

"I've never actually met him," I replied. "But he's tall, and he's got dark hair."

"If anyone's dealing they aren't going to be obvious about it," Jack said. "You have to look out for the subtle things. You know, lingering handshakes or money being sneakily passed around. And most importantly, keep your eyes open for the Stag symbol. That's your best shot at getting answers."

"This is totally legal, right?" Scott asked. "Like, we're not infiltrating a gang or anything, are we?"

"Don't worry, Scotty boy, I'll bail you out of trouble. But on the plus side, they're playing some great throwback tunes," Jack said, bopping his head with embarrassing enthusiasm.

"Please stop dancing," I said, stifling a laugh.

"But it's the remix to 'Ignition'!"

"Stop."

"*Hot and fresh out the kitchen.*"

"You dance like my dad."

"Your dad still landed your mom, so I'm not even offended."

"Yeah, and then they got divorced, remember? Now she's off in Santorini probably banging every Greek waiter who passes her."

"Your parents really are the greatest."

I'm glad one of us thought so. I was contemplating actually knocking Jack out before he attempted to put on a fur coat and chains, when someone familiar caught my eye. I stood on my toes, trying to get a better look over the growing crowd of patrons. Our eyes met immediately, and he gave me a smug looking smile.

"You've got to be kidding me," I said. "Stay here. I'll be right back."

"Where are you going?" Jack asked, following my gaze.

I ignored him and marched over to the bar, pushing past a group of college boys lining up their shot glasses with excited cheers. Jamie was there, shaking his head as if having a conversation with himself.

"What are you doing here?" I demanded.

"Hello to you too, Gia."

"You didn't answer my question."

"I'm here to have a drink with a friend. You remember Tyler." He motioned to the guy standing behind him ordering a drink. It was the same guy from outside Jamie's class the other week.

"So you and Tyler are just here for a drink. You really expect me to believe that?"

"This bar is really popular with NYU students," Jamie replied by way of explanation. He looked over my shoulder to the table where Jack, Scott, Aria, and Veronica were now watching us curiously. "You planning on introducing me to your gal pals?"

"No."

"They don't look like they're from around here."

"They're not. You must be familiar with the place. It's called Out of Your League."

Jamie looked at me musingly and said, "Hmm. Is that right next to your hometown, Rich Bitch Island?"

"It's actually the capital city."

"I knew I recognized you from the national flag."

"Oh, hey Gia," Tyler said, drink in his hand. "Nice to see you again."

"Hey Tyler." I turned my attention back to Jamie impatiently. "So are you going to tell me how you found out about thc bar?"

"You first."

"Let's call it a happy coincidence."

"Same," Jamie said. "The drummer in Tyler's band bartends here part time. I guess it's a small world after all."

I raised an eyebrow at Tyler. "Band?"

"We're still in our garage-band phase," Tyler admitted.

I gave him a polite smile that was somewhere between mild interest and "ok, cool, don't care, bye." Tyler took that as his cue to make himself look busy elsewhere and disappear.

"You're taking a *lot* of initiative for someone who claims

they don't want anything to do with Stag," I said, narrowing my eyes at Jamie.

"You know, you're right," he replied. "But I'm kind of starting to enjoy all this investigating. I think I can see the appeal now."

"Well, let's hear it then. Have you actually learned anything sitting here, or is this all just a hobby?"

Jamie placed his drink down on the mahogany bar. He was either pausing for dramatic effect or manufacturing utter bullshit in his mind. At this stage, I didn't even care which it was.

"As far as I've seen, there are no drugs being passed around tonight. Not openly anyway. But the frat boys are definitely here, Julian included. He's at the back of the bar."

I looked to where he was motioning. Beside the fireplace and people enjoying old-school Shaggy music were a few large booths, slightly hidden in the dim light. I probably wouldn't have noticed them at all if it weren't for the fact that they were clearly overflowing with college boys, laughing at each other's jokes and slapping each other's palms in intricate homie handshakes. I spotted Julian right away. He was sitting on the edge of the long, wooden table at one of the booths, his legs dangling over the edge. He was clearly enjoying a light-hearted conversation with some guy I had never seen before, fiddling with a pen in his hands. Even from across the room I could see he had the Stag symbol pinned to his shirt.

"So the frat boys are definitely up to something," I said, thinking out loud. "Has he seen you yet?"

"Nope. I was going to walk over after this beer. But he's a real charmer by the looks of it. Everyone seems to really like this guy."

"Anything else I should know?"

"One other thing," Jamie replied. "I don't know if it means anything special, but Julian keeps writing in this brown notebook. He'll work the room a little, have a few laughs, and then go and write something down."

I cast a look over to Julian. No notebook in sight. Jamie eyed my outfit up and down with a frown.

"Are you wearing pajamas with heels?" he asked.

"It's a jumpsuit! It's fashionable!"

"Right."

Says the guy dressed like a homeless car mechanic.

"Gia," Jack said, coming up beside me. "Who's your friend?"

"This is Jamie," I told him. "And we're not friends."

"Oh, you're that jerk from her psychology class!" Jack exclaimed.

"You're that bodyguard that all the gossip magazines think Gia's banging," Jamie replied coolly.

Jack looked at me with an impressed smile. "I like him."

My eyes narrowed to slits this time. Of course these two would get along. I wrapped my hand around Jack's wrist and pulled him back toward our table.

"Okay, time to go do your thing," I said. "Let me know how it goes."

Jamie cast a look over my head. "Looks like you've got bigger problems right now."

He was right. Even from deep inside the bar, I could see the familiar flashes from cameras on the sidewalk outside. There was a small group of photographers practically pressed up against the window, their shutters moving at lightning speed. Aria was shooing them away from the window with her hands, as if they were a neighbor's pesky dog begging for leftovers.

"Oh crap!" I groaned, whipping my head back around so my face was out of sight. "How did they find me?"

"Must have been *Gia Watch*," Jamie said.

Okay, someone seriously needed to tell me what the hell that was.

"It's okay, there's only a few of them," Jack told me, putting a protective arm around my shoulders. "Just keep away from the window and they'll get bored when they realize nothing exciting is happening."

"I wouldn't be so sure about that," Jamie said uncertainly, eyeing the front door.

I was expecting to see a hoard of paparazzi surrounding the place. I knew all too well how they tended to multiply in the blink of an eye. But to my surprise, that's not what Jamie meant. He was referring to the group of NYPD officers marching into the bar. Outside, I could see an officer talking to a man holding a heavy-looking camera, ushering him to get back from the building. At first, I thought the police were there just to scare off the paparazzi. But it became clear pretty quickly that they had other business in the bar. It seemed everyone else shared my confusion, because all conversation ceased as we watched the officers walk, the sounds of Ashanti's voice still crooning in the background.

The NYPD officers headed straight for the back of the bar, toward the frat brothers. I couldn't hear what they were saying, but the boys didn't look happy. Julian was one of them.

"Is it a little suspicious if we just sneak out?" I asked Jack.

"You didn't commit any crimes today, did you?"

I thought about it. Nobody had died after trying my chocolate chip cookies.

"Not that I know of."

"Good," he said. "Get the girls. We're leaving."

Without a goodbye, we left Jamie by the bar and rounded up our friends. Jack had gone into full bodyguard mode and had one arm around me the entire time, as if he were afraid the photographers would break through the glass window and launch at me. There were definitely more of them now, but half of the group was too busy arguing with the police outside to really focus on me. By now the music had been turned off, but everyone stood frozen in their spots, chatting amongst themselves with hushed excitement and curiosity.

"Yo, get off me, man!" we heard someone yell.

"Can you see anything?" I whispered, struggling to get a glimpse over the crowd ahead of me.

"No, there're too many people," Veronica whispered back.

"Someone's definitely spending the night in the slammer," Aria said.

This was *so* not the place I wanted to be photographed at.

"It's okay, they seem to only want the guys at the back," Scott told me. "We can just sneak out the front. It's fine."

"But we have to do it now," Jack added. "Before they start hauling people into police cars."

We had made it halfway to the door when every single

person in the bar turned in our direction. But they weren't looking at us. They were all watching as the group of NYPD officers marched the frat boys out of the bar, their hands cuffed behind their backs as they yelled out in protest. I counted eight boys. Julian was the third. My friends and I stood glued in our position, as if we were hoping we could be mistaken for statues.

"Alright, everybody. IDs out!" an officer called out.

Nobody moved. They were too busy watching the scene still unfolding outside.

"Did you not hear him?" the cop next to him said. "IDs out!"

Everyone snapped into action, pulling out their wallets and bags. Nervous chatter shattered the silence, everyone eager to share their own theory on what had just happened.

"Well, there goes our sneaking-out plan," Jack said.

"Gia?" I heard someone say above the noise.

My body immediately filled with dread. I recognized that sweet voice. Sure enough, Aidyn stood amongst the scattered crowd of patrons, dressed in her NYPD uniform with her signature ponytail atop her head. A second later Milo emerged next to her, wearing dark jeans, his white shirt untucked and a police badge hanging on a chain across his neck. A look of confusion flashed across his face as he eyed us and then frowned.

"Oh good," he said. "The whole gang's here."

"Hey Milo!" Aria chirped. "Long time no see. How's it hangin'?"

Milo gave his head a tiny shake of disbelief and hooked a finger at me in a *come here* motion. I walked over sheepishly, like I was being sent to the principal's office.

"What are you doing here?" he asked, leading me to off to one side.

"What are *you* doing here?"

"What do you think I'm doing here? I'm working!"

"You're not supposed to be at work yet. The doctor told you to rest."

"I've had plenty of rest! I should be back at work now."

I gave his badge a little tap with my long fingernail and

said, "Where's your uniform then, officer?"

Milo rolled his eyes impatiently. "Aidyn called me last minute. She said they had a big lead, so I had to come in."

"Oh, so if Aidyn calls then you pick up. But I guess my calls aren't as important."

"Seriously? This again?"

"Yes, this again! No wonder you couldn't talk today. You were at work when you weren't supposed to be, and you weren't even going to tell me about it!"

"I was doing desk work mostly!" he shot back, but even he was starting to look a little guilty.

"Besides, I thought this whole thing was a competition," I continued. "But evidently Aidyn doesn't count, does she?"

"We all want to make it to the top, Gia. But at the end of the day we still work together. We're still a team!"

Milo was giving me this disapproving, judgy look, which was kind of getting on my nerves. When it came to the douchey NYPD boys, it was a fight to the death. But when Aidyn was around, it was all *hooray teamwork!* I crossed my arms over my chest defensively.

"How did you know about the bar?" I asked.

"This is an ongoing investigation. I can't share those details with you."

"You're kidding, right?"

He wasn't.

"Gia, you know how this goes. I can't share confidential police stuff with you."

"You don't seem to have a problem sharing police stuff when it gets you a lead or two."

"In case you hadn't noticed, your leads are landing you right in the middle of trouble," Milo said. "I can't have my girlfriend showing up in the middle of a major arrest! They're never going to take me seriously that way!"

"In case *you* hadn't noticed, I wouldn't even be here if it weren't for you! The only reason I didn't tell you about going to the bar was because I was scared it was waste your time if it turned out to be nothing! I'm only trying to help!"

"Well, stop helping!"

"Maybe I will!"

"Fine!"

"Fine!"

"And another thing!"

"What!"

"I'm sorry."

I glared for a few seconds more, getting all the residual anger out before I too gave in.

"Yeah, okay," I muttered, eyebrows still furrowed. "I'm sorry too. I didn't mean to obstruct your justice, or whatever."

"Can we go back to being cute now?" he asked.

"Only if you tell me what just happened."

Milo thought about it for a beat, before giving a defeated sigh. "We re-interviewed the most recent victim yesterday. I guess she got tired of pretending."

"What did she say?"

"A few things. She mentioned the frat."

"Psi Delta Alpha," I said.

"Yeah," Milo replied. "How did you know?"

It was only then that I realized I hadn't even told Milo about my impromptu interview with Craig in the park. Whoops. I definitely wasn't going to bring it up now. He really should pick up his phone more often.

"It's not important," I said quickly. "Go on."

"Anyway, we did some digging and it turns out one of the guys in the frat used to date one of the girls who ended up in the hospital because of Stag. It's a long story, and I'm not sure I can tell you all the plot points. But Psi Delta Alpha are definitely involved. We just need to find enough evidence to prove it."

"So you're hauling them in without evidence?" I asked.

"They're all wearing Stag buttons and we found two of them in possession of illicit drugs. I'd say we're doing okay on the grounds for an arrest."

Well, damn. He was a pain, but Milo Fells sure was hot when he went into NYPD arrest mode.

"That tall one with the dark hair," I said. "You found drugs on him?"

"Yeah," Milo replied. "Why?"

There was no getting around it. I had to tell him about my conversation with Craig. Besides, with all these witnesses around, what was the worst he could do? I even had a lawyer present with Scott around, just in case he threatened to sue me or something. I explained the whole interrogation to Milo, who looked a little like he wanted to die when I first brought it up, and didn't even relax when I assured him I used the excuse of a criminal justice assignment. But after overcoming his *I can't believe the whole world knows about this damn investigation* rant, he finally calmed down a little.

"Jamie didn't get a chance to actually talk to Julian tonight," I told him. "Your arrest kind of got in the way. But he said he saw him writing in some brown book the whole night."

Milo nodded and said, "Yeah, that little black book. I think one of the other officers got it off him."

"Brown," I corrected.

"Black," Milo repeated. "It's black."

"Jamie said it was brown."

"Well, then I need to talk to Jamie."

I looked around the bar. Half the senior officers were now standing around talking seriously. Andrew's bar wasn't down for a party anymore, seeing as the staff had turned over their open sign to "closed," and were politely ushering irritated college students out the doors slowly. My friends were among them.

"Jamie!" I said, spotting him close to the exit. I ushered him over urgently.

"Name?" Milo said when he approached us.

"Jamie Hart," he replied, turning to me. "So this is the famous cop boyfriend?"

"The book you saw with Julian," I said, ignoring him. "What color was it?"

"Brown."

"Are you positive it wasn't black?" Milo asked. "Maybe you mistook it for brown in the dim lighting?"

"It's kind of hard to mix up light brown and black, man."

Milo and I exchanged looks. "Alright," he said. "We'll do a quick search and see if we come up with anything. You're free to go."

Jamie gave me a little finger salute and headed back toward Tyler, who was looking too sober to be enjoying the sudden excitement the night had brought.

"I have to head back to work," Milo told me. "You have a ride home?"

I was about to tell him that Andrew's was intended to be stop one on an adventurous New York night out, but then thought against it. I was actually ready for bed. The city may never sleep, but I definitely enjoyed my share.

"We'll take a cab back to my apartment."

"And Jack?"

"Jack was included in that 'we.'"

"Oh."

"Is there a problem with that?"

"Nope."

Yeah, there better not be. Especially when you show up next to Miss Perky Ponytail over there.

"We're clearing out," an older officer told us. His mouth was turned down when he looked at me. He was clearly unimpressed. "Fells, stay back a minute."

Milo's police mode kicked back in, and he quietly promised to call later. Yeah, yeah. I'd heard that one before. I gave him a little wave and headed for the door. The place was completely empty except for the bartenders, who were talking to the small group of officers remaining, Aidyn included. The excited and confused chatter grew louder as I stepped outside, walking over to my friends.

"Let's get you guys home," Scott said, eyeing the road for a passing taxi.

I had barely turned on my stiletto when a blinding flash of light went off directly in front of me.

"Hey buddy, back off!" I heard one of the officers say.

Another blinding flash closely followed, then another, and another.

"Hey! I said back off! You guys can't be here!"

I was like a deer in headlights. Beside me, people had now begun to notice what the big deal was. Or rather, *who* the big deal was. Me.

"Oh my gosh, that's Gia Winters!"

"Back up everybody!"

"Gia! Over here!"

"Look, it's Gia Winters!"

The officers were trying their best to push the paparazzi away, but unfortunately, they weren't as fast as a camera lens shutter. The damage had already been done, and now the onlookers and bar patrons had caught on as well. Everyone was pulling out their phones and getting to work, documenting my embarrassment. Jack tried to pull me behind him, as if he could shield me in some way. But there was no point.

"Hey Gia!" one of the men yelled out, putting the camera up to his eye. "Smile!"

The blinding flash went off before I could even blink.

Fourteen

Jack and I were standing in the middle of his loft. He was watching me uncertainly, one hand running through the back of his hair absentmindedly.

"It isn't much," Jack said quietly. "But . . . it's home."

The wooden floorboards didn't look as glossy as they should have, and the drapes were neither fantastic nor terrible. There was a closed door on the opposite side of the loft. Framed photos hung all over the place, but none of them told stories I understood. There was a little table stacked with DVDs near the TV, and a few magazines that I couldn't make out the title of from where I was sitting. It was probably something manly, like *Cars Are Cool* magazine or whatever guys read. But it already felt more like home than Mom's penthouse.

"It's perfect," I told him.

The whole night had been a blur, and I was just grateful to be in any place that was far away from the cameras. Everything had happened so quickly, all the buzz around me just became white noise. The police had been helpful in finding me a cab to escape, with the help of Jack, Scott, and Milo—once he noticed the cameras outside. Trust me, he wasn't a happy camper. I couldn't even properly enjoy his angry hot cop face with all that commotion. But then came the really difficult part. Pulling up at the penthouse had been a complete waste of time, considering the entire entrance was swamped with paparazzi, arguing relentlessly with the building's security. Whatever scoop they thought they had landed about me they were clinging onto for dear life. Gia Winters right in the center of a major drug bust. I had just made their careers.

Obviously, Milo had insisted I just stay at his apartment when I called him from outside the penthouse where we were sitting in our cab and watching the media frenzy. But I refused. It was kind of awkward to share a room with his father in the house. That ruled his place out.

"We've got a hotel room," Aria had reminded me. "I booked one just in case there wasn't room at yours."

"Mom's penthouse has like four bedrooms!"

"Yeah, but it's your mom. I'm kind of scared to see what she uses those other rooms for."

She had a point there. There are some doors even I hadn't dared to open yet.

"They'll check the hotels next," Jack had said. "It's just a matter of time. Unless you're willing to stay at the Holiday Inn."

Over my dead body. Scott had already gone home, and I wasn't about to call him and ask if I could stay at his place. We hadn't quite solidified our friendship enough for a sleepover just yet.

"You guys gonna hop out or nah?" The cab driver sighed, turning to look at us impatiently.

We all exchanged looks, unsure of what to do. The crowd outside the building was only growing.

"We'll drop the girls off at the hotel," Jack finally said.

"And what about me?"

"You're staying with me tonight."

And that's how I ended up standing in the middle of Jack Anderson's place, looking lost and feeling completely exhausted. Jack led me into his room with so much caution, it was like he was afraid I was going to start tearing the wallpaper off the walls with disgust.

"Welcome to the Ritz," he said.

His tone was sarcastic, but there was a nervous edge in his voice. The bedroom was plain, but oddly comforting. Not overly colorful. A small bookcase sat in the corner with books collecting dust. No photos or potted plants or anything. A laptop was lying closed on the right bedside table with the charger plugged in. Maybe he preferred the right side of the mattress to the left. I always slept on the left. His bed was roughly made, and there were a few shirts strewn on one side. The room was just like Jack. Nothing fancy, but you knew you were safe.

"I'll just fix that up," he said, grabbing the shirts off his bed and clumsily throwing them into his closet.

"Where are you going to sleep?" I asked him.

"On the couch."

"Jack, you should really let me sleep on the couch."

"Yeah, right. And then you can do my laundry afterwards."

"I'm serious."

"Relax, Princess. I've had lots of experience sleeping on couches."

I sat on the edge of the bed, watching him make a desperate attempt at tidying his room up. The mattress felt softer than it looked. Jack pulled out a gray sweatshirt from his closet and handed it to me.

"Sorry I don't have a silk robe or anything," he said. "But you can sleep in that. The bathroom's right over there. There should be a new toothbrush in the first drawer."

I eyed the sweatshirt. It smelled freshly washed, and it was definitely two sizes too big for me. Jack disappeared inside the bathroom for a second, and then reemerged a second later, holding a pair of boxers, a t-shirt, and a blue toothbrush. We looked at each other awkwardly.

"Okay," he finally said. "I'll be right outside if you need anything."

He gave his room one final look, nodded in approval, and then headed for the door. He had almost closed it completely behind him when I finally called out to him.

"Jack?"

The door opened an inch, and he stuck his face in between the gap. "Yeah?"

"Thank you," I said, clutching the sweatshirt against my chest.

He paused for a few seconds, blinking at me. "Sure," he replied. "Anytime."

I waited until I couldn't hear his footsteps anymore before taking my clothes off and pulling the sweatshirt over my head. It was so baggy on me, it was almost a dress. But the inside was warm and fuzzy, and it's all I needed in that moment. By the time I had roughly washed the makeup off my face, located the new toothbrush, and collapsed onto his bed, the entire place was silent. I couldn't even see any lights on from the crack underneath the bedroom door. Jack's sheets smelled faintly like his cologne. I wanted to drown in that smell. I buried myself underneath his blankets, listening to the sound of my own breathing beginning to slow. I was asleep in a matter of minutes.

I awoke the next morning feeling fazed, as if I had spent the last few hours in a state of sedation. No nightmares. Just complete silence. My eyes fixated on the little wooden table next to me. It didn't look familiar. It took me a few minutes to get my bearings.

I propped myself up on one elbow and reached for my phone. The time on the lock screen read 12:07 p.m. Four missed calls from Milo. One from Jack. Two each from the girls. Seven from Dad. Thirteen from Steph. Three from my mother. One voice mail. There were also a few texts that I didn't even bother reading before I skipped right to Jack's. It read: *call me when you wake up*. I dialed voice mail and put the phone to my ear.

"Hey, it's me," Jack's voice came through the receiver. *"It's like, 11 o'clock, which means you've probably got four hours of sleep to go before you finally decide to wake up. If by some miracle you do find yourself awake at this ungodly hour, feel free to raid the fridge. There's nothing fancy, but hopefully you can manage not to burn toast. I had to work, ugh. Some snotty senator needs me to keep everyone away from him in case he gets punched in the face again. Yeah, I said 'again.' Long story, I'll explain later. Anyway, I should be home in a few hours if I'm lucky. I'll call you later to check up on*

you. Text me if you need anything. And stay out of trouble! Okay, that's it. Bye!"

There was a dull ache at the back of my head as I dragged myself out of bed, but it was far from a hangover. The glimpse I caught of myself in the bathroom mirror almost made me laugh out loud. Makeup was still smudged at the bottom of my eyes, and I looked like I had spent the night in prison. If only Marie Claire could see me now. I didn't have the guts to open Jack's wardrobe and search for some more respectable clothes without his permission. I already felt like I had intruded in his space enough. So I roughly combed my fingers through my hair, worked on making myself look a little less ghostly, and headed straight for the kitchen.

Jack's invitation to raid his fridge was welcomed, considering I felt like I hadn't eaten in days. He was right; his fridge was pathetic. No fresh strawberries, no chocolate syrup, no fancy dips. Just regular milk, ham, mustard, and the basics. At least he had a jar of Nutella, the only sign he wasn't a complete robot. I put two pieces of bread in the toaster, searched the kitchen for the utensils and scooped some Nutella onto a spoon.

The loft looked even nicer in daylight. It was the kind of place where you wanted to sit when it was pouring with rain, and you could sip hot chocolate and read a book. There was a pillow and a blanket lying on the brown leather couch where Jack had slept. The door on the other side of the loft remained closed.

Jack had mentioned a few times that he lived with his uncle, but it was like the trauma from the camera lights had erased parts of my memory and I was just getting them back. I slid off the kitchen counter and put the spoon down, conscious of what I was wearing and doing. Jack's uncle didn't seem to be home, or else he surely would have made an appearance by now.

"Hello?" I called out.

There was complete silence until the toaster sprung up, almost giving me a heart attack in the process. I layered the hazelnut spread on so thick, it was sticking to the roof of my mouth. Finally, some comfort in the hellish twenty-four hours I had just endured. God bless Nutella. But my bliss was short lived because the sound of my phone ringing interrupted my nutritious breakfast, and I groaned when I saw the screen. Apparently fourteen calls weren't enough for this woman.

"Steph," I said, not bothering with a hello. "I'm safe. Seriously, you don't have to worry about me."

"Worry about you?" came the shrill reply. "I'm not worried about your safety, Gia. I'm worried about the shitstorm that's hit the papers this morning!"

"What are you talking about?"

"The *New York Times,* that's what I'm talking about!" Steph snapped. "Page two, Gia. Page. Freaking. Two. The headline says: 'Not All That Glitters is Gold.' This is a travesty!"

"It's not front page, so it could be worse, right?"

"I hope you're joking."

"Steph, are you really surprised?" I said irritably. "The fact that cameras were practically being shoved up my nose last night sort of implied it would be a news story this morning. People will read *any* gossip these days. But there's no point losing your mind over it."

If you ask me, I was showing a level of maturity that I wasn't even aware I was capable of. But apparently nobody told Steph that, because she was in full dragon-lady mode.

"Gia, the article describes a whole drug crusade the NYPD have got against a fraternity. People are chalking it up to your PTSD from the kidnapping! They're saying it was only a matter of time until you landed yourself in trouble. Does that sound like something we can just breeze past?"

I almost choked on my toast. "It says *what*?"

"It's *everywhere.* Every gossip magazine, every Facebook article, every tweet. People are starting to bet on when you'll check into rehab. You're lucky some people are trying to be sympathetic, but most are just out for blood. Don't even get me started on the jokes they're making about you dating a police officer. The photos of you outside the bar with cops all around you has been made into over ten different internet memes. And only three of them make sense! I swear this generation is so screwed up."

Oh my lord. I was a meme! This could *not* be happening.

"That's slander!" I cried. "Or, like, defamation! Can't we sue?"

"Who exactly do you want to sue? Because we can't sue the whole world," Steph replied. "No, we need to release a statement."

"Well, isn't anyone going to ask how the paparazzi even knew where I was?"

"It was a Saturday night, and you were out in plain sight at a college bar. They weren't exactly looking for a needle in a haystack. Anyone could have posted a photo online. People are watching you all the time, Gia."

"Which reminds me," I said. "What is *Gia Watch*?"

There was a short pause on the line, and for a second I thought Steph had hung up. I was expecting an "I've never heard of it," but apparently that wasn't the case.

"Right. That . . ." she replied. "It's just a silly website; I'm already working on getting it removed."

"I'm going to pretend I'm not mad that you already know what this is and ask you again," I said steadily. "What actually *is* it?"

Steph let out an impatient sigh, like she was dealing with a troublesome toddler refusing to eat their veggies.

"It's a website where people can post photos of information about where they spot you. It's sort of like a personalized live map of your whereabouts."

"So they're stalking me? What is this, *Gossip Girl*?"

"Kind of. Except it's totally legit."

"How is that legit? That doesn't sound remotely legit!"

"They're not technically breaking any rules. Besides, you're a public figure now. Your personal life doesn't belong to you anymore."

It's not like I wasn't already aware of it, but hearing it coming from someone else stung a little. So it was perfectly acceptable for people to say and do whatever just because I was a celebrity. Apparently everyone seemed to have forgotten I was also a human being.

"Where are you?" Steph asked.

"At a friend's house," I told her.

"Good, stay there. Don't go back to the penthouse, there are photographers still snooping around all over the place."

"So what, now I'm supposed to go into hiding?"

"What you're supposed to do is listen to me while I fix all the damage you've caused."

I let out a small noise that sounded a bit like laughter but was a little more incredulous.

"Are you kidding me?" I exclaimed. "I didn't cause any damage! I literally just went out to have a good time with my friends, and the next thing I knew frat boys were being hauled into police cars, and people were yelling about drugs, and then the paparazzi showed up and practically chased me away from my own home! So correct me if I'm wrong, but that doesn't sound like any of that damage was caused by me!"

"Why in the world would you want to do drugs?" Steph rambled on. "I mean, I can't even imagine the trauma you must have experienced, don't get me wrong. But drugs? The least you could do is make sure your occasional cocaine sesh with your friends is private! And not only do drugs make your brain fried, it makes you super ugly. Is that really something you want to be dealing with for a temporary high?"

"Are you even listening to me?" I replied. "I'm not on drugs! It was just a matter of being at the wrong place at the wrong time."

"Well, now we need to get you into the right place. I'm *this* close to landing you a deal with Ted Baker. Just remember, drug addiction doesn't sell luxury handbags. We need to start on damage control right away! See, this is why you need an assistant! I'm hiring one right now."

"No."

"Text me where you're staying! We need to get started right away. Call your makeup team, we need to shoot a video for your social media pages."

"No!"

"Excuse me?"

"I said no!" I repeated angrily. "I'm not in the mood to be around anyone right now, and I definitely don't want to film some stupid video so I can try to prove to a bunch of people I don't even know that I'm not some wild child."

"Gia, please don't make this difficult for the both of us," Steph replied, practically scolding me. "The sooner we fix this mess, the sooner it all goes away."

"Fix it yourself," I said abruptly, hanging up on her.

I placed the phone down on the counter and stared down at my half-eaten toast. Great. She had gotten me so riled up, I couldn't even enjoy my Nutella anymore. I was so upset, I was actually shaking a little bit. I didn't want to do damage control, and I definitely didn't want to see any pictures or read any articles about last night. I didn't want to care what people were saying and thinking, but unfortunately I did. They didn't even know me. I felt like I was an animal being put on display at the circus.

The phone screen immediately lit up again with Steph's name, and I gave a loud groan and turned the entire phone off. There. No more PR phone calls, no chance of Dad calling to disown me, no magazines asking for a photo op. Never in my life had I been so grateful for complete and utter silence.

Fifteen

I WAS PLACED UNDER TEMPORARY HOUSE ARREST BY Steph's PR team for four days. I didn't understand why I had to go into hiding, especially when all the ridiculous rumors weren't even remotely true. But seeing as I still refused to film a cheesy explanation video to plaster all over the web, I caved and stayed cooped up inside. As long as Krispy Kreme was able to deliver to my doorstep, staying out of the public eye couldn't be all bad. When my mug shot didn't emerge, the buzz died down a little. Of course, everyone was patiently waiting for my next slip-up so they could hammer the final nail into my coffin. But at least the chaos had subsided enough for me to move back into the penthouse.

I spent my time at home chipping away at the pile of schoolwork mounting and refining my part of the psychology presentation, practicing my speech to an uninterested Famous. Not that it was hard, considering my contributing part made up, like, 2 percent of the whole project. I emailed all my professors and told them that I didn't think it was a good idea to show up to class, which they enthusiastically agreed with. I was pretty sure they were more worried about me being the distraction in class rather than me being distracted myself. Even locked away, Steph had me working. When she realized I wasn't answering her calls, she showed up at my doorstep, handed me her phone, and told me *Teen Vogue* was on the line, asking about my winter wardrobe essentials. Seeing as they weren't asking about what my favourite drug was, I gave in, put on a chirpy voice and gushed about my taste in knitwear.

Mom called a few times, promising she'd be home soon, but I didn't hold my breath. At this point, I wasn't even sure where in the world she was or with whom. Aria and Veronica had flown back to LA the following afternoon after the bar debacle, forced to face the wrath of their own parents. Mike messaged and asked if he could have my weed guy's number. Dad outright *threatened* to fly down and then yelled at me about seven different times.

"I leave you alone for a month and you become a drug addict!" he'd shouted into the phone when I finally got around to calling him.

"Dad, I'm not a drug addict! I was at a bar and these guys just happened to get arrested the same night. I have nothing to do with it, I swear!"

"Gia, I will literally drop out of this movie and come down there. Don't push me."

After about fourteen phone calls of more yelling, he finally gave in and decided to believe me. That, or he really couldn't get out of pre-production. Either way, I was off the hook. On thin ice, for sure. But off the hook.

At least Dr. Norton believed that I was just trying to help out Milo's case. But just when I thought I was warming up to our sessions, she told me that I was so involved in pursuing this investigation because it was a good distraction from dealing with the things that weren't going right in my life. Basically she was telling me to get a real hobby.

Sitting at home had gotten so monotonous, I was sure I was slowly slipping into madness. The penthouse was always so quiet and empty and with no one to talk to, my mind would immediately wander to Frank Parker and that terrible night. I couldn't allow myself to think about it, and I couldn't hide away forever, no matter who hated or loved me. So I raided Mom's closet, pulled on her black lace Ellie Saab dress to channel my inner Audrey, slipped on some oversized sunglasses, and headed out. There was no better way to improve my mood than downing a colossal frozen hot chocolate at Serendipity 3. Under all that happy pink and blue lighting, you'd never be able to tell my soul felt shriveled up on the inside.

Milo was officially back to work now, which meant I was back to barely seeing him. Mr. Fells had returned to LA, and I was sad I hadn't gotten to see him since our impromptu dinner. I hadn't seen Milo since the arrests, and there hadn't been too much to say in the phone conversations. At this rate, the NYPD may as well have hired me as an honorary officer. I was probably more invested in this than half of their team. Thankfully, he managed to spare some time before his graveyard shift and join me at the elusive café. It wasn't exactly the romantic date I had been eagerly hoping for, but any chance I got him in the week, no matter how small, I would take.

The special corner table that I had requested for privacy was pretty intimate. But it didn't exactly help that Reggie and Bo, the temporary second bodyguard I had acquired from the agency, were sitting on the table right beside us and scanning the crowd like they were the secret service.

"This seems a little excessive now that I think of it," I said, watching them uncertainly.

Two burly men dressed in all black cramped into a dainty seating area is not only extremely comical, but also kind of defeats the whole purpose of discretion. They had practically broken the wiry staircase going up.

"It doesn't hurt to be a little extra careful," Milo replied. "Pretty much everyone here was gawking at you when we walked in."

"That's only because they let us skip the line when they had to wait for two hours."

"Yeah, that, and your face has been on every website and newspaper in the last week."

"Are you sure you guys don't want anything?" I asked the bodyguards.

"Pass. I'm lactose intolerant," Reggie replied.

"I already reached my chocolate quota for the day," Bo added.

"So," I said, plunging my straw into the giant goblet in front of me. "I read NYU's statement in the news the other day. It was . . . interesting."

Milo nodded and said, "They've got a reputation to maintain, so they're doing everything they can to distance themselves from Stag and the raid. But they're taking it pretty seriously. They've suspended everyone who's been arrested and put the fraternity under probation. Expulsion isn't out of the question."

"So they've shut down the fraternity?"

"Not exactly. The frat is basically on lockdown while they're being reviewed, which means they aren't allowed to hold any events or anything. NYU's even considering shutting them down for good after all the backlash they've received from the public."

That was probably the only silver lining to this whole debacle. When people weren't too busy leaving ignorant comments or pill emojis under my selfies, they were raging about how a group of college boys had somehow managed to start a drug trade under everyone's noses. At least I wasn't the only one in this sinking ship.

"But if you shut the frat down then the Stag problem goes away, right?" I asked.

"I wish," Milo retorted. "Shutting the frat down doesn't really solve any problems if we can't prove they're guilty of being involved in the first place. If they're just minor players in a bigger game, then we've just wasted all of our resources and time on them for a very small outcome. If they're the instigators, then we're just displacing the problem. It goes from the college parties to the streets, and that's a whole bigger mess to deal with."

"Damn."

"What?"

"Nothing, I just like when you go all Officer Fells on me. It's very attractive."

"Are you even paying attention, or are you just checking me

out?"

"A little of both. Are the frat boys telling you much?"

Milo shook his head. "Not really. We didn't find drugs on all of them, so we had to let some of them go."

"What about the notebook you found? That's something, right?"

"Maybe. But the task force doesn't know what exactly, and the boys aren't giving much away. Right now it makes no sense. It's just a whole bunch of numbers and letters."

"The NYPD has to have some theory," I said. "Or are all the cop shows a lie?"

"I'm not supposed to be telling you this stuff."

"You've told me basically everything else already!"

"Yeah, and I'm regretting it."

I made a symbol of a cross over my heart. "Cone of silence, I swear."

Milo's lips curved up, but it didn't quite count as a smile. "They think it's a receipt book. Sort of like a log of all the transactions between the dealers and buyers. The sarge thinks that the letters are written in code. Locations, initials of names. It could be anything."

I frowned. "It's kind of dumb for them to put it in a book. Anyone can get their hands on it then."

"It's probably a lot easier to access if it's sitting on someone's laptop. You'd be surprised at what people can hack into."

He didn't have to tell me twice. I had far too many incriminating group chat screenshots that would not only destroy my life, but those around me too.

"Anyway," he went on. "I don't think the probation will last long. There's far worse that happens in these fraternities and sororities than Stag, I'll tell you that. But I'm not worried right now. The task force is working on the case really hard. They'll crack it eventually."

"They?" I repeated. "Aren't you supposed to be helping them?"

Milo suddenly looked uncomfortable. "Um, yeah," he said, not quite making eye contact. "I'm just taking a break from the investigation for a while. They asked me to take a step back given all the media frenzy."

"But lots of cases get media attention. I don't see why they need you to . . ." I paused, a wave of panic sending ripples through my skin. "Wait, the NYPD doesn't actually think I'm involved, right? I'm not going to, like, have a SWAT team pounding on the penthouse door anytime soon?" Trust me, I can*not* pull off a prison jumpsuit.

"No, of course not!" Milo replied. They're just being . . . cautious."

So the NYPD wasn't concerned with what the media had to say about the students. They were worried about *me.* I guess I couldn't really blame them. It didn't look great to have Milo assisting on the case when a good chunk of the public thought I was involved somehow. Now Milo was paying the price for it all.

I guess he must have noticed the guilt flash across my face because he said, "It's okay! It's not like they've pulled me off for good. It's all temporary. Aidyn's been giving me updates, so I'm still in the loop on everything."

He was doing a good job of sounding optimistic, but I wasn't entirely convinced. He had wanted this case so badly, and now I had managed to find a way to ruin it for him.

"Oh, there you guys are!"

The sound of Jack's voice broke into my train of thought.

Milo glanced over my head and fought back a groan. "Well, this is a surprise," he said quietly, while Jack greeted the bodyguards.

"Did I forget to mention he'd be dropping by?" I asked innocently.

"Yeah," Milo said. "You did."

"Hey guys."

"What up playa?" I said.

We all froze for a second.

"Did you just call me *playa*?" Jack asked.

"Yes, I did," I replied in a strained voice. "Now let's pretend it never happened and move on."

I think my nervy British accent had spent too much time listening to nineties R&B that night at the bar.

"Just so you know, this privacy thing is a fail," Jack told me, taking a seat on the chair in between Milo and me. "It took me like two seconds to find the table, and pretty much everyone is talking about you right now."

"Oh, great," Milo muttered.

"Why are you dressed like an accountant at a runway show?" Jack asked me, eyeing my outfit.

"Firstly, rude," I said. "Secondly, this is couture!"

"So, Jack," Milo cut in. "Long time no see. How are things?"

"Yeah, things are pretty good, man. How about you?"

"Yeah, can't complain."

There was silence as both men stared at me, prompting me to start a meaningful conversation while I tried to find a way to evaporate.

"Milo was just filling me in on the Stag investigation," I said.

"I would say it's confidential, but I think Gia's told half the continent by now," Milo added.

"As long as it's not a bumper sticker on her car, we're good."

"You want something to drink?" I asked Jack, attempting to lighten the mood. "Or a cookie or something?"

"No thanks," he replied. "I still have PTSD after your baking session the other day."

"They weren't *that* bad!"

"Wait," Milo said, holding up a hand. "*You* baked? How did I miss this?"

"Trust me, you didn't miss much," Jack replied.

Milo shook his head, checking his watch. "I have to go. We're getting our assignments for Halloween today. All these scary clown sightings have really got people on edge, and it's still a week away."

"Will I see you later?" I asked him.

"Not tonight. I'm on patrol, so I'll be done at like three in the morning." He leaned down and gave me a quick kiss on my head. "Don't get into any trouble while I'm gone."

And with that, he was gone. Off to fight crime and save the world, as usual.

"I need to ask you something," Jack said hesitantly, as if he was still deciding in his mind.

"If this is about your clothes that I borrowed," I said. "I'm not giving them back. You can have the pants I guess. But the sweatshirt is super comfy. Of course, I wouldn't be caught dead wearing it in public. Well, maybe if I paired it with m—"

"No, Gia. Stop, I don't care about the sweatshirt. You can keep it, whatever. I need you to do me a huge favor," Jack said. "I need you to come to my mom's birthday dinner with me."

I stared at him for a few seconds, not knowing exactly how to respond. It was like someone had walked over and smacked me on the forehead.

"I'm sorry," I began. "I'm a little confused. I thought you hated your parents?"

"I do," Jack said. "I'm surprised I even got an invite, but it's her fiftieth, so she's having some huge soirée and probably needs me there to pretend we're all a happy family. Honestly, it's my dad I really hate. My relationship with my mother sort of just imploded as collateral damage."

"Okay, but I'm still confused. Why would you want to go to her birthday dinner?"

He sighed, running a hand through his hair. "Because Scarlett is making me. She's flying in especially for the party, but she said she won't go if I won't. It's still a few weeks away, so she has plenty of time to force me into this. My parents aren't easy to love, but she's so pure she somehow manages to do it anyway. I feel guilty sometimes. I don't want her to think she can't have a relationship with them just because I don't."

In that moment, two things were happening. First my ovaries were dying, but I'm going to blame it on my natural hormones and move on. Secondly, I was imagining what it was like to feel affectionate toward your younger sibling, rather than fantasizing about squashing them most of the time, like I did with Mike.

"If Scarlett's going to be there, then you won't have to face it alone!" I said. "You don't need me as backup."

"But she's not the problem child, I am! People are going to be fawning over her the whole night while I stand in the corner and drink."

"Sounds like a solid plan to me."

"Please, Gia? I would ask Scott, but he's so busy with law school. It sucks though, he'd be able to piss my father off in no time."

"I don't know, Jack," I frowned. "I want to help you out, but it just seems like a really personal event. I won't be welcome there."

"You'll be more welcome than I will, that's for sure."

I paused, dreading the question I was about to ask.

"What about Lucy? Shouldn't she be going to this party with you?"

"Lucy and I are . . ." He leaned back in his chair. "It's complicated. I think we've sort of broken up."

I take it back. *That* was like someone had smacked me in the forehead.

"You what?" I said.

"I'm fine. Really. It's not like it hasn't happened before, right?"

"How do you *think* you broke up? Don't you know for sure?"

"Well—"

"Because I'm pretty sure I would know if I wasn't in a relationship with someone anymore."

"Okay, yes. Definitive yes, we broke up."

"So you're telling me that you and Lucy broke up."

"Yes, that is what I'm telling you."

"Like . . . finito."

"That's how the Italians would say it, yes."

"And you're *sure* you broke up?"

"Are you okay? Your eye is twitching."

I looked down at my half-empty glass hoping my joy wasn't visible on my face. Am I bad person? Yes. Absolutely. But they had actually broken up! Miss Perfect with her glossy hair and her perfect apartment and perfectly toned calf muscles and that ability to eat healthy things like kale. I don't actually know if she eats kale, but I bet you she does. She just seems like a kale eater. Either way, her kale-eating days with Jack were over!

"I'm very sorry to hear that," I said. "That's, uh, very sad. She was uh . . . yeah. Very sad. I feel sad . . . ness. Sadness."

Jesus, Gia. She wasn't dead. What was I trying to do, craft a eulogy? Jack raised an eyebrow so high, it might have actually jumped off his head.

"Um, cool . . ." he replied. "So does this mean you're in?"

I looked at Reggie and Bo, as if they were my life advisors. They both gave me a *girl you better say yes* look.

"Yeah," I told Jack. "I'm in."

Jack's face lit up with a relieved smile. "Really? Thank you! I owe you big time."

"I'll remember that," I said. "Anything I should know before the big night?"

I looked at him expectantly, hoping that *now* would be the time he'd finally open up a little about his past. But he just sat back in his chair with a shrug.

"It's pretty much the usual. My father is a pathological narcissist and my mother pretends that he's not one."

I took another sip of my frozen hot chocolate. "Sounds like your average Hollywood couple to me."

Sixteen

I WAS SLUMPED ON MY CHAIR, STARING AT MY LAPTOP screen through sleepy eyes. The only motivation I had to stay focused on schoolwork was the fact that everyone in the open study area of the New York Public Library was gawking at me. In hindsight, choosing to study in one of the most frequented landmarks in the city wasn't a great idea. But that *How to Be a Real New Yorker* article on WikiHow said studying at the library was a must. Who was I to argue with the experts? Besides, sitting cooped up in the house like I was a prisoner wasn't doing me any good. I couldn't stop living because I was afraid someone would hound me for a photo. If only we hadn't turned down the E! network's offer to have our own Winters family reality show. These past two weeks would have been a gold mine.

Seeing as I was avoiding showing up to class every chance I got, I figured I should help my karmic luck and actually do some studying. But after catching up on just a week's worth of content, my brain was already drained of energy. That, and I was still losing sleep over my nightmares.

My eyes flicked up from the computer screen and were

immediately met with the gaze of at least twenty people sitting across my long and secluded table watching me in awe. It was like they had been frozen in time. I turned to face Reggie and Bo, who were standing behind me on either side, looking all mean and tough. They were perhaps the only reason no one had dared approach me and ask for a selfie or an autograph yet. No one had even dared to squeak out a hello.

The entire point of venturing out to do homework was to keep away from distractions back in the penthouse. I was clearly setting myself up for a loss. Not only did I now have dozens of eyes fixated on me, my mind couldn't focus. It was still stuck on one thing: Jack and his family secret. His mother's dinner party was only weeks away, and I was still completely in the dark. Random Google searches had turned up completely empty, but then again, "Jack Anderson father who is kind of a jerk" was probably a little vague for the search engine.

Well if Jack wasn't going to give me answers, only one other person would. And luckily, finding Scarlett Anderson online was far easier than I had imagined it would be. One glance at her Instagram page, and I immediately knew she was Jack's sister. They shared the same brilliant blonde hair and striking blue eyes that were hard to miss. Scarlett's page was simple and modest. Her bio read: *Scarlett Anderson. 21. New Yorker playing dress up in California.*

No peach emojis as captions, no blurry photos of her and her friends from drunken nights out. It was all sweet smiles and the occasional "I miss NYC" post. She was all class. She was also my last hope.

I clicked the direct message icon and said a silent prayer while I typed a message to Scarlett. I kept it honest and straight to the point. How could I help Jack survive dinner with his parents if I didn't know what I was walking into? I added my email address and a few lines of "thank you so much, I know this is really weird and I'm not a creep, I swear," and clicked send with a knot in my stomach. Maybe she wouldn't reply. Maybe she'd think it was a joke. Maybe she'd tell Jack, and he would hate me for going behind his back. Maybe she wouldn't even read it. I was really going out on a limb here.

"You've got a visitor," Reggie said, bending down so I could hear him.

I looked up to see Jamie strolling toward me, making his way past the rows of people, staring at him with a mixture of admiration and disbelief. It was like he was the sole brave soldier, on his way into battle.

"Gia," he said quietly, as if it were a greeting. "Reggie. New bodyguard. Nice to see you all."

"What are you doing here?"

"I came to say hi."

"How did you even know I was here?"

"*Gia Watch.*"

Jamie slid into the chair opposite me. I think I actually heard someone gasp from another table.

My jaw clenched. "You're kidding, right?"

"Uh, no?"

"Excuse me for a second," I said, holding up a finger while I pulled out my phone.

I didn't bother with her assistant and dialed Steph's number straight. She picked up on the second ring.

"Hello?"

"I thought you said you dealt with *Gia Watch*!" I hissed as quietly as I could.

"I did deal with it! We shut it down last week!"

"Well apparently you failed big time, because it's still up and running. Get it taken care of. NOW!"

I hung up before she could launch into a bunch of wild marketing schemes and placed the phone down beside me. I narrowed my eyes at Jamie.

"What?" I asked, almost giving up on keeping my volume levels low.

"Nothing." He snickered.

I fought back an eye roll. "So what are you really doing here, anyway?"

Jamie pulled a piece of paper folded in half out of his notebook and slid it across the table toward me like we were in some shady business meeting.

"What's this?"

"It's an invitation I got to a frat party."

"And you want me to congratulate you on having a social life?"

"Just read it."

I unfolded the paper. There were Greek symbols printed at the top of the page, with a cartoon police badge on one side, and an animated prisoner in a pinstriped jumpsuit on the right. The invite read:

BACK BY POPULAR DEMAND!
They came, they tried, they failed!
In honor of our ban being lifted, we're
inviting you to celebrate our victory with us.
Theme: Cops vs. Robbers
Date: November 18th
Time: Party o'clock
THE PDA BOYS ARE BACK IN
BUSINESS.

I leaned in closer across the table so Jamie could hear my whispering.

"What the hell?" I said. "I thought they were on probation? NYU was even thinking about shutting them down!"

"They're still on probation," Jamie replied. "The frat is still suspended, but that only lasts for a month. And as for shutting them down, we all knew that was never really going to happen."

"Isn't a cops and robbers party a little distasteful given their . . . situation?"

"Tact isn't exactly what these boys are known for. Either way, I think we need to tell the cops."

"Uh, why?"

"What do you mean 'why?' This invite was slid under my door last night! Isn't that a little strange to you?"

I blinked at him. "Should it be?"

"It's not every day you just get an exclusive invitation to a frat party delivered to your door," Jamie said in a stage whisper. "Especially if you don't even know them!"

"So maybe it wasn't for you?" I shrugged. "Maybe it was for Craig."

Jamie flipped over the invite to reveal his name scrawled at the bottom of the page in blue pen.

"I think there's a reason they invited me, and I think that reason is that bull symbol. Maybe they saw me at Andrew's and remembered me or something. Isn't your boyfriend on this case? Shouldn't you tell him?"

"And say what? It's just a flyer for a party!"

"Before you started asking around about that button, I'd never had any interaction with the PDA. And now they're personally inviting me to their party! They only let you in if you're tight with some of the boys or if they want something from you. And since I don't know any of the brothers, I'm guessing it's the latter."

I looked down at the invite. The party was the day after Jack's mother's birthday. By then, the NYPD could have completely solved the mystery. And the last time I was even *close* to the frat boys, my face had ended up on every newspaper and Milo had gotten temporarily thrown off the investigation. So, yeah, involving the NYPD was the last thing I wanted to do at the moment. The PDA boys were smarter than they seemed, and this party was a good way to prove they were up to something. I was pretty sure Steph had already roped me into an event for *Variety* that same night, but I could always just stop by later on.

"Okay, fine," I said begrudgingly. "But I don't think we should involve the cops right now. We don't know anything yet and telling them could ruin everything."

"*We,*" Jamie repeated. "So does this mean you're coming?"

"I don't know if we're even going to find anything. But yeah, I'm coming."

"Good," Jamie said with an approving nod. He flicked his eyes to my laptop. "Are you studying for psych?"

"Well, I *was,* before you came over and distracted me."

Jamie pulled out his own laptop and opened the lid with a small smile. "I'll study with you."

Wow. A month ago he would gladly have thrown me off the Brooklyn Bridge without someone even asking him to, and now here he was, voluntarily sharing air with me.

Guess they all come around when they want something from you.

Seventeen

My first Halloween away from home had come and gone with little activity. While Milo was off defending the streets from bad guys and drunk teenagers in search of adventure, I sat on the sofa all night trying not to drop butter chicken on any of the white cushions.

Halloween back in LA had always been a grand affair. Mike and I would fill the mansion with jack-o'-lanterns and hang skeletons from every tree branch. Of course we never really got trick-or-treaters; security wouldn't let them past the gate. But sometimes if they were really lucky, Dad would make a quick appearance outside, pose for a few photos with little kids with face paint on and their excited mothers, then disappear back inside the house. But this year, everything was different. There were no over-the-top decorations, no wild high school parties with my best friends, no candy that would last until Easter. It was just me, Famous, and the sofa.

I guess it wasn't all bad. I had a decent supply of chocolate in the penthouse, and watching *Hocus Pocus* while Famous slept on my lap was actually pretty fun. Staying home also meant staying out of trouble. The last thing my "party girl" image needed was another paparazzi ambush at a Halloween bash. I think I had officially reached my quota of scandals for the year.

School was still proving to be a struggle, and I had spent the whole of mid-term break forcing myself to study. I was in a vicious cycle of my own creation, missing classes just to catch up on previous classes I had missed. My grades were still hovering around average, but there was so much to learn that it seemed almost impossible to fit it all into my brain.

Surprisingly, the only class I *wasn't* completely struggling with was psychology. I hadn't quite wrapped my head around the endless list of theories and fancy words, and missing class wasn't helping much with that. But it was the only subject I was actually interested in learning about, and even the idea of our group presentation at the end of the semester was starting to become a little less terrifying. Of course, I couldn't actually share this minor sense of relief with my group members. If I was lucky, I'd get a small nod of acknowledgment from Jamie in class or a reluctant smile from Michelle as she hurried past me on the stairs. Hannah probably had a voodoo doll of me stashed somewhere in her heinous bag collection. Either way, it was clear that I hadn't won them over with my winning charm just yet.

With my time spent focusing on school, and Milo busy at work per usual, we didn't get around to seeing each other much. Every time I did see him, it felt like an alarm clock was ticking above out heads, waiting to remind me how little time I actually had before he'd be pulled away for work again. But after lots of rearranging of schedules, we finally found a night that was free for both of us when Milo had texted and said he had some exciting news to share with me. I figured he had finally been allowed back on the task force or, better yet, cracked the Stag investigation. Milo was finally going to get the recognition he so deserved.

When the concierge told me Milo was on his way up, I was practically bursting with anticipation. I all but pounced on him when he walked through the door, running toward him with childish excitement. It hadn't even been that long, but with Milo, I never knew when I'd see him next.

"You're a little riled up today!" Milo laughed when I finally released him from a comically exaggerated hug.

"Is that a gun in your pants, or are you just happy to see me?"

"Seriously?"

"What? I always wanted to use that line."

Milo shook his head, amused. "What's this?"

He motioned toward the dining table that was perfectly set, complete with a lit candle stand in the center.

"Well," I replied. "I thought we may as well do date night properly."

Milo looked hesitant. "You didn't cook, did you?"

"Relax. Val did all the cooking. But I watched her with my own two eyes. I'm obviously exhausted."

"Oh, you really shouldn't have," he said, feigning a touched look. "Should I thank the chef personally?"

"She's off duty, actually. Just you and me tonight."

Milo pulled off his leather jacket and draped it over the arm of the sofa. "I'm so sorry about the last few weeks. I can't seem to get a day off."

"It's okay!" I said, hoping it sounded more convincing than it felt. "Don't worry about it."

"Halloween was terrible. Some guy threw up on me twice. But Aidyn had it even worse. Everyone thought she was just in an NYPD costume and almost every creep out there tried to feel her up. It was disgusting."

"Ugh, gross."

He glanced at the giant *Congratulations!* balloon floating beside the dining table in the distance. Famous was bouncing around the string, staring up at it with wonderment and excitement.

"So what's the balloon for?" he asked.

"It's for you!" I told him cheerfully. "Famous! Stop trying to eat the balloon!"

"For me?"

"It's in case you got promoted or something!"

"Promoted? Why would I get promoted?"

"Well, you said you had some good news," I explained. "So I

figured it had something to do with work."

"Gia, you're adorable. But at this rate, they aren't going to care even if I save the president from a burning building."

"Oh," I said, not bothering to mask my disappointment. "So what's the news then?"

"Two things!" Milo said, looking excited. "I'm a long way away from a promotion, but I'm officially back on the task force!"

"Seriously? I knew it! That's so amazing!"

Relief washed over me. It looks like I hadn't screwed up his whole career after all.

"Plus," Milo continued, "one of the guys we arrested finally caved and told us that the black book was a list of customers. So that's a huge breakthrough for us!"

"Milo, that's incredible!" I exclaimed. "You've basically solved the case."

"It's good," he told me, "but not good enough for the task force. This is a bigger operation than we first thought, but they're not saying who else is involved. We can't really arrest the rest of the frat boys without any proof of their involvement. We searched the frat house and came up clean. But if they continue to cooperate and give us proper names of customers, not just the initials, then we can try and make our way through them to get some more information. But right now, our focus is on getting the dealers."

Note to self: never become a cop. I lose my patience riding the elevator to the penthouse every day. There was no way I could handle actual police work.

"Wait," I said. "So what's the second piece of exciting news?"

Milo broke out into a wide smile. "You know my brother Chris? Well, he's coming to the city soon and he really wants to meet you!"

"Oh my gosh, that sounds awesome!" I replied. "I can't *wait* to finally meet him."

I always enjoyed when Milo talked about his older brother. All this time had passed and I still hadn't even met the guy. At least Milo had given me some warning before springing another family introduction on me. Now I knew to wear appropriate pants.

"No, wait, that's not all," Milo went on. "He's proposing to his girlfriend while they're visiting, because she loves New York. And he wants us to be there when it happens!"

"That's *so* romantic! But what if she says no?"

"She won't say no," Milo assured me. "They're obsessed with each other. I'm surprised it took him this long to actually put a ring on it. But he said he needs your help planning the proposal. I told him you're an expert on all this Hollywood-style romance stuff."

He was right. If there was anything I was good at, it was this. All my years of watching romantic comedies were finally paying off. "This is the best news I've heard all week!" I exclaimed. "When is he proposing?"

"He's planned it for the night of the seventeenth," Milo replied. "I think it's the anniversary of their first date or something corny like that."

"That's only a couple of weeks away!"

"I know, it's crazy. Plus, this means you get to be my date to the wedding!"

I was practically jumping up and down now. "Oh, this is so exciting! I love weddin—" I suddenly let out a gasp, clapping a hand over my mouth in realization.

"What?" Milo asked.

"I can't do that night."

"Why not?"

"I, um, have a really important dinner."

Milo waved a hand dismissively and said, "Just tell Steph you can't be her show pony that night. Reschedule dinner with Karl Lagerfeld or whatever."

"Okay, first of all, you can't just reschedule dinner with Karl Lagerfeld. Like, that doesn't just happen," I explained, slightly appalled at his suggestion. "And it's not for Steph."

"So what then?"

I glanced at the floor. "It's for . . . Jack."

Milo blinked at me. "Jack," he said in a strangled voice.

"Yeah. He invited me to his mother's birthday dinner, and I

promised him I'd go."

Milo paused, thoughts clearly running through his mind. "I thought he hated his parents."

"He does," I said. "Which is exactly why I need to be there to support him."

"You need to be there," Milo repeated, clearly struggling to cope. "Why?"

"It's a long story. Super boring. You don't want to know the details. Any chance your brother wants to propose the day after?"

"You're kidding, right?" Milo said, half-laughing. "You want my brother to reschedule his proposal?"

Yes.

"No."

Milo put his head in his hands like he couldn't believe this was actually his life.

"I don't understand," he said. "You're choosing Jack's party over my brother's proposal?"

"Don't say it like that! I'm not choosing it *over* anything. He asked me first."

"You do know how important this is, right?" Milo said.

"Yes," I replied, growing impatient. "But this is really important to Jack as well."

"Gia, he doesn't even like his parents! Why do you need to go? *I* probably know more about his life than you do."

"I know plenty about his life, actually. And you can run all the background checks you want on him, as I'm sure you have already. But I don't care. He's my friend and he asked me to be there for him, so I'm going to be there. Sorry."

"Fine."

"Fine."

There was a tense silence in the air for at least a minute as we both contemplated our next move: Pretend like we both weren't a little pissed and move onto dinner, or launch into a huge argument. Yep. Launch into an argument.

"I can't believe this!" Milo practically exploded. "Literally the *same* night."

"It's not my fault!" I insisted. "I didn't ask his mother to turn fifty the same time your brother wanted to get engaged!"

"This is so typical! Of course Jack would find a way to ruin it."

The conversation basically continued in that vein as we yelled at each other from across the sofas and stomped around a little like children. It was like reliving every one of my parents' arguments, only this time I couldn't shut the room door and put on a Hilary Duff movie to escape. At one stage, we even started yelling about things that had nothing to do with anything. I swear I remember saying something about Tom Ford's new lipstick collection, but to be honest, all the words started to mesh together after twenty minutes of arguing.

"I don't love working fourteen-hour days!" Milo exclaimed. "I have no social life and no time for myself. But it's my job, and I was hoping you'd respect that."

"I do respect that! Why do you think I'm constantly trying to help you out? I don't even see why this is such a huge deal. You cancel plans all the time! I deserve a free pass."

"I never cancel on anything important."

"Oh yeah? What about that Marc Jacobs Fashion Week After-party?"

"I had work!"

"So you say . . ."

"I did! Besides, I just can't do the whole fake smiling on the red carpet, wear a rented tux, and hope you don't spill anything on it charade."

His words stung a little more than I thought they would. "It's not a charade. It's my life!"

"You're so lucky that you don't have to worry about things like paying bills and making rent! Not all of us get offered fifty grand to promote detox tea on Instagram!"

My jaw dropped open. "First, it was sixty grand," I told him. "At least get your statistics right before you attempt a burn. Second, is that what you think I do all day? Sit around and post photos of meal replacement drinks?"

Milo let out an exasperated groan. "No, I'm not saying that!"

But he totally was saying that. I was so deeply offended that he thought so little of me. I mean, come on. After all of this time he should know how I get when I skip a meal. The very idea of promoting that was a direct insult to my entire existence.

"Maybe I just want a boyfriend I can actually see without an appointment. I feel like I'm invisible sometimes!"

"Oh, you are the furthest thing from invisible, trust me."

I narrowed my eyes to slits. "What is that supposed to mean?"

"We can't go anywhere without it being a news headline!" he said. "I want to be able to walk down the street and hold your hand and not read about it in ten different newspapers the next day. I want to buy you a pretzel and kiss you in Central Park without a pack of paparazzi capturing every moment."

Well, jeez. He never *once* even offered to buy me a goddamn pretzel.

"So what, that's my fault?"

"No, but it's not mine either. I didn't choose this life."

Somewhere between us, Famous started barking curiously.

"Really?" I went on. "Because you sort of did choose it when you chose to date me. I told you from the start that it wouldn't be easy, and you were up for it. But I can see you're obviously regretting that!"

I sank onto the sofa, crossing my arms protectively across my chest. This boy had some nerve coming over after I had watched Val cook for almost two hours. All of that effort was completely wasted.

"Gia," Milo sighed, his voice softening. "I don't regret it. But you and I come from very different worlds, and sometimes it can be a little overwhelming."

I looked up at him. "Has Aidyn met your dad?"

A look of irritation flashed across Milo's face. "How is that relevant?"

"Would you just answer the question, please?"

"Yes," he replied abruptly. "She has. Again, how is this important?"

"It's important to me!" I told him. "The only reason I met your dad was because he walked in on us making out, and you couldn't hide me in the closet the whole night!"

"That's ridiculous, Gia. Of course I was going to introduce

you to my dad. I literally just asked you to meet my brother!"

"Your dad was in the city for *days*, and you didn't even mention him. Why were you so scared to introduce me? Let's not even pretend like you weren't. What, are you ashamed of me or something? Do I embarrass you?"

"Of course not!" Milo replied, sinking into the sofa opposite me.

"Well, then why?"

"You won't get it."

"Try me."

"Because," Milo said. "You're Harry Winters's daughter. You spent your whole life living in a mansion in LA. I'm not the guy who dates you, I'm the guy you hire to guard your front gate. I just felt like my family was so ordinary in comparison. I was going to introduce you, I promise. But it wasn't *you* I was embarrassed by."

I was surprised enough to let my anger soften. That hadn't been the reply I was expecting.

"Is that what you think of me?" I asked him. "That I'm a spoiled brat who was going to complain about your dad's pasta not being *al dente* enough? Because honestly, we've been dating for a while now, and I would hate to think that was your opinion of me."

"No, it's not at all what I think about you," Milo said with frustration. "I told you, you wouldn't get it."

He was right; I didn't get it. I did, but I didn't. Never before had I felt completely resentful for having money and the title of fame hanging above my head. It used to feel so great, like I was untouchable or invincible. But more and more, it felt like some kind of toxic chemical, poisoning every stream of my life.

"I bet having a girlfriend like Aidyn seems a lot easier right about now."

Milo leaned forward, looking directly into my eyes. "I *promise* you, nothing is going on between us two."

Truth be told, I didn't even think there was. I didn't for one second believe that he was off at work making out with her in the file room or going on secret dates while they arrested robbers. I trusted him, but it was stupid insecurity just rising to the surface, and I couldn't push it back down. I was jealous because she got to spend all day with my boyfriend, and she didn't even realize how lucky she was. Or maybe she did, who knows. And I was hurt because even though he'd never admit it, he did miss Aidyn. Maybe not her specifically, but their relationship. He was right. Sometimes ordinary was a lot less hassle.

"And since we're on the topic," Milo said. "I want to know what's going on with Jack."

His comment caught me so off guard, it took me a while to respond. "I . . . We're not talking about Jack."

"We're *always* talking about Jack," Milo said with an eye roll. "It's like I'm the third wheel in my own relationship! Are you really going to pretend you don't know what I'm talking about?"

My cheeks flushed, and I raised my head up high, hoping it displayed confidence I wasn't feeling.

"You've got it all wrong," I told him.

"There's just something hanging in the air every time you guys are around each other," Milo went on. "I try to ignore it, but it always feels like you guys have some huge secret that only you two are in on and I'm not allowed to know! That's not just friendship, Gia. Can you honestly look me in the eye and tell me that's not true?"

I opened my mouth to try and defend myself, then closed it again. What could I say? I guess we had just never talked about it so openly before, and now that it was out there, I wondered how we ever managed to ignore it in the first place. Jack was an extremely complicated person in my life, and I wasn't sure if that was his fault or mine. Being with Milo was like cooling rain on a scorching summer day. Comforting and appeasing. But every time I was with Jack it felt like the room was on fire. It was heated and exciting, and you could practically see sparks flying around us. I had been trying to pretend that this was never going to affect my relationship with Milo. But of course it would, and it had been, even if I hadn't quite noticed. I had convinced myself that my feelings for Jack had disappeared. But maybe it had just been pushed under the rug. I spent half my life lying to myself. I'll wake up early and finish that assignment. I totally don't need therapy. I'm definitely going to start working out. Flamin' Hot Cheetos are actually very nutritious. All lies.

The biggest lie I kept telling myself was that Milo and I were meant to be. That all the other stuff just didn't matter. I kept pretending that the clock on our relationship had started ticking when I had arrived in New York, but it hadn't. Jack and I may have had history, but Milo was there for it all. I had an embarrassingly huge crush on him the moment I went all British on him in the police station the first day I saw him, and it had only grown from there. Our relationship began that night he kissed me at the frat party. It had solidified itself when he kissed me again after helping to save me from Frank. We weren't in the honeymoon phase anymore. He was my first serious boyfriend, which meant I needed to be serious about him. I was hurt by the words we had flung at each other. I was ashamed that most of them had been true. If we wanted to, we could brush past it. But we had been trying to fit a circle into a square for a long time, and it just didn't seem worth the pretending anymore.

I hugged my legs to my chest, as if they could shield me from what was coming. "I think we should break up," I said. My voice sounded wobbly, like it would give way at any time.

There was silence for a few seconds. "What?"

"I said I think we should—"

"Gia," Milo said sharply, and I finally looked at him. "This is just some stupid fight! We don't have to break up!"

"It's not just a stupid fight," I replied. "This is the first time we've really been honest about how we feel, and I think that's important. Don't you?"

Milo practically slid off the sofa and knelt on the floor beside where I was sitting.

"This is a huge overreaction," he told me. "This is like that time you almost kicked me out because I said *Sleepless in Seattle* was actually kind of stalkerish."

"I'll admit that wasn't one of my finer moments," I said. "But I don't want to be in a relationship with someone if we feel like we need to cut people out of our lives just to make each other happy."

"I would never ask you to cut Jack out!"

"But it would be a lot less complicated if he weren't around. And it's not even about that. I know you're busy, and maybe I haven't been that understanding. But I never see you anymore, and every time we do see each other, we fight!"

"So we'll fight less!" Milo said simply, as if he had just cured world hunger in one sentence.

I gave my head a defeated shake. "It doesn't work like that."

"I know you're upset," Milo reasoned. "But all of this stuff is *so* not important! We can work this out, I promise."

"I think this is what's best for us. For me. Maybe I'm being selfish but . . . I don't know. I think this is the right thing to do."

Milo didn't seem convinced. "But what if we love each other?"

"Do we?"

"Don't we?"

"Is that how you really feel? Be honest."

For a second, he looked lost for words. Like he wasn't quite sure what the correct answer was.

"I don't know," he admitted. "But I care about you."

"I care about you too. Like, a lot. But I don't think that's enough right now." I pulled him close in a tight hug before he could say anything else. "If you try and convince me then I'll change my mind. And I don't think I can right now."

Milo held me in obedient silence, giving me a tight squeeze as I fought back tears. It almost made me angrier that he was still so perfect at a time like this. Seriously, what was wrong with me? Was my brain self-combusting?

"I should go," he finally said, slowly pulling away. He rose to his feet, but I stayed curled on the sofa. "I hope you change your mind."

So did I, but somehow I felt that wasn't likely. A switch inside me had just flipped. Maybe I was being crazy, or maybe, for the first time, I was being sensible. The jury was still out on that one. Milo grabbed his jacket and, in three long strides, left the penthouse. He didn't even pet Famous on the way out. It was eerily quiet for a few long seconds; the only thing you could hear was my sniffling. Then a loud popping noise came from behind me, and I had to actually clutch my heart to stop it from escaping out of my rib cage. I turned to see Famous standing next to what was the congratulations balloon, barking at its rubbery ruins in surprise, as if he hadn't just caused it to burst himself.

I get it. It's all a big metaphor, and I'm a genius for working it out. Dr. Norton would be so proud. I flopped onto the sofa and pulled a pillow to my face, letting it crush the tears streaming down my cheeks.

I was in a city full of eight million people, yet I was still completely alone.

Eighteen

I WENT INTO FULL HERMIT MODE RIGHT AFTER THE breakup. It was like my body physically needed time to adjust to the changes. It wasn't just a breakup for me, it was an entire process of grieving. I stayed in bed for almost the whole of the next day. I canceled a photo shoot with *Cleo* magazine and numbly listened to Steph yell at me for it. I didn't show up to therapy with Dr. Norton. I barely slept at night. I skipped class again. I watched *Roman Holiday* and cried when Princess Ann had to leave Joe Bradley. None of these new cheesy rom-coms were doing the job, so I needed to go full old-school romance. I listened to John Mayer on repeat. I made Val buy so much chocolate, I may have actually given myself diabetes. Oh well, it would be one on the list of many other problems I had.

Those first few days followed the same routine. Lying in bed, showering late in the after, and watching *When Harry Met Sally* on repeat. It took five days before I finally hauled myself out of my cocoon of misery and had a long pep talk with myself. This was ridiculous. I was being completely unreasonable. I was living life before I met Milo, right? I would surely survive after him. It had been a difficult choice to break up, but I knew it was the right one. I had gone from dating Brendan to immediately falling for Milo with no time in between to just be by myself. Not to mention the whole raging-feelings-for-Jack debacle in between. Maybe I needed this time to just be alone and happy.

By this stage, Jack had gotten fairly suspicious that I had been ignoring him at every turn and hadn't left the house in almost a week. Apparently Reggie had told him I was having some kind of existential crisis, or I was just back to sneaking off without him. But that was unlikely considering there weren't any new photos of me crossing the street or eating a hot dog or whatever. He had messaged me with a few *hello, u alive* texts that went unanswered, but I ultimately had to tell him when he announced he was coming over. I was in zero position to see anyone, least of all Jack.

Milo and I broke up.

The three dots that indicated he was typing appeared and disappeared at least four times before his reply finally came through.

Are you okay?

I stared at his message for a while. How exactly was I supposed to respond to that? Of course I wasn't okay! I literally found a gummy bear in my bra two days ago! I was beyond not okay.

Yeah, I just need some time. xx

Jack didn't send me any other messages. He did call a couple of times, but I didn't pick up. I think he got the hint because he sort of backed off after that.

Even though I had finally managed to be an upright human being again, Milo hadn't completely left my mind. I hadn't changed my phone wallpaper. I hadn't deleted any photos. I hadn't removed his number off my phone. It was like nothing had changed, but the world still felt lopsided. Had he told Aidyn? Was she going to make her move? Just thinking about it made me lose the air in my lungs. I thought about replying to his message at least a hundred times in the week that followed the breakup, but I never got around to pressing send. The worst part was, I wasn't even sure what I was really upset about. Was I really even mourning the relationship anymore? Deep down,

I knew there was a good reason for why I had done it. I was maybe even the slightest bit relieved, which only made me feel more guilty.

I inevitably didn't show up to my next few sessions scheduled with Dr. Norton, although that was perhaps the time I needed her the most. But what exactly was she going to tell me that I didn't already know? The person I really wanted to speak to was my mother, but when I had called her voice had been completely warped as she yelled that the reception was terrible. There was no chance in hell I was going to Dad for love advice.

In the meantime, the city was preparing for the holiday season, even with over a month to go, and the chill in the air only added to the excitement. Of course, I'd be home in LA for both Thanksgiving and Christmas, but New York had its own charm this time of year. The questions about Milo were still whirling around at the back of my mind, but he was no longer all I thought about. I started feeling like myself again, which was such a relief.

I was reluctantly settling into my seat at the back of the lecture room on Friday morning when my phone flashed with a message from Jack. It read: *Hope you aren't leaving me hanging tonight.*

Jack's mother's birthday. I had been so busy tending to my broken heart that I had completely forgotten about the dinner. Jack would surely understand if I didn't show up, right? He didn't even want to go himself! I had almost made my peace with being a terrible friend when I noticed an unopened message from Scarlett sitting in my inbox, almost a week old. I clicked on Scarlett's email with my heart beating fast against my chest.

Hey Gia,

Thank you so much for messaging! I cannot wait to meet you in person once I'm back in New York. I've heard so much from Jack, it feels like I've known you forever.

I know my brother can be a little secretive about our family. Ironically, he shares that trait with my parents. But you're right. If you're going to be at my mother's dinner, you deserve to know the whole story.

The truth is, my father is not a particularly affectionate man. Growing up, Daddy was always tough on Jack. I don't know why, but he never treated me quite as harshly. But no matter what my brother did, he was always a disappointment. Jack is probably one of the smartest people I know, but he was never interested in the whole Ivy League thing. Not that he had a choice in the matter. His life plan was set out for him. Be a good son, get into a good college, date a business partner or family friend's beautiful and rich daughter, get married, take over the family business.

I guess he decided it was all too much one day, and he left. Jack always used to tell me that one day he'd just pack a bag and leave, but I never really thought he'd do it. At first, staying with my Uncle Tom was supposed to be a temporary arrangement. Daddy yelled a lot but said that he'd be back begging for forgiveness in a couple of days. But when it had finally been weeks and he refused to come back, I just knew he was never coming home.

They made a deal. As far as my father was concerned, Jack wasn't his son anymore. If he ever needed a parental signature, he'd sign it, and Jack would be present for any major events that would involve publicity. Not that there were many; my parents are very private people. But the rest was up to Uncle Tom. He's the one who put Jack in his new high school, and it was his buddy who worked at the agency who helped Jack get a job. I always wondered if my mother was as heartbroken as I was over the matter. But she kept so quiet about the whole thing, sometimes I think she never even noticed he left.

Seeing my parents after such a long time is going to be hard for Jack, but I am so grateful you're going to be there for him. I hope this answers some of your questions.

You're a good friend, Gia. My brother is lucky to have you in his life.

Best,
Scarlett xx

And just like that, I now had the answers I was so desperately searching for. I had always thought of Jack as some man of mystery. An enigma. But he wasn't some huge question mark, he was just a boy from a broken home. And tonight he needed me to be there for him.

I crafted a text back to Jack.

I'll be there. xx

Sure, I had made the promise, but for some reason, I hadn't planned any part of the evening. I mean, I had been a little busy tending to my broken heart, after all. With less than six hours to piece something together, I called every contact I had in the fashion industry and somehow managed to get my hands on an incredible Paolo Sebastian gown that almost made my heart stop when I laid eyes on it. Its dusty blue silk flowed almost like flower petals around my legs, and the pale, golden embroidery on the top made me feel like a princess. It was the first time in a long time that I actually felt a surge of pure happiness rush through me. Unfortunately, that was knocked out of my system pretty quickly when Tony arrived with his hair and makeup team.

"Darling, you look like shit. No offense," he had said, eyeing me with disgust. I was definitely going to be taking some offense, Tony.

When the time finally came for the dinner party, I was actually feeling calm. It was like the emotional roller coaster of the past few weeks was beginning to slow down and stabilize, and I almost felt excited. I looked beautiful, I felt beautiful, and it was a beautiful night in New York City. Worse things could happen, that's for sure. I carried this attitude with me when I walked through the gold-plated doors of a Gramercy Park building, where I almost immediately laid eyes on Jack, pacing impatiently by the golden elevator doors.

He didn't spot me right away, but he must have heard the sound of my heels against the marble floor because he eventually turned and cast his eyes on me walking toward him. For a second, he just stared.

"Hi," I said.

"Hi."

"I made it."

"Yeah, you made it."

We both blinked at each other for a few minutes. For some reason, it felt weird being around Jack. It was a feeling I couldn't quite describe. Something just felt different.

"You look stunning, Gia," he said, motioning toward my gown. "You look like . . . well, you look like a princess."

I was about to crack a joke, but for some reason decided against it.

"Thank you," I replied simply, eyeing his perfectly fitted tuxedo. "You too, Jack. Minus the princess part, obviously."

"Thanks."

What were we doing? It was like we were awkwardly standing by the punch table in the school gym, waiting for one of us to ask if the other wanted to dance. This wasn't us! We thrived off insults, sarcasm, and banter. This was too normal. Too rehearsed.

"How are you feeling?"

"Suicidal."

"Jack."

He gave a strangled laugh and said, "Look, I'm here to support Scarlett, so that's what I'm going to do. Nothing more, nothing less."

"You survived fifteen years with your parents."

"Barely."

"You can handle one more night. I believe in you."

"Thanks," he said. "I think I'm going to need that faith."

Jack extended his arm out a little, pushing the elevator button with his other hand. It opened immediately, revealing a well-dressed man.

"Shall we?" Jack asked.

I weaved my arm through his elbow in reply and let him lead me into the elevator. The man seemed to know exactly where we were headed, because he pushed a button without even asking, giving us polite smiles. Boy, would I hate to have *that* job. Although, apparently pushing buttons is a talent of mine, so who knows? I might need to look into that.

"Hey, I'm sorry about you and Milo," Jack said after a few moments of silence.

The elevator man stood completely still, staring at the doors as he pretended he was invisible.

"Yeah," I scoffed. "Right."

"No, I'm serious. I know I gave him a hard time, but he's an okay guy. And he made you happy so . . ."

Wow. He chose *after* the breakup to warm up to Milo? Typical.

"Um, thanks."

More heavy silence followed, as the elevator continued smoothly upwards. I shifted from one foot to another uncomfortably.

"So," I said as casually as possible. "How are things with you and Lucy?"

"Good, I guess."

"Oh?"

"I mean we're not back together or anything. But we're . . ." Jack trailed off. "I don't know, it's complicated."

"Oh."

So they weren't back together, but they were clearly *something*. It wasn't quite the answer I was looking for, but I didn't exactly have the right to be affected by his relationship status in any way, no matter how messed up it was. After the long and tense ride up, I was relieved when the elevator doors let out a small "ding" and parted, revealing a set of huge mahogany doors ahead and a slender woman dressed in a Ralph Lauren gown standing there with a clipboard in her hand. There was a sharply dressed doorman standing a little behind her.

"Here we are!" Elevator Man said with rehearsed enthusiasm.

Jack and I thanked him and stepped out, walking toward the woman apprehensively. I was suddenly nervous, but my emotions were nothing compared to Jack's. His whole body went rigid beside me, and his jaw was clenched so tight, I was scared he was going to snap it.

"Good evening," the woman with the clipboard said, flashing a million-dollar smile. "Name please?"

"Jack. Um . . . Jack Anderson."

The woman looked up from her clipboard and blinked

at us with surprise. It was a name she clearly recognized but wasn't expecting to hear. I knew then that our names weren't on that clipboard. But it didn't make a difference, because we were getting in either way. After the initial shock, the woman regained composure and the smile reappeared on her face, albeit not as steady as before.

"Welcome," she said, and right on cue, the doorman pulled open one of the large doors to let us through.

Jack stared at the open door for a few seconds, completely still. In that moment, all I saw was fear.

"Jack," I whispered, "you can do this."

He nodded, a little too quickly. "I know. Yeah. I—I can do this."

He took ahold of my hand and weaved his fingers through mine, giving it a tight squeeze. He kept his eyes on the open door the entire time, breathing in and then exhaling heavily. I looked down at our hands, trying to ignore the electric currents shooting through my veins. Jack didn't let go until I had basically dragged him inside, where we were met almost immediately by a waiter holding a tray of champagne flutes.

"Oh, Jesus, yes!" Jack exclaimed, grabbing a glass. "You may as well leave the tray here."

I picked up my own champagne with what I hoped was a little more grace and elegance. It was clear we weren't going to find red plastic cups at this party.

"Getting drunk probably isn't the best idea," I told him, the moment the waiter disappeared.

"Take a look around. You might want to reconsider that thought."

I did look around, and honestly, it was super fancy. Wealth isn't exactly a new concept to me, but even we didn't have gold practically hanging off the velvet drapes. It was the complete opposite of Lucy's apartment, which had been modern and fresh. These people were old money for sure. Grand paintings hung on the walls, and above us was a huge chandelier, completely lit up. Across the marble floor, there was a large staircase curving upwards with shiny golden railings. The mahogany furniture and the decor seemed a little old-fashioned, but more in a regal than outdated way.

As for the people, well, Jack had done a good job describing them. Middle-aged women wearing necklaces so heavy, it was a wonder their necks were still intact. I had never seen so many perfect updos in my life. In LA, we tended to let our hair down a little more. But these women were all business and no fun. Not unless you count a game of croquet or something. The men weren't much different. They were spread out across the room, drinks in one hand and cigars in the other. They all wore perfectly tailored suits and had a similar look of smugness on their faces. All in all, it wasn't a big party. There were probably twenty-five people at most, including myself and Jack. In a way it was good; less snobs to deal with. But it was weirdly intimate, and I felt like a complete outsider.

Jack gave a quiet groan. "Oh lord, here we go."

I followed his gaze to the woman walking toward us with a huge smile on her face. Based on that alone, I knew that couldn't be his mother. Nevertheless, it was someone he recognized, because he was audibly groaning as she approached us, adjusting her mink fur that was draped over her gown. Seriously. She was wearing mink fur like she was the villain's girlfriend in a 1940s noir movie.

"Jack!" she exclaimed, pulling him toward her for an extremely forced kiss on the cheek. "Goodness, gracious. I barely recognize you. You're so handsome!"

Jeez lady, at least buy him a drink first.

"Eleanor," Jack said, with such a lack of enthusiasm that it was almost embarrassing. "You look lovely."

"How long has it been?"

"Oh . . . I'm not sure."

"Years!"

"Yes, probably."

"Dennis! Dennis, look who it is, it's Jack!"

A little sigh escaped from the middle of Jack's fake smile. He extended his hand toward the man who had come by Eleanor's side.

"Jack!" the man said with surprise, shaking his hand. I almost laughed at how comical his mustache looked when he spoke. "Wow, it's been so long. We don't see much of you around here these days."

"Uh, yeah. Things have been a little busy." Jack motioned toward me and said, "This is Gia."

"Gia," Eleanor repeated, sizing me up with a curious smile. "Wonderful to meet you."

Oh lord, what was I supposed to do? Curtsy?

"Charmed," I replied airily.

"Eleanor and Dennis have known my parents for years," Jack explained.

"And I mean *years*," Eleanor laughed. "I was *much* younger when we first met Amelia and Carter."

"So you're Jack's . . ." Dennis trailed off, waiting for me to finish.

"Friend," Jack and I said in unison, exchanging a look.

"Friend," Eleanor said, her smile tightening. "How lovely!"

If they knew Jack, then they had to know about Lucy. I waited for one of them to bring her up, but they never did. And if they knew who I was, they didn't seem to be keen on bringing that up either.

"Your father mentioned that you'd been living away from home for some time," Dennis said. "He was delighted that you wanted to make something of yourself on your own."

Jack looked confused. "I'm sorry, I'm not sure what you mean."

"Oh, you're just being humble now," Eleanor said cheerfully. "Your parents were so pleased when you told them you wanted to live on your own and learn about the business without the family's help. I think it's absolutely wonderful."

"I agree," Dennis nodded. "I wish Henry had some of your sense."

Eleanor touched my hand lightly. "Henry is our son," she explained. "Bless his soul; he's such a smart boy. But sometimes he needs a little bit of a push. He's a wonderful young man though. Last year, he surprised Dennis and me with a two-month Scandinavian cruise!"

"Oh!" I said, forcing fascination on my face. "That's . . . awesome!"

"These two boys were quite close growing up," Dennis added, looking at Jack. "You should definitely get in touch with him, I'm sure he'd love to hear from an old friend."

"Absolutely," Jack replied. "I'll get right on that. Now if you'll excuse me, I should go wish my mother a happy birthday."

"Oh of course!" Eleanor said brightly. "We'll chat more at dinner."

"I can hardly wait," Jack said, practically yanking me away from the couple.

"Let me get this straight," I said, watching Jack down the remainder of his champagne in one big gulp. "Your dad told his friends that you moved out because you wanted to become a businessman without your father's help?"

"Yeah, apparently."

"But it's a flat-out lie!"

Jack shrugged, handing a passing waiter his empty glass. "It takes a lot to shock me when it comes to my father."

At that moment, Scarlett walked in the room and Jack's face immediately lit up. Scarlett was twice as beautiful as her photos. She was wearing bright red lipstick and a red and white dress that I recognized as Oscar de la Renta. Her blonde hair bounced around as she rushed over to us in excitement.

"Jack!" she exclaimed with delight, throwing her arms around his neck. "You made it! You actually came!"

"I told you I would."

"I know, I know," she replied, pulling away. "But I was convinced you would back out last minute."

"I was tempted, trust me," Jack said. "You can thank Gia for my presence here tonight."

Scarlett enveloped me into a tight hug, which made me feel weirdly warm and fuzzy.

"Gia, you're here!" Scarlett said. "It's *so* great to finally meet you. I can't tell you how much it means to have both of you here."

"Anytime."

Except probably never again.

"And that dress," she gushed. "It's breathtaking. You have to let me steal it off you sometime."

"Just say the word and it's yours."

It was barely mine. I really needed to ease up on my promises.

"I'm wearing a tux!" Jack said. "Isn't anyone going to comment on that?"

Scarlett and I looked at each other. "No," we both said.

"Tough crowd, jeez." Jack nudged his sister playfully. "So, are you enjoying tonight's festivities?"

She gave an eye roll and said, "Please. I was hiding in the kitchen a minute ago, staring at the clock for entertainment."

"Well you signed up for a night of boredom and fake pleasantries," Jack said teasingly. "Enjoy it."

"Oh hey," Scarlett said, as if she suddenly remembered something important. "The Fieldses aren't here! Did Lucy say her parents were going to come?"

"Her parents weren't invited," Jack replied. "Lucy told me the other day."

"What? No way!"

"But didn't you say your parents were old friends?" I asked them.

"There was a little love lost between them when they realized Lucy's parents weren't as hell-bent on torturing me," Jack replied. "Their so-called friendship is basically a sham."

The siblings continued talking about the guest list and the surprises that it carried, but I was stuck on Jack and Lucy. Of course they still probably hung out. Why wouldn't they? They were old friends, and they had broken up a thousand times. But they had always gotten back together. It was only a matter of time, right?

"Jack," Scarlett whispered, her smile dropping as she looked behind his shoulder.

We both followed her gaze to the couple that walked into the room. My Google searches might have come up short, but I knew in a heartbeat that these were Jack's parents.

Amelia Anderson was the walking definition of grace. Her hair was dark brown and completely free from any grays. She wore a simple but elegant Reem Acra gown, her short sleeves falling off her shoulders elegantly. I recognized it immediately, because it was the gown my mother had described as "way too modest" for her own tastes. In that moment, I wished Mom was there to see how wrong she was. The diamond necklace wrapped around her neck was practically blinding the room. She looked regal and completely, utterly stone-faced. Seriously. There was not an expression in sight.

Carter Anderson, on the other hand, looked completely at ease in his perfectly fitted tuxedo. His hair was almost all gray, but his age didn't show much on his face. Like Jack, his smile was pleasant but just a tad smug. Like they had been told a secret about you but weren't going to shout it from the rooftops just yet. He had what looked like Bourbon in one hand and a cigar in the other. It was like stepping into an episode of *Mad Men*. He smiled and said something to the man beside him, as if they were sharing an inside joke. It wasn't until Jack's mother wrapped her arm around his wrist in what can only be described as alarm that he stopped and noticed we were there. The three of them stood gaping at us for a few seconds. The whole episode took about ten seconds total, but it seemed like the world was moving in slow motion. I reflexively slipped my free hand into Jack's and gave it a squeeze. I'm not sure if it was an encouraging "you can do this" or a "please don't die or anything" gesture, but it took a moment before he squeezed back. It was the man beside Jack's father who broke the trance first and approached us.

"Wow," he said, eyeing Jack up and down as if he were looking at a wax figure. "Jack. Long time, no see. You look great, kid."

"Thank you," Jack managed to reply, looking pale.

"You were just a boy the last time I saw you," the man continued. "What was it, fourteen? Fifteen?"

Jack was struggling to keep upright at this stage. He looked about ready to jump out of the window.

"Fifteen."

"Wow." The man gave me an absentminded smile and a nod of acknowledgment, clearly lost in thought. He dropped his gaze to Jack's hands, one of which was still interlocked with mine. "What are you drinking?"

"Uh, nothing right now," Jack said, regaining a bit of confidence in his voice.

"I'll get you something." The look he gave Jack was almost as if he understood he'd need a bit of liquid courage. "Scarlett, be a dear and give me a hand, would you?"

Scarlett blinked at us, looking hesitant to leave. The Andersons were now slowly walking toward us, and with every step they took, I could practically hear Jack's heart beating faster.

"Of course," Scarlett said, giving us an apologetic look before trailing behind the man.

I could practically hear Jack's heart beating as we came face to face with his parents. The four of us stood staring at one another silently, almost willing one of us to break the silence. Finally, it was Carter who took the leap.

"Well," he said. "I can't say this isn't a surprise."

Seriously? *Those* were his opening words? No "Hello Son, sorry for being a jackass all those years ago." No "hey man, how's it hanging?" Not even a simple "hi."

"Happy birthday, Mrs. Anderson," I practically squeaked with courage I didn't know I had within me. "I'm—"

"Gia Winters," she cut in with what I presumed was her attempt at a smile. "I know who you are. Thank you for coming. It's lovely to have you here."

I've got to hand it to the woman. She had the same level of affection as a piece of barbed wire, and she was reuniting with her estranged son and his uninvited plus-one celebrity friend who showed up with no prior warning, but she was still a gracious host. That skill only comes from years of pretending to like the people around you. Dad could learn a few tips from this woman.

We plunged back into silence, but nobody was bothered about my presence anymore. Jack and his parents seemed to be engaged in a staring competition.

"Miss Winters," Carter finally said, pulling his eyes away toward me. "Do let me know if there's anything you need. Any friend of my son's is a welcomed guest here."

On the word "son," Jack flinched beside me. His dad walked away before I could meekly offer a thank you, his mother perfectly in time beside him. Jack pulled his hand out of mine and ran it through his hair, somehow managing not to ruin its style. He exhaled deeply, and I realized that he must have been holding his breath the entire time.

"Ja—" I began, but he was already escaping.

"I need a drink."

I watched him walk away just as Scarlett reappeared. It's a good thing Jack went off for his own drink, because she had returned with no glass in her hand.

"Gia, seriously," she said with a sigh. "You don't know how glad I am that you're here right now."

"Who was that man with your parents?"

"Johnathon Hughes. He's my father's business partner and probably the only person he actually considers a friend. He's been around my family for as long as I can remember. He's also one of a handful of people who know the truth about why Jack left. I don't even think his wife knows. Although, let's face it, my father's version of the truth was probably a little skewed."

"Excuse me, Miss Anderson," a waiter interrupted us quietly. "Dinner is served."

"Oh great," Scarlett whispered to me. "I'll go hide the knives from my father."

Good thinking. At this rate, I was surprised Carter wasn't roasting his son and serving him on the dinner table with an apple shoved in his mouth. I found Jack downing the contents of his heavy crystal glass, standing secluded in a corner as everyone headed toward the dining room. It took a large refill of his drink and a bit of coaxing before we eventually followed, being ushered to our seats by the waiters.

In the dining room, one long table sat underneath yet another enormous chandelier, candles and flower petals delicately placed in scattered patterns around the plates. At first I was surprised to see that Jack and I were seated next to his parents and Scarlett, but it quickly made sense. He was still a part of the Anderson family as far as most people knew, and his parents were determined to keep the facade going. To my left sat a tall British man, who turned out to be a lot friendlier than he looked. His wife sat directly opposite him—next to

Scarlett—and was wearing a pearl necklace with so many layers I actually had to look away before I ripped it off her. Johnny Hughes and his wife sat strategically at the other end of the long table, no doubt taking care of business from across the room.

"He owns some steel factory," Jack leaned in and whispered to me, motioning toward the British man. "Apparently my father's in talks about setting up a huge deal with him. I can't wait to watch him kiss his ass all night."

I didn't bother asking how Jack knew who the man was. I also didn't comment on the fact that Jack had never once referred to Carter as "my dad." It was always "my father." Scarlett, Jack, and I stayed silent the entire first course, eyeing each other with anxiety as we forced scallops down our throats.

Dad had attempted to throw a few of these sit-down dinners for his friends and colleagues, but they had a very different vibe to this one. This was some next level fancy, and it was clear I didn't fit in. My knife kept making scraping noises as it hit the china plate, and it took me less than a minute for a pea to go shooting off my plate and almost jumping right into the flame of a candle. Thankfully, Jack's father was so busy smooth-talking his new potential business associate that he didn't seem to notice. That, or he was excellent at pretending I didn't exist.

But when the main course was brought out and placed in front of me, it made it a little difficult to pretend I wasn't there.

"Pigeon," the waiter said, when I asked him what kind of cooked bird was resting alongside the mushrooms.

"Pigeon," I repeated weakly. "Awesome."

"You aren't on one of those Hollywood diets are you, Miss Winters?" Carter asked me. "You know, veganism, gluten-free, or whatever else is in fashion these days."

The way he said my name made me want to throw my pigeon at his stupid, smug face.

"Of course not," I said with a smile, piercing a mushroom aggressively with my fork. "I almost had this exact dish for breakfast this morning. What a coincidence!"

Carter smiled back. "Excellent!"

For someone who lived in New York and saw dirty, grimy

pigeons flying around all the time, you'd think he'd be less excited about eating the damn things. Of course, I had no problem eating chicken, which was still technically a bird. But pigeons were a step too far for me. I glanced at Jack's plate. Apparently he didn't share my reluctance. I stared down at the bird with disgust, praying that it would magically transform into an In-N-Out double-double burger.

"So tell me, Jack," the British lady, Maureen, said in her posh accent. "Are you working with your father?"

Jack looked at his parents, and then at me. I gave him a tiny *I don't know* shrug.

"No," Jack replied. "I'm in private security."

"Private security?" William, Maureen's husband, repeated.

"Yes. I'm a bodyguard, actually."

I snuck a glance at Carter. He didn't look at all happy that Jack was chipping away at his fantasy family story.

"A bodyguard!" Maureen said, looking uncertain. "Why not the family business?"

"I don't think it's really aligned with what I want to do in life."

"Jack has never really been sure about what that is," Carter said with a humorless laugh.

"Well, I suppose not everyone has to follow the same path as their parents," William said, a little unconvinced. "But a bodyguard . . . How fascinating."

Fascinating was definitely not the word he had sitting at the forefront of his mind.

"Gia, dear," Maureen said cheerfully. "You *must* tell me what it's like to have grown up with Harry Winters as a father. Every day must have been an absolute adventure!"

I placed my fork down beside me, relieved that I now had an excuse to escape the pigeon.

"Um, it was great. I guess I don't see him like the rest of the world does; to me he's just my dad. But it was definitely an eventful childhood."

"Your mother is a model, is she not?" William asked.

Oh, come on, William. Like you don't already know.

"She was. She's more of an actor now."

"I'm sure I'm not familiar with any of her movies," Carter said flippantly.

Jack cut his gaze to me. He looked like he wanted to say something but then decided against it. I narrowed my eyes ever so slightly.

"Oh, I doubt that," I said.

Carter looked up from his plate. "Excuse me?"

"She's had a lot of cameos lately. It's hard to miss her."

I offered my explanation with a look of complete innocence on my face, but it was evident that the tension had just risen a notch at our end of the table. Only Maureen and William hadn't quite caught on yet.

"Amelia, you were telling me that Scarlett works in Los Angeles now, weren't you?" Maureen asked, taking a sip of her red wine.

"Yes, that's right. She's been doing a marketing internship with a big firm there."

"And how are you enjoying that, Scarlett?" William asked.

Scarlett glanced at her parents, as if asking for approval to speak. "I'm loving it. It's a lot of work, but I'm really enjoying myself. LA is so different from New York City, but it's been quite easy to adjust."

"That's lovely!" Maureen said. "Of course, William and I have never been to the West Coast, but now it seems that we just have to visit!"

"You really should. The people, the place. Everything! I'm sure you'll love it."

"I don't care much for Los Angeles," Carter said, and I refrained from rolling my eyes. "I've gone many times for business, and I've never really enjoyed myself. Everything's so plastic and gaudy. The Walk of Fame is just a dirty sidewalk, and the people are all bizarre, if you ask me."

Scarlett and I locked eyes. She looked like she was waiting for a UFO to abduct her.

"No disrespect to you, of course, Miss Winters," Carter added quickly.

Actually, I'm starting to think he meant a lot of disrespect.

"Well, in the immortal words of Soul Kid," I said. "'We got

more bounce in California than all y'all combined,' so . . ."

Beside me, Jack almost spat out the sip of wine he had in his mouth, struggling to control his laughter. Scarlett put her napkin to her lips, no doubt to try and hide her huge smile.

"Soul Kid . . ." Maureen said thoughtfully. "I'm not sure I'm familiar with his work."

"He's a modern-day Shakespeare. Trust me."

"Then it looks like you won't be able to escape Los Angeles for a while, Carter," William said with a hearty laugh. "What with Scarlett living there now, and your son seeing Miss Winters."

Jack and I froze, exchanging fleeting looks as we contemplated whether or not to correct him. We both decided against it and went back to the birds on our plates. Carter obviously shared the same view, because he swiftly ignored it and moved on.

"Scarlett's time on the West Coast will be temporary, I assure you. She'll be back home the moment she gets this internship out of her system. Besides, that's no environment for a girl to be working in," Carter continued. "She doesn't need to be running around in heels getting coffee for those men. I know what those ad guys are like, and they're no good, trust me."

"You're too right, Carter," William agreed. "No place for a fine lady like your daughter."

"Which is why men like you and I work so hard. So we can ensure that our children don't have to endure the hardships we did."

At this point, I wasn't sure what I was most offended about. Was it the fact that Carter was completely undermining his own daughter's love for her job by reducing it down to fetching coffee? Or how both men were deciding where a suitable workplace was for a "lady," right in front of her? Maybe it was the way Carter was trying to pretend that he was actually doing his children some huge favor by sucking up to business partners and neglecting them their entire lives. To top it all off, Amelia looked like she had turned off her hearing for the entire conversation. She was just sipping her wine gracefully, staring at the wall in front of her with what looked a little like boredom.

Sitting at that table, the only thing running through my mind was how Jack had managed to survive fifteen whole years with these two. I could barely get through the main course. I was almost disappointed that the rest of the table couldn't hear the disaster of a conversation we were being forced to endure. Although given how uptight everyone looked, I'm sure they were all Team Carter on this one.

"I think it's amazing what Scarlett's doing," Jack finally said. We all looked at him with surprise. "I mean it's pretty obvious that my father's hard work has given us a lot of luxuries. So, moving across the country at twenty-one and away from a lot of these comforts is actually a very big deal. Everyone starts at the bottom, right? But my sister really enjoys what she's doing, and she's not afraid of working hard. Besides, there are sleazy men everywhere. Even in your business trade. Not like that should stop a *lady* from doing what she wants."

In that moment, Scarlett, Maureen, and I had to physically put a hand over our chests to stop our hearts from bursting through. Jack met his father's steely glare with a look that was almost challenging. He was steady as a rock, and here I was ready to launch my pigeon at Carter, Angry Birds style. One thing was for sure, Carter was not happy.

"You're right," he said, forcing a cold smile. "I should commend my daughter on having some ambition in life. At least she knows what she wants to do. Unlike some people, who would much rather waste their lives away without any direction."

"Oh, you know how kids are these days!" Maureen said, waving her hand dismissively with a chuckle. "My boy was convinced he was going to be a rugby player until one fine day when he decided to give it up for music. Now he's a lawyer!"

"It's so hard to keep up with this generation," William added. "Always changing their minds."

Carter was staring so intensely at Jack, I was afraid he was going to burn a hole through his skull with his laser vision.

"Exactly," he said. "Sometimes they insist on doing things their own way, even when they know you're right."

"Or maybe," Jack said, placing his knife and fork down at

the table with a clatter. "They're tired of being suffocated, and would much rather be disowned than be forced to live their lives as miserable as their parents'!"

Carter's expression had become so scary, I actually cowered back in my seat a little. Jack didn't look at all afraid though. He was glaring right back at his father, daring him to continue.

"It's a shame," Carter said quietly, after a few seconds of heavy silence, "that sometimes our children are so ungrateful for what we give them. Oh well. I suppose they all come running back eventually."

Jack gave a humorless laugh that sounded a lot like Carter's. "I assure you, Father. You won't be seeing me running back any time soon."

"Jack!" his mother said sharply, her tone implying a warning.

"And what makes you think I'd even let you back in this house if you did?" Carter replied angrily. A few more people down the table briefly turned to look in our direction.

"What makes you think I *want* back in this house? The only reason I'm here tonight is for Scarlett. You know? The loyal daughter who, for whatever reason, hasn't gone insane yet living under the same roof as you two!"

"Jack, that's enough!" Amelia said. "Do not speak to your father like that!"

By now, most people at the long dinner table were now watching the argument unfold.

"You'll have to forgive us for the little family outbreak," Jack said to William, not looking one bit apologetic. "Usually we don't speak at all. This is sort of a big occasion for us. We're pretending we're a happy family so my father can bleed your company dry."

Carter slammed his open palm against the table, causing me and everyone else in the room to jump in our seats. The whole dining room plunged into silence, eyes glued on Carter. Jack didn't look the slightest bit fazed.

"How *dare* you disrespect me in front of my own guests?" Carter demanded. "I want you out of this house right now! And don't ever think about coming back! Not for your mother, not for your sister, and *definitely* not for me!"

Jack calmly placed his napkin on the table beside his half-full plate and pushed his chair back as he stood. "Lucky for you," he said to William, "Carter Anderson is a much better businessman than he is a father."

He took one last look at his mother before he spun on his heel and walked out of the dining room.

Nineteen

It was like a tornado had hit the room and left a mass of destruction in its wake. We were all just sitting in its debris, listening to Jack's footsteps echo against the marble floor. Carter looked like he had ruptured a vein in his forehead. Scarlett looked completely stunned. Amelia had a dead-behind-the-eyes Medusa stare on her face. Maureen and William no longer looked hungry. Johnathon Hughes ran a hand over his face with a sigh. Eleanor and Dennis were mentally naming an island in Henry's honor.

Now what? Were we all supposed to go back to dinner and pretend that whole spectacle hadn't happened? Not likely, bud. Carter Anderson could take his pigeon and shove it where the sun don't shine. I threw my napkin on top of my untouched food, said a little mental apology to the poor bird's ghostly spirit and stood. Everyone looked at me.

"Great party," I said, meekly giving Amelia a thumbs-up. "Happy birthday."

Oh, dear god. I practically sprinted out of the dining room before Carter threw a plate at my face, almost tripping over the hem of my gown a few times. Jack was nowhere to be seen, but my guess was he hadn't gotten too far out the door. Wow, could this night have been any more of a disaster? Not only did the Anderson family basically malfunction in front of a room full of high-strung rich folk, I had to deal with all of this on an empty stomach. He couldn't have had a meltdown after they brought out dessert?

I eventually found Jack angrily pacing by the elevator. The woman in the gown was no longer waiting outside. The doorman was, but he was so still and quiet, he may as well have been a part of the wall.

"Jack!"

He stopped pacing for a moment, looking at me with a deflated look on his face, and then went right back to pacing. Oh boy. Damage control was going to be tough.

"Jack," I said softly, catching onto his arm so he would stop.

He hung his head in his hands and groaned. "I can't believe I just did that."

"It was freaking amazing!"

"I don't give a damn about Carter, but Scarlett's going to hate me forever!"

"No she's not!" I pulled his hands away from his face. "Look at me. She's not going to hate you at all. What you did back there was incredible. You stood up for her and you stood up for yourself."

Jack sighed. He looked like a scared kid again.

"I think I want to go home," Jack said in a quiet voice. "My home. Not here. This was never home for me."

"Okay. Let's go home."

I pushed the elevator button, and the golden doors opened immediately. The elevator man was nowhere to be found. Just empty space. Jack and I stepped in, both breathing an audible sigh of relief when the doors closed in front of us and the sight of the Anderson penthouse disappeared out of view.

"I was really hoping things would be different," Jack said. "With him. My father. I don't know, I guess I just thought after all of this time he would be different. But he hasn't changed at all."

"You're much better off without him," I told him. "Honestly, you don't need people like that in your life."

Jack didn't reply. He just stared at the elevator doors blankly as we continued our slow descent. I hated seeing him like this. He was always smirking and teasing me and cracking lame jokes and dancing really badly in bars. *That* was the Jack I was used to.

"He's right ,you know," he finally said.

"About what?"

"About me having no direction. I mean, look at me. I left my own house and cut off all ties with my parents to prove a point, and where did it get me? I'm not doing anything great with my life. I haven't proved anything! I have no clue what I even *want* to do. I'm just a bodyguard!"

"Are you kidding me?" I asked incredulously, and he looked away from the doors at me. "Jack, you're probably one of the most accomplished people I've ever met! You talked about how brave it is for Scarlett to leave behind all those luxuries, but you did it at fifteen! You were just a kid. Nobody knows what they want at that age, but you knew what you *didn't* want and you stuck by it!"

"Yeah, bu—"

"But what? Who cares if you don't become a millionaire on your own, or end up on the cover of Forbes or something. You made sure you would be nothing like your father, and that's something you should be proud of. You had to grow up a lot faster than you should have, and you *still* took the time to care about your little sister. If I went a year without talking to Mike, I don't even think he'd text me to check if I was alive! Your dad may still think you're some lost little boy, but you're not. You're smart and loyal and caring. You put your own pride aside and actually showed up tonight, even though you knew it was going to be a disaster. You grew up to become an incredible man, Jack. Not because of your father but *in spite* of him. And if he can't accept that, then it's his loss and not yours."

Jack just stared at me for a few seconds. I think he was a little overcome with what I had just said. To be honest, so was I. I hadn't planned on giving him an entire speech, and I was afraid it was a little overkill. But I had meant every word.

But then he finally blinked, and his body came alive again. He took one stride toward me, wrapped his arm around my waist and kissed me. Just like that. Just kissed me. Jack Anderson was kissing me. For a few seconds, I was too in shock to do anything. But then my brain eventually caught up with my heart, which was pounding against my chest, and finally kicked into gear as I kissed him back.

It wasn't slow and romantic like I had always imagined it would be. It was intense and clumsy. It was almost urgent, like we were afraid someone was going to tear us apart in a few seconds. Jack ran his hands up and down my back as he closed the space between us. It was like he wasn't sure where the best place was to put them. I curled my fingers into his suit jacket and pulled him closer. It was like everything was going in slow motion, but we were rushing, making up for all the lost time. In that moment, I knew. I knew what I had known deep down all along. Why Milo and I could never be perfectly right for each other. I hadn't done it intentionally, and I had done my best to fight it. From the bottom of my heart, I wanted to feel for him the way I thought I did all this time. But I was hopelessly and embarrassingly in love with Jack, and now that his fingers were in my hair and his lips were pressed against mine, I knew that *this* was all I had hoped for the entire year.

It had just never seemed like a realistic possibility. It's not like Jack ever gave me an indication that he wanted more. I mean the sexual tension was pretty obvious. And sometimes it felt like he hinted at it. But I had just chalked the flirting up to a hobby of his. Some people like to knit. He likes to flirt. He feels the same way. He feels the same way. He feels the same way!

And then all too quickly, he pulled away and took a big step away from me, as if he was about to burst into flames. We were too overwhelmed to look at each other, so we both concentrated on the golden doors again, both of us steadying our breathing and lowering our heart rates. Yeah right, like that was going to happen any time soon. I was so glad there were no mirrors in the elevator or else I would have been forced to see how much color had filled my cheeks. I stole a quick look at Jack, running a finger over my lips. They felt like they were on fire. Jack was looking at that floor, breathing in and then exhaling heavily. I wanted to ask him what he was thinking, what he was feeling. But I wasn't brave enough.

Had that really just happened? Had Jack just kissed me? I hadn't, like, died, and gone to heaven already had I? Because I wasn't even sure I was going to be let in at this point, especially after making Reggie skip all those Starbucks lines for me. I'm pretty sure Baby J doesn't approve of that kind of stuff.

I turned away, trying to hide the smile creeping up on my face. I had never felt complete euphoria before. Not like this. All those months of denial, loneliness, and jealousy had led to this moment. I couldn't hide what I felt any longer, and I didn't have to anymore. Not from myself and not from him. I could feel the floor beneath me settle to the ground level, but I was on a complete high.

The elevator doors were already open as we stood there, and I quietly retrieved my bag from the floor. I could feel Jack looking at me, but I kept my gaze on the floor. It had actually happened. I wasn't dreaming.

"Gia," Jack finally said quietly. "I'm sorry. I shouldn't have done that. Can we just pretend that didn't happen?"

The golden doors slowly closed, hitting against each other with the same weight that had dropped onto my heart. Wait. *What?* I finally looked up at his grim expression. What was that on his face? Guilt? Confusion? Regret? Either way, it all added up to one thing. Rejection. Every sense of elation escaped my veins as the realization hit. The shiny walls suddenly felt like they were caving in, and I couldn't breathe. Slamming my finger on the button, I bolted out.

"Gia!"

I marched across the marble floor toward the concierge, fighting back the sick feeling that was growing at the pit of my stomach. It was like I had just risen to the very top of happiness, only to come crashing all the way through the floor a second later.

"Gia Winters," I told the man at the front desk. "Tell them to bring my car around. And tell them to hurry."

The man at the concierge flicked his eyes behind me, but I didn't turn around.

"Now, please." My voice sounded strained.

"Gia, wait!" Jack said, grabbing ahold of my arm gently.

I whipped around, yanking my arm out of his reach. I couldn't handle the feeling of his skin on mine in that moment.

"Don't touch me!"

Jack put his hands up in a surrender motion, backing away a little. "Okay, but please just talk to me."

"No. I'm done talking. I'm done listening. I'm just done, okay? I don't want to do this anymore."

"I'm sorry. Tonight has just really messed my brain up, and I guess you were just . . . there . . . and—"

"Did you not hear me?" I said fiercely. "I'm *done!* I'm really sorry that you had a crap night, but I'm not sure telling me I was a convenient option is a really good apology!"

"That's not what I meant!"

"Well, what *did* you mean?"

"I just . . . Can't we just pretend this didn't happen?"

"No," I said firmly. "I'm finally done pretending. All the jokes and all the banter were fun, don't get me wrong. But I can't keep doing this anymore."

"What are you talking about?"

"You know what."

"No, I really don't!"

"Jack, come on! You know how I feel about you!"

Jack blinked at me for a few seconds in silence. He opened his mouth, and then closed it again.

"Gia," he finally managed. "We're friends, right?"

"Are we?" I demanded. "Because you don't seem like just a friend when you get jealous of my boyfriend. You don't seem like just a friend every time you make a flirty comment or stare at me a little too long. You definitely don't seem like just a friend when you decide to kiss me after probably the most important dinner you've had in the last decade! I don't want to keep pretending we're something we're not, because honestly, I don't want to be just friends with you!"

"What do you want me to say?"

"I don't want you to say what I want to hear! I want you to say how you feel!"

"Yes!" Jack exclaimed. "Okay? Yes, I have feelings that are more than . . . friendly. But things are complicated!"

So I hadn't imagined the whole thing, and he really did care somewhere deep down. Too bad he was too much of a robot to actually acknowledge it.

"Gia," Jack sighed, daring to take a step closer. "I know you're mad that I kissed you—"

"No, I'm mad that you kissed me and then tried to act like you would have done the same to a lamp if it had been standing next you. You're living in this fantasy land where it's so much easier to pretend than actually deal with your feelings!"

"Oh right," he said sarcastically. "Because you've always been living in reality?"

I narrowed my eyes with anger. "What is that supposed to mean?"

"Don't you think you're being a little hypocritical?"

"Why am I a hypocrite?"

Now it was Jack's turn to walk away. He headed back toward the elevators, even though I knew he wasn't planning on taking a trip up. He was just physically trying to escape what was ahead of him.

"I don't want to talk about this right now," he muttered.

I hurried after him, the sound of my heels echoing on the marble floor. I didn't care that the man at the front desk was watching us intently as if his favorite TV show was on. I was ready to battle.

"No, we're going to talk about this now!" I called out after him. "Stop running away. You always tell me I'm so immature. Well, maybe it's time we both grew up!"

He abruptly stopped, spinning around to face me, and my heel skidded against the floor. Now Jack looked pissed.

"Don't act like I'm the only one to blame here," he snapped. "You had a boyfriend up until a few weeks ago! What was I supposed to do?"

I looked at him with disbelief. "I'm sorry, were you expecting me to sit around and wait for you? Because you weren't exactly open about what your status was. You still aren't! For all I know, you and Lucy are still together!"

"We're not!"

"Oh right, I forgot. It's *complicated.*"

"What did you want me to do?" Jack exclaimed. "I don't have the right to tell you who you can and can't date!"

"No, you don't. But if you were ever interested, then maybe you should have actually stepped up and told me! Instead, you just decided to sulk every time I talked about Milo, with *zero* mention of you having a girlfriend back home!"

"When was I supposed to do all of this, huh? When you were already with Milo? My window of opportunity was pretty slim."

"I'm giving you a window of opportunity now!"

"Besides," Jack continued, "you didn't exactly make a move either! Aren't you going to take responsibility for that?"

"Okay, fine!" I said. "But that was only because I thought you didn't like me! You were so hot and cold."

"I was your bodyguard! I was working for your dad!"

"So you're saying you *did* like me?"

Jack gave an exasperated noise that was somewhere between a groan and a sigh. "What do you want from me, Gia?"

"I want you stop acting like this was nothing! If you don't feel the same, then fine. I can't change that. But you can't just turn around and apologize like it isn't a big deal or it didn't have any meaning behind it. I hate to break it to you, but I don't think we were *ever* just friends, and I think you're scared to admit it! I can't be friends with someone I'm secretly in love with!"

For a second, we were both stunned. It was like when an elastic band snaps right in between your fingers, and for a moment you need to re-evaluate your entire life. I had never actually said that out loud before. I had only *just* accepted it in my own brain. Honestly, this is the kind of stuff I should be talking about in therapy. We were seriously overpaying for those sessions.

"You're not in love with me." His look of anger had almost turned to pity. "You just think you are."

"I didn't mean I was in love with you," I said haughtily, although my confidence was wavering a little. "It was just an expression. You know . . . whatever. Besides, you don't get to dictate how I feel! You can barely manage your own emotions."

"If you're expecting some big declaration of love back, then I can't give that to you," he said. "Sorry to disappoint."

At this moment I was pretty sure I felt anything but love for him. He was being so cold and hostile; like it didn't even matter that I was literally ripping my heart out and handing it to him.

"You know what I want?" I replied. "I want to feel like myself again! Before I met you, I was waking up every morning and just *living* my life. I was silly and childish, sure. I still am! But so what? At least I knew who I was. But ever since you came waltzing through the front door, I think about you *all* the time. What you're doing, where you are, if you're with Lucy, if you're thinking about me. I spend all this time thinking about you when I could be thinking about Milo, who's sweet and kind and I *really* like. But he's not you. I could be thinking about myself! I don't even know who I am because I spend so much time lying to myself about what I want and how I feel. And maybe that's not your fault. But we're both to blame for this stupid game we keep playing with each other. I just want to be a normal, functioning person again. And I just can't do that with you always on my mind!"

The guy at the concierge was probably filming this whole event and sending it to his family group chat. I wouldn't even hold it against him. Jack's expression softened as he took a step toward me and put a hand on my cheek. I didn't pull away this time. I didn't have the energy. Jack tilted my head up a little so I was looking right into his eyes. His face was so close, we were practically breathing the same breath.

"I can't," he practically whispered. "I want to. But . . . I just can't."

He was wrong. He could; he just wouldn't. He wanted to, but he still chose not to. Maybe he didn't think it was worth it. That I was worth it. I was disappointed and exhausted. This whole thing wasn't fair to Milo or Lucy, and it definitely wasn't fair to us.

"Can we just stop?" he said, pleading with me.

He sounded so much like a little kid that I almost laughed. It was like he genuinely believed everything would magically be solved if he hit pause on our life. I had never cared about Jack more in my life, and never wanted to hate him as much as I did in that moment. Enough was enough. I had made a fool of myself for long enough.

"You're right; I think it's about time we stopped," I said simply. "Goodbye, Jack."

Once again I headed for the exit, silently promising myself that I would never lay eyes on Jack Anderson again. If this was love, then I didn't want it. If this was love, then I was better off pretending I had it with Milo, who actually cared about me the way I had always dreamed. If this was love, then it freaking sucked, and I would make sure I never made this mistake again. Because I guess that was what we were going to call this whole thing. A mistake.

I had almost reached the doorman when I heard Jack's voice call out behind me.

"Would it have even made a difference?" he demanded angrily. It took me a few seconds before I turned to look at him. "Would it have even made a difference if I had told you how I felt back then? If I had said, 'Don't choose him. Choose me.' Would you have actually done it?"

We stared at each other in heavy silence.

"Well, I guess we'll never know," I replied quietly.

It was safe to say that Jack and I were well and truly over before we had even begun.

I slunk back into the penthouse feeling completely drained and defeated. Another night of silence and despair. Yay for me. What I desperately needed was Dr. Norton and her fancy couch. It was about time I started appreciating that some stranger wanted to hear me complain about my problems. But what I found waiting for me on the plush sofa was actually better than a therapist. It was my mother. Her tan was so impeccable, she almost radiated light amongst all the white furniture. Her blonde hair was in immaculate beach waves, and she still looked ready for a runway even though she was dressed in silk pajamas.

"Surprise!" she exclaimed, jumping up in excitement. "I'm back!"

For a minute I just stood there, trying to figure out whether she was actually there or just a hologram. Her smile dropped a little as Famous barked enthusiastically.

Her shoulders dropped a little in disappointment. "Aren't you surprised?"

I ran to her in reply, flinging my arms around her and pulling her into a tight hug. "Mom! You're really here!"

"Okay, you're crushing me." She laughed, attempting to hug me back while I basically had her in a death grip. "Gia, sweetie. Are you crying?"

My chest heaved in between sobs. I was so happy to see her but so incredibly heartbroken with everything that had just happened. I had forgotten just how much I missed her and just how alone I felt without her around.

"Gia," she said, pulling away with concern. She sat me down on the sofa beside her. "What's wrong?"

I told her everything. I told her about hating Hannah and the coffee incident and about my sessions with Dr. Norton. I told her about meeting Milo's dad and the breakup. I told her about Aidyn and Lucy and the terrible drug rumor. And, of course, I told her about the god-awful dinner party, the kiss, and the huge fight Jack and I had just had. The entire time she listened in silence, nodding occasionally and asking basic questions only for the purpose of getting more detail. By the time I finished, I was dying to hear what she had to say.

"I'm so sorry, kid," she said, exhaling deeply.

"For what?"

"For not being there when you needed me. You've obviously been going through hell, and I haven't been around to help you at all. God, I feel so terrible."

Honestly, she *had* been MIA and it would have been nice to have had some backup. But she was here now, and that's all that mattered. I needed all the support I could get.

"It's okay," I told her. "I just really missed you. I don't know what to do about any of this. My whole life is a mess!"

"Babe, your life is not a mess."

"Mom, did you not hear anything I just told you? I have literally zero friends, I'm single as all hell, and the guy I'm in love with is a jackass. The world still thinks I'm on my way to rehab, and I've been to, like, three classes this semester."

"All of those have easy solutions." She shrugged. "First of all, this Hannah girl is a total psycho. Next time, pour the coffee on her head instead of her bag."

"Yeah, because *that's* going to win me friends."

"Who cares about winning friends? You have friends! They may not be here with you, but at least you know you can count on them no matter what. If you need to actually put in effort to win people over, most of the time they aren't worth it anyway. So stop trying so hard. It's a tough city, but you're tougher. If people want to be friends with you, let them make the effort."

"Okay . . ." I said. "Bu—"

"As for this whole drug debacle," Mom continued. "Who the hell cares what they think? Am I supposed to stop living my life because the guy who sells donuts from a cart thinks I cheated on my boyfriend with a Hungarian dancer? No!"

"Wait, what?"

"I mean, he wasn't even Hungarian!"

"Okay, I feel like we need to discuss this a little more."

"Forget what they think!" Mom said sternly. "People are always going to have an opinion. You just have to get used to filtering it out."

"But it's not that easy!"

"I never said it was easy, but it's something you have to do. And seriously, you *need* to start showing up to school. I get it. It sucks. Trust me, there's a reason I never bothered with it and took up underwear modeling instead. But you're a lot smarter than me, and you can't let yourself get distracted with all this other nonsense!"

I groaned. "I've been trying, I swear! But things have just been so out-of-control lately."

"Well now that I'm solving all of your life problems, that really isn't an issue anymore," Mom told me matter-of-factly. "No more excuses from now on, okay? Seriously, your father is going to kill us both if you fail any classes. Not to mention, you've got finals coming up! He probably sleeps with a ticket to New York under his pillow, waiting to hop on a plane the moment I screw up with my parenting."

"*Fine*," I said begrudgingly. "I promise I'll go to class."

"Good." She gave me a satisfied nod. "Now, the final problem."

"The biggest problem."

"The *smallest* problem," Mom corrected me. "I'm sorry you and Milo broke up. I liked him. And not just because he's hot."

"Good lord."

"I mean, he is *really* hot."

"Can we stay on track please?"

"But if you aren't giving a hundred percent in a relationship, then there's no reason to be in it, now is there? I think you did the right thing by breaking up. I know it was hard, but I'm proud of you. It was a very mature thing to do."

I was grateful for her saying that, but I still felt like crap. Was I a bad person for still caring about Milo? Or did it make me a bad person to *not* care? Either way, the whole thing pretty much sucked.

"As for Jack . . ."

I pulled a cushion off the sofa and buried my face in it. "Can we just not mention his name ever again?" I asked in a muffled voice.

Mom pulled the pillow out of my grasp and threw it on the sofa opposite us.

"No, we're going to talk about him," she said firmly. "You know I love Jack, but the boy is an idiot."

"Yeah. That's my entire problem in a nutshell, Mom."

"He's obviously crazy about you, but he just can't say it."

"But why not?" I wailed childishly. "If he likes me so much then what's the problem?"

"There's obviously something holding him back. Love is a scary thing, kid. Especially when you haven't had a lot of it in your life. If his parents are as bad as you say, then no wonder he's a little messed up."

Jeez. This was like Dr. Norton's dream conversation.

"But he's had a girlfriend on and off for half of his life!"

"Yeah," Mom replied. "But she's a safe choice. Less risky. He doesn't have to open up if she already knows him so well."

You know things are bad when my mother starts to sound wise. Even with her questionable taste in men, she was still giving me some pretty decent advice about boys.

I flopped onto the cushions with defeat. "So what do I do? Just cut him out of my life forever? That's it. No more Jack?"

I guess Mom couldn't conjure up a witty enough response in time because she sort of just sat there with this sort of sad, almost pitying look on her face.

"Gia, people are going to be letting you down your whole life," Mom finally said, stroking my hair comfortingly. "Especially when it comes to love. But we can't stop living every time someone disappoints us, right? If somebody wants to be in your life, they'll fight for a spot. Trust me."

Maybe that was what I was afraid of. Jack didn't seem like he was up for fighting for that spot.

Mom leaned in closer with a little sigh. "Look, I'm not going to give you one of those *you're just a kid, you don't know what love is* speeches. I wasn't that much older than you are when I met your dad, and I'm still convinced he was probably the greatest love of my life."

"So then why did you guys spend so much time fighting? Why did you get divorced?"

"Because sometimes the person you love isn't the person you're meant to be with."

That idea sunk deep into the pit of my stomach. I felt like I had swallowed a bag of rocks. I guess that was my sad truth. I was just a girl, standing in front of a boy, asking him to love her. And he had said no.

"You want some hot chocolate?" Mom asked with an encouraging smile. "I got this cool Spanish cocoa thing, and we have fat-free whipped cream in the fridge. Let's use it all up!"

"As exciting as that sounds, I'm going to have to pass." I

forced myself off the couch, letting my perfect gown fall around my legs. "I think I'm just going to sleep."

If Dr. D showed up in my nightmares tonight I was going to straight-up punch him in the face. I was in *no* mood to deal with him.

"Get some rest," Mom said, pulling me into another tight hug. "Tomorrow you and I are hanging out the whole day! We can get the full spa treatment done if you want. And we can paint our nails and watch *Gilmore Girls* reruns!"

"Mom, I'm not waking up in 2002. Nobody even watches that show anymore."

"Don't knock it 'til you've tried it. I blame that show for my coffee addiction."

Well at least I had something to look forward to, even if it involved flared jeans and flip phones. I collapsed onto my bed the moment I shut the room door behind me and buried my face into my pillow. I was fast asleep within ten minutes, my gown and makeup still on.

That night I didn't have any nightmares. No Frank Parker, no dark warehouse, nothing. It seemed that even the man I hated most in my life no longer wanted anything to do with me.

Twenty

Heartbreak is a funny thing. It kind of feels like someone turned off the lights in your soul, and if you pay close attention you can actually feel your body aching from the pain. Heartbreak from rejection is a whole different ball game. I woke up looking like death in a human form and feeling about as bad as my reflection looked in the mirror. Not bothering to remove my makeup from the night before was a mistake I was definitely never going to make again, and I was lucky I hadn't accidentally ripped any of my gown during my slumber.

Honestly, I was expecting the waterworks to turn on before pancakes had hit the table. But surprisingly, no tears came. I knew I wasn't over Jack in just one night because I was pretty certain my heart had actually been crushed in three different places. But I genuinely didn't want to sit at home and wallow the whole day, even though Mom had practically encouraged it. The idea of staring at my plain bedroom ceiling all day while I cried myself into oblivion sounded horrible. Maybe it was because I had been doing it a lot lately, or maybe I just really hated that stupid bedroom décor. Either way, I wasn't in the mood to sit and mull over the thousands of "what ifs" swimming in my mind.

Even with the overwhelming trauma from last night, the day ahead turned out to be one of the best I'd had in a long time. Mom's mission to keep me distracted meant that I was allowed to raid her closet and borrow any pair of heels I wanted. After much deliberation, I settled on a pair of Alexander McQueen boots that were far too flashy for her wardrobe. There was no chance I was giving them back.

Mom's idea of keeping me busy also meant that we had zero time to stop and breathe before launching into another activity because we were running around the city from the moment we left the penthouse. We didn't really do much more than visit about a hundred cafes around town, where Mom would pick at a piece of cake while I tried not to inhale the slice whole. I think we lost a few hours in Bergdorf's, but the loss was completely worth it. At some point, we ended up having a conversation with Lenny Kravitz in Dumbo, and I honestly can't even tell you how that started. One minute we're sipping matcha tea by the Brooklyn Bridge, and the next Mom is telling Lenny she likes his velvet jacket. I couldn't remember the last time we had spent the entire day together. Every time Mom came to visit in LA, she was always fully booked up with spa treatments, meetings, or glamorous events. It was nice to have her just to myself for a while.

It was past six when Mom and I finally placed our shopping bags on the floor of the penthouse and declared the day a success. How she managed to still look energized after a major outing *and* a dose of jet lag is a mystery to me.

"Up, kiddo!" Mom instructed, the moment I sank into the sofa. "Hair and makeup will be here in like ten minutes!"

"What? Why?"

"The *Variety* party is tonight! Now that I'm back in the city, you and I can go together. It'll be fun!"

Crapola. No wonder Steph had been messaging and calling all day. It had gotten so annoying, I almost threw my phone in the Hudson at one point. It then occurred to me that I had not one, but *two* parties to attend. The PDA party was that night and, in my emotional turmoil, it had completely slipped my mind. I mean, Jamie wouldn't die of disappointment if I were a no-show. I didn't know for sure if he was even going to be there or not. Not to mention, I was by no means emotionally equipped for a party in my current state, let alone two. No way, José. Alright, there was a slight way, José. What was my alternative? Getting all dolled up just to vacantly stare at camera flashes all night, pretending to be chummy with supermodels? No thanks.

Besides, PDA were almost definitely involved in this whole Stag thing. I might even come across something useful for Milo's investigation. If anything, I owed him that. It was the least I could do after springing a surprise breakup on him and secretly being in love with someone else. You know, all that minor stuff. At least this way I could deal with the guilt burning up my insides.

"Actually," I said to Mom, "can I meet you there?"

"But you're my date," she replied.

"I know! I'll just be a little late! I have to stop by another party first."

"What party?"

"A frat party."

Mom looked like she both surprised and slightly impressed. "That sounds exciting! Can I come?"

"God, no."

"I'm going to pretend I'm not offended by that."

"I'll bring you back a cute frat boy, I promise."

While Mom underwent her glam process, I began one of my own. I laced up my thigh-high boots and put on my leather skirt, pulling a navy NYPD t-shirt over my head. It was almost long enough to cover my skirt completely. Milo had bought it for me as a joke in my first week of officially moving cities, along with a shiny police badge that looked like it was made for toddlers. He had said it was the only time we'd ever be able to match our taste in fashion. Of course, I had never actually worn it, and looking down at it now sent a wave of sadness through my body. But it was only fair that I would wear it the night I tried to make things right for Milo. Poetic justice, or whatever my English teacher had always been yapping on about. I clipped the plastic police badge onto my skirt, and impatiently waited while the makeup team hurriedly worked their magic on my face.

"Did you say frat party or bachelor party?" Mom asked, eyeing my outfit up and down as I headed for the front door.

She was sitting in between a team of stylists and makeup artists, buzzing around the place with urgency and excitement.

"I'll change later, I swear! Leave my dress on my bed."

"I got your back, kiddo," Mom called out over the sound of the hair dryer. "Have fun! Don't do anything I wouldn't do!"

What *hadn't* my mother done? Steph was probably going to murder me for being late, especially with a rushed hair and makeup job. But in the meantime, I pushed her out of my mind.

I took a taxi to the frat party, hoping to avoid the extra attention from the partygoers by pulling up in a town car. The party was in the East Village, at some apartment building that looked an awful lot like the row of buildings right beside it. I tipped the driver extra as a thank-you for either not recognizing me at all, or not saying anything about it if he did.

I hugged my arms around myself and walked toward the party, cursing the chill in the air. The two boys standing at the top of the stairs were wearing NYPD shirts similar to mine. They had clearly lost some kind of bet to be waiting out in the cold while the party was raging inside.

"Invite?" one of them asked in a bored voice.

"I don't have one."

"It's invite only."

The other one squinted at me. "Holy shit. You're Gia Winters."

Wow. That was quick. The boys exchanged looks as if they needed each other's confirmation that they weren't dreaming.

"Is there any chance you want to let me in?" I asked with a sweet smile. "I'm freezing out here."

It took them a few more seconds to snap out of their trance.

"Yeah, of course!"

"Sorry! Come on in."

I was expecting them to simply let me through then continue ogling at me from behind. But they were practically tripping over their own feet while rushing alongside me to lead the way. Even without their help, I knew where the party was from the moment I stepped inside the building. The muffled sounds from the apartment at the end of the corridor was growing louder with each step. How these boys were planning on having a frat party without getting a few thousand complaints from their neighbors was beyond me. The door was already wide open, so I walked right in. The two boys from outside gently squeezed past me and rushed through the large crowd in excitement.

The apartment was much larger than I had anticipated, but that was probably because the couches had been pushed to the corners to allow more room for dancing. It was hard to tell exactly what it looked like with most of the lights off and fairy lights in its place. Above the plasma TV on the wall hung a velvet banner with Greek symbols that I presumed read Psi Delta Alpha. A makeshift bar lay on what looked like a dining table, holding red cups stacked in perfect pyramids. A small DJ booth had been set up in the corner of the room, where a lanky guy with headphones far too big for his face was mixing away on his MacBook with the concentration of a neurosurgeon. Toward the back, the apartment floor seemed to shift down a little onto a lower deck of sorts, and I could see at least four red doors, all closed. I took a wild guess that they were bedrooms. Almost everyone was dressed in some form of a police uniform, with the odd few wearing jeans or a tight black dress. There were more NYPD logos in this apartment than in an actual police precinct.

Nobody seemed to have noticed I had walked in, which was a luxury I knew wouldn't last long. I spotted a familiar face standing against the wall, sipping a drink out a plastic cup with an unimpressed look on his face.

"Waiting for someone?" I asked him.

Jamie looked at me with surprise, then curved his lips up. "Look who decided to show up."

"I thought about bailing. But why miss a good party, right?"

"I was going to ask if you were coming after class this week, but you ran out of there so quick I didn't get a chance."

"Yeah, sorry. I was in a rush."

"So," Jamie said, eyeing my makeshift police uniform. "Did you steal this outfit off your boyfriend?"

I involuntarily flinched on the word "boyfriend," giving him a tight smile to cover it up.

"What are you supposed to be, anyway?" I asked, ignoring his question.

Jamie looked down his black sweater, black jeans and black combat boots. "I'm a robber, obviously!"

"Obviously?"

"I'm wearing all black! It's like the universal thief uniform."

"Shouldn't you be wearing a mask? Or, I don't know. . . a beanie or a balaclava?"

"You know that there are sorority girls here, right? I'm not letting a balaclava ruin my chances tonight."

Couldn't argue with that logic.

"I thought NYU doesn't have frat houses," I said, posing it more as a question than a statement.

He leaned in a little closer so I could hear over the music.

"They don't," he replied. "But PDA do things a little differently. They usually rent a place every semester and make their own frat houses. Sometimes it's an Airbnb, sometimes they just rope some poor landlord into their whole innocent act. Most of the guys just stay in the dorms like everyone else. The whole thing is pretty dumb if you ask me."

"How do you know so much about these guys?"

"If you want any kind of social life at NYU, you're bound to come across the PDA at some stage. You learn about them pretty fast, trust me."

Our conversation was interrupted by the sound of the music being abruptly cut off, and all the lights turning on above us. Everyone looked equally confused as we did, groaning and calling out for the music to be turned back on. A guy wearing the exact gray NYPD shirt as the boys outside jumped onto a table, knocking over a few empty red cups in the process. He looked out to the crowd with a wide smile on his face.

"Ladies and gentlemen," he said dramatically. "We have a *very* special guest here tonight, all the way from Hollywood.

We'd like you to give Gia Winters a round of applause and welcome her to our celebration tonight!"

On cue, people began cheering and clapping the moment my name left his lips. They were all looking around, trying to spot me in excitement and surprise. It took about three seconds before their eyes collectively found me, and the cheers kicked up a level in volume. Oh, great. It's not like I didn't see this coming. I hadn't bothered with a fake mustache or a trench coat and oversized sunglasses. In fact, I had practically demanded I be let in because of my celebrity status. But even so, dread rushed through me when I saw the drunken college kids clapping like I was the night's entertainment.

"Welcome to the PDA!" the frat brother announced loudly, hopping off the table with a fist pump to the air.

The music immediately turned back on to the delight of just about everyone in the room around us. Jamie and I looked at each other with the same lack of zeal as the apartment went back to darkness.

"Guess we're giving up on the whole stealth thing for tonight, huh?" he said.

Oh yeah, big time. People weren't even bothering to be subtle or polite anymore. The flashes from their cameras were blinding me even from afar, and it seemed like everyone had somehow traveled an inch closer through their dancing, just to get a better snapshot or closer look at me. Guess this wasn't so different to the *Variety* party after all.

"Gia Winters!" The same frat brother from the table came sauntering over, the arrogant look still on his face. "I have to say, we're pretty honored to have you here."

Directly behind him were the two boys we had met outside, looking embarrassingly pleased with themselves. It was as if they had personally dragged me into the party as a gift for their king.

"Thanks for letting me through the security team," I replied simply.

"What brings you to our party tonight?"

There was a hint of genuine surprise alongside the curiosity in his tone.

"I heard that PDA runs the party scene at NYU. I thought I'd come see for myself."

The three boys exchanged looks that were a mixture of both pride and conceit.

"Well, then you heard right," King of the Frat Douches said. "If there's anything you need tonight, come find me. I'll be waiting."

Yeah, you'll be waiting a long time, bud. He gave Jamie a quick once-over and sent a sleazy wink in my direction before disappearing into the crowd again, his two friends at his side. With every fiber of my existence, I hoped that these guys were involved in Stag just so I could watch someone throw their asses in jail. I practically needed a shower after just one conversation.

"I'm starting to think this party was a bad idea," I said.

Jamie moved his head to the rap music playing. "At least the DJ knows what's up. How bad can it be?"

"Really bad" was my go-to answer. And it was made even worse by a slightly drunk Zoe appearing out of nowhere with a half-full plastic cup in her hand. She was dressed in a black SWAT t-shirt, tiny leather shorts, and heeled combat boots.

"Gia!" she exclaimed with delight, throwing her arms around me in a sloppy hug.

I gave her an awkward pat, trying desperately to avoid the contents of her cup from falling all over me.

"Hey, Zoe."

"I am *so* excited you're here!" She pulled away with a giant smile on her face. "I haven't seen you in, like, forever!"

"Yeah, things have been sort of crazy."

"I get it, don't worry. I'm totally going to die in my finals. I am *so* not prepared!"

Zoe's high-pitched giggle confirmed that this was definitely not her first plastic cup for the night. She locked eyes with Jamie and immediately straightened up, consciously running a hand through her hair. I fought back every urge to roll my eyes.

"Jamie, this is Zoe," I said. "She's my unofficial tour guide at NYU. Zoe, this is Jamie. He's in my Intro to Psych class."

"Oh my gosh, no way!" Zoe gushed. "That's so cool!"

Honestly, the level of coolness was a little disproportionate to the excitement she was showing. But the way she was sizing up Jamie in his black attire, it was clear she would have had the same reaction if I had said we were both collecting garbage together on the weekends.

"I've never seen you at a PDA party before!" she yelled to him over the music.

"Uh, yeah. They're not usually my thing."

"It can be a little full-on sometimes. But no one parties harder than the PDA, right?"

"Right," Jamie said, casting a quick glance at me. "So, who wants another drink?"

I practically shot my hand in the air and said, "Me! For the love of God, please."

Zoe held up her red cup. "I've still got some left."

"I'll be right back." Jamie raised his eyebrows at me, then disappeared into the crowd.

Zoe grabbed onto my arm the moment he was far enough and gave it a little squeeze. "Oh my gosh, he is *so* hot! Is he single?"

"Er, I'm not really sure."

"Aren't you guys friends?"

I was beginning to envy Jamie getting swallowed up by all the drunk college kids.

"I wouldn't really say we're friends," I told her. "More like casual acquaintances."

"Ugh, how come I don't have any hot casual acquaintances? And plus, your boyfriend is perfect. You're so lucky."

Oh boy, she didn't know the half of it.

Jamie returned with two plastic shot glasses in hand. "Drinks!"

Zoe grabbed one from him and downed it in one big gulp.

"I'll get you a refill!" She marched away before we could reply.

"She seems nice," Jamie said.

"She's a hugger. But she means well."

Beside me, someone else's flash from their phone went off, and I dug my nails into my palms.

"Time to get down to business," I told Jamie. "We need to

get our hands on some Stag."

"Boy, you sure know how to have a good time."

"Someone here definitely knows something, I guarantee it. We just need to find out who we can get the good stuff from."

"Slow down, Walter White," he said. "We can't just walk up to people and ask them if they have any of 'the good stuff.'"

"Why not?"

"Because they'll think you're a narc!"

"Look at this crowd! I'm surprised they aren't handing them out as party favors."

"I don't want the frat brothers to know we've been asking around about it. Just lay low for now. Let them come to us."

"And what are we supposed to do in the meantime?" I retorted. "Wait around and do shots?"

"You know what your problem is?" Jamie said.

I folded my arms across my chest. "Oh great. More life lessons."

"You're too uptight! You don't know how to just have a good time."

"We're not here to have a good time," I reminded him. "We're here to get information, and then get out."

"We literally just got here! You're not going to get any information from anyone standing in the corner looking all pissed off. Just relax!"

"I am relaxed!"

"Yeah, clearly."

"I'm not really in a party mood, okay?"

"Well this isn't exactly my ideal Saturday night either, but the music is decent, and the booze is free. So just chill out."

"Whatever," I said, deciding I could no longer hold back the eye roll.

"When was the last time you had fun?"

"I have fun all the time!"

"No, like *real* fun!" Jamie said. "When you don't have something nagging at the back of your mind. Or you're not just faking it for the cameras or to make your publicist happy or something. I'm talking stupid, mindless fun."

I opened my mouth to reply, but then closed it again.

I could have come up with a lie, but it wouldn't have been convincing at all. My mind had drawn a complete blank. How was this possible? Had I really not had proper fun in so long that I couldn't even remember it? As if I wasn't already having a terrible time, I now had to admit that Jamie Hart was right about my life.

"It's not as easy for me, okay?" I said finally. "I can't have the same fun other people can."

"Yes you can! You can have way more fun than anyone else because you can actually afford it!"

"Believe it or not," I told him, "money isn't always the answer to every life problem."

"Yeah, but it's the answer to most of them. I don't see any reason why you can't give yourself a night off and actually let loose a little."

This whole *Jamie making actual sense* thing was getting a little annoying. I had reached a new level of pathetic if I couldn't even remember the last time I had just enjoyed myself completely without some kind of stress or anxiety eating away at my insides. Not since moving to New York for sure, and probably right before Dad had announced we were getting bodyguards way back in March. I looked around the room. These people weren't worried or anxious or sad or annoyed. They were partying without a care in the world. If they could do it, then why couldn't I?

"Fine," I sighed. "Give me the damn shot."

Jamie handed over the little cup and watched me down its contents, looking pleased with his act of persuasion. As the liquid sent a trail of fire down my throat, I made a silent vow to myself. Tonight, even if it was just for a little while, I wasn't going to think about Milo or school or Steph or Frank Parker. I *definitely* wasn't going to think about Jack. I was going to have fun. Stupid, mindless, fun.

As it turns out, that's pretty easy to achieve at a rowdy college party. One shot turned into two, which eventually turned into four. And before I knew it, Jamie and I were standing in the middle of the living room, surrounded by a circle of people while we sang along to "In Da Club" like our lives depended on it. The *Variety* party didn't flash across my mind once. Jamie was actually a pretty decent dancer, and he knew all the lyrics to just about every hip-hop song that played. Zoe offered to teach me her twerking moves she'd picked up from YouTube tutorials, but we were both so bad at it, I think Jamie actually ruptured an internal organ from laughing so hard. I didn't even really mind that people were taking videos and photos of me. After a while, even they got a little bored of it when they realized I really wasn't that extraordinary. So this was what actual fun felt like, and it was amazing.

It was almost midnight when Jamie pulled me to one side and pointed toward the red doors at the back of the apartment.

"Gia, look," he said, holding my arm unsteadily. I wasn't the only one who had one too many cheap vodka shots.

I looked to where he was pointing to see one of the PDA brothers climbing down the small set of stairs onto a lower deck and disappearing behind one of the doors.

"I saw him hand some guy a little clear packet with a bull symbol on it."

My brain went on high alert mode, even though it was still a little fuzzy from all the partying.

"What? When?"

"Just now!"

"Are you sure?"

"Positive."

I looked at the red door thoughtfully. It felt like there was a thick fog pushing against my mind.

"We need to get behind one of those doors," I said.

"Agreed," he replied with a clumsy nod.

We were a little sloppy for spy work. But damn it, we were going to give it a try anyway. A moment later, the PDA brother emerged from behind the door, and Jamie snapped into action.

"Come on!" Jamie hissed.

"Where are you going?"

"I have a plan!"

He roughly pushed past a couple making out beside us and practically ran toward the end of the apartment. I followed as quickly and inconspicuously as I could in my four-inch

Tom Ford heels. Jamie clasped his hand on the frat brother's shoulder, saying something that made the guy groan. I couldn't hear over the music, but I tiptoed closer. The two boys began laughing together as if they were old friends, but Jamie locked eyes with me and jerked his head violently toward the door, motioning for me to sneak past them and into the room. I nodded, lowering the police cap on my head further over my eyes to shield my face in the dim light.

A second later, they were heading toward the dance floor, still enjoying whatever was so amusing to them. Jamie had his arm around the other guy's shoulders in one of those bro hugs, and he shot me a quick thumbs-up as he passed me. The frat brother had left without locking the door behind him. When I was sure nobody was watching, I crept inside.

The room illuminated to reveal two couches and a slightly worn-out beanbag placed in front of a medium-sized flat screen TV. The back of the room was lined with a long wooden desk that carried a held a series of books lined messily against the wall. A tall stack of video games lay on the floor below the TV, and a mini pool table was placed to my right. Right above it on the wall was a banner with Greek symbols, identical to the one in the living room. Underneath were a series of headshots of the PDA brothers, tacked to the wall in neat rows. There were about thirty faces smiling back at me. This wasn't a bedroom. It was a hang out spot.

Three knocks hit against the other side of the door, just loud enough to hear over the muffled sound of music. I hesitantly opened the door a tiny bit and eventually swung it half-open when I saw Jamie looking back at me through the crack.

"Your plan worked," I told him as he shut the door behind us. "What did you say to that guy, anyway?"

My ears were ringing a little from the sudden drop in volume.

"I just told him we were out of drinks and then made some joke about Danny being a lightweight."

"Who's Danny?"

"I don't know, there's usually some guy named Danny at these things. I took a stab in the dark."

Jamie looked around the room, nodding to himself as he took it all in. We were both way in over our heads, and not nearly sober enough for the task ahead.

"So where do we start?" he finally asked.

"You take the left, and I'll take the right?"

"Sounds good."

I rummaged through the junk on the right side of the desk. Trust me, there was a lot of it. Essay drafts and mismatched pieces of assignments lay scattered all over the table. I was by no means a model student, but at least I could find my homework if I needed to. There was an open packet of Sour Patch Kids sitting in the corner and a banana that had definitely been in the room a few days too long. I recoiled and tried my luck with the books. I didn't even know what I was looking for anymore, and every little thing seemed just a little funnier than it actually was. I guess we can thank the cheap alcohol for that.

"Find anything?" Jamie asked, kneeling down to check the cupboards below the desk.

"Nope." I flipped through the pages of a very complicated looking textbook that was covered in dust. "There's got to be *something* in this room!"

"Holy shit."

Jamie was frozen, staring at the contents hidden behind the open cupboard door.

"What?" When he didn't respond, I walked over to see for myself. "Holy shit."

Jamie and I had come face to face with the mother lode; a giant plastic bag full of tiny packets, each one marked with an orange bull logo. Even through all the packaging, I could see the tiny orange pills. There were at least a hundred of them.

Jamie reached his hand into the cupboard to pull out the bag, but I caught it midair.

"Don't!" I exclaimed. "We don't want any fingerprints on it."

"Right," he said, pulling his hand back to his side. "My bad. What do we do with it?"

"I don't know." I pulled out my phone from my leather skirt and handed it to him. "Maybe we should take a picture of it or something."

"Why, you want to tweet about it?"

"Uh, no. I was going to give it to the cops."

"Sure, sure."

"Just take the photo, would you?"

Jamie chuckled to himself as he obediently snapped a few shots of the plastic bag.

"This is insane," I said, opening the cupboards on my side of the desk just to be sure I hadn't accidentally missed a giant bag myself.

"These guys are a real piece of work."

The cupboards were filled with random junk, so I moved on to the drawer just above them. It, too, contained random pieces of paper, half-ripped envelopes, and capless pens. I was about to close it and move on when my hand landed on a small, brown, leather-bound notebook.

"What color was that notebook you saw at Andrew's bar again?" I asked.

"Um . . . brown, I think," he replied, still gawking at the bag of drugs in front of him. "Why?"

I held up the notebook to show him. "Does this look familiar?"

Jamie rose to his feet and took the notebook from me, examining it. "Kind of. I don't know, I can't really remember. I only saw it for a second."

"The police found a black notebook on Julian that night. Milo said it was a list of customers."

"Would they really keep an inventory?" Jamie asked, unconvinced. "They don't seem like the type of guys who want to keep their accounts in order."

"That's what one of the frat brothers told the police when he had been arrested."

Jamie handed my phone back to me and flipped open to the first page of the book, where three columns had been roughly drawn in blue pen. The first column didn't have a heading. The second and third were labeled R and S, respectively. The unlabeled column had a list of letters, two at a time. The next two listed numbers that I couldn't make any sense of. A good quarter of the notebook had been filled in this way.

"Any guesses on what this is?" I asked.

"No clue," Jamie replied. "Maybe it's part two of the inventory."

"Maybe you're right. Milo said he thinks the letters in the black notebook are initials. Maybe this is just part two?"

"But what do these numbers mean?"

"I have no idea. Some of these initials keep repeating."

"Maybe they're regular customers."

I studied the columns, trying to decipher what it all meant. The drinks were making me feel a little light-headed, but there was definitely some link to the black notebook. Only the numbers didn't seem to align with an inventory. None of them were high enough to represent any proper earnings. I looked at the wall of photos for more inspiration, hoping it could give me a clue.

"What are you thinking?" Jamie asked, following my gaze.

"I don't know . . ." I mumbled. "I don't think these are customers."

"You think these are the frat brothers?"

I looked down at the book again thoughtfully. "What do you mean?"

Jamie and I walked closer to the wall, standing directly in front of the head shots. He flipped to the first page of the notebook and ran his finger down the list.

"J.H.," he said, looking back up at the wall. His eyes settled on a photo and he gave himself a satisfied nod. "Julian Horowitz."

"The guy who got arrested?"

"Yeah."

I looked down at the notebook and chose another set of letters at random. M.B. matched with Max Baker. R.C. matched with Reed Cooper. D.G. was David Gomez. Tyson West, Connor Dunn, Kyle Chapman, Greg Butler. The list went on and on, and the names continued to match. We had cracked the first column. They were the PDA brothers.

"So what do these numbers mean then?" Jamie said. "Or these headings?"

"I don't know about that, but it definitely has something to do with dealing rather than buying."

"I can't believe this is actually happening," Jamie said. "But not all of these PDA members are in this notebook."

"Maybe not all of them are dealing."

"And I can't figure out who L.M. is. He keeps showing up but there's no one on the wall with these initials."

I scanned the photos just to be sure. You could still hear gleeful shouts and laughter above the music from the living room. Jamie was right. There was nobody on the wall with those initials.

"Horowitz . . ." he said quietly, looking lost in thought.

"What?"

"Horowitz. Julian Horowitz." Jamie closed the notebook and scratched his stubble thoughtfully. "Craig once told me that he has a step brother he completely hates. He always used to go on about how much of a pain in the ass he is. I can't remember his name, but he used to call him Horror-witz as a joke."

I was beginning to catch onto the same train of thought, but it was so ridiculous the idea was refusing to completely form in my mind.

Jamie looked at me, dead serious. "That's why Craig knows Julian. They didn't have a class together, like he said."

"What are you getting at?"

"I think Julian and Craig are step brothers."

We both let that revelation hang in the air for a few seconds, contemplating if it was just crazy enough to be true.

"What's Craig's last name?" I asked him, pulling the notebook away from his clutch.

"Montgomery."

"There's no C.M. in this notebook."

"But there's an L.M. that's still unaccounted for. M could stand for Montgomery."

"But that still doesn't explain the L." I shook my head, even though somewhere deep down I believed he was right. "Jamie, we're drunk! We don't know what we're saying. Besides, Julian isn't the only person in New York with the name Horowitz. It could just be a coincidence."

"Yeah, but it all matches just a little too well to be a coincidence. Come on, it's definitely suspicious. Maybe that's why I was invited out of the blue! Because of Craig."

He was right. The fog around my thoughts was beginning to clear a little, and things were starting to fall into place. It would mean Craig had a legitimate link to Julian, and it explained the Stag button on his bag. He could easily have left that invite under his own door for Jamie. He just pretended not to know anything when I started asking around about it because he was suspicious of why we were asking. He wasn't a member of the PDA, which meant no one would really suspect he was involved. With Julian out of the picture, he could step in and take charge. It was a radically wild theory, but somehow it made sense.

The sound of the doorknob turning sent a jolt of panic through both Jamie and me. We froze, staring at each other as the door opened a fraction.

"Nah," we heard someone call out over the pumping music. "It's in the kitchen!"

"Hide the book!" Jamie hissed frantically.

"Where!"

"Anywhere! Hide it!"

I flailed for a few seconds, my body unable to keep up with the thoughts racing through my brain. The door remained open just an inch, while the guy behind continued whatever conversation he was having. I pulled the t-shirt away from my body a little bit and tried to shove the notebook into my chest. It smacked me on the chin.

"Ow!"

"What are you doing?" Jamie whispered fiercely, watching me in disbelief.

"I'm trying to hide it!"

"It's not going to fit in there!"

I thrust the notebook in his hands with urgency. "You hide it then!"

Jamie rolled his eyes and scanned the room.

"Dude, I said near the sink!" the guy said, and the door opened an inch wider.

"Oh my god!" I hissed, practically jumping up and down in

panic.

Jamie ran to one of the sofas and roughly shoved the notebook under one of the seat cushions, pressing down on it just to be sure that it was completely hidden. The door swung completely open and the frat brother that Jamie had fooled before stared at us for a few seconds in surprise. Jamie and I were like statues, daring only to move our eyes to glance at one another, and then back at the frat brother. I identified him from the photos as one of the two Adams in the frat. He looked at me, then Jamie, then the cupboard door that remained wide open, revealing the large bag of Stag.

Adam backed out of the room without a word, slamming the door shut behind him. Jamie and I didn't move for a few seconds, registering what had just happened.

"I think he saw us," I said finally.

Jamie looked like he was ready to strangle me. "No *shit*, Sherlock!"

Almost immediately after, the door opened again. Adam was back, but he wasn't alone. This time he had brought the sleazy guy who had spoken to me before, Max. Two more frat brothers I had seen in passing throughout the night also followed. It wasn't until Craig walked into the room that my heart actually did a backflip. We had been right all along.

Craig closed the door behind him, drowning out the drunken cheering.

"Well," he said, looking from me to Jamie. "This is awkward."

Twenty-One

JAMIE LOOKED LIKE SOMEONE HAD PICKED UP THE Chrysler Building and hurtled it at him. Actually, he looked like he was struggling to stay awake, but that was probably just the alcohol starting to wear him down. I couldn't blame him.

"Craig, what the hell, man?" Jamie said incredulously.

"I think you should sit down."

"I think you should tell us what's going on."

Craig's expression darkened, and for some reason I felt a tingle of fear run down my spine.

"Sit down."

It wasn't a polite suggestion. It was a command. Jamie and I looked at each other briefly as we reluctantly obeyed. I carefully lowered myself onto the seat cushion, which held the notebook buried beneath it. I felt like the sofa was about to explode any minute and expose it. Craig and his band of PDA boys remained standing in front of us, looking all business and no play.

"Now would be a very good time to start talking," Jamie said impatiently.

"I could say the same thing to you," Craig replied. "How

much have you two figured out about our Stag operation?"

"I think it's pretty safe to say we didn't see *this* little surprise coming," I mumbled.

"You acted like you didn't know this entire time," Jamie said. "That day in Central Park, you didn't say anything."

Craig gave a little bark of laughter. "What were you expecting me to say? You show up randomly with Gia Winters of all people and start asking me all these questions. Was I just supposed to confess everything to you guys?"

Well, damn. I really thought he had bought that criminal justice research paper excuse. Guess not.

"Is Julian your step brother?" Jamie asked.

Craig's lips curved into the tiniest hint of a smirk. "Honestly, I would have been disappointed if you hadn't eventually made that connection, Jamie. You really gotta start paying more attention when I talk."

"Is that how you got involved in this whole thing?" I asked him. "Julian brought you in on it?"

"I guess you could call it a joint effort. We had the idea, but Julian knew he had the PDA brothers to back it up."

"That's right!" one of the frat brothers said proudly.

Read the room, dude.

"Julian didn't have the right mind-set for the business, right from the very start," Craig continued. "It took a lot of effort to make these things, and he was happy to just hand over the product to any hot girl he saw at a bar or party. He was wasting our potential, and it's that carelessness that got him arrested."

"Hey, that's not fair!" Max exclaimed angrily. "We wouldn't have any of this without Julian's help. He sacrificed a lot for his PDA brothers and for you, even though you weren't even one of us."

"Yeah! Julian is a hero!" Adam added.

"Julian is a dick, and you all know it!" Craig snapped. "So you can spare me all this brotherhood bullshit."

Well, gee. If I had aimed a camera at the boys, I was guaranteed to make a killing in the reality TV industry. The Real Frat Boys of New York City was a show just waiting to happen.

"Can you guys go fight in an alleyway some other time

please?" I said. "I have places to be."

"Yeah, what are we even doing here?" Jamie asked. "I can't have just *randomly* been invited to this party. So do you want to just get to the point already?"

The energy in the room was tense. The PDA boys may have been in business with Craig, but the angry looks on their facces made it obvious the interaction ended there. The boys took a few seconds to suppress their frustration before continuing.

"We have an offer for you," Max said. "Jamie, we'd like to invite you to become part of the team. It's easy enough. We just give you a certain number of packets to push, and you sell them each week. And you get a cut of all the earnings."

Jamie and I gaped at each other in surprise. I think I had to physically push my jaw up back toward the rest of my face from fear of losing it to the floor forever. Craig was just standing there looking at us both calmly, as if they were offering me a job as a car salesman.

"You want us to become drug dealers?" I asked, barely able to comprehend the sentence I had just spoken.

Craig laughed and shook his head. "Not you, Gia. Just Jamie."

"Why now?" I said. "You live with Jamie and you never once thought to bring him on board this whole time?"

"Normally I don't mix business with personal," Craig replied. "Julian was family, so I couldn't really avoid that. Plus, he was the one who had all the street connections. But now that you and Jamie know more than we can help, we figured that this would be a win-win for everyone."

"So then what's Gia's part in all of this?" Jamie asked.

"Yeah, what do you want from me?"

"You're too much of a risk," Max replied simply. "Your boyfriend is in the freakin' NYPD. When you started asking Craig all these questions, then showed up at Andrew's Bar, we figured something was up. When we invited Jamie, we guessed you'd probably come too."

"The media loves you, Gia. They're always looking for a new headline about you," Craig went on. "If you say a word about this to anyone, and we mean *anyone*, we're leaking a story. And trust me, your reputation won't recover from this one."

I could practically feel my insides shriveling up, remembering the media shitstorm that followed the night at Andrew's. I didn't even want to think about what the papers would say about me if this got out.

"Are you forgetting about the part where my boyfriend is a cop?" I said. "What makes you so sure I won't go to the police right now and tell them everything?"

The boys all exchanged grim glances. This possibility had definitely crossed their minds during the risk assessment.

"I think we can persuade you not to," Craig said vaguely. He pulled out his phone and pulled up a low-resolution photo of Jamie and I looking into a . . . wait, what was it? A cupboard?

Seeing the confusion on our faces, Craig said, "Little insurance policy. That cupboard over there is equipped with a small nanny cam, courtesy of eBay. We have all the fuel we need to make you look like you're just as guilty as the rest of us."

Crapola. Crapola. *Crapola!* Of course they would have a camera. I was actually a little bit impressed with their foresight. Maybe they weren't as dumb as I thought. Luckily, Jamie finally found his voice.

"Yeah, sorry, but I'm not really interested in dealing illegal drugs," he said, shaking his head.

"Well, I guess that leaves us with a slight problem," Craig replied with a grim nod. "Keeping quiet."

"I'm not going to say anything, man," Jamie told him. "Honestly, this whole thing was mostly a joke for me. Sure, I was a little curious. Then I really just wanted to know why I got invited to this party. But trust me, I'm done. You don't have to worry about me."

"It's not really you we're worried about, Jamie."

All eyes fixated on me. What, did they want me to sign a nondisclosure agreement or something? They could add it to the pile practically falling off Steph's desk.

I shrugged, trying to play it cool. "I'm not going to say anything either. Obviously you guys have thought this thing through. Kudos. Bravo. Ya' really got me."

"What if we don't believe you?"

"Well, that sounds like your problem, not mine."

I leaned back against the sofa, as if I was already bored with the conversation. In all honesty, I still felt sort of light-headed, and I wasn't entirely confident that these boys wouldn't try to completely destroy my reputation. But I was kind of tired of being held ransom to the media. No matter what I did or *didn't* do, the rest of the world would always have their opinions about me. Besides, the PDA brothers were nervous, and I knew they had more to lose here than I did.

"By the way," I said. "You guys didn't consider one teensy little scenario. I still have the upper hand here," I said.

"Oh yeah? How'd you figure that?" Max said. "Got any superpowers laced into those sexy boots?"

"Actually, I have something better." I smiled. "Your little brown notebook."

Jamie whipped his head around to face me with surprise. Obviously he wasn't a fan of my newfound confidence. The four boys gaped at me for a few seconds, processing what I had just said. Craig stalked over to the wooden desk without a word, throwing open the drawers and roughly pulling apart the contents as he rummaged through them.

"It's not here."

A look of panic flashed across the boys' faces.

"That's impossible!" Adam exclaimed. "It's been in there like, all week!"

"Well, it's not in there anymore!" Craig practically growled back.

Their attention turned back to me and Jamie, who was having not nearly as much fun as I was.

"Where's the notebook?" Craig demanded.

"Maybe if you asked nicely I would give it to you. It was a *very* interesting read. Which reminds me! Craig isn't your real name, is it?"

"What?"

"Your real name. What is it?"

"I . . . That's . . ." Craig looked flustered. "That's not important."

"Come on, *Craig,*" I probed. "Let's hear it. What are you

afraid of?"

Craig's eyes were burning into mine with fire. "Fine! I changed it to in high school to my middle name. You know how hard it is to get through high school with a name like Linus? There! Are you happy? Can we move on now?"

The frat boys snickered, but Jamie and I were too busy connecting dots in our minds. Linus Montgomery. L. M. Even inebriated, we weren't bad at this whole detective thing.

Craig, or should I say Linus, was clearly done with my games. Not only did I have his precious notebook, I had just undermined his authority in front of his henchmen. He leaned down closer to me, giving me a steely glare that actually made me a little nervous. Beside me, I could feel Jamie's body tense a little.

"Gia I'm not some criminal mastermind," Craig said in an eerily calm tone. "I'm not going to kidnap you and throw you in some warehouse. But I guarantee you're not leaving this room until I get that notebook back."

"If you guys are smart enough to start your own drug trade at school," I replied steadily, "you're smart enough to know you can't *make* me do anything. Who do you think you're messing with, huh? I'm Gia freakin' Winters! So go ahead and leak that bullshit story, but be prepared for hell to rain down on you. I have access to the best lawyers in this city and *lots* of money to spare."

The boys in the back of the room were eyeing each other uncertainly. They knew I was right. They were completely powerless here, nanny cam or not. Even eBay couldn't save them now. Only Craig was nodding to himself thoughtfully.

"You're right," he said. "We can't do anything to you. But we can hurt *him*."

Before I could even blink, he had dragged Jamie off the couch and thrown a fist directly at his cheek. He groaned in pain, holding onto the edge of the couch to steady himself. It took me a few seconds to overcome the shock before I jumped off the sofa and kicked into action. Somewhere from the living room, people were chanting "kiss, kiss, kiss!"

"Are you insane?" I screamed.

Every one of the frat boys was staring at Craig in surprise. Adam and Max didn't look like they necessarily minded this new strategy, but panic and confusion were still evident on their faces.

"Where's the notebook, Gia?"

"What the fuck, Craig!" Jamie yelled, clutching the side of his head. His lip was bleeding.

"Where's the notebook?"

I had to do some quick thinking. I could just whip out the notebook from under the couch and call it a day, but I couldn't let a piece of evidence like that go. Besides, I didn't like Craig. He was either more fearless than the others, or just plain stupid. Either way, he was a straight up d-bag, and it was worth overcoming my questionable lying skills to see him thrown behind bars. Plus, who names their kid Linus Craig Montgomery? Like, that's just setting him up for a loss in life. Amongst all the scrambled thoughts racing across my mind, I pulled out what I hoped was a convincing lie.

"It's in the NYU library!"

Craig froze, narrowing his eyes at me suspiciously. "How did you get your hands on it in the first place?"

"One of your PDA boys sold you out!"

"Which one?" Max said angrily. This was his jurisdiction.

"Like I remember his name, jeez!"

Jamie was resting his head on the couch cushion, sitting on the floor. He was still groaning softly beside me.

"I don't believe you," Craig said. "Why would he give you the notebook?"

"I don't know," I replied. "After looking at the notebook, it's pretty clear not everyone in PDA is involved, which is probably why you've had to start recruiting outside the fraternity. Maybe he wasn't okay with what was happening. Or maybe he just thinks you're a grade-A asshole!"

"Why would you put it in the library and not give it to your boyfriend?" Max asked, still skeptical.

"I have my reasons," I told them, trying to keep the shakiness out of my voice.

"I don't believe her," Adam said doubtfully.

"If the cops had your notebook, you wouldn't be standing here right now. Whether you believe me or not is up to you."

The boys fell silent, weighing up the likelihood of my story being true. There were definite plot holes, but I was counting on them taking the risk.

"Where in the library?" Craig finally asked.

"I just threw it in the returns box."

"It could be on any shelf right now!"

"Look, I'm telling you everything I know. I can't give you any more than that."

"Grab the Stag," Craig said to the frat boys, and one of his henchmen obediently ran over to the open cupboard.

"Where are you going?" I asked, watching them all head for the door.

"I meant what I said," Craig replied roughly. "You don't leave until we get that notebook."

"This is ridiculous!" Jamie said, propping himself up to a standing position.

"You can't do that! That's, like, false imprisonment!" I yelled as the boys filed out the door. The sound of blaring rap music flooded the room.

"Oh yeah?" Craig raised his voice over the noise. "Watch me."

And with that, the door slammed shut behind him.

Jamie ran to the door, giving the handle a hard yank. It didn't budge. He pressed his elbow against it, banged his fist against the wood and screamed some colorful curses. The door remained locked.

"You just *had* to piss him off," he said, wheeling around to face me with a steely glare. "Why couldn't you just give him the notebook instead of making up that insane excuse?"

"Insane? That was some of my best lying!"

"Well done! You've really nailed it this time!"

I pushed him aside and tugged on the doorknob. Once again, nothing happened.

"HELP!" I screamed, slapping my palms against the door.

"HELLO? ANYONE? HELP!"

Only the sound of people singing along to Rihanna responded to my calls for help. I yelled a few more times—rattling the doorknob so hard it almost fell off. It was no use. We were well and truly stuck.

"The library's probably closed," I said, talking more to myself than Jamie. "They'll have to be back soon."

"Maybe," he responded. "Or maybe they'll be back five hours from now. And in the meantime, we're just stuck in here! This is all your fault!"

"My fault?"

"Yes, your fault! Ever since you asked me about that stupid Stag button, everything went to shit!"

"Oh right, because you didn't do anything to help? You're the one who brought Craig to Central Park out of the kindness of your heart. And you're the one who told me about this party!"

"Okay, fine! I may have contributed. But whatever's happening right now is completely on you!"

"Can we stop arguing and try to get out of here please?"

"Sounds good to me!" Jamie held out his palm toward me. "Give me my phone."

I looked at his palm with a mixture of annoyance and confusion. "Why would I have your phone?"

"Because you bet that random guy you could guess the exact population of Australia and then when you looked it up, you were, like, forty-five million off?"

"That wasn't me; that was Zoe!"

"Awesome," Jamie said sarcastically, dropping his hand to his side. "So, Zoe has my phone."

I gave an exaggerated sigh and reached for my phone.

"I only have like 3 percent battery," I told him. "But it should be enough to make a call."

I ignored the twelve missed calls from Steph and pulled up my contact list, scrolling through the favorites. I *really* should have bothered to charge my phone after spending the whole day out. On top of that, the service in the room was terrible, but hopefully manageable for one phone call. My finger hovered over Milo's name as I stared at my screen for a few seconds in realization.

"What?" Jamie asked, watching me.

"I can't call my boyfriend."

"Why not? Isn't he a cop?"

"Um, yeah. I just can't call him."

Jamie was giving me a look that told me his facial injuries weren't the only cause of his current pain. But I couldn't help it. I couldn't call Milo. It would be the first time since the breakup, and I couldn't hear his voice without emotionally preparing myself. What would I even say? "Hey, remember me? Your ex-girlfriend who literally just broke your heart and is now calling for a favor?" No, thank you.

"Call 911 then!" Jamie said.

"But . . . what if they send Milo?"

"Oh my god, are you kidding me? I don't care if there's trouble in paradise, just call the goddamn police!"

I blinked at him in silence. He was right. I should just call Milo and get us out of this god-awful place. But somehow my body was struggling to catch up with my brain.

"Gia!" Jamie gave an exasperated sigh. "Okay, fine! Call one of your friends. That blond guy!"

"Right! Jack!" I reflexively flicked to his name and then froze again, my finger suspended above my phone.

"Now what?" Jamie asked, studying my face.

"I can't call him either."

"What, did you two break up too?"

"It's . . . complicated."

Jamie squeezed his eyes shut for a minute, no doubt trying to teleport to his happy place. I let him take his time. I didn't want him to strangle me. Unfortunately, my battery was less patient and had now dropped to 1 percent.

"Gia," Jamie said, trying desperately to sound calm. "I don't care if you call the National Guard or the freakin' White House. Just call *someone!*"

"I'll call Reggie!"

"Yes! Reggie! Call Reggie!"

I dialed Reggie's number, impatiently tapping my heel against the floor as it rang. The sound of his voice mail eventually filled my ears. I hurriedly crafted a simple but direct text to Reggie. It said: *SOS LOCKED IN FRAT HOUSE. PDA ARE EVIL.*

And then I added a lot of shocked-face and pill emojis and clicked the button to share my location so he would know the exact address. God bless modern technology. Jamie and I were watching the message send when my phone screen went completely black and lifeless in my hands. We blinked at it for a few seconds.

"Did it send?" Jamie asked.

"I don't know. It was definitely sending."

"But we don't know if it actually sent?"

"No."

I pressed the home button. Nothing happened. I pressed the lock button. Nothing happened.

"Well this is just GREAT!" Jamie yelled, livid.

He kicked at the door, but it remained firmly locked in place.

"I'm sure it sent," I said, trying to convince myself of the best.

"Well you better hope your emojis didn't slow it down, or else you'll be spending the night in a makeshift frat house!"

"Yelling at me isn't going to solve your problems!" I snapped. "You're getting on my nerves."

Jamie let out a humorless laugh, pacing in front of the door.

"You're unbelievable. You think that because you've got this perfect life, you just have everything figured out. You don't even bother to worry about the consequences to things you say and do!"

"That is *way* out of line."

"Is it? Because it sounds pretty accurate to me! Little Miss Millionaire has her daddy or her publicist bail her out of every situation. She doesn't even need to use her brain!"

Even with all the commotion from outside, I could practically hear something inside of me snap. I marched right up to Jamie and glared at him, still having to look up a bit even though I was in high heels.

"You think my life is so perfect?" I demanded, and Jamie

raised an eyebrow. "You think I'm so lucky? You don't know the first thing about my life! So let me tell you just how *lucky* I am. I spent most of my childhood either watching my parents fight or being taken care of by nannies while my parents were out at parties or on movie sets. I spent my teenage years watching the details of their divorce being plastered on every newspaper, and only seeing my mother twice a year with difficulty! That is, of course, only if she could squeeze me in between hair appointments. My dad became a complete control freak, and don't even get me started on my brother."

"Yeah—" Jamie began dismissively.

"No, listen!" I said angrily. "On the biggest night of my life, some lunatic kidnapped me, almost killed my dad, and then shot my bodyguard right in front of me. I'm still afraid to go to sleep because every night he makes a guest appearance in my dreams. And even now, half the world thinks I made the whole thing up! I'm definitely going to fail finals, and I've just about given up on next year too, what with my publicist constantly shoving more contracts down my throat every day! My two best friends live on an entirely different coast, and they've probably made new friends and soon they'll forget all about me. I dumped the only truly decent guy I think I've ever met. And for what? Some jerk with the emotional maturity of a four-year-old! So if I have to hear about how lucky I am, or how perfect my life is *one* more time, I am going to well and truly LOSE. IT."

Jamie looked slightly alarmed for my mental health now. "Okay, I didn't need a whole rundown."

"Now," I said firmly, "you stay on that couch, and I'll stay on this one. Unless of course, you want me to continue?"

"Uh, no. I'm good, thanks."

I stalked over to the couch without the notebook, aggressively rearranged its pillows, flopped down, and waited for my adrenaline to drop a little. Jamie didn't say anything. He reluctantly sat on the other sofa, eyeing me with the same caution a deer would show around a mountain lion. I clenched my eyes shut and focused on breathing in and out, trying to block out the sounds from the party and my own heartbeat pulsating in my ears.

At some stage I think the breathing exercises, alongside the panic and exhaustion, helped put me to sleep. Because when I opened my eyes next, it felt like it had only been a few minutes. But I knew it had been far longer. My head felt heavy, and my vision was slightly distorted. Jamie was still sitting on the other couch, looking half-asleep as he mindlessly stared at the TV screen.

"How long have I been asleep?"

Jamie flicked his eyes from the TV to his watch. "About an hour and a half," he replied, sounding utterly uninterested.

"Did Craig come back?" I asked.

"Nope. I think the neighbors complained, because I could hear some yelling going on and they eventually turned the music down. But don't even bother shouting for help again. I already tried that and it didn't work. Those people out there don't even know what their own names are anymore."

A wave of disappointment crashed over me, and I felt the panic rising back in my throat. But I forced it down, trying to keep positive. Where were the frat boys? Surely they would have been back by now.

"So . . ." I said, just to avoid my own thoughts. "Anything good on TV?"

"At this time, there're only pornos and random shows about truck drivers."

The image on the TV screen showed a pair of burly men dressed like lumberjacks riding a gigantic truck across a land completely covered with snow.

"I see you decided to go with the truck drivers then."

"I'd already seen the pornos."

Jamie finally looked at me, giving me the closest thing he could to a smile. I gave him one back. Apparently the only ice left in the room was now being driven over by lumberjacks.

"I found a phone charger, by the way," he told me, pointing below the TV to where a bunch of wires were lying close to a outlet. "I was going to grab your phone but . . . you know."

He would have to basically reach into my skirt to get it, which might have been an awkward conversation to have later.

I pulled out my phone and plugged it into the charger. The red battery symbol appeared immediately, and I gave a sigh of relief.

"Now we just need to wait until it turns back on, and we can get out of here."

With nothing else to do, I slunk back to my couch and collapsed onto it. It was at least five full minutes before Jamie finally said something.

"I always believed you. You know, about the whole the Golden Globes thing. I always believed you."

I looked at him with surprise. "Really?"

"Yeah. I never believed for one second that you made the whole thing up."

"Oh . . . well. Um, thanks."

I wasn't really sure what to say. This was probably the first decent conversation we'd ever had. But apparently Jamie wasn't done pulling out the surprises.

"I think I owe you an apology, Gia. I was kind of a jerk to you, and I shouldn't have been. People were always talking about you, and your face was just *everywhere.* I guess I thought I already knew you before I had even met you. And for some reason, it sort of pissed me off when you didn't really match the description I had made of you in my head. I know that makes no sense, but I'm sorry. I think I was honestly just a little sick of everyone talking about you all time, even though it's not really your fault."

Well, whaddaya know? I guess Jamie Hart did have a heart after all.

"If it makes you feel any better," I told him, "you're not the only one who's sick of it. And I'm sorry too. You weren't completely wrong about me. I think I've just been feeling a little lost since I got here, and I'm still trying to figure out what version of myself I like best."

"You're allowed more than one version."

"Yeah?"

"Yeah." Jamie gave me a nonchalant shrug. "And if you ever wanted to hang out, I'd be down. I can't help you with your love life drama, but I know some good spots around town."

I raised an eyebrow, giving him a victorious grin. "Are you

saying you want to be friends?"

"No," Jamie replied, but he was smiling a little. "I'm saying if I'm not going to make any money off you, you might as well buy me a drink. Anything but coffee! I don't want to risk the third-degree burns."

"Deal."

My phone let out a little chime, interrupting our little bonding session. Jamie and I were off the couches in a millisecond, eagerly waiting to see if our escape route was finally within reach.

"Four missed calls from Reggie," I said, reading the screen. "The text must have sent!"

"Call him back!"

My finger had barely found the call button when the door swung open, sending Jamie and I back on our feet with alarm. I let the phone fall out of my hands as I watched Craig, Max, and Adam enter looking completely exhausted and equally frustrated. There was no sign of the other two boys.

"Okay, I'm done messing around," Craig announced, slamming the door shut behind him. It hit the frame with a slight rattle. "Give me the notebook. NOW."

Jamie and I exchanged a contemplative look. We could just give him what he wanted and be out of here in a second. But if Reggie knew where I was, then he was coming. And even if we did give them the notebook, I didn't really trust them to let us just walk out with a wave goodbye. That book was basically the key to everyone involved in the entire Stag business. It was a vital part of Milo's investigation. I wasn't sure what the right move was.

"It wasn't in the library?" Jamie asked Craig.

He had made the decision for me. Craig was done playing the game, but Jamie wasn't. And I was so insanely grateful.

"Don't give us that bullshit!" Max replied. "Just give us the notebook!"

"You know this is the twenty-first century, right?" I said, stalling for time. "Have you ever heard of a computer? It might come in handy next time you want to hide important information like this."

"You know how easy it is to hack into files?" Craig asked, looking at me as if I had just suggested we all join a salsa dancing class. "The whole point of the notebook was to protect ourselves. Do you think I'm an idiot?"

"Do you really want me to answer that?"

"That's it!" Craig declared, practically stomping closer to me. "I'm done with you."

"Whoa, whoa, whoa!" Jamie stuck an arm out in from of me, as if creating a barrier between Craig and I. "Back off, man. Back. Off."

The sound of music abruptly cutting off caused us all to freeze, as we heard a mixture of groans and protests coming from the rest of the apartment. We all looked at each other for answers, as if we weren't standing in equal confusion. The door burst open and one of the frat brothers from before appeared, looking frantic.

"The cops are here!" he yelled. "Real ones!"

And with that he disappeared, leaving the door wide open.

Twenty-Two

JAMIE AND I DIDN'T EVEN HESITATE. WE BOTH LAUNCHED ourselves at the door, not even bothering to remove the notebook from its hiding spot. The frat boys didn't know it was there, which meant we could always come back for it. Only, the PDA boys were ready for us and were standing by the door like a barricade. Adam swung his fist at Jamie but missed. Jamie swung back and *didn't* miss.

"Where do you think you're going?" Max asked as I squeezed past him.

I felt him roughly wrap one arm around me from behind, trying to slide the other hand up my skirt. Uh-uh. Not today, Satan. Not today, or ever. I stomped down directly on his foot, piercing it with my stiletto heels. He yelled out in pain, and I took the opportunity to swing my head back to try and head-butt him just like Jack had taught me. I was off by about an inch, but it didn't matter. At that point I was just flailing, looking for any way to cause him harm. In the movies, they always make the fight sequences look so slick. In real life, it's mostly just a lot of unintelligent screaming and clumsily throwing your hands around. Beside me someone let out a grunt, but I couldn't tell if it was Jamie or not. I didn't stop to check. Instead, I whirled around, looked Max right in the eye and gave him a thunderous slap across his cheek.

"OW!" he cried out, putting a palm over his injury. "You bitch!"

But I wasn't done. This dude had pissed me off one too many times that night. I placed one hand on his shoulder as if to lock him into position, and with all the power of Queen Beyoncé, I lifted up my knee and aimed it right at his groin. You know. His Dolce and Gabbanas. Not that they're remotely worth as much. Max keeled over with a groan and dropped to his knees right in front of me. It was a position I found extremely satisfying.

"Touch me again," I told him, "and you'll be kissing your reproductive system goodbye."

I guess the threat sort of worked, because he just looked up at me in this pathetic *I will never feel joy again* kind of way. I, on the other hand, felt *fabulous.* Exhausted and emotional, but completely exhilarated. But my feelings of victory were short-lived when I saw Jamie still struggling with the two boys. They were sort of throwing punches in every direction, like it was a cartoon fight where everyone ends up in a giant hazy ball and all you can see are limbs sticking out. I decided that clawing at Craig's smug face was probably worth ruining my manicure over and launched myself at him, tugging him away from Jamie. I was yelling, he was yelling. We were basically all yelling, and there were hands and french-manicured nails scratching in every direction. And then suddenly the police were yelling, prying us apart from one another as they rushed into the room.

"Alright, alright. Let's break it up!"

A group of officers dressed in almost identical outfits to some of the ones I saw earlier began breaking up the fight, tearing us away from each other.

"Okay, party's over, people!" a tough-looking officer said. She grabbed Craig by the shirt and practically hauled him to one side as he resisted angrily.

The cop next to her pulled me out of the room, firmly instructing that I calm down. Another officer was holding

Jamie back, talking his anger down. Jamie shrugged his arm off roughly, but didn't attempt any more hits. His face was flushed, his lip was bleeding again, and his left cheekbone definitely looked like it was beginning to bruise. But he was still a step up from Craig's bleeding nose, which I caught a glimpse of before he was pulled to one corner of the room. Max was being held up by two officers practically peeling him off the floor. There was so much commotion and noise from the police, I hadn't even noticed Reggie burst into the apartment and launch toward me.

"WHOSE BODY DO I HAVE TO BREAK?" he announced to the now almost empty apartment, standing in his warrior stance.

"Sir!" the officer next to me said sternly. "I'm going to need you to calm down."

"Reggie, I'm okay!" I told him, still a little breathless from the fighting. My heart was still crashing against my chest with the adrenaline coursing through my body.

Reggie placed a hand to his broad chest and let out a sigh of relief. Amongst the chaos, my eyes settled on a familiar face. It felt like a wave of emotion crashed over me as I watched Milo rush toward me, pushing past his colleagues in alarm. By now even Max had been hauled out the front door, and I could still hear the officers yelling instructions to whoever was left in the house.

"Gia! Are you okay? Are you hurt?" Milo exclaimed, scanning me with alarm.

While the officer next to me tried to convince Reggie not to kill any of the frat boys, Milo put a protective arm around me and pulled me to one side. I wasn't sure what to say or how to say it. We hadn't spoken since the breakup, and this wasn't exactly how I expected we would ever reunite.

"Milo, I'm fine," I finally said, as steadily as I could. "I'm not hurt or anything."

Unless you count my feet, but the footwear had been my own choice. And the scratch on my arm was bleeding a little. My hair looked like a train wreck, but I don't think you can count that as an injury. Milo looked unconvinced.

"Reggie called me and said you were in trouble," he told me. "He saw your message a while after you sent it, and when he called back you didn't answer. We didn't know if you were still at the same location you sent him, but we checked *Gia Watch* and—"

"What?" I said sharply.

"*Gia Watch.* Oh right, you have a stalker website, in case you didn't know."

"I thought it was shut down!"

"It definitely still exists, because there are like a bunch of photos of you from tonight on there. Only now I think it's called *Winters Watch.* Anyway, no one posted about you leaving so we thought we'd try our luck."

"It was smart of you to check," I told him.

"Thanks," Milo said, looking a little more at ease. "You know, noise complaints are sort of my specialty."

Even though it had been weeks since I last saw him and it hadn't exactly ended as well as I would have liked, I broke into a smile. He was just that type of guy—the kind that made you want to love him. And I did love him, just not in the way I should have. I pulled him into a hug, but it wasn't filled with romance and longing. It was genuine, and it was grateful.

Oh my gosh!" I exclaimed, suddenly remembering the notebook.

I peeled away from Milo and rushed back into the room where Craig was standing in one corner listening to two officers with evident annoyance on his face. On the other side was Jamie, talking to an officer with a small notepad in his hand. I pulled the large seat cushion off the other sofa and threw it onto the floor. The pesky brown notebook sat exactly where I had left it a few hours before, looking completely innocent. Craig was glaring at me from across the room, his jaw clenched. I handed the notebook to Milo with relief, giving Craig a little victorious smile as it slipped completely out of his control.

"What's this?" Milo asked.

"You know that brown notebook from the bar?" I replied. "The one Jamie saw?"

"The one we never found?"

"We found it."

I explained everything, from that day at the library when Jamie showed me the invite to a few hours ago, when we had found the bag of pills and the notebook. I told him how I lied to throw Craig off, and how the coded initials matched most of the names on the wall.

"This is incredible Gia!" Milo said, looking up from the pages. "But . . . why did you do all of this? I mean I know you have a gift for investigating things when I *really* don't want you to. And I wish you had told me about all of this sooner. But why go through all the trouble of getting this?"

"For a lot of reasons," I said truthfully. "And I didn't do it alone, Jamie helped. He's actually not so bad once you get to know him."

"So, you don't need me to have him arrested anymore?"

"The idea isn't completely off the table, but I thought I'd give him another shot."

"How generous."

"Honestly, you were the main reason, Milo," I said. "I wanted to help you. You're a great cop, and you deserve to be recognized for more than just helping old ladies cross the street."

Sure, it wasn't as altruistic as that, but I had done a lot of lying tonight, and this was the truth. Now he could finally get the credit he worked so hard for.

"I don't really know what to say," he replied quietly, clutching the notebook tightly. "Thank you."

"You're welcome."

"Look, I know this isn't the right time or place to say this, but . . ." Milo began, and my stomach filled with dread. I already knew where this was headed, and I wasn't sure I had the answers figured out. "I think it's worth giving us another try. I mean, okay we fought a little. And I know I'm always busy and I could have been a little more sensitive to your . . . status. I'm sorry for everything. But I promise, I can try and be a better boyfriend."

"Milo stop," I said firmly. "You don't need to apologize. A lot went wrong with us, but a lot also went right. You were amazing. You're sweet and considerate. You're the perfect boyfriend."

We both looked at each other, saying things with our eyes that we probably couldn't say out loud.

"But . . ."

"But . . ." I sighed. "I guess you aren't perfect for me."

And maybe that was the issue. I was always looking for perfect where it just didn't exist. Perfect hair, perfect body, perfect family, perfect boyfriend, perfect love. Living in Hollywood had always taught me that anything less just wasn't acceptable. But there was no such thing as perfect, and no mansion or amount of money could change that. Maybe I was crazy. I was probably never going to find anyone as great as Milo. But I knew deep down, there was another problem that hadn't been fully addressed. Jack. As much as I hated him in that moment, unless I woke up tomorrow after the Men in Black wiped my memory of him completely clean, that little dilemma wasn't going to solve itself. He was always going to be the "but" at the end of the sentence. Milo looked a little disappointed, but I think he knew deep down that this outcome was inevitable.

"Don't be a stranger, Gia Winters," he said.

He gave me one final, dimpled smile before he switched back into cop mode, disappearing out of the room. As cliché as it sounds, we really were better as friends. Maybe that wouldn't happen right away, but I couldn't live in a world that didn't have Milo Fells in it. He was a good person, far better than half of the people I had ever met, and I truly wanted the best for him. Truly. Plus, it goes without saying that being friends with a NYPD police officer could come in handy. I clearly seem to land myself in dangerous situations a lot. Like, way more than the normal amount. Oh man, I need to get my life sorted out.

I was exhausted and slightly emotional, but I answered the police's never-ending list of question with as much detail as I could. They eventually took mercy on me, strongly recommending I go home and "try to stay out of trouble." They didn't have to ask me twice.

"Hey," Jamie said, catching up to me just as I was about to

go find Reggie. "Found your phone."

I took it from him with a sigh of relief. "Thanks."

"So, I guess we make a pretty good team, huh?"

"I guess we do."

"I'm going to need to apply for a new roommate now, aren't I?"

"No shit, Sherlock."

Twenty-Three

Needless to say, the story about the PDA fight made front news coverage for the whole week, as did the slightly questionable videos of me dancing. Funnily enough, the nanny cam footage never saw the light of day. Apparently, kneeing a guy in his ding-dongs and then clawing at another dude's face doesn't go down too well with the NYPD. But holding someone in a frat house as a prisoner is even less favorable, so I didn't really get more than an eyebrow raise at the end of it all. That, and the brown notebook had basically cracked the entire Stag investigation, so they kind of owed me.

When Reggie finally dropped me back home, it was past three in the morning. Mom was up and waiting when I returned. After the initial panic-stricken hugs I received, she calmed down when she saw I was in one piece. The thirty-six calls I got from Dad the following morning I could have done without. It seemed that even halfway across the country, I still managed to find new ways to torture the man.

On the plus side, the Stag investigation had led to the closure of the PDA frat, and the fight against the Greek system was growing in momentum every day. I had all but given up on proving to the internet and press what side of the scandal I was on. Haters were gonna hate, no matter how hard my PR team worked. That now included Zara, the adorable new assistant I had just hired. Steph had sent me a list of potential candidates, but I insisted that I ultimately got the final say. If we were going to work together, then there was going to be *huge* change in strategy. There were going to be huge changes in my life all around, starting with the woman in the mirror. Actually they started with the mirror itself, because I moved it around when I redecorated my entire room. I couldn't keep seeing the penthouse as "Mom's place" anymore. My heart belonged in California, but New York was going to be home for the next few years, and it was about time I made it my own. So, I got rid of the stupid beige sheets and replaced them with pink ones, tossed out the Eiffel Tower picture above my bed, and hung a canvas painting of Audrey Hepburn in its stead. There, just like old times.

Any minute I wasn't turning my room upside down, I was studying. Like actually studying and only planning my birthday celebrations for next month *a little.* Okay a lot. The psychology presentation had gone off without a hitch, much to my relief. The nerves just disappeared once I realized I actually knew what I was talking about. Professor Michaels was so pleased, I was afraid he would start quoting movies again. Hannah definitely still hated me, but even she had given a half-hearted "Good job, Gia." Even so, I was never going to pass with my attendance rate, so Mom had to go in and beg my professors. Half of them reminded her that special consideration wasn't given to students based on celebrity status. The other half asked for an autograph. Either way, they all eventually agreed to pass me if I aced the finals. With the fear of having to repeat classes at the forefront of my mind, I hunkered down and got to work. And trust me, there was a lot of it. It felt like I had five years' worth of readings and lectures to catch up on, and not enough brain space to store it all. But once I started to understand what the professors were droning on about, I actually found the content interesting. Well, some of it, anyway. Mom was right. I was a lot smarter than I gave myself credit for. Maybe next time I was invited to some fancy cocktail party I could even survive one conversation without making a complete fool of myself.

Not that I even had anyone to invite to those parties. Except maybe Jamie, who I guess was the first proper friend I had made since moving to New York. At least I had my mother for company. After spending months on her European adventure, it seemed she was done with all the hot, younger men and partying. Well, not entirely. I'm pretty sure she had a new life goal to date Tom Cruise, who she casually described as "looking pretty good these days." I wholeheartedly agreed. Plus, he wasn't a twenty-two year old Italian model, so I was fully on board. Before, I couldn't get one second alone with my mother, and now she was always around, asking if I wanted to go to the Russian Tea Room or help her go rug shopping. It was an unfamiliar feeling, but it felt great.

I even started showing up to my sessions with Dr. Norton. It took a lot of whining and, at times, physical pushing from Mom to get me there, but I knew it was the right decision. I was slowly working on breaking down the mental block and trying to keep an open mind. Dr. Norton was definitely surprised, but she made a point not to show it much.

"I'm ready to talk about Frank," I told her. "I don't really know how to do this whole doctor-patient thing. But I don't want to spend the rest of my life running away from my nightmares and being afraid. What happened, happened. And it's time to move on now. So I'm ready to ask for help, if you'll give it to me."

Dr. Norton had just stared at me for a few seconds, and then given me a soft smile.

"Okay," she said. "Let's talk."

And we did. It was a little awkward at first, and I spent the first few sessions eyeing the exit. But I eventually found myself actually not hating the tight bun on her head anymore. How did she even get that bun so perfect anyway? My hair just fell out every time I tried. Talking about the Golden Globes incident wasn't easy, and despite Dr. Norton's encouragement, I wasn't fully convinced I would ever truly move on from it. But asking for help didn't make me feel as weak anymore. It was actually a big relief.

I even surprised myself by telling her about Milo and Jack. I wasn't planning on relaying the entire saga, but once I started, the words just began to spill on their own.

"Falling in love hurts," I told her. "I'm not sure it's worth the hype."

"Falling in love means allowing yourself to be vulnerable with somebody else," she had replied. "It means not only embracing your faults, but sharing them. Falling in love hurts, but it's *definitely* worth the hype."

It was a nice explanation, but I was yet to be entirely convinced.

I was finally starting to warm up to New York, but the city was anything but warm. It had already snowed a few times, and even running to the car in the icy weather was a feat. Mom usually visited for the holidays, but this year we were doing things differently. Mike and Dad were coming to visit Mom and me, and we were going to spend Christmas in New York. And even though I missed LA with every fiber of my being, there really is no better place to celebrate the holiday season than New York City. The manic shopping rush, the chilly wind, the Rockefeller tree, the Saks decoration display. There was nothing quite like it. It was like everyone was taking time out of their busy schedules to collectively shove each other out of the way for holiday sales. It was a beautiful thing really.

Well, I suppose not *everyone* was taking time out of their schedules. Apparently Jack was so busy, he hadn't bothered to call or text even once since our fight. Whatever. I probably would have deleted the message or ignored the call anyway. It's not like his stupid sweatshirt haunted me every time I opened my closet or anything. I mean, how hard is it to just pick up the damn phone? You literally have to tap at like, five buttons! To be honest, I'm not sure what I was expecting. Okay, yes, I am. I wanted romance and sunshine and cute little birds chirping around my head. Seriously, was that too much to ask? But for all I knew, he and Lucy had reconciled and were gazing at each other lovingly somewhere.

But I tried not to think about that too much. For the first

time in a long time, I actually felt like I had some control over my life. I had finalized my campaign with Covergirl, Drake had referenced me in his latest song, and my friendship with Aria and Veronica was as strong as ever. It was going to take a little more than geography to tear us apart. All in all, things could have been worse. And maybe it was the holiday spirit or the fact that my family felt whole for the first time in a long time, but I was happy.

In fact, I was so immersed in my newfound happiness that I didn't even bother yelling about the New York traffic, which was at a complete stop. Poor George was trying to hold in his own road rage while aggressively pushing down on the horn every two seconds, as if the cars in front of him would magically disappear if he pressed hard enough. Reggie was in the seat next to me, tapping his foot impatiently. He and Bo had been my constant companions since the frat party media frenzy, but seeing as it was Christmas Eve and I would only be out for a few hours, I gave Bo the day off. But from the way Reggie kept deeply sighing, I think he might have needed that vacation more.

When the car horns were eventually too loud to drown out with Michael Bublé Christmas carols, I scooped Famous up in my arms, clutched him against my chest and told George that Reggie and I would walk the rest of the way home. We were only a few blocks away, and thankfully it wasn't snowing.

"This isn't so bad!" I cooed to Famous, adjusting his Ralph Lauren doggy sweater.

It was real bad. The air was so cold, my eyes were beginning to water, and I could practically see my nose turning pink. Maybe that's why Rudolph had such a shiny nose. Maybe all he needed was a Ralph Lauren sweater too.

"So, are you doing anything fun Christmas?" I asked Reggie, who was concentrating on navigating a path through the crowded sidewalk.

"Seeing my mother," he replied gruffly.

"Oh that's fun!"

"No, it's not. Trust me."

"If it makes you feel any better," I told him, "my brother is visiting, and he decided it would be a good idea to play a little prank on me. He stole my credit card and bought forty-seven vegetable dicers off of one of those infomercials. So now I have that special delivery to look forward to."

Reggie made a sound that was somewhere between a laugh and a grunt. "Holidays," he said simply. "They can be tough."

Ain't that the truth.

We were almost home and away from the merciless cold when we saw an unexpected visitor walking out of the penthouse building and in our direction.

"Scott?" I called out in surprise.

He did his best to look surprised, but somehow, I wasn't quite convinced.

"Hey Gia!" Scott said. "Fancy seeing you out and about!"

"What are you doing here?" I asked him.

"Oh, you know . . ." he began weakly. "Finishing up some Christmas shopping."

I glanced up at the skyscraper ahead. "You were shopping in my penthouse building?"

"Erm . . . no. I was saying hi to the doorman! He's an old friend. Paul and I go *way* back."

"You mean Phil?"

"Right. Paul is, um, a nickname." Scott rubbed his gloves together awkwardly. "Anyway, what are you doing here?"

"I live here, remember?"

"Oh. Right."

Reggie had his *I don't trust this dude* look on his face, and honestly, I couldn't blame him. The way he was animatedly grinning and stumbling over his words, it looked like he had just finished burying a body in the lobby bathroom.

Of course, I had my own theory of why Jack's best friend would be "shopping" right outside where I lived.

I narrowed my eyes. "Did Jack put you up to this?"

Scott feigned a shocked look, shaking his head a little too intensely.

"What?" Scott said, his voice going shrill. "No! Of course not. Jack doesn't even know I'm here!"

Oh boy. If this is what I sounded like when I lied, then we

had a serious problem. I looked at him pointedly, waiting for the inevitable to occur.

"Okay," he said. "He might have an *inkling* that I'm here. He just wants to talk, Gia."

My stomach dropped. I had known from the start that Jack was behind it, but hearing it validated suddenly made me feel sick. Or happy. I couldn't tell which one.

"So he sent you to do the talking for him?"

"No, he just thought you wouldn't hear him otherwise. In my defense, I told him it was a bad idea to send me over!"

"You can tell him I'm not interested in what he has to say," I said firmly. "I hope he reimburses you for wasting your time."

"I know he can be a pain," Scott said. "And he's handled this whole thing *so* badly. But he's miserable, Gia. Honestly, he hasn't been the same since you guys stopped talking."

"I don't care." I did care.

"Trust me on this. I've seen Jack go through a lot, and he hasn't been this down in a long time."

I'm not going to lie, that did make me feel a tad better.

"He honestly just wants to talk," Scott continued, making use of my silence. "Please just hear him out?"

Scott was looking at me with better puppy-dog eyes than Famous, his gloved fingers locked into a praying position. People passing by probably thought the Salvation Army had taken on a new approach to getting holiday donations or something, so I reluctantly nodded.

"Fine," I said begrudgingly, and Scott gave a relieved sigh. "Tell him to message me."

"That might not be necessary . . ."

I froze, staring at Scott with frantic eyes. He looked back at me with a smile that was both apologetic and hopeful. And that's when I noticed that Jack was standing a little ahead of me, his blond hair intermittently popping into view amongst the sea of people on the sidewalk. He was pacing back and forth impatiently, occasionally rubbing his bare hands together to keep them warm. We finally locked eyes, and I felt the air leave my lungs.

"Nope!" I said, with a swift headshake. "I'm not doing this."

I was ready to leave, but Scott was too quick.

"Please, Gia? Just listen to him! He's already here."

Yes, I could see that. Thanks, pal! Not only was he here, he was now pushing past selfie sticks and lost tourists to get to me. Why did people keep springing these surprises on me? How hard was it to plan ahead and give a sista some warning? All this time, I had been waiting for the moment where Jack and I would finally talk again, but I hadn't once anticipated what I would actually say when it happened. I was hoping to throw a drink in his face and do a lot of hair flipping, but I didn't have a drink and my hair was trapped underneath all the layers I was wearing. I could feel his eyes burning into me, but I wasn't quite ready to look up at him.

"I'm just going to head off . . ." Scott said slowly. He gave me a tiny pat on the back for encouragement as he walked past me. It was his way of either wishing me luck or begging to still be friends after this all blew up in our faces.

It took probably a whole minute before I finally forced myself to look at Jack, who was staring right at me, looking equally uncomfortable.

"Thanks for the ambush," I said to him shakily. "Good plan."

"I'm sorry, Gia. But I knew if you saw just me standing there, you'd turn the other direction."

"And you didn't think to pick up the phone and call? Or message? A letter would have done the job."

Jack sighed, putting his hands in the pockets of his black coat. "I should have called."

"Yeah, you should have." I readjusted Famous's position in my arms as he squirmed around. "What do you want, Jack?"

"I want to talk."

"Yeah I heard. But you had a month to talk and you didn't. Radio silence! Nothing! Nada. Niente." If I knew any more languages, I would have thrown in some more just to really strengthen my point. But I think he got it.

"I didn't think you wanted to listen!" Jack replied. "The last time we spoke, you made it pretty clear you never wanted to see me again."

"Yet, here we both are."

We both fell silent, staring at our feet and letting people gently bump past us as they continued their day. Thankfully people seemed too busy to notice I was around, or maybe they had just stopped caring.

"Cool," I said. "Good talk. Let's do this again, never."

"No, please, Gia! Five minutes. That's all I want, I swear. And then if you don't want to talk to me ever again, you don't have to. I promise."

"Three minutes," I told him. "Reggie, start the clock."

"Got it."

"Dude!" Jack said, giving Reggie a betrayed look.

He shrugged in reply and said, "Sorry, man. I work for her."

I carefully handed Famous to Reggie, choosing to ignore the subtle groan he emitted when I did. Poor Reg. He was getting real sick of my drama and even sicker of my dog. Jack led me gently to one side of the sidewalk, where we were a little safer away from the foot-traffic.

"I thought about calling a lot," Jack began. "I think I must have picked up the phone a thousand times. I even came to your place after I heard about the whole frat party thing. But I couldn't actually bring myself to ring your doorbell."

I could imagine him standing in the grand lobby, evaluating his next steps uncertainly. I could have passed him for all I knew. He could have been waiting on the couches one day while I rushed to the car. Just the thought of it made my heart do a star jump.

"Look, I just came to say I'm sorry," Jack said. "I hated how everything went down that night, and I wish I could take it all back. But all I can do is apologize, so here I am. These past few weeks have been so weird not talking to you. Everything feels empty. And you were right. I shouldn't have passed the kiss off like it was nothing, and I *was* avoiding my feelings. It was selfish and cowardly, and I'm not proud of it. I'm just a little screwed up. But that's not an excuse, and I should never have treated you like that."

He was saying all the right things and ticking all the boxes. But it wasn't enough. I wanted it to be enough, but it wasn't.

He *still* hadn't said what he was really feeling, and we were still hanging in limbo.

I swallowed the lump that was rising in my throat and avoided his bright blue eyes, hoping the disappointment wouldn't make me cry. "Um," I said, my voice trembling the slightest bit. "Thanks. But I really have to head home now. So—"

"I went to see my father last week."

I looked up from the dirty sidewalk with surprise. "What?"

"I don't know what came over me, but I just wanted to see him. It had taken me years to build up the courage to even be in the same room as him, and I didn't want that to be my last shot at fixing our relationship."

"So . . . what happened?" I asked, against my better judgment.

"Nothing. We ended up right back where we started, only this time I didn't yell back when he told me what a disappointment I was. I don't know what happened, but all the anger just wasn't there anymore. You were right. I don't need to prove to him that I'm worthy anymore." Jack looked down at the ground. "You were right about a lot that night."

"So what does Lucy think about all of this?" I could barely say her name without an eye-roll.

"Lucy will always be special to me," he replied. "She was there for me when I really needed someone. But it's been over for a long time, and we both knew it. Just because I'll always love her doesn't mean I have to be *in* love with her."

My heart was doing that thing again where it felt like it was going to throw up. Or maybe that was me. I felt like I was going to throw up

"We weren't together when your dad hired me," Jack explained. "We were still talking, but we weren't together. We only got back together when I came back to New York and you were with Milo. I think I was a little scared to admit how I felt because you were the only person besides Lucy that I'd felt something meaningful with."

"Oh," was all I managed to say.

Honestly, I was sold. All that time convincing myself

I didn't want him anymore and I was better off had gone completely to waste. I wanted him more than ever, and it kind of annoyed me that my brain wasn't putting up more of a fight.

"Don't get me wrong, it wasn't love at first sight or anything. When I first met you, I kinda hated you. You were really annoying, and all you did was complain. I thought you were spoiled and bratty an—"

"Okay, I think your three minutes are up. Bye!"

"But then . . ." Jack said. "I don't know, I just started enjoying being around you. I found your lame jokes funny and the fact that you secretly order hot chocolate instead of coffee because you like the taste better but you don't want to seem uncool. Even though we spent all day together, I missed you when you weren't around."

Heat flushed my cheeks. "What are you trying to say?"

Jack took a deep breath, like he was preparing himself for battle.

"Gia Winters," he said. "I'm in love with you. Like, big time. I'm sorry it took so long for me to get there. But I'm here now, and I'm not even a little bit scared of it."

Oh my god. He loved me. He loved me! He loved me, and I loved him, and we loved each other. By this stage, my heart started to completely fail. Like, I'm pretty sure I developed some kind of arrhythmia that could kill me. But at least I would die knowing that Jack Anderson loved me!

And in one swift motion, my euphoria dropped and I felt like I was standing in that elevator again, disappointed and lonely. Everything was too much in too little time, and I couldn't look at him any longer.

"It won't work," I said, pushing past him and heading toward the penthouse.

I didn't know if Reggie was following, but I kept going.

"Gia, wait!" Jack stood in front of me, blocking the path. I turned to escape from the side, but he held onto my arm. He looked both hurt and confused. "Talk to me!"

"It won't work," I repeated. "We're going to annoy the hell out of each other and fight over everything! You love me *now*, but that could change in a day. I don't want to wait around until you finally decide you can handle it."

I had watched enough Steve Harvey love advice videos to recognize textbook emotional unavailability when it was glaring right back at me.

Jack was beginning to look desperate. It was a look I had never seen on him before. "What do I have to do to make things right?" he asked.

"Go home."

I continued walking, bumping into a woman without even apologizing. I was cold and sad and confused and kind of angry at myself. Wasn't this what I wanted? And now I had it, and I was voluntarily throwing it back in the universe's face.

"You're the one who told me not to run away from my feelings, but now you're doing the same!" Jack's voice came from behind me.

I could still hear him clearly over the sound of chatter and traffic. I pulled my coat tighter around me and ignored him. I had clearly lost my mind. We hadn't even started a relationship yet, and I had already deemed it a failure. If I was just going to walk away then what had all of this even been for? Breaking up with Milo, fighting with Jack, declaring our love. Dr. Norton would *definitely* be hearing about this.

"'You know what's wrong with you, Miss Whoever-You-Are?'" Jack called out loudly. I could barely hear him over the street rush. "'You're chicken! You've got no guts!'"

I stopped dead in my tracks. I knew what he was doing. I knew those words.

"'You're afraid to stick out your chin and say, okay, life's a fact. People do fall in love. People *do* belong to each other. Because that's the only chance anybody's got for real happiness!'"

I turned to look at him, completely oblivious to the rest of the world rushing past me on either side. Jack took a few steps closer, then stopped, his eyes blazing into mine.

"You watched *Breakfast at Tiffany's*?" I said, although it sounded less like a question and more like a statement.

His shoulders went up in a half-hearted shrug. "Only like fourteen times."

Not only had he watched it, he had learned the lines to my very favorite scene. The grand climax, the most vital part. The moment when everything falls apart and comes right back together again. I knew each word by heart, and now so did Jack.

I marched over to him with fierce determination in my eyes. "Things aren't always going to be easy," I declared. "I'm going to get on your nerves a lot. I'm going to be bratty and spoiled and complain about stupid things, like my eyeliner wings not matching. But you're not allowed to bolt the moment things get tough. I know you think you're screwed up, but guess what, buddy? So am I! So that's not a valid excuse anymore."

"Did you just call me buddy?"

"Is this the road you really want to take right now?"

Jack shook his head firmly. "You're right, sorry. No running away, I promise."

"There'll be cameras everywhere," I continued, "prying into every personal detail of our lives. That means dark sunglasses, fake moustaches, taking separate cars and going to events where you have to pretend to be friends with people you hate. It's annoying and frustrating, but it's my life, and I'm not apologizing for it. Can you handle that?"

Jack nodded.

"And no using your charm on other girls. No winking or flirty comments or that little half-smile thing you do."

"Look, I can't help if girls fall in love with my natural charm. I mean I'm n—"

"Jack!"

"Okay, okay. No flirting, I promise. All smiles, both half and full, are reserved for you."

"You're definitely done with Lucy?"

"Definitely."

Scott had told me not to give up on Jack. From the bottom of my heart, I wanted to ignore that advice, turn on my heel, and never look back. But I couldn't. Somewhere deep down, I knew that even though he had let me down before, he hadn't given up on me either.

"Can I say something now?" Jack asked.

"If you must," I replied.

"I'm sorry for being a jerk. Like, really sorry. I'm working on it, I swear."

"You really put the Jack in *jackass*, don't you?"

Jack's lips curved up. "Was that a joke?"

"Maybe."

"Does this mean you're going to be the funny one in the relationship?"

"Does this mean you're going to *be* in the relationship?"

"I'll keep a bag packed by the front door for those times when you annoy me."

"Wow," I said. "I really hate you, you know that?"

"Yeah," he said, closing the space between us. "I know."

And then he kissed me. And I let him. And it was just like the elevator kiss and yet absolutely *nothing* like it. There were no question marks hanging above us anymore, just a full stop. Maybe even an exclamation point. But we both knew what we wanted now. Each other. Even though it was freezing outside and I was wearing stilettos that were doing nothing to keep my feet protected, my entire body was filled with warmth. I didn't care that we were making out in the middle of a sidewalk where people were probably going to knock my eye out with a selfie stick. I didn't care that someone passing excitedly whispered, "I think that's Gia Winters!" I didn't care that the photos of us would be on the cover of every tabloid the next day. I only cared about Jack and the way he made my heart want to explode.

When I finally pulled away, we were both a little breathless but completely content. We still had our arms around each other, like we were planning on never letting go.

"Be honest," Jack said. "The *Breakfast at Tiffany's* move was what sold you, right?"

"If anything, it was cheating!" I told him. "You know Audrey is my weakness."

"Well, thanks to you and Audrey, I had *Moon River* stuck in my head for a week and a half."

"Does this mean you might actually be a fan of classic romance movies?"

"I'm not gonna lie, they're pretty good. And they're a perfect example of how this whole 'just friends' thing can never work between a guy and a girl."

"You don't actually believe that, do you?" I asked him with amusement.

Jack gave me his winning smile, which was now reserved only for me. "Why? You want to be my friend?"

I grinned in reply. "Not even a little."

And then we pressed our lips back together, and the world stopped spinning once again.

For as long as I could remember, I believed in the magic of Hollywood. I believed it every time Audrey ended up with her true love. I got butterflies every time I watched Ryan Gosling and Rachel McAdams kiss in the rain. I was in awe of the way Clooney could smoothly deliver a line and a wink in a sharp-looking suit. I was basically in awe of Clooney's general existence, to be fair.

Movie romance was passionate and grand, and I had always wanted it for myself. But somewhere along the way, I had forgotten about those miracles. Watching my parents fall apart woke me up to whatever was hidden behind the shiny facade of stardom. Real life wasn't like the movies, and it was a disappointment. It was messy and complicated and frustrating. I had momentarily forgotten that happy endings could exist. Until now, of course.

They say it takes a lot of luck to make it in Hollywood, and I think that's true. It doesn't matter how talented you are, how nice you are, or how many puppies you've saved from burning buildings. All it takes is a little luck to turn your life completely around. But if you ask me, that's not just true for being a celebrity. It's just a fact of life. I had had my fair share of bad luck this year, and I was beginning to think it would never turn around. Which to others might seem nuts, because I had always been the girl with *all* the luck.

Maybe it was the spirit of Christmas or the work of that random psychic lady I once passed on the street. But standing on that dirty, cold sidewalk with my arms wrapped around Jack, I was feeling pretty damn lucky.

Acknowledgments

I have to extend a huge thank you to everyone at Amberjack Publishing for giving me a voice in the crazy world of book publishing. A special mention goes to my wonderful editor Jenny, who has always been as invested in my stories as I am.

Thank you to all my friends in New York for letting me in on the city's secrets and making sure I never got lost on the subway. The city will always be my second home in my heart.

I am forever grateful to my parents and sister, who never fail to remind me how proud and excited they are. I am so appreciative of all that you do for me and your never-ending support.

Finally, thank you to all the readers. I've come a long way from being a shy sixteen-year-old girl, sitting alone in the back of the library with a notebook in her hand. From one bookworm to another, I am forever grateful.

About the Author

Saba Kapur is a twenty-two-year-old author currently living in Melbourne, Australia. *Lucky You* is her second novel, and the sequel to *Lucky Me*, which is an ode to her favourite things: fashion, romance, and mystery.

Born in India, Saba spent her childhood in Indonesia and Kiev, Ukraine. She has recently graduated from Monash University with a degree in Criminology and International Relations. She is currently pursuing her passion in the field of criminal justice.

In her spare time, Saba enjoys reading, laughing at her own jokes, and pretending she's Beyoncé. Her parents still won't buy her a puppy, but she's working on it.